The Reckless

Legacy of the King's Pirates 6

MaryLu TYNDALL

The Reckless

Legacy of the King's Pirates 6
by MaryLu Tyndall

Library of Congress Cataloging-in-Publication Data is on file at the Library of Congress, Washington, DC.

ISBN-13: 978-0-9991763-7-5
E-Version ISBN: 978-0-9991763-6-8

Cover Design by Ravv at raven.com
Edits Lora Doncea, EditsbyLora.com

The words of the reckless pierce like swords, but the tongue of the wise brings healing.
Proverbs 12:18 NIV

Charm is deceptive, and beauty is fleeting; but a woman who fears the Lord is to be praised.
Proverbs 31:30 NIV

CHAPTER ONE

May 1694, English Harbor, Antigua

How could any sane woman enjoy being a trollop? Surely it was the most demeaning trade that ever existed. Adjusting her over-tight corset, Reena Charlisse Hyde, daughter of Captain Edmund Merrick Hyde, Earl of Clarendon, had hoped the night would conceal what her wench's dress would not. She was not so fortunate. The seaman sitting across from her in the jolly boat had not stopped staring at her chest since they'd left the docks. How she longed to slap the drool-soaked leer from his face. Instead, she flung her unbound dark hair over her exposed skin. It did naught to sever the locked aim of his gaze. The poor man seemed in a trance. She glanced at the officer sitting at the head of the boat, then at the four sailors rowing on either side, and finally at the ten trollops perched upon the thwarts, giggling and chattering like a harem of geese. Would anyone notice if she pushed the seaman overboard just for the enjoyment? If only to put the poor man out of his misery. She smiled at the thought. Which he must have taken as encouragement, for his gaze lifted from her chest to her face, ever so briefly, returning her smile. Holding back the sudden urge to vomit, Reena snapped her gaze away and spotted a shadowy hulk rising from the dark waters of the bay.

HMS *Viper*.

Her destination. And where her beloved Freddy was—the man she intended to marry.

Lanterns winked at her from fore- and main-masts, adding a modicum of light to the half-moon that dribbled milky foam over rippling wavelets. The scent of brine, moist wood, unwashed men, and cheap perfume curled Reena's nose. Behind her, on shore, stood the ominous stone walls of Fort Berkeley and beyond, the town of Antigua, nothing but shadows at the midnight hour.

The sailors pushed the oars through the water, grunting and groaning and splashing a few of the trollops. They only giggled louder. Were they truly happy to be servicing a bunch of stench-encrusted, ignorant sailors? *Nay.* Reena glanced over their faces—at least what the moonlight would afford—and decided it was all a farce, an act which they had to perform in order to survive. Her stomach soured at the thought, and she reached down to ensure the pistol was still strapped to her left thigh and the knife to her right. They were.

The sailor's eyes were still on her chest.

Women had so few options in this world for survival. How much better was it to be a pirate than a prostitute? If she had the time, she'd recruit these ladies to join her crew on board the *Reckless*—as she'd done with Jo—and give them a chance to be free, independent, and beholden to no man. She didn't have the time.

The hail came from HMS *Viper,* and the "Oars up" command from the officer at the prow echoed over the waters. The sailors lifted the tips of their oars above their heads as the boat drifted to thud against the thick hull of the Royal Navy Ship of the Line.

Reena should be frightened. She wasn't. Instead, she was beyond excited to finally see Freddy. How long had it been? A year, two months, and five days. Seemed like she'd spent an eternity tracking him across the West Indies.

A rope ladder was tossed overboard. The officer climbed aboard as two men peered over the railing from above.

"Come now, ladies, Get yer bums up and be off to yer night o' pleasure." One of the sailors in the boat chuckled as he assisted the first trollop. The craft wobbled beneath her rather excessive weight, but she managed to grab hold of the rope and hoist herself up. The sailor slapped her on the bottom as she ascended.

The second woman smiled his way. "Yer a wry one, ain't ye?"

"I'll show ye just how wry if ye'll wait for me atop." He shoved her, taking liberties once again with his hands.

Reena stood, gained her balance, slapped away the hands that reached for her, and proceeded toward the ladder. If the foul sailor touched her bottom, he'd find a knife in his gut.

Gritting her teeth, she followed the last woman, who seemed to be having trouble remaining upright in the teetering boat. Two of the sailors reached to assist her, and Reena took the opportunity to skirt around them, leap onto the side of the rope, and skitter up like the pirate she was.

Amid the laughter, the men made a lurid comment about how anxious she was to take her pleasure.

But she didn't care. She was on the deck of a Royal Navy ship. Much easier than she thought.

Sailors and marines on watch glanced toward the women, and she scanned their faces, looking for her love. Not there. Even so, her heart rate ratcheted, knowing he was close. She allowed herself to be herded with the other women down a ladder to the berth. But before they even landed on the deck below, a horde of sailors, reeking of rum and sweat, advanced toward them like starving dogs to slabs of meat.

She pushed through the throng, slapping away groping hands as she went, peering at faces—most of which leered back at her as if she were a chest full of gold. The chink of money being exchanged echoed through the dank air as some of the sailors retreated with their prizes to the corners. Others sulked to sit in chairs and wait their turn, while others played cards, seemingly uninterested. Someone began playing a fiddle and men gathered around to sing.

Freddy was nowhere to be seen.

Two sailors approached, their eyes scouring over her like holystones on a deck. She shook her head and gave them the look she oft gave her crew—the one that sent them scurrying to task in fear. It had the same effect on these men.

With a frustrated sigh, she turned and surveyed the rest of the deck, purposely avoiding the harlots entangled with their men.

Where are you, Freddy? She didn't know how much longer she could remain amidst such sordid activities. Had her information been wrong? Had he received a commission instead of being tossed down with the common sailors?

She proceeded toward the far corner, weaving around chairs, tables, and hammocks. More hands reached for her, more salacious offers flung her way.

Finally she came to the end of the row of hammocks and peered around a temporary bulkhead. Lantern light flickered over a man sitting on the floor, his back against the hull, his head dipped into a book.

Freddy! He looked good. Healthy, strong…her Freddy!

In one swift move, she dashed toward him and lowered to her knees by his side. Then before he could even look up, she fell against his chest. His book flew to the side. Air expelled from his lungs in a grunt. She drew in a deep breath of him, his scent of leather, oak, and moss, sparking memories of happier times—laughter and love and adventure.

"Miss! Miss!" He shifted beneath her and grabbed her arms.

Unable to control herself, she showered his face with kiss after kiss.

"Miss!" He shoved her back and shot to his feet. His gaze landed on her chest, and he looked away. "I'm not interested. Find another sailor."

"I do not want another sailor. I want you, Freddy."

The grunts and groans, laughter and music faded into the background as Freddy slowly and methodically turned to stare at her. Inky black hair hung to his shoulders in stormy waves, dark stubble clung to his chin and circled lips that now flattened in disbelief—or was it frustration? He blinked, his eyes the color of sea moss, assessing her as if she were a monster risen from the deep. She had hoped to see pleasure…excitement…in their depths, but instead they narrowed yet again.

"Reena! What are you doing here?"

She stared at him, hurt and dumbfounded. "Faith now, Freddy! I'm here to rescue you."

"Rescue me? Thunderation!" Frederick raked his hair back and stared at the woman sitting on the deck by his feet, the woman he'd been trying to avoid—had *successfully* avoided for over a year. "I have no need of rescuing, Reena!" Reluctantly, he offered her his hand.

Her fingers wrapped around his and she stood, a captivating smile curving her lips—the one that always made him agree to anything she wanted. "Of course you need rescuing, Freddy." She eased beside him. Her eyes—the color of a gold doubloon and just as brilliant—stared up at him with an innocence he knew was a farce.

She smelled of coconut and lavender… a refreshing change from sweat and bilge water. He breathed it in as memories swirled about him, stirring him, soul and body. *Nay.* He nudged her back.

She pouted, then released a sigh. "You cannot honestly be happy in *this* navy with all the rules and regulations and—"

A sailor stumbled past the bulkhead, a giggling trollop in his arms. He dove his head into her neck, grunting and groaning like a pig at trough, before he glanced up and saw Frederick.

"Apologies, Preach." He smiled like a boy caught at mischief, then dragged the woman to a corner.

Other unsavory sounds emanated from across the deck, and Reena scrunched her nose. "Such baseborn behavior!"

He frowned. "When did baseborn behavior ever offend you, Reena?"

She laid a hand on her heart. "Ouch, you wound me, Freddy. I thought you'd be happy to see me."

She truly *did* look wounded. And lovely. And beautiful as always with her silky hair spilling to her waist like a mahogany waterfall, her regal cheekbones, full lips that were now pouting again, and those glistening almond-shaped eyes edged by a forest of lashes. But he knew better than to let her beauty appeal to his manly instincts to protect, to defend. This woman was as strong and determined as any man. Which is why he'd had to leave her—to run as far away from her as he could.

Before she destroyed him.

Against his will, his gaze lowered to the creamy mounds protruding from her low neckline. He slammed his eyes shut and rubbed them. "Why are you dressed like a harlot?"

"How else was I to get on board?" She shrugged. "And why did that man call you 'Preach'?"

Frederick stooped to pick up his Bible, closed it, and brushed off the fine leather cover. "Because that's what I am to these men. I preach the Word of God to them."

She cocked her head and smiled as the grunts of carousal continued all around them—laughter, a discordant fiddle, curses, and what sounded like fisticuffs in the distance. "'Twould seem they haven't quite embraced your godly admonitions."

Frederick growled. He wanted to tell her he'd been making progress, that several of the men had turned from their wicked ways. But in truth, he was not sure he'd been doing any good at all.

"Forsooth, you're fooling yourself if you think to follow in our parents' footsteps," she continued, placing a hand on her hip. "We are not like them, Freddy. No amount of Bible reading and preaching is going to change that."

He grabbed the cross around his neck, seeking solace…and wisdom. And mostly strength to resist this woman, who from the leap of his heart, still owned a piece of it.

"We have to get you off this ship," he said.

"My thoughts exactly. I have a plan." She peeked around the bulkhead before facing him with the confidence of any captain. "We both go above and then I—"

"Nay." Frederick groaned. "*We* do not do anything. I am staying. You are leaving."

"Don't be ridiculous." She looked at him as if he'd told her the moon was made of cotton. "I did not come all this way to leave without you." She grabbed his arm and leaned in to whisper. "I will distract the watchman while you slip overboard. You can still swim, can you not?"

Frederick set down his Bible and shrugged from her grip, if only to keep her touch from driving him to distraction. "I have a better idea. You stay with me until the women are done, and then you will leave with them."

She flattened those luscious lips of hers. He could see her mind spinning behind her eyes, forming a plan. A devious one, no doubt, from the expression of victory that claimed her features. But then her face softened, and she waved a hand through the air. "Very well."

She looked up at him, and if he didn't know her well, he'd think tears were forming in her eyes. She fumbled with a lock of her hair and lowered her gaze. "I shall just have to resort to drastic measures."

"What drastic measures?"

"Why, throw myself overboard, of course."

"You cannot swim." He blew out a sigh and stared at her. "If I don't come with you, you intend to kill yourself? Come, now, such feminine theatrics are beneath you."

He'd meant it as sarcasm, but her expression grew serious. "I would do anything to have you, Freddy."

"Frederick." He crossed his arms over his chest. "You are far too strong a woman to end your life like a coward."

"We shall see." Then grabbing her skirts, she spun on her heels and disappeared behind the bulkhead.

"Thunderation!" Frederick started after her, but she had already vanished into the mob of sailors dancing and carousing like schoolboys in their first brothel. Averting his eyes from the debauchery, he shoved his way through, and up the ladder. A blast of salty wind struck his face as he scanned the shadowy deck. Where had she gone?

There. Talking to Midshipman Wilson. But why? Glancing over her shoulder, she pointed in his direction.

Wilson frowned, nudged Reena aside, and started toward him. But it was the smug look on Reena's face that gave

Frederick pause, that all-too-familiar look of victory that always preceded some impending disaster of her own making.

Before he could do or say anything, she darted for the bulwarks, gripped the ratlines, turned and smiled his way…

And jumped overboard.

Frederick's heart seized.

The splash halted Midshipman Wilson and sent him to peer over the railing. Frederick stripped off his shoes and waistcoat and joined him.

"What in the…?" Wilson was gaping at the dark water.

Grinding his teeth in frustration and knowing full well he was making a huge mistake, Frederick leapt on the railing and dove into the bay.

CHAPTER TWO

*T*he silky, warm waters of English Harbor caressed Reena from all sides even as the darkness kept her hidden from sight. No doubt those on HMS *Viper* would believe she was drowning. Precisely what she wanted.

She hated deceiving Freddy like this. She hated putting him in danger. But the stubborn man had left her no choice.

Sounds, muted and distant, pulsated past her ears, along with the gush of water as she swam through the bay. She'd purposely not worn petticoats and had donned a cotton gown and light shoes that wouldn't come off or weigh her down. But that gown became chain-mail, tangling and weighing heavy on her legs. Her corset pinched. Her lungs ached for air. But she had to get far enough away from the ship. Finally, she headed toward the surface, broke through, and waited to hear the splash she longed to hear.

Just when she feared she'd underestimated Freddy's love for her, the splash sounded, hollow and distant—yet full of promise.

Shouts ensued, followed by the midshipmen calling for lanterns. The sharp report of a musket cracked the air.

"Deserter! Deserter! There! Shoot him!"

Being as quiet as she could, yet loud enough for Freddy to hear her, she called for help and splashed lightly. Where was he? She spun, her face barely peeking above the water.

Another shot echoed across the night.

Surely they hadn't hit him? *God, if you're there. Please, God, No!*

The slightest rustle of water, a breath, barely perceptible. There he was, his head poking above the black waters, scanning his surroundings. He'd come for her. He still loved her!

"Over here!" she attempted to sound frantic.

He started for her. More shots ricocheted over the bay. One of them far too close.

She dove under, hoping he'd do the same. He did—and grabbed her leg. She feigned a fearful struggle, dragging him away from the ship. Gripping her waist, he sped for the surface.

They both gulped in air. She clung to his neck, longing to kiss his wet cheek, happy to be so close to him.

He struggled to keep them both above the surface. "Hang on! We're going back."

"Nay! They will shoot you!" She breathed out while clawing at his shirt.

As if to prove her point, another shot sped past them in an eerie whine.

Confusion stole the desperation from his face as he glanced at HMS *Viper*, then back at Reena.

"Wait, you're treading water!" He released her.

"Nay, I'm not." Reena slipped beneath the surface again, chastising herself for being so careless.

He dove after her and brought her up again. This time she thrashed and kicked and clung to his neck. "Please don't let me drown."

"Shh…Shh. I will not, Kitten. Hang on."

He'd used his pet name for her! She couldn't help but smile.

He started for the *Viper*, dragging her along. Sailors scrambled over the sides and descended the rope into a jolly boat.

"Find him and shoot him!" one of the officers shouted.

Freddy halted, his breath coming hard, resignation finally sinking in.

"Hold on." With one hand wrapped around her waist, he used the other to swim to shore. She did her best to act frightened and keep from helping him, but the jolly boat had pushed off from the ship and would soon be upon them.

She kicked her feet, but still they made little progress. Finally, she pushed from him and shouted, "Hurry!" then dove into the water and swam with all her might.

"You can swim!" Frederick growled as he dragged himself onto the beach. If it wasn't for his gasping lungs and exhausted limbs, he'd grab the woman crawling out of the water beside him and throttle her.

As it was, all he could do was sink onto the wet sand and gather his strength…*and* his temper. Waves tumbled over his feet, reaching foamy claws toward his arms, attempting to drag him back into the bay. He deserved it—and worse—for falling for this goose-brained woman's schemes. How could he have been so thick-headed? He could hear her breathing beside him, hear her moan as she crawled over the sand.

And then he heard something else.

Men's voices, the slap of oars in the water.

By all that was holy! He was a deserter. And they wouldn't hesitate to shoot him on sight.

Frederick opened one eye. A crab skittered toward him and halted, staring at him as if to mock his stupidity before dashing away.

Reena flipped over, gazed at the stars, and started laughing. *Laughing*! "Egad, that was delightful! Just like old times, Freddy, eh?" She managed to say between heavy breaths.

"Nay. Not at all." He wanted naught to do with old times, especially not those with this woman. Pushing himself upright, he lunged for her with every intention to strangle her.

She rolled out of reach. "Now, Freddy, your temper, remember?" Her voice teased.

"I'll show you my—" A shot split the night sky.

"There. On the beach!" A voice echoed over the water. Close. Too close.

More shots ripped past them. One hit the sand by her feet. Lantern light bobbed in the darkness, growing brighter and brighter.

He grabbed her hand, jerked her to her feet, and headed for a patch of palms.

Shots peppered the sand. No time to think. No time for rage. Barely time to run.

Frederick dove into the brush and stepped on something sharp. Pain spiraled across his bare feet. He kept running, Reena by his side.

Pistols cracked the darkness. The sound of a boat scraping the sand.

"This way!" Reena jerked him to the right across a swampy inlet. He sloshed through the warm water, his toes sinking into mossy silt one minute and tripping over giant roots the next.

He didn't want to follow her, but where else could he go? Certainly not back the way he came.

The sound of voices grew louder behind him.

Mayhap they would give up soon. After all, he was a mere topman and not worth the effort. Frederick held back a curse. Unfortunately—due to an increase in recent desertions—the Royal Navy had halted all shore leave and given orders to shoot anyone abandoning ship. Just his luck.

They emerged from the swamp onto a sandy strip littered with a sharp plant that poked and jabbed Frederick's feet.

"Ouch, woman. Can you not find a spot without thorns?"

"Cease your whining, Freddy," she retorted, halting at the edge of the brush and gazing over a sandy cove that extended to the sea. Waves, laced in moonlight, curled toward shore where ficus and palms stood like sentinels beside a foam-splashed cliff.

"Where are we going?" Frederick asked.

"*Shh.* Follow me." She started across the sand.

"I'm not following you another step. Do you know what you've done to me?"

At this, she spun to face him, one hand on her hip, her expression lost in the darkness. "I have saved you, you mule-headed buffoon."

"You have—" Sloshing sounded behind him.

Someone shouted, "Up ahead!"

"Come." Reena took his hand once again and dragged him across the sand. He snagged it back but followed nonetheless. At the edge of the beach, they rounded a cliff that did further damage to his feet.

A boat waited on the other side. Three men cloaked in shadows stood beside it.

"Abraham." Reena approached and gripped the hand of the largest one, a black man, who greeted her enthusiastically.

"Dis him?" He gestured toward Frederick.

Only then did Frederick see the shadow of a ship anchored offshore—a *familiar* ship.

"Aye. 'Tis him. Abraham, meet Freddy Carlton, son of the infamous pirate captain Kent Carlton. Freddy, Abraham—my quartermaster."

Ignoring the man, Freddy gestured toward the ship. "Whose?"

"Ours, of course. The *Reckless*."

"Reckless, indeed. If you think I would sail away with you, you've—"

A volley of musket shots thundered behind them.

"Shove off!" Reena ordered her men then grabbed the boat and helped push it from the sand. In one swift move, she leapt inside as the other two sailors jumped in behind her. The man called Abraham held the prow steady.

Reena extended her hand toward Frederick. "Coming, Freddy?"

"Frederick, not Freddy." He huffed as more shots rang behind him.

He reached for his pistol, then remembered he didn't have one. One glance at the cliff revealed the shadows of several men. If he stayed, they'd catch him. Yet going with this woman might be just as dangerous.

Grinding his teeth, he sloshed through the surf. A musket fired in the distance.

Pain seared his left shoulder. He fell into the boat with one thought blaring through his mind. He was surely going to die.

CHAPTER THREE

*R*eena entered her cabin and gestured to the sailor guiding Freddy to a chair. Fred, her parrot, shifted over his perch, squawking, "Take no prisoners, take no prisoners."

"I don't need help. 'Tis but a flesh wound." Freddy, stubborn as always, jerked from the man's grip and moved to the side, pain tightening his face as he scanned his surroundings.

Abraham dipped his head beneath the low beams and marched through the door, followed by two more of her men, who stopped short to ogle her.

She glanced down, temporarily forgetting her revealing gown. "What are you looking at, you pig-faced rats. Get back to work! Call Brodie. Tell him a man's been shot." Snatching her waistcoat from a chair, she eased into it and covered her chest.

Freddy hobbled to a chair, leaving bloody footprints on the deck.

"Tell him to bring salve and bandages as well," Reena added. Shrugging off a sudden wave of guilt, she faced Abraham. "Weigh anchor and raise all sail. We need to get far away from the Royal Navy. Set a course north-northwest."

"Raise all sails!" the parrot exclaimed.

"Ye alrigh', Cap'n?" Sedley, her bosun, pushed past the departing sailors, addressing her, but his eyes were on Freddy. He adjusted the ever-present blue kerchief tied around his neck and hopped back and forth as if he were standing on hot coals. The man was almost twice her age and skinnier than an anchor chain.

"Aye, all is well. Back to your duties." She nodded toward Abraham, who gave her one of his *I hope you know what you're doing* looks before he grabbed Sedley by the collar and dragged him off.

Michael came bursting through the door, his blond hair sticking out in all directions.

Reena gave a heavy sigh and placed a hand on her hip. "And what are you doing up at this hour?"

Ten-year-old Michael rubbed his eyes. "I couldn't sleep. I was worried about you. Is this him?" He blinked and stared at Freddy.

Freddy only cocked a brow at him as if he were an oddity.

"Aye. Now back to bed." Reena reached out to grab the boy, but he spun and darted to Freddy.

"Are you the famous pirate captain Freddy Carlton?" The boy's eyes lit up in wonder.

"I'm Frederick Carlton, lad, but I'm no longer a pirate."

Michael's gaze dropped to the gunshot wound on Freddy's shoulder. "You're hurt." Then with all the gentleness of a nursemaid, the boy brushed his hand over the bloody area.

"Enough." Reena took him by the shoulders. "You can talk to Captain Carlton tomorrow. Now, out." She gave him a slight shove out the door and closed it behind him.

"So, you took over as captain." 'Twas more of a statement than a question as Freddy lifted his hand and stared at his shoulder curiously.

Reena sashayed back to her desk and toyed with the feathers of a quill pen. "What did you expect after you left me? Was I to go live with my parents? Take up some tiresome skill such as knitting, painting, or playing the pianoforte?"

He snorted. "Now *that* I would have loved to have seen." But his jovial tone soon soured. "I hope you're quite pleased with yourself. The Royal Navy will hunt me down for desertion. Should they find me, at best they will lash me, at worst, they will court-martial and hang me."

"Hang 'im by the yardarm!" Fred squawked.

"Then we shall ensure they do not find you." Reena spun to face him, a grin on her lips. "And aye, I am quite pleased with myself. I have saved you from a life of drudgery and misery. A measure of thanks would be in order."

"Thanks!" He spit out. "I'm shot and my feet are in shreds!"

"A small pittance to pay." She shrugged.

"Mayhap for you!"

Ah, but the man was handsome. And it was so good to see him, especially here in this cabin where they'd shared many a good time—many a *loving* time. She approached him, unable to keep her distance for another minute. Kneeling before him, she took his hands in hers. "I missed you so much, Freddy. Tell me 'tis good to see me again. I know you have missed me. Your eyes betray you."

Freddy slowly pulled his hands away and closed those eyes. His lips twisted and turned and finally flattened into a snarl. "I was doing well, Reena. I was making a life for myself."

"Poppycock." She shot up. "We already had a wonderful life together."

Shouts echoed from above, along with the thunder of feet as Abraham woke the crew to their tasks.

Freddy opened his eyes, but there was none of the affection, the spark, the light of love that she'd seen moments before. It was as if a monster had absconded away with her Freddy and left a carcass of loathing behind.

"If that were true"—his tone was heartless—"*If* we had a wonderful life together, I would not have left."

A crack etched its way across Reena's heart, ripping away flesh, spilling blood and hope onto the floor. Against her will, a mist covered her eyes, and she turned her back to him.

A knock rescued her from betraying her weakness.

"Enter."

The door creaked open and in walked Brodie, a black satchel in hand. Wiping her eyes, Reena gestured toward Freddy.

The young Scot shook his head. "I didna know ye'd hae injuries, Captain, or I wouldna be weel into me cups."

"Bottoms up. Bottoms up," Fred squawked.

"Hold your feathers," Reena said to the bird then turned to Brodie, smiling. "When are you not well into your cups?"

He gave her that charming grin of his and laughed. "Aye, that." Stumbling over to Freddy, he plopped down beside him. "Off wit' yer shirt." He attempted to help Freddy, but the stubborn man would have none of it. Instead, with great difficulty and obvious pain, Freddy tore the shirt over his head.

Freddy had always been well-built and strong, but Reena was not prepared for the extra muscles he'd obtained whilst in the navy—muscles that rounded his arms and rippled down his stomach. Power. Sheer power. Add to that honor, kindness, and love. Such a wonderful man! And she would have him. Despite the cross hanging around his neck. By God, she would have him.

⚓

Pushing the besotted fool's hands away, Frederick attempted to rise, but the throbbing in his feet forbade him. Above, sails snapped as they filled with wind, and the brig jerked and started on its way, evident by the rush of water against the hull.

"You have naught to fear from Brodie," Reena said. "He does his best work inebriated."

"Comforting," Frederick snapped back, though for some reason, most of the pain had left after the young lad, Michael, had touched him.

"Ach now, hold still, Captain Carlton." Brodie slurred as he examined the gunshot wound on Frederick's shoulder. "Shot clean through," he announced as he opened his satchel, put away the knife, and pulled out a small bottle, bandages, and a jar.

The Scot was young—mayhap mid-twenties—with red hair and blue eyes that would be the crisp color of the Caribbean if they weren't hazed with alcohol.

Without warning, he poured liquid from the bottle over Frederick's shoulder. He might as well have stuffed hot coals into the wound, but Frederick forced back a shout of agony, closed his eyes, and growled instead.

"Weel, 'tis a strong man we hae here, jist as ye said, Captain." Brodie continued his ministrations. Despite his fumbling, he made quick work of Frederick's shoulder, bandaged it up, then moved on to examine his feet.

While the drunken surgeon patched up the cuts and scrapes, Frederick distracted himself from the pain by glancing at Reena. *Reena…*he could hardly believe she was standing before him. Or more like fidgeting before him as she shuffled parchment on her desk, moved trinkets around, picked up her pistol and set it down again. A parrot as big as a bottle of rum sat on a tall perch beside her desk, moving side to side, as fidgety as she. Reena Hyde, nervous? Nay, that wasn't the woman he knew.

He'd hurt her with his harsh comments. He knew it. And despite hating himself for the pain he caused her, he had no choice but to be callous. For his own sake. And hers. *Thunderation!* She'd stolen him off a Royal Navy Ship! Her courage, her bravery, her *foolishness…* this woman would be the death of him. He thought he was in the safest place possible—a place she could never reach him. But the woman never failed to surprise him.

A lantern hanging above trickled golden light down her lustrous dark hair that tumbled to her waist and then rolled over her curves, so evident even with the waistcoat she'd donned. It glistened over her high cheeks, the delicate line of her jaw, and those…sweet lips. He gulped. Gads, but he *had* missed her! Not a day had gone by in which he had not thought of her, prayed for her, and wondered how she fared. Hoping beyond hope that she was not getting into trouble, that she had gone home as he'd told her to do, spent time with her parents, and took up a womanly skill. And most of all, committed her life to God.

Aside from the parrot, the cabin looked much the same as it had the last time he'd been here, save for a few feminine touches—a crystal vase of fresh flowers on the desk, a spill of lace and silk peeking from within a fine Flanders chest, a painted porcelain tea set on a rack attached to the bulkhead, and a comb and jars of perfumes and ointments strewn haphazardly on a table perched before a looking glass. But the large oak desk, mahogany sideboard, racks of books, and heavy twenty-pounder perched before the bed—the bed, he gulped and snapped his gaze away—were all the same.

"Egad, man!" He jerked his foot from the so-called doctor's ministrations.

"Ach now, quit bein' sich a goose-livered squid." A waft of rum drifted from the man as he reached in his bag for more bandages.

"Mayhap if you were sober, you wouldn't dig your nails into my wounds."

The parrot squawked. "Fetch the rum!"

Reena looked up and smiled.

Brodie applied the last bit of salve to Frederick's foot and bandaged it up before gathering his things and rising. The deck canted and the man stumbled sideways, but caught his balance, and swerved to bow before Reena with an exaggerated flourish. "Weel there be anythin' else, Captain?"

She laughed and waved him off. "Out with you, now, Brodie. Go sleep it off."

After the man left, Reena circled her desk and started toward Frederick.

He leapt to his feet, winced at the pain, and held up a palm to stop her. She wasn't the only one whose heart felt like it had been keelhauled. "What do you want from me?"

Halting, she stared at him. Sorrow clouded her expression, but only for a moment before she gave a half grin and the twinkle returned to her eyes. "It has come to my attention that there is a vast amount of hidden treasure to be found on Saint-Domingue."

Frederick growled and rubbed his eyes.

"I'm serious, Freddy. I have a very reliable source who told me its exact location. This could be the prize of a lifetime, and I need your help to get it."

"Aye, thar be treasure," the parrot interjected. "Thar be treasure!"

Retreating, Reena grabbed a peanut from a bowl on her desk and handed it to the bird. "Hush now, Fred."

"Fred? You named your parrot after me?"

Reena shrugged. "The cabin was so empty without you. What else was I supposed to do? Besides,"—she gave the infernal bird a piece of mango—"he's much nicer than you are. He agrees with everything I say."

"You mean, he mimics everything you say." Frederick huffed. "Which is what you always wanted of me." Before she could respond, he added. "Since you already have a Freddy in your cabin, what need have you of me?"

She gave him a sideways grin. "Among other unmentionable things, he cannot help me dig up treasure."

"Alas, you ruined my life for treasure, then?" He ran a hand through his hair. "And stop calling me Freddy. My name is Frederick."

She pouted and twirled a strand of her hair. "You'll always be my Freddy."

"I will never be *your* anything, Reena. Can you not understand that?"

At this, she turned her back to him and walked to the stern windows where gray lit the horizon, announcing the dawn of a new day. The brig leapt and Frederick balanced on the deck, ignoring the pain in his feet. It was no match for the pain in his heart.

"'Tis not simply the treasure, Freddy. But the adventure." She swung about, eyes moist but sparkling with excitement. "Just like old times."

Frederick ground his teeth. "I told you when I left a year ago that I had renounced piracy. Hence, we can no longer be together."

She crossed her arms over her chest and faced the windows again. "Because you committed your life to Jesus?" Spite filled her tone. "Does He not want us to love each other? Isn't God love? 'Tis what my parents always said."

"Aye, God is love." Frederick hesitated, searching for the right words. "But love within boundaries. And we broke every one of those boundaries."

She waved a hand through the air. "Bah! How can love have boundaries?" She straightened her shoulders and fisted hands at her waist. "No matter. I will not let you go. I can't. We are meant to be together, you and I. I've known that since we were little when we played pirate on board our parents' ships."

Unbidden memories swamped him of chasing a brown-haired girl around his father's brig, the *Restitution*—of sword fights with broken broom sticks and pretending to fire old empty pistols. How many times had they raced up the ratlines, stood in the crow's nest, the wind blasting through their hair, and stared over the turquoise Caribbean.

He shook off the happy memories. "Even if we were meant for each other, 'tis certainly not God's will that we pirate."

"Ah, I knew you would say that." She smiled. "Being the righteous man you are now. But this particular treasure only belongs to thieves. Hence"—she cocked her head—"'tis not stealing."

Frederick could only stare at her in wonder. "'Tis the taking something that is not ours, Reena. If you cannot understand that, then you know naught of God."

"I know everything of God," she shot back. "His ways were pounded into me since birth."

"Jesus rules. Jesus reigns," Fred squawked.

"Hush now, Fred!" Reena shouted.

"Seems the bird knows more than you do." Frederick arched a brow. "But knowing and following are two different things."

Reena sighed. "Look what following God has done for our parents, Freddy. They are poor, hated, and shunned by many. And they are growing old and feeble. I want to live life to its fullest before that happens. Like we used to do." An urgent appeal filled her eyes.

He wanted to tell her that their parents were none of those things, but he sensed the futility of doing so. "And this treasure will help you do that?"

"Not the treasure exactly." She leaned back against her deck. "But the delight of finding it, the adventure. While we are still young. Let us not waste our youth on piety and prudeness." She spun a strand of hair around her finger and smiled. "I want to be young and beautiful forever. And I want you by my side."

The brig pitched over a wave, sending its timbers creaking and groaning. He shifted his stance, sharp pains shooting up his legs—wounds from this misguided woman he'd once loved. "Don't you understand, Reena? You will not be young and beautiful forever. And when this life is over, where you end up for all eternity is what is most important."

"I know. I know. I'll burn in hell." She huffed.

"Burn in hell. Burn in hell," the parrot repeated.

Ignoring the bird, Frederick grew serious. "It is a real place, Reena. I have seen it."

"Aye, that infernal nightmare that caused you to leave me. I am well aware," she snipped.

"That was not the only reason."

She flattened her lips. "Alas, I have no intention of going to hell, Freddy. I simply wish to enjoy my youth and beauty while I have it. Then I shall repent right before I die."

The pain in Frederick's heart turned to sorrow. The woman had not changed a bit this past year. Not for all his praying and fasting and pleading with God. Mayhap the Almighty would not listen to the likes of him. Mayhap he was too evil, had made too many mistakes—was far too much like his father. He blew out a sigh. "I will pray for you, Reena. But as soon as we make port, I'm getting off this brig."

She plucked her pistol from the desk and slid a finger down the barrel. "That's the thing, Freddy, I cannot let you do that."

CHAPTER FOUR

Shadows light and dark shifted over Reena's eyelids—back…and forth, back…and forth—urging her to rise from her bed. When the sun had finally peered over the horizon, she had begged Freddy to lie down with her for at least an hour or two of sleep. Like they used to do after a wild night of adventure. But, much to her dismay, he refused. In fact, he insisted on sleeping elsewhere and—from the look of disdain in his eyes—as far away from her as possible. So, she had sent him to Abraham's tiny cabin. Mayhap the quartermaster's snoring and smelly close quarters would drive Freddy back to her bed where he belonged.

And still the sunlight swayed over her eyes, light…dark…light…dark. Ecstasy…misery…ecstasy…misery. Both of which consumed her heart at the moment. Freddy was finally back on the *Reckless* with her, just as she had dreamed he would be again one day. But he was not the same Freddy. He did not drink. He did not laugh. He did not seek adventure. And he did not seem to love her anymore, if that was possible. If this was what Jesus did to people, Reena wanted naught to do with Him.

Against her will, tears filled her eyes. Not even the sounds of the sea dashing against the hull or the creak and groan of the brig brought her any comfort. What was she to do? She could not live without Freddy. Nothing made sense without him. Nothing. In truth, she had only gone through the motions this past year as she sought him across the Caribbean. After he'd left and the crew abandoned her, the first thing she'd done was set out to prove him wrong. To prove that she could be as good a captain as he had been.

"Absurd!" he had said in this very cabin on that direful night. "A pirate crew will not listen to a woman. Go home, Reena. Seek God, be good, set sail with your parents, and do good to others instead of harm."

"You forget, Freddy, that my mother captained an entire crew of pirates when she went searching for my father before I was even born."

He had looked at her with a mixture of disappointment and sorrow. "Indeed. I have not forgotten. And you are your mother's daughter?" He raised his brows. "But what is she doing now?"

Reena had no desire to talk about what her mother was doing. She'd wanted to prove herself to Freddy, to pretend she wasn't in agony over him leaving. "I am as capable as you are, and you know it. There's naught you can do that I cannot. A crew will respect me. You'll see. And after I gather one, I shall come and get you. Wherever you are, wherever you hide. I *will* find you."

Tears spilled from her eyes now as they had done back then on that fateful day. She'd finally broken down, swallowed her pride, and begged. "Don't leave me, Freddy. Please, don't leave me."

Pain had etched across his green eyes, and for a moment she'd thought he intended to take her in his arms and forget his foolish notion to leave. But then he'd turned and, without saying a word, marched out the door.

And out of her life.

Reena opened her eyes, wiped them, and turned to stare at the very spot where, that night, she had melted into a pool of despair. She'd cried for hours, her tears saturating the deck where she lay. Even now, she was surprised there weren't stains upon those very planks to memorialize her agony.

Wings flapped. "Get up ye lazy seadog!"

"Hold your feathers, Fred," she managed to growl as she swung her legs over the side. She had more than proven herself. She'd recruited a crew who obeyed her every command, who respected her, who fought by her side. Truth be told, some of them were here for the treasure she got them, but some had become her friends.

Feet pounded above deck as Abraham's voice echoed over the ship. Another voice sounded, a familiar one, a commanding bass tone that caused her soul to leap within her. *Freddy.*

Jumping to her feet, she donned her breeches, flung a shirt over her head, eased into her waistcoat and tied it tight—all with a new leap to her step, new hope, new determination that she would not lose Freddy again. Never again.

She strapped on her belt, slid in her sword and two pistols, then tied a scarf around her waist and one over her head. Out in the companionway, she made her way to the ladder leading above when Michael came toward her, two mugs in hand.

"Captain! Captain! I have your chocolate."

"Good lad. Bring it above deck."

The boy nodded and slid behind her.

A blast of briny wind struck her as she emerged onto the quarterdeck and marched to the tiller where Abraham stood, thick arms crossed over his bare chest and feet spread against the heaving deck.

She followed his gaze up to the fore topsail where several of her crew were working to loose canvas that appeared to be caught in a jackstay. And right there in the middle of the yard stood Freddy, directing the men to task. Her heart swelled to near bursting as she watched him issue commands and her crew obey him without question. He had traded his navy attire for breeches and an open-collared shirt that flapped in the stiff breeze. Several strands of his dark hair had loosened from his tie and waved over his jaw. He looked like the pirate she remembered, and she felt she would melt for joy on the spot.

"Captain…" A child's voice brought her out of her daze. "Your chocolate?" Beside her, Michael held up a mug. "I crushed cacao beans and added sugar just how you like."

Reena took the mug and scruffed his hair. "Good lad. Thank you."

Michael beamed and shifted his gaze to Freddy.

Gliding along under towering peaks of white canvas, the *Reckless* crested a wave then plunged into the trough, sending a spray of sea foam over the prow. The sun, nearly at its zenith, lit the blue waters in glittering bands as far as she could see. Oh, how she loved these seas.

Abraham glanced her way, sunlight glinting off his silver tooth. "Yuh got yer man, now, Cap'n. Wha' ya goin' t' do wit' him?"

Reena sipped her chocolate, enjoying the sweet, smooth taste. "He's going to help me get the treasure on Saint-Domingue, of course."

"Not wha' he tol' me last night."

"Indeed?"

"Can I talk to him now?" Michael asked, his eyes still on the infamous Captain Carlton.

She smiled. Mayhap she'd exaggerated a few tales about Freddy. "When he climbs down. Then you can give him that cup of coffee you made for him." It had not escaped her attention that the other mug was filled with steaming coffee.

This seemed to satisfy the lad as he stood and waited.

"What did Freddy say to you?" she asked Abraham.

"Dat he's leavin' as soon as we make port."

Sunlight angled over the scar on Abraham's right bicep— the brand of his former master.

"Pay him no mind. He's merely confused."

"Him didn't seem confused t' me. 'Cept he slept on de deck."

The brig plunged over another wave, and Reena caught her balance before taking another sip of chocolate. "But there are two bunks in your cabin."

"Him insisted." Abraham shrugged.

Reena could make no sense of that. Even the Royal Navy provided hammocks.

"An' he asked me fer a Bible dis mornin'." Abraham nodded and smiled. "I like dis man."

Reena frowned. "He fancies himself a preacher, but he's not. He's a pirate and always will be."

"Hmm."

Under Freddy's direction, the sailors untangled the canvas, and it dropped and flapped in the wind as they pulled on the halyards. Freddy began his descent, and she wondered that he could do such a thing with bandages on his feet. But that was her Freddy. He was born to sail, born to pirate these seas.

"Did you tell him where we were going?" Wind whipped her hair in her face and she snapped it aside.

"Aye."

Bilge water. She'd wanted that to remain a secret for now, at least until she could pierce that shield he'd erected around his heart with her charm and beauty.

The wind shifted, leaving the foresails floundering.

Handing her mug to Michael, she gripped the railing, glanced across the main deck, and shouted orders to the topmen. "Braces ease. Trim your sheets! Trim the bowlines!" The men scrambled to do her bidding, some hauling ropes, others leaping into the shrouds.

Abraham descended onto the main deck and began shouting further orders, while Freddy grabbed the backstay and slid to the deck. He landed with a thud that must have hurt his wounds, but his expression revealed no pain.

He glanced up and headed her way, lips flat and jaw stiff. Reena braced herself for the incoming storm.

Michael stared up at her. "Why does Captain Carlton look so angry?"

⚓

Frederick could not take his eyes off Reena. He'd noticed her as soon as she'd emerged from the companionway, dressed like a pirate, weapons and all. Not that she'd ever dressed like a proper lady, but the breeches were new. How could someone look so beautiful and so fierce at the same time? He heard her shouting commands with all the authority and confidence of any good captain, and he watched in shock at how her crew rushed to do her bidding. They respected her. Some even seemed to fear her. She had changed this past year. No longer the needy seductress he remembered, she had become strong, confident—in command.

She glanced up at him then, her hair blowing in the wind behind her, her jaw firm and her eyes filled with a sorrow he knew he had caused. She'd always been so playful, fun-loving, like his pet name for her—kitten. But now, she was more like a cat—a predatory cat. Grabbing the backstay, he slid down the rest of the way, doing his best to gather his fury once again. He made his way across the deck, ignoring the pain in his feet, and accidentally bumped into a sailor on his way to the quarterdeck ladder.

"Pardon, Cap'n," the man said in passing.

Frederick stopped and glanced at him over his shoulder, and the man did the same. Nay, not a man—a woman in sailor's garb with dark hair and large brown eyes. She stared at him as if he were as much an oddity as she, before she turned and continued on her way. She stopped at one of the swivel guns mounted on the starboard railing and issued commands to the men hovering around it to polish it and clean out the powder chamber. A woman master gunner? Of all things.

Leaping onto the quarterdeck, Frederick marched toward Reena, fully intending to unleash his fury upon her, but the young boy approached him, mug in hand.

"Captain Carlton! Captain Carlton! Your coffee."

Frederick could not resist smiling at the excitement beaming from the lad's innocent face. Indeed, it had the curious effect of melting away a portion of his anger.

Besides, the coffee smelled good. He grabbed the cup and took a long swig. "Thank you, boy. Michael, correct?"

The boy's face lit as bright as a dozen candles. "Are you here for good, Captain Carlton? Did you really do battle with two Navy Frigates, outgunned and outmanned, and nearly sink one and blew apart the mainmast of the other?"

With a sigh, Frederick gazed toward the horizon where the sun scattered gold pellets upon the waves. Aye, he had. But it was not something he was proud of nor wished to brag about to this impressionable child.

"I did. But I shouldn't have. 'Twas wrong of me."

He expected to see disappointment on the boy's face, but instead he only smiled and nodded.

"Thank you for the coffee."

"If you need anything, Captain Carlton, I'm at your service." Turning, Michael started off, shouting over his shoulder, "Anything at all. I can get it for you."

Reena swung about and offered Frederick one of those smiles that used to make his heart as pliable as dough. A blast of wind spun around them, fluttering her hair about like liquid silk.

Swallowing a lump of desire, he looked away. "Turn the brig around at once."

She cocked her head and took a step closer. "I no longer take orders from you, Freddy. You lost that privilege when you abandoned me."

"I never abandoned you. I quit pirating. You didn't."

She arched a brow. "Yet, here you are again. On a pirate ship."

He forced back a growl. "By no will of my own. Now, turn this brig around and take me to Kingston posthaste."

"Back to Mother and Daddy's?" She teased, then glanced over the deck where Abraham fired off orders. "Your parents are probably off sailing with mine, saving the world."

"Mayhap, but I will wait for them in Kingston."

"Sounds horribly dull."

"Alas, you have limited my choices. I cannot show my face at any British port, thanks to you."

"Then you certainly can't go to Kingston." She chuckled. "'Tis one of the largest Naval ports in the Caribbean!"

"You can leave me ashore, far from town. I'll make my way home without being seen."

"Why not avoid the British altogether and join me at a French port?" Her golden eyes flashed. "To go after treasure."

A cauldron of frustration and fury bubbled in his gut as he stared at the woman. He fisted his hands to keep from cinching them around her neck. Then taking a deep breath, he calmed his voice enough to say, "You are not understanding me, Reena."

"I'm the only one who has always understood you, Freddy."

"Frederick! Call me Frederick or Preach, but I am no little boy anymore."

She gave him a seductive look. "You most certainly are not."

His body warmed simply by the way she looked at him. Thunderation, but the woman would be the death of him. Moving to the quarterdeck railing, he gripped the cross around his neck and stared down at the crew, some attending duties, others whittling wood or playing cards—a strange sight after spending so much time on a Royal Navy ship where no man was idle.

Sails flapped overhead. The deck canted, and he grabbed the railing as memories penetrated his thoughts…memories of commanding this brig, of battles at sea, the thunderous blast of cannons, the ring of swords, the smell of gun smoke. The thrill of capturing a prize and then spending their ill-gotten fortune on feasting and dissipation.

The love he'd shared with this woman.

Why did those memories thrill him so? Why did he not loathe every moment of his past with this woman instead of thinking back on it fondly? Was he too much like his father to ever change? Too much of an accident to be of any good?

He closed his eyes against a burst of wind. *Help me, Father. Help me.* He'd felt so strong when he'd left the cabin that morning. God had spoken to Him through his Word, through the story of Joseph in Genesis where a beautiful woman, the wife of Joseph's employer, had tempted him. But he'd resisted and run from her, only to be accused of ravishing her later on. However, in the end, God had elevated Joseph to the highest position in Egypt for his faithfulness.

Then the Lord had led Frederick to this verse in 1 Corinthians:

There hath no temptation taken you but such as is common to man: but God is faithful, who will not suffer you to be tempted above that ye are able; but will with the temptation also make a way to escape, that ye may be able to bear it.

Frederick closed his eyes. He would remain strong. He must.

"Haul the foresheet to windward!" Reena shouted beside him.

He blinked then watched Abraham carry out her orders without question, his black chest gleaming in the sun like polished onyx.

"Your quartermaster is a good man. You chose wisely."

"A compliment?" Her tone was sarcastic. "My heart is all aflutter."

He frowned at her. "I'm serious. Where did you find him?"

She hesitated for a moment as if pondering a curt reply, but then her eyes shifted to Abraham. "A slave ship."

Frederick leaned sideways on the railing and studied her. "You boarded a slaver?"

"Not an actual one, but a ship heading from Puerto Rico to Hispaniola, transporting a group of slaves. I thought they were merchants"—she glanced back down at Abraham—"but I found a cargo more precious than gold in her hold. Ten slaves. I freed them. Abraham, and"—she pointed to a black man hauling on a line—"Samuel joined my crew."

A gust of wind struck Frederick, cooling the sweat on his brow, and he leaned both arms on the railing and glanced over the brig once again. "And the rest of these men? The lad?"

"Michael? An orphan I found on Providence Island."

"And your besotted surgeon?"

She chuckled. "Indentured servant escaped from Barbados."

Frederick pointed toward the bosun he'd met last night in her cabin, the skinny, fidgety fellow. "And him?"

"I found Sedley on a deserted island. Put there by his pirate captain for stealing."

"And the woman?"

"Ah, you saw Jo." Reena stood up proudly. "She's my master gunner."

Frederick couldn't help but chuckle at Reena's beaming expression, so like a little girl proud of herself for successfully completing a school lesson.

Yet, she must have sensed his skepticism, for she added, "Do not be deceived, she's the best gunner I have seen."

"And where did you find such a prize?"

She bit her lip. "A brothel, if you truly wish to know. She had been beaten terribly."

Sorrow stole Frederick's grin. Yet, he was hardly surprised at any of these stories. Despite her flaws, Reena had the biggest heart of anyone he knew. 'Twas one of the reasons he had loved her. "Still rescuing the downtrodden, I see."

She gave him a sassy grin. "I rescued you, eh?"

"Touché, Kitten." He looked at her sternly. "However, you *will* take this downtrodden man to Kingston."

She studied him a moment with those golden eyes sparkling in the sunlight as if she were masterminding a devious plot.

"I will," she finally said. "If that is what you desire."

He frowned. She never gave in that easily.

Facing the main deck, she glanced up at the sails, then down at the horizon, and shouted to helmsman standing behind her at the tiller. "Watch your luff, Fletcher."

She faced Frederick. "After one short stop at Saint-Domingue," she added curtly.

He tightened his grip on the railing.

She shrugged. "'Tis on the way to Jamaica."

"I refuse to help you steal treasure."

She raised a brow. "Then do not. In the meantime, to prove I am not lying, I want you to co-captain with me."

Frederick released a heavy sigh. "You cannot resurrect the past back to life, Reena."

Turning, she gripped the railing and shouted across the deck. "Crew! All hands on deck!"

Everyone stopped what they were doing and turned to look up at her.

"This is Captain Carlton." She gestured toward Frederick. "Until we arrive in Kingston, he is co-captain of this brig. You will obey his every command, just as you would mine."

The crew responded as she hoped. "Aye, aye! Huzzah for Captain Carlton! Huzzah for Captain Carlton!"

She smiled sweetly at him. "See? You can trust me."

Sunlight reflected off something on her finger, and he squinted against the blinding light. 'Twas the pink pearl ring he'd given her so long ago—the ring that bespoke of promised marriage and faithfulness.

Guilt beat down upon him hotter than the fiery rays of the sun.

She followed his gaze. "Nay, I have not taken it off. I'm holding you to your promise, Freddy."

He grimaced and shifted his stance. "And I'm holding you to yours to take me to Kingston."

CHAPTER FIVE

Reena stood at the bow of the *Reckless,* one hand on the handle of her pistol, the other on the hilt of her sword, and her legs firmly positioned on the deck against the heaving of the brig. To her left rose the island of Tortuga, an infamous pirate haunt until ten years ago when all forms of piracy were outlawed and the capital of Saint-Domingue was moved from Tortuga to Port-de-Paix on the mainland. She'd been too young to enjoy the mad frivolity of that pirate haven, though the cliffs and mountains rising from the sea still resembled the turtle for which it was named.

To her right, sat the island of Hispaniola and the French colony of Saint-Domingue with its bustling capital Port-de-Paix—her destination.

Behind her, the sun set in a glorious array of crimson and gold waves spreading across the horizon. Oh, how she loved the Caribbean—its clear, turquoise waters, cleansing trade winds ripe with the scent of life, its many islands, secret coves, tall cliffs, and sandy beaches. She loved the feel of the ship bucking beneath her feet and the wind in her hair, the smell of salt, fish, wood, and tar. She loved her freedom most of all— defying her sex and pirating these waters as well as any man. She never wanted it to end. Which is why she simply had to get her hands on that treasure. Not for the doubloons and jewels she'd heard it contained, though the wealth couldn't hurt. But for something far more precious than money.

Speaking of something more precious than money, she heard Freddy shout an order behind her to one of the crew. His rich, deep voice sent a spiral of joy down her back. He was taking on the role of captain as she'd asked. She didn't think he would, but then how could he not? He was a born leader, a born commander, and one of the best pirate captains she'd ever known.

Which is why she simply had to persuade him to come along on their adventure tonight, to experience the rapture of fighting side by side again. Then, surely he would change his mind and stay with her.

The brig plunged over a wave, showering her with sea spray. Plucking the spyglass from her belt, she held it to her eye and brought into focus the city of Port-de-Paix, several miles off their starboard bow. Good. She leapt down the foredeck ladder onto the main deck and examined her crew.

"All hands, lay aloft to lower tops and sheets! Fletcher," she shouted to the helmsman at the whipstaff. "Four points to starboard." Glancing back over her shoulder, she gestured to a small inlet. "Bring her into that cove up ahead."

The man nodded and moved the staff as sailors leapt above to adjust sails.

"Abraham, put Bellamy on the lead and line. And then gather Sedley, Cobb, and Baines and meet me in my cabin."

Nodding, Abraham shouted further orders to the crew, sending them scrambling to do her bidding. She glanced up on the quarterdeck where Freddy stood, shoulders back, arms crossed over his chest, hair blowing in the wind behind him. Like the captain he was. She smiled, but he only shifted his gaze away to the approaching land.

Bilge water, but the man was annoying. She raised her voice to him. "Captain Carlton, you have the helm. Anchor her in that cove, if you please."

Even from this distance, she saw his jaw flex. "Aye, Captain," he responded, but she thought she saw a hint of a smile cross his lips.

Down in her cabin with her men assembled around her, she informed them of her plan to retrieve the treasure and assigned them their individual tasks. All of them were excited, save Abraham, who gave her his usual glower.

After the others left, he spoke up. "One of dese days, Cap'n, de good Lord's not goin' t' let yuh get away wit' stealin'."

"Steal the booty, steal the booty!" Fred squawked.

Reena tossed the bird a peanut. "'Tis not truly stealing this time. But"—she smiled his way—"I shall take your words under consideration."

Sails cracked above as the brig veered to starboard, and Reena gripped the edge of her desk. "Now away with you. I must change my attire. Have Jo come assist me."

Opening her wardrobe, Reena gathered a chemise, petticoats, silk stockings, stays, and a gown of lavender taffeta, and laid them on her bed with a sigh. She loathed donning these confining layers women were expected to wear, but there was naught to be done for it. She had a part to play tonight, and she couldn't do so looking like a pirate.

A rap on the door brought her master gunner Jo into the cabin, a grin on her face at the way Reena was staring at the gown.

"I should be so lucky to 'ave sich a lovely gown, Cap'n. 'Twill look lovely on ye."

Reena removed her breeches. "You may have it when I'm done with it, Jo."

"Me?" Jo chuckled. "Wearin' sich a fancy dress? Nah, Cap'n. 'Twouldn't suit me, an' I'd be gettin' soot an' such all over it from the guns."

Fred whistled, causing them both to laugh.

After slipping on her chemise and petticoats, Reena sucked in her breath while Jo laced up her stays.

"Wish I could join ye, Cap'n."

"I need you here, along with Brodie." Reena caught her breath. "Just in case Captain Carlton tries to sail off with my brig."

"'E wouldn't dare. 'Sides, the crew is loyal to ye. They wouldn't let 'im."

Reena hoped she was right about that, but if she'd learned one thing in her year as captain, 'twas that pirates were not to be trusted.

"I owes ye everythin'." Jo finished the final lace and tied it tight. "If not fer ye I'd be dead or beaten up agin by sailors."

Reena spun around and smiled at her friend. "'Twas my pleasure to take you from all that misery."

"Ye not only gave me my freedom, but ye gave me a life as well." Jo shifted her moist eyes away.

"'Tis a pirate's life fer me!" Fred said.

"And I would do it again. For you and any woman."

Muffled commands filtered down from above, and the brig jerked to larboard as the purl of water softened against the hull.

Reena wiggled, placed a hand on her middle, and tried to find her breath. "I had forgotten how uncomfortable these things are." She plucked the gown from her bed. "Help me get this blasted thing on."

After Jo helped her on with the lavender mantua, she combed and pinned Reena's hair up in a fashionable bun, completing the coiffure with a pair of jeweled pins. Finally, Reena added a gold necklace she'd pilfered from a prize ship.

The grinding of the anchor chain echoed through the cabin. Good. They were there.

"Lud, but ye are a sight, Cap'n. Why would Cap'n Carlton ever want to leave ye?"

"I have no idea." And, as she caught her reflection in the looking glass, she truly didn't.

Without so much as a knock, the door opened and in walked the man in question as if he owned the ship and was, indeed, the only captain. She'd call him on it if he wasn't so…so… Freddy.

"Apologies," he muttered when he saw Jo handing her a pair of lacy gloves. "I didn't realize you were dressing." He shifted his gaze and started to back out the door.

"No need, Captain," she responded with alacrity. "'Tis not like you haven't seen—"

He cleared his throat so loud, she stopped mid-sentence.

Fred whistled again. "Seen it all, seen it all."

"Jo knows everything about us, Freddy. JoAnna Hewe, may I present Captain Frederick Carlton. Freddy, this is my master gunner Jo."

To his credit, he dipped his head. "Charmed."

"Charmed, are ye?" Jo laughed, and if Reena didn't know her better, it appeared as though her face pinked.

Brodie entered behind Freddy and smiled, his eyes latching upon Jo. "Weel, who wouldna be charmed tae meet sich a fine woman?"

"Oh, hush now, the both of ye." Jo stared at Brodie. "That tongue o' yers always flatters when ye're into yer cups."

"I didna have a drink yet today, lassie." He winked at her.

"What is it, Brodie?" Reena asked, drawing his attention her way.

"I came to fetch Jo, Captain. There's an issue wit' one of the guns on the port side."

Nodding, Jo headed for the door, chuckling. "Charmed. I like 'im, Cap'n. I like 'im a lot."

Reena smiled and tugged on her gloves before facing Freddy again. When she did, she found him looking at her as if he'd never seen a woman before. Not in a salacious way, but in the way one would look at an angel floating down from heaven.

Mayhap he was seeing such a thing. The man claimed to have visions of heaven and hell. Surely it wasn't the sight of her in a gown that had him so befuddled. He'd seen that before. But the poor man was having trouble breathing. Finally he coughed, ripped his gaze from her, and marched further into the room. "Unusual attire for a raid."

"I'm an unusual woman." She moved to the cabinet against the bulkhead to choose her weapons.

He huffed his agreement while he stared out the stern windows where darkness pushed the last streaks of sunlight beneath the horizon.

Opening her cabinet, she grabbed a pistol, set her leg on a chair, swept up her skirts, and stuffed it in the small scabbard strapped to her leg. Then she slid a knife down the inside of her boot.

Coughing, Freddy turned his back to her.

Chuckling at his unexpected modesty, she gathered shot and a pouch of gunpowder from the cabinet.

"What do you plan on doing—fight an army?" he asked.

Fred shifted over his perch. "Fight t' the death, says I!"

"Hush your feathers." She smiled at the parrot then shrugged. "You never know what we may come across." She stuffed gunpowder in a pocket attached beneath her skirts, then settling the fabric around her legs, she sidled up to him with a smile. Ah, she could smell his scent of leather and oak and wished she could bottle it and bring it with her for comfort.

"I forgot about your birthmark until I just saw it again," he said as she drew close.

Now it was her turn to be embarrassed. She ran her fingers over the back of her neck. "I could swear my father made a bargain with God before I was born to brand me with a cross."

Freddy smiled. "Seeing it gives me hope for you."

"'Tis just a birthmark," she shot back, but then let out a sigh, regretting her harsh tone. She leaned back against her desk. "If I don't return, I suppose the *Reckless* is yours once again. Do with her as you wish. My only request is that you distribute what wealth I have among the crew and set them ashore someplace decent where they can find employment."

He stared at her curiously.

"That is unless you plan on jumping ship and swimming to shore—abandoning me once again."

Fred flapped his wings. "Walk the plank! Walk the plank!"

"Would you blame me?" Freddy said. "After you kidnapped me against my will?"

"Kidnap, rescue, it's a matter of perspective." She gave him a seductive smile as she circled him, admiring his transformation to pirate once again. "I must say, if 'tis possible, you make an even more handsome pirate than before."

She expected him to laugh or perhaps smile at her compliment. Instead, he whirled about and grabbed her by the wrist. "Quit playing games, Reena. You have my word I will not jump ship, but only if you take me to Kingston after this ridiculous—What do you mean *if* you don't come back?"

Snagging her hand from him, she fingered a wayward curl. "I said there was treasure on Saint-Domingue. I didn't say it was going to be easy to steal."

"I thought you weren't stealing. Oh, thunderation! Where exactly is this treasure?"

"Underneath Antoine du Casse's estate. In the wine cellar, if you must know."

Freddy grabbed the cross around his neck and paced over the Turkish carpet. "Antoine, the nephew of Jean-Baptiste du Casse, the governor of Saint-Domingue, the infamous—and I might add—*brutal* pirate? You intend to abscond with his treasure right beneath his nose?"

She smiled. "Sounds exciting, doesn't it?"

He halted. "You're mad."

"Indeed. What pleasure otherwise?"

"Mad as an old boot!" Fred screeched.

Abraham appeared at the door. "We's ready t' go, Cap'n."

Clutching her skirts, Reena swept past Freddy, intentionally brushing against his arm. "You have command, Captain."

He growled under his breath as she followed Abraham out the door. They were halfway down the companionway before he called out.

"Wait!"

Wiping the smile from her face, she returned to her cabin where she found him strapping a baldric over his chest and stuffing pistols and knives within.

Memories assailed her of countless times in the past when she'd watched him prepare for a battle or raid. Finally, he plucked one of her cutlasses from the cabinet and slid it into his scabbard, then grabbed a bandanna from her desk and tied it around his head. Her insides melted at the sight.

She feigned a frown. "What are you doing?"

"I'm coming with you. What kind of man would I be if I allowed a woman to put herself in danger alone? Even though 'tis your own doing."

She hid her smile with a grimace. "You don't think I will succeed?"

"Nay, I fear you will."

CHAPTER SIX

*F*rederick could not believe he had somehow agreed to participate in a raid. He had promised God he was through with this life—the life of a freebooter and member of the Brethren of the Coast. Just fancy words for "pirate and thief." But how could he allow Reena to be killed? He would have to answer to her parents, Captain Merrick and Lady Charlisse, as to why he did not accompany her. Besides, the thought of losing her caused his insides to feel like they were being trampled by a herd of pigs.

But now as he helped pull the boat onto the sandy beach and lent a hand to assist Reena from the craft, he wondered if she had done this on purpose, exaggerated the danger in order to get him to join her.

She started to lead them across the beach, but he nudged her behind him and forged ahead. A half-moon flung creamy light over the shadowy scene as he plunged into the dense foliage fringing the edge of the shore. Wind hissed through palm fronds, crickets chirped, and the mad dash of waves filled his ears. Shoving aside branches and leaves, he tried to ignore the throbbing in his boot-clad feet. Pain caused by Reena— both physical and emotional. Only God knew what other pain she intended to cause him this night.

Why had the woman put on such a lovely gown only to traipse through the muddy jungle? Had she lost all reason? Especially when it came to Antoine du Casse! The man would just as soon slit her throat as look at her.

Which was why Frederick had come along.

Footsteps sloshed behind them—the shifty-eyed Sedley, and two other sailors Frederick had not been introduced to yet. All of them armed to the teeth and seemingly excited about their adventure. Abraham had wanted to join them, but Reena insisted he stay with the ship now that Frederick was going. Even so, Frederick could not deny a spike of thrill at the thought of taking a risk again, embarking on some half-cocked adventure as he had done so often in the past with this woman. But 'twas only emotions, and he'd learned over the past year not to allow his emotions to rule him anymore. Instead, he would be ruled by the Spirit of God. That was the sign of a mature man, of a godly man.

At her direction, he made a right turn down another path which finally opened to a dirt street that was busier than he expected at this late hour of night. Intermittent street lamps spread cones of light far into the distance as if the maker of light had left bread crumbs to follow. A group of sailors, laughing and speaking French, entered a pub across the way, while several servants wove around pigs skittering about. A carriage rambled by as a pianoforte entertained them from a distance.

"This way." Reena wove her arm through his and entered the avenue, sauntering down the street as if they were on a Sunday stroll through the park. Her crew kept slightly behind them.

Frederick only hoped they looked like Frenchmen and didn't draw too much attention. It had been a while since he'd been in a sword fight, and he didn't relish engaging in one again. Especially not with a wounded shoulder.

Reena glanced up at him and smiled—one of those pleased-with-herself smiles. He gave her a look that said *be careful*, but it was lost on her as she sauntered down the street, smiling at passersby and holding her head up so high, you'd think she was the governor's wife.

Suspicion took over any enjoyment Frederick might have of the evening. What was she up to? His uneasiness only increased as they walked right up to a carriage parked before the tavern, Bonne Chance. Immediately upon arriving, a man in a black livery opened the door and she promptly climbed in.

Frederick could only stand and stare at her as Sedley pushed past him and entered while the two sailors climbed on back.

"Freddy, hurry—get in." She gestured for him to climb up. "This is our ride."

"Our ride? To where?"

"To Antoine's estate, of course."

Frederick leaned in to whisper, "You are taking a carriage to the man's house from whom you intend to steal?"

"How else can I carry the treasure away? Get in. We shall be late."

Frederick felt like laughing, but the situation was far too serious to do so. "Do you have an appointment to pilfer the man's goods?"

She smiled. "In truth, he invited me to supper."

If Frederick weren't such a fool, he would not have gotten into that blasted carriage, not listened to the woman's foolhardy plans, not allowed himself to be driven to the vast estate of Antoine du Casse.

He especially would not have gotten himself involved in something that was completely against everything he believed.

But he *was* a fool. A fool for Reena, for he could not allow her to get captured—or worse, killed—without at least trying his best to protect her.

So, here he sat in a fancy phaeton with leather seats and blue velvet curtains, being jostled here and there as they ascended a hill over a bumpy road. Peering through the tiny window, he stared out over the landscape, which at the moment was naught but a jungle of gloomy shadows. A moment ago, however, he'd had a good view of the flickering lights of Port-de-Paix and the vast black ocean beyond, its waves laced with silver moonlight.

The scents of wildflowers and loamy forest blasted over him in the cool evening breeze as the carriage bounced around a curve. The slight thud of boots and lift of the carriage told Frederick that Reena's two men, Baines and Cobb, had leapt off the back as instructed.

Which meant they were close to the estate.

He should be anxious, excited—feel the usual thrill that accompanied such an adventure.

Instead, he felt angry and morose.

Leaning forward, elbows on his knees, he studied the woman sitting across from him, a true lady by all appearances with her posh gown and jewels sparkling around her neck. He'd never seen her look so lovely, and if he admitted it, the sight of her had taken him aback. It still took him aback as she smiled at him, her eyes sparkling with excitement in the lantern light.

"You can still turn around, Reena, pick up your sailors, and head back to the ship. Forget this reckless plan."

Beside him, Sedley snorted.

Removing her muddy boots, Reena pulled out a pair of satin slippers from the pocket beneath her skirts and put them on. "I see it shall take a while for you to return to your old self, Freddy. But never fear." She took one of his hands in hers. "Your zeal will return."

Pulling away, Frederick leaned back on the seat with a huff. "I have plenty of zeal, Reena. For the right things."

Before she could respond, the carriage turned onto a gravel pathway. Through the window Frederick spotted the white columns of a large two-story home with circular steps leading to a wide front porch and mullioned windows on either side.

The carriage jerked to a stop. The horses snorted, and Reena arched a brow at him. "I can count on you, right, Freddy? To do as I asked."

Against everything within him, he clenched his jaw and nodded.

A footman in a white periwig opened the door and situated the steps. A gloved hand appeared, and Reena took it, winked at Frederick, and stepped from the carriage.

Frederick followed her, Sedley behind him. Flickering lantern light shimmered over marble steps and lit a wide French porch bedecked with carved wooden furniture. On either side of the double door stood two men armed with muskets and swords, both barely offering a glance to the newcomers. The front doors swept open to a short, stout man in a butler's livery with red, puffy cheeks, a thin mustache, and a scowl on his face.

"Mademoiselle Hyde. A pleasure to see you again."

Again? Frederick withheld a growl.

Reena only smiled in return and handed the man her cloak. "Merci, Girad."

The butler scanned Frederick and Sedley with an uplifted nose that wrinkled as if he smelled something disagreeable. Frederick returned the stare with equal repugnance, wondering yet again why he was even here.

Reena waved a hand toward Frederick. "These are my men, Girad. Can you see them to a sitting room to wait for me until I'm ready to leave?"

Girad cleared his throat. "Mademoiselle, I fear they shall have to wait outside. Monsieur du Casse does not approve of armed men in his house."

Frederick shifted his stance. *Good.* Then they *all* could leave.

Reena didn't flinch. Didn't even bat an eye. "Then you may inform your master that I have no intention of traveling through such a dangerous city without protection. Hence, they will stay in the house where I can easily call them, or I will be forced to leave immediately." She gave a tight smile. "I'm sure you do not want to disappoint Monsieur du Casse. He has been so looking forward to our dinner, I am told."

Girad shifted his droopy eyes between her and Frederick. His lips twitched as if he had an itch he could not scratch, but finally, he nodded and the snap of his fingers brought another man to his side. "Take these men to the servants' hall."

After firing one last angry glance at Reena, Frederick followed the man down the hall to the right, down a set of stairs, and into a room dimly lit by two candles perched on a long wooden table surrounded by chairs. Decks of cards lay about, along with a tattered chess board and several old books. Along one wall, a sideboard stood, housing plates, cups, trays and silverware. The servant retreated out the door and turned before he shut it. "You will remain in here, monsieurs, until your lady is finished."

Frederick closed his eyes for a moment and attempted to reel in his fury. He wanted to shout, pluck out his sword, grab Reena, and leave this hideous place. Instead he charged to the cold hearth and kicked the bricks. She knew this vile Frenchman…had been here before. No wonder she was so familiar with the layout of the house. How long had she been consorting with the nephew of a pirate? What sort of relationship did they have?

And why did he suddenly feel jealous at the thought? *Thunderation!* He kicked the bricks again as the chink of glass sounded behind him. Swinging about, his eyes narrowed on Sedley, helping himself to what looked like a bottle of brandy he'd found in the cupboard.

"No more of that." He ordered the man after Sedley slammed the liquor to the back of his throat.

"Ah, come now, Cap'n. Ye can 'ardly 'xpect me t' turn down free brandy?"

"I can and will. I need all your wits tonight."

Sedley stared at him, seemingly debating whether to obey him or not. But Frederick took a step toward him, placing his hand on the hilt of his sword. Sedley smiled.

Strange fellow. Medium height, hair as light as white sand, stained blue neckerchief around his neck. And nervous, always nervous.

"Tell me, Mr. Sedley, how did you come to sail with Ree…Captain Hyde."

He shrugged. "Found me on a deserted island."

"Why did your captain leave you there?"

"He were a mean ol' cur, he were. Didn't like me face. That's wha' he said."

Frederick studied him with suspicion. "Captain Hyde said it was for stealing more than your share of a prize."

A flicker of fear appeared on the man's face, but then it was gone. "That's wha' the captain accused me of. But it weren't so." The man fidgeted and walked to examine one of the old books, though Frederick doubted he could read.

Moving to the window, Frederick eased back the curtains and stared into the darkness, waiting for the signal.

The signal that once again would make him a thief.

CHAPTER SEVEN

"*A*ntoine, dearest, how good it is to see you again."
Reena sashayed into the sitting room that was all aglitter. Candlelight fluttered over a velvet stuffed settee, several matching chairs, and a polished mahogany table. A plush rug centered the room while exquisite paintings lined the walls above walnut wainscoting. Antoine du Casse rose regally from his seat, glass of port in hand, and approached, bowing elegantly before her. He took her hand and placed a kiss upon it, delicate and sensual.

"Mademoiselle Hyde, you look ravishing as ever. How long I have waited to see you. Pray, what has kept you from me?"

Reena withdrew her hand, resisting the temptation to wipe it on her gown. Instead, she moved to the windows and stared out into the night. "Why, Antoine, you know how busy I am pirating the seas." Turning, she offered him her most charming smile.

Setting down his glass, he slunk up behind her and fingered a curl dangling about her neck. "Someday I wish to pirate those seas with you, if you'll allow." His hot breath rippled down her neck as the scent of his lemon pomade curdled the contents of her stomach.

She moved from him. "And yet I have informed you in no uncertain terms that I work better alone."

"*Mais*, I have a ship of my own. Think of the two of us sailing side by side, ravaging these *sauvage* seas. Such amusement we would have! Such excitement!" He reached for her, but she smiled and shifted away.

"Aha, *ma chérie*. You play the *coquette* with me, *non*?"

"I wouldn't dare, Antoine. I am here, after all, am I not?"

This did not seem to appease the man for he moved to pour more port into his glass. He also poured her a glass and brought it to her, halting to study her curiously. He was not unattractive. Tall, fine boned, dark hair, with a strong chin and deep-set brown eyes. But he was a bit of a dandy for her liking, and there was something sinister behind his gaze that always gave her pause.

However, he had not hid his interest in her, not since the day they had met out at sea and she had bested him in a battle for a prize. When he boarded the *Reckless* and saw that a lady captain had outwitted him, he'd fallen at her feet in near worship. Since then, he'd called on her many times to visit his estate where he wooed and charmed her and begged her to become his mistress. For his uncle would never allow a marriage to a British pirate.

But Reena would be no man's mistress. No man's save Freddy's. And even with Freddy, she wished to be bonded in marriage rather than toyed with as a plaything on the side. Not that Freddy would ever do that. He'd promised to marry her and would have done so—if he hadn't recommitted his life to God.

Antoine handed her the port, and she sipped the sweet, pungent flavor. "I'm simply famished, Antoine. When do we eat?"

"Soon, *ma chérie*." He moved to sit on the sofa and patted the spot beside him. "What have you been up to? Or are you allowed to tell me?" He chuckled.

She gave him a sardonic smile. "I have not attacked any French ships, if that's what you mean, Antoine. But should one loaded with gold pass my way, I cannot deny 'twould be tempting."

"I would expect nothing less."

Good, then he wouldn't be disappointed when she robbed him blind. Speaking of, what were Baines and Cobb up to? She glanced out the window, wondering if she should have chosen more reliable men.

"You seem *nerveux*. So unlike you, *ma chérie*. Come sit."

'Twas more of a command than a request, and Reena knew not to play games with this volatile man. As amusing as it was to act the coquette while stealing his gold, she must be extremely cautious and conceal her emotions. After all, 'twas during one of his drunken tirades that he had revealed the treasure he stored below in his wine cellar. All she'd had to do that night was nestle up to him and suffer a few kisses before he'd told her all about the treasure chest he'd stolen from a Spanish merchantman, full of gold, silver, and jewels. But apparently, there was something else within this particular chest, something that—when he'd described it to her—she knew 'twas worth far more than all the gold in the world.

Setting her glass down, she eased beside him on the sofa, knowing he would probably attempt to take liberties as he usually did. But she also knew that within seconds his attention would be diverted elsewhere.

He inched closer, his eyes traveling over her as if unraveling each thread of her gown in his mind. "Mademoiselle. When are you going to give yourself to me?"

When she joined the Catholic church and became a nun. She gave him a coy smile.

He leaned in so close, his hot breath violated her chest. Her nose wrinkled at his bergamot cologne.

Hurry, men!

Antoine nibbled on her neck. Cringing, she allowed him.

A loud *boom!* came from outside, rattling the windows.

Finally.

⚓

The expected explosion thundered in Frederick's ears, followed by shouting and retreating footsteps. Moving to the door, he slowly opened it and peered outside. More shouts in French echoed through the halls and bounced off the high ceilings of the mansion.

"Come." He motioned for Sedley to follow, then slipped into the hallway and turned right, trying to remember Reena's directions. At the end of the hall, he opened a door that led to the servant's stairs.

Footsteps pounded up them from below—fast.

Shutting the door, he pushed Sedley into the shadows just as it burst open and two servants, carrying clubs, dashed through and darted down the hall.

Frederick slipped down the stairs before the door shut, Sedley behind him. They sped down two flights, then through the laundry room and kitchen. A few scullery maids and cooks glanced at them curiously as the scent of lamb stew made his mouth water. Smiling at them, he proceeded calmly as if he were meant to be there, then once out of sight, fled down another set of stairs into the cellar.

The smell of mold and moist wood struck him along with a mist of cool air as naught but shadows and gloom surrounded him. Grabbing a lantern from a table, he reached in his pocket, struck flint to steel, and lit it.

Pushing past him, Sedley rushed ahead, wove around two floor-to-ceiling racks of wine and headed toward the far end, where Reena had told them the treasure was buried.

Holding the lantern aloft, Frederick followed and found the man already prying up the floorboards with his ax.

Shouts above sounded muffled and distant. A musket shot cracked the air.

"Hurry." Frederick plucked out his knife and pried off another board…then another. Sedley made quick work of the rest, and Frederick held up the lantern and shook his head at the sight. Just as Reena had described—a wooden chest engraved with Catholic crosses and pictures of ships and snakes, crisscrossed with leather straps and locked by an iron bolt.

Sedley blew out a low whistle.

Running his fingers over the cross around his neck, Frederick begged for forgiveness, then gestured at Sedley. "Take that end."

Together he and Sedley hefted the heavy chest from its resting place, then carried it with great difficulty around the wine racks and up the cellar stairs. At the top, Frederick gestured for Sedley to set it down while he listened for the sound of carriage wheels.

Instead he heard footsteps, soft footsteps, descending from above. Drawing his sword, he waited.

Sedley's twitching only increased.

The swish of silk sounded as Reena appeared in the stairwell.

"There you are. Come, let's hurry," she whispered calmly as if they were having tea at an afternoon soiree. "Antoine has gone outside with his men to investigate the explosions as we guessed he would."

She turned and moved back up to the pantry, where thankfully, no staff remained. Still calm, yet quick, she opened the servants' entrance doorway leading to the back of the house.

Holding fingers to her mouth, she whistled and within seconds, the snap of reins and rattle of wheels sounded. Their landau appeared out of the darkness and stopped before them.

It only took Frederick and Sedley a few minutes to heft the chest onto the back.

The driver Reena had hired nervously shouted, "*Se dépêcher*! We must go!"

Sounds alerted Frederick, and he whirled to find two men, swords drawn, bursting around the corner into the back courtyard.

He drew his own blade and advanced.

Reena did the same.

"Get in the carriage!" Frederick ordered.

"I will not leave you." She took a position by his side, not an ounce of fear on her face.

"Then you will lose your treasure and we'll both be put in jail. Now go! I can take care of myself."

The men advanced, grins on their faces. Where was Sedley? Frederick quickly glanced around. Nowhere in sight. Coward. And what of Cobb and Baines?

The first man slashed at Frederick while Reena took on the second.

The hideous scrape of metal rang through the air. Frederick swooped down to strike the man's legs, but his parry met him with equal strength. By his side, Reena dipped her blade in defense as her attacker attempted to thrust her through.

Another man sprang around the corner, saw them, and shouted behind him in French.

"I am leaving!" The driver snapped the reins and the landau lurched forward.

Distracted, Reena glanced toward him, intending to say something, but her attacker slashed her arm. Shrieking, she heaved her blade toward the man's middle. Blood appeared on his waistcoat. She bashed him over the head with the hilt of her sword.

"Go, Reena. Please! No sense in both of us being captured."

Breath heaving, she pressed a hand over her arm. Blood seeped between her fingers. Still, she stood her ground, her terrified gaze traveling from him and back to the now five men advancing upon them.

Finally, she dashed for the moving carriage and leapt onto the back. "I will come back for you!" she shouted as the landau disappeared into the night. The last thing Frederick heard was the rattle of wheels over the cobblestones and the victorious grunts of the men about to put an end to his life.

CHAPTER EIGHT

"*B*last it all! We are going back for him." Sticking her head out the carriage window, Reena shouted at the drive. "*Arrêtez*! Stop immediately!"

But the man only snapped the reins harder. The horses sped around a curve, tossing Reena back into the carriage and across the seat.

Sedley took her arm to help her up, but she jerked from him. "Where were you? Did you not see those men attacking us?"

"Nay, Cap'n. I was tryin' t' convince the driver t' stay. He woulda left long ago if not fer me." His gaze shot to the trees racing past the window. "We can't go back." His voice rang with alarm. "It be a death sentence and ye knows it."

She did know it. But she didn't care. She'd finally gotten Freddy back, and she was not going to lose him again.

Turning aside, she lifted her skirts, plucked the pistol from the scabbard on her thigh, and once again, stuck her head out the window. This time, she leveled the gun at the man. "Stop at once or I'll shoot!"

The driver, whose hearing miraculously improved, uttered a curse and pulled back on the reins. The horses slowed and finally stopped. Cobb and Baines leapt off the back.

"Why is we stoppin', Cap'n?"

Reena jumped from the carriage, pistol still pointed at the driver. "We are going back to get my friend."

The driver uttered a string of French in such rapid succession that she had a hard time understanding him. But she understood enough—she would have to shoot him because he wasn't going back to face certain death.

Sedley tugged on his neckerchief. "I don't knows wha' he said, but methinks I agree."

Frowning, Reena studied the surrounding jungle, then stared up at the moon as if it held the answer to her dilemma.

But she hadn't time to ponder it when shouts preceded the thunder of horse hooves coming from behind them.

"*Dépêche-toi!*" The driver gestured for them to get back in the carriage or he would leave without them.

More frustrated than she'd been in a long while, Reena grabbed hold of the carriage window just as it lurched forward and hoisted herself inside.

The rest of the journey was a blur of jungle, cobblestone streets, shifting lanterns, bawdy music coming from pubs, and the stench of pig droppings and human refuse.

She paid the driver, who uttered a curse before he left them in a cloud of dust. Sedley, Cobb, and Baines, with many a complaint, carried the chest through the jungle to the beach where a jolly boat awaited to take them to the *Reckless*.

Reckless. The words painted on the bow scraped against Reena's guilt as they rowed toward the brig. Reckless, indeed. An accurate description of her life, of each adventure she'd undertaken. And now, she'd been reckless with the one man she loved. Only God knew what he was enduring at the depraved hand of Antoine.

"Put it down there," Reena ordered the men carrying the treasure chest into her cabin. "Now, out with you!" The sailors scrambled to escape her fury as she clawed at the pins holding up her hair and tossed them onto her desk. Dark strands tumbled over her shoulders as she gripped the edge, attempting to contain her anger whilst coming up with a plan to get Freddy back. Preferably alive.

"There be treasure thar!" Fred announced.

She heard Abraham enter. She could tell because of the peculiar light sound of his footsteps, though the man had to weigh well over fifteen stone.

"It seems dings didn't go as well as yuh expected."

She spun to face him, her anger growing at the look of reprimand on his face. "Do you see Captain Carlton standing here with me?"

"Beware the Cap'n's fury!" Fred bellowed.

Despite the parrot's warning, not a speck of fear appeared in Abraham's gaze as he crossed thick arms over his chest and dipped his head toward the treasure. "Nay, but looks t' me like yuh got what yuh was after."

Reena ran fingers through her hair, found another pin, and flung it to the deck. "But I lost the most important thing."

"Wha' did yuh dink would happen, Cap'n?"

"Certainly not this." Reaching around her back, she tried to tear through the buttons. "Summon Jo. I must get dressed."

"No need, Cap'n. I'm here." The female voice preceded the woman who marched in with more authority than her station. Behind her, Brodie entered, rubbing eyes that finally landed on Reena. "Anyone injured?"

Reena waved him off. "Nay. Go back to bed."

"There's blood on your sleeve." He pointed to her arm and started for her.

"Just a scratch. Jo, come, help me off with this," Reena turned her back to the woman. "And out with the rest of you!"

The shuffle of feet sounded, and Michael dashed around her and into her arms. "You all right, Captain?"

"Aye." She embraced the lad, finding unusual comfort in his concern.

"Where's Captain Carlton?" Stepping back from her, he looked around the cabin, his gaze barely grazing the treasure chest.

"Don't you worry. He'll be here soon enough. Jo, come!" She turned her back to the master gunner once again.

"Your arm." Michael pointed to her wound.

"Dina fash yerself, lad. She says she's all right," Brodie handed a bandage to Jo. "Fer when she comes tae her senses."

Before Reena could offer a retort, Michael reached up and touched her wound. 'Twas a mere second, and then he withdrew his hand and smiled.

"Wha' yuh dink t' be doin', Cap'n?" Abraham said.

"Why, rescue Freddy, of course. Again. Though this time 'tis my fault and my fault alone." Her only consolation was that she knew Freddy. He was tough, strong, defiant. He could withstand much before he would falter. And she intended to get him out before that happened. Of course she could bargain with Antoine for his release—use the man's attraction to her—but she knew the Frenchman, knew his prideful fury, and he would just as soon gut her than deal with someone who had stolen his treasure from beneath his nose.

Freddy had risked himself for her. She still could not believe it. This was *her* quest, not his. He could have easily run off and abandoned her when Antoine's men attacked. Instead, he allowed her to escape. Surely that meant he still loved her.

Brodie grabbed Michael and headed for the door. "Come, lad. There's things ye ought nae tae see at yer age."

Michael nodded in her direction. "You'll find him, Captain Reena. You'll both be safe." And the declaration, no matter how naive, brought an odd comfort to Reena.

Jo finished untying the back of the gown, and Reena glanced over her shoulder to find Abraham still standing there.

"Do yuh have a plan, Cap'n? Or are yuh jis' goin' t' charge in dere and get yuhself killed?"

Fred skittered back and forth on his perch. "Muskets to the tops!"

Reena sighed. "Have I ever gotten myself killed? Now, allow me to get dressed or I'll do it in front of you."

The stubborn man grimaced, the darks of his eyes piercing her.

She allowed the gown to slip from her shoulders, and that's all it took for him to turn and march out.

Minutes later, she felt like herself with her breeches, boots, waistcoat, headscarf, and assorted weapons stuffed in appropriate places. Jo had placed a bandage on her arm and Reena stretched it, suddenly realizing it no longer pained her— and just as well.

There was no time to waste in rescuing Freddy.

The fist struck hard and solid. Frederick's head snapped to the side, and he gripped the arms of the chair he was tied to.

The metallic taste of blood filled his mouth and trickled from his lips.

"I will ask you one more time, monsieur." Antoine du Casse stood above Frederick like Goliath towering over David. But Frederick was much closer to being a David—with the power of God on his side—than this French pimp was to being a Goliath.

"Where is the pirate witch? Where is her ship anchored?"

"I don't know nothin'." Frederick answered, mimicking uneducated speech. 'Twas best if Antoine thought him a common sailor than someone close to Reena.

At Antoine's nod, his man punched Frederick in the stomach. All air fled his lungs as a burst of pain radiated through him.

"Go get the iron." Frederick heard him say in French. Had he interpreted correctly? Iron?

"Now, monsieur, you *will* tell me, or I'll have you stripped and locked in the gibbet by the docks where the pirate wench can watch your carcass rot."

Frederick swallowed. Not the best way to die. And he had no doubt the nephew of the governor had the power to do such a hideous thing.

Antoine leaned over and cocked his head. "Hmm. Look how handsome you are. I would wager the *femme fatale* will come back for such a prize."

Frederick shook his head. "Jist joined 'er crew last week. She won't risk anythin' fer the likes o' me."

The man fisted Frederick across the jaw again so hard, the chair tipped and crashed to the floor. His head thudded against the stones. His vision blurred and confusion mottled his thoughts.

Where was he? Why was he here?

He shook his head as his chair was hoisted up so fast, it caused a new wave of dizziness. The ropes on his right hand had loosened.

Black shadows slithered around Antoine, around his waist, between his legs and circling his head. Frederick squeezed his eyes shut. He must be seeing things.

When he opened them, they were gone. But something far more frightening filled his vision. A branding iron—glowing red.

"Where is she? Or I'll mark that pretty face of yours."

Frederick had never considered himself attractive, though more than one woman had declared him so. It had never been of import to him. But at the moment, he found he did not relish being mutilated.

Two men dashed into the cellar, out of breath, their gazes wandered from Frederick to Antoine.

"*Oui?*" Antoine glanced their way, giving Frederick time to wiggle his right hand free from the ropes.

They replied in French, and though Frederick didn't understand all the words, he knew they'd lost Reena. She had gotten away.

Despite himself, he smiled. The action sent a spiral of pain across his cheek. Enhanced further when Antoine must have noticed and struck him again, followed by a string of French expletives, which sent the men fleeing back out the door.

If only the branding man would leave as well. But he remained, holding the simmering iron, awaiting his master's orders.

Leaning over, Antoine gripped both arms of the chair until his face was inches from Frederick's, and he could smell the brandy on his breath.

"Then what use have I for you, monsieur? Your mistress has left you." He pushed from the chair. "Take him to the docks and put him in the gibbet." Halting, he turned and grinned. "But brand him first. Let him die marked as a slave to Antoine du Casse!"

The shadows reappeared, slinking around Antoine, but this time, eyes appeared within them—small-slitted reptilian eyes that smiled at Frederick in victory.

The branding iron sizzled beside his ear.

And all he thought to do was utter, "Jesus, Jesus, Jesus."

"He calls to God." Antoine laughed as he directed the man to continue.

The shadows around Antoine jolted backward into the darkness of the cellar, releasing the man for a moment. A look of confusion crossed his face for the briefest of moments, and he shifted his shoulders as if a weight had been removed.

The branding iron drew closer. Frederick struggled against the bonds that held his left hand and feet.

Antoine's eyes met Frederick's, and something sinister glazed them again. "Do it!" he shouted at the brander. The shadows returned.

The red-hot iron filled Frederick's vision. Terror numbed his mind. Was this to be his fate? *Lord?*

A surge of unusual strength rippled through him. Shoving his feet against the stone floor, he forced his chair up, grabbed the handle of the branding iron with his right hand and thrust it against the brute's chest. The man screamed and fell backward. Frederick snatched the iron and seared the ropes on his other hand, then swung around and slammed the chair into Antoine and his remaining henchman.

The rope sizzled and smoked. Pain etched across his wrist, and the chair dropped to his feet which were, unfortunately, still bound to it. The action nearly toppled him. The branding man was still moaning and gaping at his chest. Antoine and his brute charged Frederick.

He backed against the stone wall as hard as he could. The chair splintered into pieces, and his legs broke free. He swung the iron, striking the brute. The man fell backward with a moan.

Shock registered in Antoine's eyes as he backed away and fumbled for a knife clipped to his belt.

Frederick kicked him in the stomach. Antoine flew backward against a rack of wine bottles. The rack teetered. Two of the bottles crashed to the floor, one struck him on the head.

The eerie chime of a sword being drawn turned Frederick around to see the branding man coming his way. He thrust his sword at Frederick but Frederick met it with the iron. A blood-curdling *clang* echoed through the room as the man chuckled and forced Frederick back.

One more second and the brute would overpower him, but Frederick leapt to his side and struck the man's head with the iron. He toppled to the floor.

Moaning, Antoine struggled to rise. Frederick placed his boot atop his chest, pinning him to the ground as he plucked the knife from his belt.

"A pleasure, monsieur." Frederick mocked.

Then flinging the iron away and gathering Antoine's sword, Frederick mounted the stairs, opened the door, and fled into the night.

CHAPTER NINE

Something was amiss. Port-de-Paix was up in arms. Literally. Normally at three in the morning only a few people would be about, a brothel or mayhap a tavern still open for business, but it would be quiet, hushed, sleepy throughout most of the town. Instead, Reena exited the jungle onto a street that was full of armed men—bands of them—dashing about, banging on doors, and diving into alleyways.

She slid back into the shadow of trees, Abraham and Brodie doing the same. She hadn't wanted to bring their surgeon along, but Brodie insisted. In truth, he was just as good at fighting as he was at doctoring, and she might have need of him this night.

Another group of men darted by, the clap of their boots on the cobblestones sending a spike of fear through Reena. Surely Antoine wasn't looking for her. He would have assumed she'd be back on her ship by now, not hiding in town.

Her breath stopped. *Freddy.*

"He escaped," she whispered to Abraham standing beside her.

A breeze fluttered the leaves above them as a night bird uttered a shrill warning.

Brodie joined her on her other side. "Aye, Captain. But where would he go?"

More armed men appeared around the corner.

Where, indeed? "He must be making his way back to the *Reckless.*"

Abraham shifted his stance. "If I was him, I'd be hidin' out till Antoine calls off his dogs."

"I agree." Reena rested her hand atop the hilt of her cutlass. "Then we shall simply have to find him first."

"Hmm." Abraham interjected his usual indeterminate groan.

"Weel, they will be lookin' fer ye tae, Captain."

"They're looking for a woman, Brodie. Not three men."

"Ach now, if he's headin' to the ship, wouldna be best to wait fer him at the beach?"

"Nay," Reena said. "He needs our help, and I won't risk him getting caught again."

A chorus of katydids swept away Abraham's groan as Reena burst from the jungle and led them down the street, unsure even where to start.

The firing of a pistol cracked the night sky, followed by shouts and the chime of blade on blade.

"I believe we've found him, gentlemen." Drawing her sword, Reena darted into the night.

Frederick had been so close to the jungle lining the southeastern part of town—so close to freedom. Within feet. Feet! But then six men had come out of nowhere—materializing from the darkness, specters armed with every manner of device with which to kill a man.

Six to one. Not great odds, especially when he was sure one of his ribs was cracked and his face was battered. Not to mention the gunshot wound throbbing on his shoulder and his sore feet. All wounds caused by Reena. But who was counting?

Raising his sword, he scanned the swarthy lot of Frenchmen who no doubt would rather be in bed with their wives or mistresses than out here with him. But men who were equally afraid of the wrath of their master.

He grinned, the grin that always seemed to set his enemy on edge. "*Allons-y*, let us play, then."

One man spit to the side. Another chuckled. The rest hesitated. And in that hesitation, Frederick swerved his blade at the first man, thrusting him backward, then grabbed the pistol from his belt and fired at the man beside him.

Gripping his leg, the man yelled and hit the dirty street like a sack of rice.

One down, five to go.

Lord, if this is how I am to die, let me go down with honor and prevent me from taking a life.

The smell of gunpowder pinched his nose as two men advanced toward him, one with a sword, the other a knife—evil intent in their eyes and malevolent grins on their faces.

He swept his blade up to meet the first man's sword. The chime echoed through the night air. The other man thrust a knife toward him. Frederick leapt to the side. Pain sliced him as he spun and met the first man's sword, steel to steel. Left then right, he parried, ignoring the pain pulsating through his body. Slashing this way, diving, leaping, he drove the two men backward. A sword came at him from the right. He jumped out of the way. Another sliced him from behind. He whirled, swung his blade and drew a line of blood over the man's chest. Roaring, he fell backward.

Frederick heard—rather than saw—the whiz of a sword heading toward him. He ducked and swung blindly around, striking his opponent in the legs. The man dropped. Two more swords came at him.

He shoved one of them away with his blade, but the other was heading straight for his heart.

This was it. "Lord, take me home," he managed to whisper when a shot exploded in his ears.

The attacker dropped his sword. His eyes widened and he stumbled backward, a red stain advancing over his coat.

Frederick didn't have time to seek out his rescuer before another man charged him. He raised his blade and swung to attack, wondering why the other men weren't advancing upon him as well.

Chimes that weren't from his sword rang through the air. Reena appeared at his side, cutlass drawn.

The man before her chortled. "A woman!" as if the very idea were ludicrous.

She charged him, brandishing her sword with more skill than most men he knew. The poor fellow didn't stand a chance. But Frederick couldn't worry about her at the moment as another man came at him from the left.

Enough of this. He swung his blade ferociously, catching the attacker off guard. Snagging the hilt of the man's sword with his blade, he jerked it from his grip and sent it flying through the air. Then holding the tip of his cutlass to the man's throat, he said through gritted teeth, "Go tell your master he will never brand me."

Eyes alight with terror, the man darted off. Frederick turned to assist Reena, but she had already bested her man and sent him fleeing as well. Beyond her, Abraham and Brodie had done the same with the others.

She sheathed her blade and smiled his way.

Frederick wanted to throttle her, shout at her, run from her, but most of all, at the moment, he wanted to take her in his arms and kiss her.

But he had no time for any of that as a pistol shot ricocheted off the dirt by his boots.

"This way!" Reena shouted.

But Freddy had already grabbed her hand, dashed across the street, and dove into the jungle. Brodie and Abraham followed as they wove around trees, bushes, and vines, tripping over rocks and roots. Bullets whizzed past their ears along with the creak of branches and swish of leaves.

Not a word was said.

Freddy increased his speed and they soon emerged onto the beach where a boat and two sailors from the *Reckless* waited.

Without hesitation, they splashed through the surf, leapt into the craft, and the sailors shoved off into the dark waters.

"Put the lantern out," Freddy ordered, and one of the sailors immediately doused it. Then grabbing an oar, Freddy plunged it into the wild surf and helped force the boat through the incoming waves. Even in the dim light, Reena could see him grimace in pain.

Thankfully, a cloud swallowed up the moon, effectively hiding them, though Reena thought she saw a band of armed men emerge onto the beach.

More bullets peppered the air, one hit the side of the boat.

"Faster!" Freddy whispered.

They struck the hull of the *Reckless* with a hollow thud. Grabbing the rope, Reena climbed aboard first and tied the craft to the bulwarks. Freddy soon followed, along with the rest of them. No time to lift the jolly boat on board.

Freddy marched across the deck and shouted orders to the waiting crew. "Hands to stations for making sail. Up the anchor!"

Reena should be angry that he'd stolen her authority, at least temporarily. But in truth, she thrilled at watching him take command. Just like he used to do. In fact, she'd been smiling ever since she'd seen him single-handedly fighting off six men. He'd not lost an ounce of his skill with a sword during his year in the Royal Navy.

"Topmen aloft! Up tops and sheets!" Freddy continued.

Abraham repeated orders and sailors scrambled into the shrouds.

Sails flew into the night as the anchor chain ground out a macabre tune.

"Where to, Captain?" Fletcher said from the tiller.

"Jamaica," she replied as Freddy stopped beside her on the quarterdeck. Was that a smile on his face?

Reena fisted hands at her waist. "You must admit, Freddy, that was quite enjoyable."

Wind tossed his hair behind him as he gazed aloft where sailors followed his orders. "I'll admit nothing of the kind. I wouldn't have been in that fight at all if not for you."

She smiled. "You may thank me later."

"Thank yo—thunderation, woman!" He turned to face her, his lips flat, his eyes aflame, and she got the feeling he wished to strangle her.

Fear jolted her as she retreated and braced herself for his fury. Not that he had ever struck her, but his anger—the shouting, the look in his eyes—had always been unnerving.

A moment passed as he glared her way. But then slowly, he lowered his gaze and released a deep breath.

Reena allowed herself to breathe as well, more than pleased that he'd learned to control his temper this past year.

Abraham continued to issue commands as flapping canvas caught the wind in a thunderous snap. The brig jerked forward.

Freddy turned to face the sea again. "I was doing quite well on my own."

"Indeed. But what pleasure is there in going it alone? Come, let's have Brodie tend your injuries." For she'd taken note of the blood on his lip and red swollen marks on his face. Not to mention that he kept holding his chest. And limping. Well, the limping was due to previous injuries. *All* her fault.

Instead of defying her, he followed her down the companionway and into her cabin.

"Avast! Sword fight! Sword fight!" Fred squawked from his perch while Reena lit a lantern.

Freddy sank into one of the chairs, a grimace on his face— that handsome face that in the light looked as though it had been trampled by a horse.

"What did that beast do to you?" Reena knelt before him. "Oh, my poor Freddy."

"Poor Freddy, poor Freddy!"

"I'm not your poor anything." He shoved her hands away. "And I'm not Freddy!"

Guilt battled against the agony in her heart at his repeated rejections. Rising, she backed away as Brodie entered, medical satchel in hand. She wanted to apologize, to beg Freddy for another chance…to ask him why he'd risked himself for her.

Yet she did none of those things while Brodie stooped before him and opened his satchel.

"Be still, man." The surgeon examined Freddy's face and winced. "Ach now, how many times did they batter ye?"

"I lost count."

"Nothin' tae do aboot it, save clean the cuts. Here, let me help ye off wit' yer shirt."

Pushing Brodie away, Freddy tore off the garment himself, but Reena could tell by his expression and the sweat on his brow that his pride had cost him dearly.

Brodie pressed fingers onto his chest. "Pardon, laddie, I know this hurts."

Yet Freddy's expression was steel.

"Ach, a bruised rib. I'll bind it tight, but ye must rest, Captain Carlton, for it tae heal."

Brodie got to work spreading salve on the cuts on Freddy's face and then wrapping his chest. He checked the gunshot wound on his shoulder and scrapes on his feet before pronouncing them to be healing well.

Relieved it was nothing serious, Reena grabbed a flagon off the shelf and poured rum into two mugs.

More shouts echoed from above, followed by the roar of sails. Yet even the soothing sound of the sea rustling against the hull did naught to calm Reena's angst.

She sipped her rum. When she had rounded the corner and saw Freddy fending off at least four attackers at once—quite successfully, she might add—she couldn't deny the leap of her heart. The scene transported her back to a time when fighting side by side with Freddy had been a common occurrence. Indeed, Freddy had been the one who taught her how to sword fight in the first place.

Brodie packed his bag and stood. The deck shifted, and he stumbled slightly. "He wull live, Captain," he said, starting for the door.

"Thank you for your help tonight," Reena shouted after him.

He waved a hand over his head as he passed through the door.

Freddy shifted his gaze from her to the treasure chest.

The brig rose over a wave, its timbers creaking and groaning—like her heart was doing, longing to fall against his chest and feel those thickly-muscled arms embrace her…to feel his heart beating beneath her ear.

"You risked your life for me." Even saying the words caused her to blink away a mist that threatened to cover her eyes. She offered him a glass of rum, but he shook his head and blew out a sigh.

"What was I supposed to do, Reena? One of us was going to get caught. Better me than you."

She stared at him, unsure how to respond.

He arched a brow. "Does that surprise you?"

"Aye." Reena sat back against her desk and took another sip of rum. "The way you've been acting… Well, I didn't think you…"

He held up a hand. A fresh burn mark sizzled on his wrist. "Before you get the wrong idea, I would have done the same for anyone. 'Tis my duty as a Christian."

The rum sped a bitter trail down her throat even as the cross hanging around his neck mocked her. "Indeed? So you would have sacrificed yourself for Sedley, Cobbs, or Baines?"

"In a heartbeat," he answered, but she knew him well enough to see his hesitation.

"Come now, Freddy, I know you still love me." She twirled a long strand of her hair and smiled his way. "Why not just admit it so we can get on with things."

"Reena loves Freddy. Reena loves Freddy," Fred said.

"Hush your feathers," Reena chastised the bird, then tossed him a peanut.

"I see you acquired your precious treasure." Freddy nodded toward the chest. "You must be very happy."

"I am."

"But you have made a fierce enemy of Antoine du Casse." He rubbed his cheek and winced.

"Bilge water." She huffed and waved a hand through the air. "He'll recover."

"Scalawag, scalawag!" Fred said.

Freddy shook his head. "If you actually believe that, then you are, indeed, mad. From my brief experience with the man, he doesn't react well to betrayal."

Setting down her glass, she approached him and took his hand. "I am truly sorry, Freddy. I didn't mean for you to get hurt." She glanced at his wrist. "He burned you."

"Nay, though he intended to. I did that to myself. In order to escape."

Reena gently squeezed his hand, gazing into those green eyes she'd missed so much. "It does you great credit to have escaped the man. But somehow I knew you would."

He pulled his hand from hers and gestured toward the chest. "What is in it? I'm surprised you haven't already opened it and been dancing about with your gold and jewels."

Frowning at him, Reena rose and grabbed a boarding ax hanging on the wall, swung it above the chest, and brought the full force of it down onto the iron lock. *Clank*! It split and fell to the deck. The lid was heavier than she thought, but worth the effort when lantern light spilled over the contents and brought them to life in waves of glitter and glisten—gold doubloons, sparkling jewels, silver candlesticks, a gold chalice, an emerald-encrusted crucifix, bars of gold, emeralds from Columbia…

Fred squawked and shifted across his perch. "Shiver me soul. Yo ho ho, hand o'er the treasure!"

Even Freddy inhaled a breath.

"It appears you are now a wealthy woman. If Monsieur du Casse doesn't kill you before you can enjoy it."

"Your lack of confidence cuts me to the quick, Freddy." She winked at him and removed the treasure, setting the cups, plates, coins, and jewelry on the deck, seeking the one item she desired most of all.

There—a tall, dark bottle. Seemingly worthless when compared with the other items in the chest. Gripping it, she stood and nearly squealed with glee.

But pirate captains didn't squeal like girls.

Freddy pushed against the chair arms and rose with difficulty. "I need some sleep before the sun rises. I shall leave you to your treasure, Reena. I'm sure you will be very happy together."

"Wait, Freddy." She uncorked the bottle and tipped it over. Nothing came out. "This is far better than treasure."

"Unless there's a Bible in that bottle, I doubt it."

She frowned, turned, and slammed the bottle against her desk. The glass shattered in pieces on the deck. And there it was! Carefully reaching into the shards, she snagged the paper. Glass sliced her thumb, but she didn't care.

"What are you—you've cut yourself." Freddy took her hand, and before she could stop him, he grabbed a neckerchief from the desk and wrapped it around the wound. So touched by his tender care, she nearly forgot about the paper.

"Thank you." She studied him, spotting a hint of affection hiding behind his indifference.

He backed away. "What is worth injuring yourself over?"

Reena unrolled the parchment, took one quick glance and smiled. "'Tis a map."

Freddy's jaw tightened. "You risked everything— including my life—for a map?"

"Not just any map, Freddy. 'Tis the map that will lead us to…" Her eyes lit up brighter than all the jewels combined. "The Fountain of Youth."

Whistle, whistle on the clock
Treasure is behind a rock
Two steps back and five steps east
Eight toward the south, beware the beasts

CHAPTER TEN

*F*rederick leaned on the railing and gazed over the vast gray waters of the Caribbean. A strip of gold with hints of saffron appeared on the horizon as if the Creator had dipped a brush in paint and dribbled it over the edge of the sea. Ribbons of that paint now spilled onto the waves, bringing the water to life in a myriad of blues, greens, and violets. He smiled and drew in a deep breath, instantly regretting it when pain radiated across his chest—reminding him of his bruised rib, battered, swollen face, gunshot wound, burned wrist, and sliced feet. All injuries acquired since Lady Reena Hyde had sailed back into his life. Still his smile remained. Which made him question his own sanity. All these years, he'd thought *her* mad, when it appeared he was the one who'd lost his wits. For what rational man would enjoy the company of a woman who not only tore his heart into shreds but his body as well?

"Oh, Lord." The brig rose over a wave, and he tightened his grip and bowed his head. "What am I doing on a pirate ship? With this woman? Forgive me for my weaknesses, for…" Thunderation, he had stolen treasure! Fought off the men who were trying to get it back. What kind of preacher did that? "…for stealing. Father. I don't know what's happening to me. I want to do Your will, be holy, preach the Gospel like my parents, but I keep slipping away."

'Tis your father's pirate blood in you.

He'd heard that voice before… incriminating… condemning. Yet always fired with arrows of truth that embedded deep into his soul. His father, the infamous Captain Kent Frederick Carlton, had been one of the fiercest pirates ever to sail the Caribbean. He had enacted a host of atrocities—murder, thievery, and rape. The latter sent a putrid taste into Frederick's mouth. He was the product of such an encounter—a ravishing, a violation of all that was sacred. He was illegitimate, a misbegotten child, an accident that had ostracized his mother from her family, sent her living the life of a pauper in the service of a poor minister of God.

Of course his father had changed after his encounter with that God. He'd attempted to make up for his past. His mother had married him, an act Frederick still could not fathom. But that didn't change the fact that he'd been born out of violence.

The brig pitched over a wave, foamy claws reaching up the hull as more sailors appeared on deck. Abraham also emerged from a hatch, spouting a string of orders before making his way to Frederick.

"G'day, Cap'n Carlton, Yuh's up early."

"Couldn't sleep."

"Cap'n Hyde has dat effect on people." He smiled and glanced over the sea. "But de good Lord be workin' on her. I knows it."

"The good Lord?" Frederick didn't hide the surprise in his voice.

"Aye, yuh here, ain't yuh?" He chuckled. "I never dreamt I'd see de day she'd allow a preacha on board."

Freddy crossed arms over his chest. "I'm no preacher."

"Not wha' she says. Though I's sure she'll try t' keep yuh from yer callin'."

That was an understatement. A gust of wind swirled about them, and Frederick gripped the railing and studied the quartermaster. He wouldn't have assumed he was a believer, but now that he looked at him, there was a peace about Abraham and something in his eyes that bespoke of inner joy.

"If you're such a godly man, why are you sailing with a pirate?" Frederick asked.

Abraham scratched his graying patch of black hair and chuckled. "Dat's a question I ask the Lord ever' day. I s'pose 'cause she needs me. An' now she needs yuh."

Frederick shook his head, squinting at the sun peeking over the horizon. "Then you don't know Reena Hyde very well. She doesn't need anyone."

Abraham only humphed in reply, and Frederick drew a deep breath of the sea air, instantly regretting it for the pain etching across his chest.

"Tell me, Abraham, how did you come to be on the *Reckless*?" Though Reena had told him she'd rescued Abraham from a slave ship, he wanted to hear the man's story.

"I were a slave on a sugar plantation. My master were…" He hesitated then rubbed the brand on his right bicep Frederick had noticed a few days ago—a large S with an R in one of the circles. "Cruel. I lived five years under 'is whip. And den he sol' me t' another plantation owner on Jamaica. Cap'n Hyde attacked de ship I were sailin' on." He smiled and the sunlight lit his teeth like the white sands of a Caribbean shore, save for a single silver one on the bottom row. "Pertiest sight I ev'r seen, her comin' down in de hold, sloshin' through the stink an' slop an' unlockin' our chains. She let every las' slave go. I vowed dat day dat I would always protect her." Shouts from above drew his attention for a moment before he continued. "I never forget dat moment 'cause she look straight in my eyes, smiled, and asked me t' join her crew. Taught me everythin' I know 'bout sailin'."

Frederick shook his head. The woman was a dichotomy—a pirate with the heart of a saint. In truth, she intrigued him, fascinated him… which is why after he'd returned to God, he had to run as far away from her as possible.

Yet now, he felt himself being sucked deeper into her seductive mire with each passing day. He stared out over the turquoise seas, their foamy waves kissed with gold by the rising sun. "You've led a difficult life, Abraham. Even now, 'tis not easy sailing with Reena."

Abraham laughed.

Frederick faced him. "Yet, for all your heartache, you still worship God?"

The big man shrugged. "Not God's fault. 'Sides, He's done give me *eternal* freedom by sendin' His son t' die fer me so's after dis short life, I can be wit' Him forever."

Frederick grimaced. This ex-slave's faith was putting him to shame.

"Yuh's here fer a reason, Cap'n Carlton. Mebbe ask God wha' it be."

"I'm here because Reena captured me," Frederick growled.

"Ahh," he leaned toward Frederick, a twinkle in his eyes. "Dere's always a deeper purpose wit' God." Then, slapping the railing, he marched away, shouting orders as he went.

A deeper purpose? What could that possibly be? Frederick thought of his vision of Antoine, how the shadows slithered about the man. Demons. Frederick had seen them before, but only in dreams when he'd been asleep. Never awake. Was God trying to tell him something? Could He still use Frederick, despite the circumstances of his birth? But how could He when Frederick had already succumbed to his father's love of pirating?

Reena had been right. Aside from his injuries, he'd enjoyed himself last night, the adventure, the excitement, fighting side by side with her. His father's blood pumped strongly through his veins. Far too strongly.

He hung his head again. "Forgive me, Father. Help me. Strengthen me. Tell me what I'm doing here."

He waited several minutes, but no response came… save the sounds of wind and wave.

"Fountain of Youth, Fountain of Youth," the parrot was squealing as Frederick ducked his head beneath the beams and entered the captain's cabin.

Reena stood behind her desk, studying a piece of parchment laying on top. Abraham, Jo, Brodie, and Sedley circled the desk, equally enthralled.

"Bilge water! 'Tis just a section—a piece of a larger map." Reena shoved from the desk and turned to look out the stern windows where the sun was slowly sinking behind foam-capped waves. "I had hoped the legend wasn't true."

Frederick had spent most of the day above, directing the crew, navigating their way to Jamaica, and then resting in his cabin when his rib pained him overmuch.

"Ach now, did ye search the chest? Mibbe there's another bottle?" Brodie gestured toward the open trunk where gold and jewels sparkled in the lantern light.

"Aye," Reena spat out. "I was told the entire map would be here." She spun around, saw Frederick, briefly smiled, and then continued. "Instead, it appears 'tis naught but a puzzle we must solve to find the rest."

Frederick approached the desk. "The rest?"

Sedley's eyes skittered in delight. "A map t' the Fountain o' Youth, Cap'n. Imagine that." He stared down at the parchment. "Livin' ferever young."

Frederick huffed. "All of us are already going to live forever."

Abraham nodded. "Amen."

Grabbing a bottle from the desk, Brodie took another sip.

"Ye been drinkin', Cap'n Carlton?" Sedley chuckled. "Livin' ferever?"

"He's talkin' aboot heaven or hell, goosebrain," Brodie shot out with a sneer.

The deck tilted, forcing them all to grip the edge of the desk.

"Oh yeah," Sedley shifted his feet and glanced sheepishly at Frederick. "Forgot ye were a preacher."

"He's not a preacher." Reena circled the desk and approached him. "He's a pirate, and he's going to help me find the Fountain." She smiled up at him, then frowned when her gaze landed on his swollen eye. She reached up to caress it, but Frederick caught her wrist.

"I'm not a pirate, and I'm not helping you with anything. You're taking me to Kingston, remember?"

Her pert little nose scrunched, even as she shifted her eyes away. "Of course, but I meant along the way, since you are here."

"We are to go to Kingston straight away." Frederick returned in a severe tone. "You gave me your word."

"Ye took the word of a pirate?" Brodie laughed and took another drink.

"Double-dealin' swab!" Fred interjected.

Ignoring both Brodie and the infernal parrot, Frederick approached the desk and studied the piece of yellowed, stained parchment. Shaped like a square, it had a quarter of a circle drawn in one corner. Several odd shapes had been sketched in what appeared to be random locations, along with the words:

"Whistle, whistle on the clock
Treasure is behind a rock
Two steps back and five steps east
Eight toward the south, beware the beasts"

He laughed. "What foolery is this?"

"'Tis a riddle we must solve," Reena replied in a curt tone. "And these"—she pointed to the various shapes—"are land masses in the Caribbean."

"How can you possibly know that?" Frederick shook his head, ignoring the hurt look in her eyes.

She raised her chin. "I have it on good authority."

"Burn and sink me!" Fred chirped.

"Indeed." Frederick shook his head. "A pirate's authority may not be the most prudent thing to rely upon."

"She's right." Jo leaned both hands on the desk and stared at the map. "This one looks like Saint Vincent an' 'ere"—she pointed to another shape—"is shaped like Dominica."

Brodie smiled at her. "A wise *and* becomin' lass, a rare find."

Jo looked at him oddly, then pressed back a wayward lock of her hair.

Wind whistled through cracks in the stern window panes, singing a mournful tune.

Reena halted, her brow furrowing. Moving the map aside, she glanced over the chart spread beneath it. Her gaze shot back and forth for several minutes before she pointed to the Fountain map. "Which makes this one where the X is—Saint Lucia. And it sits atop the city of Castries." Her voice grew with excitement. "Excellent work, Jo. That has to be where the remainder of our map is located. Or at least the next piece."

The master gunner returned Reena's smile.

Abraham humphed.

Reena tapped her chin. "And my guess is the rhyme refers to a building, an old one. Perhaps a tavern."

Frederick withheld a groan of frustration. "How do you know these maps are genuine or that they even lead to anything?"

"You've not heard the legend of the Fount?" Her surprised gaze shot to him, then traveled over her crew.

When no one responded, she leaned forward, hands gripping the edge of her desk, her tone somber. "'Tis a love story. I've heard but pieces of it." She stared at the map. "Some years ago, a pirate fell in love with a French nobleman's daughter who was visiting their holdings on Martinique. I believe the lady's name was Marie Bauffremonts, if I remember correctly. The lady returned his affections, but her father had promised her to another—a cruel man of title and wealth. Before her father could whisk her back to France for the wedding, she ran away with the pirate, and they spent a year sailing the Caribbean loving each other."

Reena's eyes met Frederick, a deep sorrow within them.

"The nobleman pursued them relentlessly," Reena continued. "And the pirate knew he'd eventually catch them, for the man had the ear of the King and unending resources. But the pirate had a secret…"

She leaned forward, candlelight shimmering in her gaze as she took them all in. "He knew how to find the Fountain of Youth."

Sedley scratched his head. "'Ow did 'e know that?"

Frederick shared a disbelieving glance with Abraham, while Jo and Brodie seemed mesmerized with the story.

Reena continued, "An old pirate who claimed to be a descendant of Ponce de León divulged the secret one night when they were both well into their cups."

Brodie took a sip from his flask. "Why didna he find it then?"

Reena shrugged. "Apparently he tried, but couldn't find it and ended up believing it was indeed a myth. Regardless, the pirate and his lady knew that if they could find the Fount and drink from it, then her father would not be able to separate them forever."

"Good plan," Jo said. "Even if she got caught an' forced to marry, she'd outlive 'em all."

"Aye, and then she could find her love, and they could be together forever."

Frederick bristled. Precisely what Reena hoped would happen to them.

"Wha' happened?" Brodie asked.

"On the way to find the Fount, her father attacked the pirate's ship. The pirate knew he was defeated, so before their ship was boarded, he told her he'd find the Fount and then leave her a map in a secret location only she would know. The pirate barely escaped with his life." Grabbing a lock of hair, Reena twirled it around her finger, a cloud of despair hovering over her as if 'twas her own story she told. "Alas, brokenhearted, he found the Fountain, drank of its waters, and then spent years trying to rescue his lady love. But her husband locked her away out of his reach."

"What a sad tale," Jo offered, glancing at Brodie.

"Aye, and as the years passed, the pirate found he'd rather die than live forever without her, but 'twas too late, you see. No matter his attempts, death escaped him. Hence, he returned to the Fount to bargain with the angel who stirs the waters there."

Angel? Frederick jerked slightly… enough to draw Reena's questioning gaze. Angel… waters. Sounded much like the pool of Siloam in the Bible.

Brodie scratched his chin. "Ach now, an angel?"

Reena nodded and gripped the edge of her desk again. "But the waters were nearly dried up."

Jo flung a hand to her mouth.

"He had to keep the fountain flowing just in case his love escaped and found her way there. But the angel said the only way to do that was for him to dive in, sink to the bottom, and remain there until his love came to drink."

Abraham huffed. "Yuh's tellin' me him's sittin' at de bottom o' de Fount now?"

Reena flattened her lips. "Aye, legend says 'tis his tears that fill the fount, waiting for his love to return."

Frederick blew out a sigh. "And if she doesn't come and dies? Why can't he leave?"

Reena gave him a cross look. "At the bottom of the Fount, there's no sense of time, and once he leaves, the Fount dries up."

Jo dabbed at her eyes. "Tha' is the saddest story I e'er heard."

"So why more than one map?" Frederick asked.

Reena pushed from the desk. "The pirate feared that either the lady's father or husband would force the information about the Fount from her, and he didn't want such cruel men to drink from its waters. Hence, he created a map and divided it into sections, then left riddles on them leading to places he and his love had visited."

"Humph." Abraham said.

"But where were the first one found?" Jo asked.

"I don't know. But it ended up in a treasure chest that Antoine plundered off a Spanish Galleon."

Frederick wanted to say the story was hogwash… but he remembered the pool of Siloam and its healing waters stirred by an angel. Things like this *were* possible in God's kingdom. Abraham seemed of the same mind as he swallowed hard and glanced out the stern windows.

"Sounds like poppycock tae me," Brodie said.

Reena shrugged. "'Tis but a legend, of course, but I believe it bears some truth."

Jo nodded. "I agree wit' ye, Cap'n."

Sedley tugged on his stained neckerchief. "I dunno, Cap'n. Seems farfetched t' me." His gaze latched onto the treasure chest. "Fortune be better t' 'ave then livin' ferever. What ye goin' t' do wit' all them jewels an' gold?"

Reena barely afforded the treasure a glance. "I'll take my share and Freddy will have his, then you may divide it up amongst the crew as usual."

Sedley rubbed his hands together.

The brig pitched. Frederick spread his feet apart for balance and crossed arms over his chest. "I want no share of your ill-gotten booty, Reena, though I can now see 'twas never about the treasure, was it?"

She gazed up at him curiously. "Treasure I can always get, but eternal youth and beauty? That's priceless."

"I still can't believe you risked all our lives for a legend, a part of a broken map that leads nowhere."

She pursed her lips, her golden eyes sparking. "It doesn't lead nowhere. It leads to the greatest treasure of all." She glanced over the group. "Let's take a vote, shall we? Who is in favor of seeking the Fountain of Youth?"

Brodie arched a brow, took a sip of rum, and said. "Soonds grand tae me!"

Jo shrugged. "Never dyin' sounds worth lookin' into, Cap'n."

"Aye," Sedley said, still staring at the treasure.

Abraham released a heavy sigh. "I agree wit' Cap'n Carlton. Seems a far-fetched quest fer only a legend."

Reena shifted her gaze to Frederick.

"I say you're mad," he said.

"That's four to two." She gave a smile of victory. "'Tis settled. Abraham, chart a course to Saint Lucia at once."

It took every ounce of Frederick's strength to keep his anger from reaching his tongue and firing arrows of fury at Reena. Instead, he spent the next minute trying to contain himself, lest he say or do something he would later regret.

Fred bobbed his head up and down from his perch. "Heigho, to the map we go!"

"See, Freddy?" Reena gave him a coy look. "How can you argue with your namesake?"

⚓

"That's wha' I said. She be givin' an extra cap'n's share t' Carlton." Sedley leaned closer to his fellow sailors. "I don't know 'bout ye, but I didn't sign up to serve two cap'ns an' lose part of wha's comin' to us."

"Me neither!" Baines said as curses filled the air. "He only bin on the ship a few days, and he gets a cap'n's share. Not if I gitsa say in it."

"Speak to her, Sedley," Abbot said, his expression one of sorrow. "Talk sense into her."

Sedley took a sip of his ale. He could and she might listen if he told her the crew was unhappy. Cap'n Carlton didn't want the treasure anyway. But they didn't need to know that. Especially Baines, who held a great deal of influence with the men.

Sedley sighed and shook his head. "She won't listen. She be blind when it comes t' Carlton. Methinks they were lovers in the past."

"Well, I fer one ain't gonna sail wit' two captains."

"Aren't ye forgettin' she saved yer sorry carcass from the noose, Baines?"

"An' I were grateful." Baines adjusted his stained waistcoat. "But this be business. She's violatin' the articles we signed." He leaned forward, gazed over all of them, his foul breath saturating the air.

Sedley resisted the urge to cover his nose.

"I says we take over the brig," Baines offered in a malicious whisper.

Eyes grew wide. Wilson guffawed. "Mutiny? Yer mad, Baines. She got too many loyal who she saved."

He sat back. "Mabbe. Mabbe not when we tells them what she done. I can git enough on our side. The rest will 'ave t' join us or die."

"Aye, sounds fair t' me," Clark added.

Baine's eyes twinkled in malevolent delight. "We can 'ave the ship an' all that booty fer ourselves."

"Wit' ye as captain, I assume?" Sedley smiled.

"Aye! I be the only one qualified. But as captain, I will divide any booty we get equally betwixt every man."

"Hear, hear! I'm wit' ye then, Cap'n Baines."

Sedley leaned back in his chair and took a swig of ale that was tasting sweeter and sweeter with every sip.

CHAPTER ELEVEN

Reena knew something was amiss the minute she stepped on the quarterdeck. For one thing, several of the crew glanced at her nervously and then shifted their eyes away. For another, half of them seemed to be missing. Shrugging off the sensation, she took her position beside Abraham and gazed over the glittering Caribbean. 'Twas another gorgeous day in the West Indies. A wind, ripe with promise, fingered through her hair while rays from a glowing sun warmed her face and neck. The sounds she'd come to love—the slap of waves, the creak of tinders, and flap of canvas filled her ears with delight. Here, upon the sea, she was free. Here, she could defy the restraints placed on her gender and do whatever she pleased, love whomever she wanted, live whatever adventure came her way. And if everything played out according to plan, this grand life would never have to end.

Shielding her eyes from the sun, she glanced up at the massive sails drifting like white clouds over a cerulean sky. With topsails furled and a considerable list to larboard, the *Reckless* rippled through the sea on a course due east.

Grabbing the backstaff from the binnacle, she turned her back to the sun and used the instrument to determine its angle above the horizon. Then plucking a compass from her pocket, she checked the reading.

"Fletcher," she addressed the helmsman at the tiller. "Veer another point to starboard."

"Aye, aye, Cap'n," the man replied. "One point to starboard."

Reena faced Abraham. "We should be at Saint Lucia by tomorrow."

"Humph."

"You disapprove?"

"Aye."

"Because?"

"I dink yuh should take de man t' Kingston like yuh promised, an' stop chasin' fantasies."

"Indeed? Fantasies. Well, I shall just have to change your mind about that. And as far as Freddy goes, he doesn't yet know what he truly wants."

"An' yuh do?" Abraham gave her that look that always made her feel like a little girl caught in some silly indiscretion.

"Of course." Wind flung a strand of her hair in her face, and grabbing it, she twirled it around her finger. "That's why God created Eve. He saw that man needed assistance to get through life."

"Hmm." Abraham smiled, then focused on a group of loitering sailors on the main deck below. "Holmes, Paxon, back t' work!" he shouted, sending them scurrying.

The odd sound of whistling rose on the wind just as Jo leapt up from a hatch. She smiled at Reena before she headed toward the ten-pounder on the starboard quarter. No doubt to clean and inspect it. Another reason Reena adored the woman. She was thorough and meticulous about the guns. And for good reason. They must always be in perfect condition should they come across an enemy—or even better, a worthy prize.

The brig rose then plunged over a wave, and Reena planted her feet apart for balance. Closing her eyes, she swayed with the shifting of the ship, a mesmerizing dance of love. Which brought her thoughts to Freddy. She hated to disappoint him, but Saint Lucia wasn't that far out of the way. Well, in truth, it was a bit out of the way. But she wanted him by her side. She wanted to stir the flame of adventure she knew he possessed within—the one his God had squelched.

Yet now he was furious with her. Yesterday, he'd given her that look of rage she knew too well before he had marched from her cabin. For a moment, she expected his temper to return, for him to draw his sword and try to fight off her entire crew, demanding they take him to Kingston. But Freddy was no fool. She was still in command of this brig, and he knew it. No matter how much he hated that fact. Surely, he would come to his senses soon. Had she not seen sparks of the old Freddy in his eyes—his lust for adventure, sword fights, treasure, and the sea? And most of all, his lust for her. Soon, with maps in hand, they would be on yet another adventure, seeking the Fountain of Youth. Then once they found it and drank their fill, they would sail these seas and love each other forever.

'Twas a dream come true and the only one Reena desired. For no other man would satisfy her. And she could not keep any man—even Freddy—if she were to grow old and die. She could not keep any treasure either, for she would lose all her strength, and those stronger than her would steal it away. 'Twas the way the world worked. Youth was everything—youth, strength, and beauty. Another reason not to follow the God of her parents. How cruel a joke He played on His creation to give them but a few years of youth and vigor before time slowly drained both away like leeches that sucked the blood and life from a man overcome with illness.

Michael darted up the quarterdeck stairs and approached, the wind tossing his wheat-colored hair every which way, and a huge smile on his face. "Heard you found the map you been looking for."

"I did at that, Michael. And"—she raised her brows at him—"that means we shall soon be on another adventure."

"A treasure hunt!" The lad nearly leapt out of his shoes. His eyes landed on her backstaff. "You promised to teach me about navigation, Captain Reena. I so greatly want to learn."

"You are *most anxious* to learn."

"I am most anxious to learn," he repeated with a smile.

"Aye, I will teach you, I promise. Allow me to attend a few things, and I shall call upon you soon." She tapped him on the nose. "You're such a smart lad and a good learner. Soon you'll be the captain of your own ship."

"I'm too young for that, Captain." He laughed, but his face grew red at the compliment. "Maybe Captain Carlton can teach me how to sword fight?"

"No need to bother the captain. I can teach you. I'm just as good as he is."

The lad looked at her, blue eyes sparkling. "I know you are, but I heard he fought bravely yesterday at Port-de-Paix. And he's got injuries to prove it. Can he teach me how he fought off so many?" He sliced the air with his arm like a cutlass.

Reena was not offended. She knew the lad desperately needed a father. Abandoned by his own family on Providence Island, he longed like any child to find someplace where he belonged, a family, a home. She'd done her best to be a mother to him, but she also had to be his captain and ofttimes, the two conflicted. In truth, the lad needed a man's influence, and Freddy was just that man.

Speaking of, the man himself leapt up from the hatch in all his masculine glory and marched across the deck as if he owned the brig—a born leader, confident, strong, able to make quick and wise decisions. All those qualities wasted on a mere preacher.

He gripped the railing and gazed over the sea as if pondering jumping over rather than dealing with her. Then he gazed up at the quarterdeck, spotted her, and ascended the ladder.

She braced herself for his temper.

Michael darted to him. "Captain Carlton, Captain Reena says you'll teach me how to sword fight."

Freddy looked at her with his usual disapproval, though she caught the hint of a grin on his lips…especially when he stared down at the boy. "She did, did she? Well I suppose I will have to accommodate her, then. Her being the captain." He winked at Reena, and even that small gesture sent a thrill down to her toes.

"Now? Can we do it now?" Michael leapt from foot to foot.

"I need a word with your captain first. But soon, I promise."

The warm exchange and the kindness with which Freddy treated Michael did odd things inside of Reena she dared not admit.

Michael started to leave, but suddenly halted, closed his eyes for a moment, then glanced over the brig. Something in his eyes gave Reena pause. No longer glistening with exuberant youth, they seemed suddenly older…wiser. He looked up at her, then over to Freddy, then down at the swords at their sides.

"Are you all right, lad?" Freddy asked him, placing a hand on his shoulder.

Michael nodded, gave a tight smile, then stepped back to take a spot by the helmsman with a stance that stole his youthful innocence.

Reena didn't have time to consider his odd behavior as Abraham shouted to the crew to get back to work. Odd. Even though they were pirates, most of them usually attended their duties without complaint.

And there was that whistling again. She glanced over the brig, seeking its source. Jo and a few of the gun crew were cleaning one of the guns, the topmen were aloft, adjusting sail, other sailors were either holding lines or coiling them, while the rest skittered about nervously. Sedley appeared from below.

Freddy took a stand beside Reena. "Alas, I had hoped *and prayed* you would reconsider breaking your promise to me. But I see you are set on your course."

Blast his navigation skills! "Never fear, we are still going to Kingston. I'm merely stopping at Saint Lucia first." She knew he was frowning, mayhap even grimacing. She knew that his temper could erupt at any moment. She also knew she should say something to placate him, but the crew was acting strangely again. Why were at least half of them below decks? Even when not needed for the running of the ship, they were usually above deck, playing cards, whittling, or dancing to a fiddle. 'Twas far too hot and putrid-smelling to stay below all day.

Freddy seemed to notice as well. She felt him stiffen beside her. Gripping the railing, he gazed down across the deck as the wind shifted, flapping the sails, and the brig groaned over a wave.

Several men emerged from the hatchway, cutlasses in hand. Before Reena's mind registered what was occurring, her instincts caused her to grab Michael and shove him behind her.

"Stay close to me," she told the lad as she drew her sword. Abraham and Freddy did the same.

Blood pounding through her so loudly she could barely hear the sea gushing against the hull, she glanced down at close to thirty armed men, some with muskets, some pistols, some axes, and Baines, her top rigger, leading the pack.

"What is the meaning of this, Baines?" she roared, though she could quite tell it was a mutiny—a tragic event she had thus far avoided. She'd always kept the crew in line, always kept them teetering on a razor's edge between fear and respect. Why, half of these cogheads owed her their lives!

"Stand down, Baines!" Abraham shouted. "While yuh 'ave a chance."

Several sailors, vile grins on their faces, slowly mounted the ladders to her left and right, leading up to the quarterdeck. She quickly scanned the remainder of the crew for those who might still be on her side. Back by the foredeck swivel gun, two sailors pinned Jo's arms behind her back. Other men, not part of Baines' pack, had frozen in place, staring wide-eyed at the proceedings. The topmen slowly descended the shrouds.

Wheeling about, Baines addressed the crew. "Cap'n Hyde were not goin' t' give us our proper share o' the booty she hauled in yesterday." Several groans and moans rumbled through the sailors as he pointed his blade at Freddy. Sunlight glinted off the steel, stabbing Reena in the eye. "She were goin' t' give what's due us t' this newcomer. And I says, o'er me dead body!"

"Aye, o'er our dead bodies!" the mutineers shouted, while others on deck shrank back, their faces filled with horror. Baines shouted to them, "Those what come wit' us will be spared. Those what don't, will die by the sword."

Freddy groaned beside her, gripping his cutlass tight. "Thunderation, of all the…"

Terror like she'd never known clawed up her spine. With thirty armed men, Baines could easily subdue the rest of the unarmed crew. Still, would no one stand with her? Would no one put up a fight?

Freddy nudged her behind him as if he could protect her. The sentiment warmed her heart, but it would be of no use. "Men, I am not your captain," he shouted. "I don't wish to be your captain. I fully intend to get off this brig in Kingston. I do not want any share of treasure. You have my word, you will receive your proper shares according to the code you signed. Hence, I urge you to cease this nonsense at once and get back to work. Or you'll have to answer to me and my blade."

At first, silence, save the creak of wood and flap of sail, invaded the ship. But then Baines laughed as if someone had told a joke. His men soon followed suit. "We's gettin' our proper shares, wit' or wit' out yer permission, *Cap'n*." He dipped an exaggerated bow before Freddy.

Pushing past him, Reena tossed her chin to the wind and scanned the crew. Aye, she had made a fatal error in favoring Freddy with the treasure. But who had disclosed her intentions? The treasure was worth a vast amount, and hence their shares would be so large, they wouldn't have noticed. *Sedley*. But the man was nowhere in sight. Commotion drew her gaze to the hatch where Brodie's head appeared, followed by the rest of him, his hands bound behind him and a cutlass at his back.

Indignation welled inside of her, and she gripped the railing again and shouted to her mutinous crew. "Hendrick!" A middle-aged sailor with a gut as round as the capstan stared up at her. "You'd be dead if I hadn't dragged you out of that sewage pile in Barbados, sleeping in your own vomit. And you, Eris." She gestured to another man, this one young and sturdy as a mast. "I paid your gambling debts just as your debtors were stringing you up. I paid in full and took you aboard my ship, expecting naught in return." She scanned the deck for others she had saved. "And what of you, Northwick? Your last captain left you for dead on a beach in New Providence with your leg half blown off. And what did I do? I brought you aboard my ship and Brodie there"—she nodded toward the surgeon, still bound and held at sword point—"patched you up and gave you a wooden leg so you could live a normal life." Drawing a deep breath, she allowed her fury to speak for her. "How can you betray me, thus? How can any of you betray me? I order you to arrest Baines and those with him and lock them in the hold!"

"Yuh 'eard de captain!" Abraham held his sword aloft. "Or yuh'll 'ave t' face me first."

"And me!" Freddy once again took a stance of protection before her.

"And me," Michael added with more courage than a lad should possess.

Though warmed by the chivalry of her friends, Reena could take care of herself. She was the captain of this brig, after all. And she'd need no one to defend her against her mutinous crew.

The *Reckless* slid into a trough, flinging foam into the air and sending black squalls over the deck. Above them, the sun whipped rays of searing heat upon the scene. Sweat slid down her back, and she shifted her stance, leveling her blade before her.

Though many of the sailors seemed to ponder her words, none of them rushed to subdue the mutineers. No doubt they realized some of them would die in the effort, for Baines had recruited the most bloodthirsty of her crew.

Brodie struggled against his bonds and looked up at her with a glazed haze of sympathy. Freddy's jaw was as stiff and unyielding as the steel of his blade—growing stiffer as the sailors proceeded onto the quarterdeck.

It appeared there was naught to be done but fight for their lives. Three blades—though capable blades—against thirty pirates. Not great odds.

Was this to be the end of her life? To die as she had lived—by the sword? Wasn't there something in the Bible about that? Mayhap 'twas God's judgment on the life she had chosen—her rejection of the principles she'd been taught from youth. But there was no time for regrets as the men advanced.

Abraham took a stand before her while Freddy protected her rear. He shoved Michael against the quarterdeck railing. "Stay there and don't make a move."

Reena leaned toward Freddy. "If you're on speaking terms with God, now might be a good time to inform Him of our predicament."

"Trust me, He already knows." Freddy leveled his blade before him.

Three men advanced from the right, four from the left. Reena could see the hesitancy in their eyes. They were attacking their captain, after all. Not to mention three expert swordsmen. Failure on their part would mean certain death. Their confidence, however, came from numbers, as more men ascended the ladders behind them.

A rain of blades swooped down upon them like flashes of lightning.

Abraham took on the first two men, while another two attacked Reena. With her cutlass in one hand, she drew her knife with the other and parried with them both, ducking and whirling and spinning to keep them off guard, diving toward one, while thrusting her knife toward the other. The hiss of steel echoed through the air. Shouts blared from the rest of the crew, some offering encouragements, others curses.

She glanced at Freddy beside her, engaged with three men. One sliced his arm. He thrust the man through his leg. Screeching, he fell, flipped over the railing and landed on the deck below with an ominous thud.

Reena ducked just in time before one of her opponents struck her chest. Blindly rushing the other, her knife hit its mark in the man's side. He toppled to the deck. Still more came. And more and more.

And she knew what she'd known from the beginning. 'Twas hopeless to continue. It would only end in their deaths, and she couldn't bear it if her last vision was one of her friends being run through with the sword.

Another mutineer came at her, cleaving downward with his cutlass. There was no time to react. This would be the end. She knew it. The sharp edge of steel advanced toward her…down…down…down, slicing a wedge of death in its path.

But then a light, bright as the sun caused her to blink. A mighty blade, gold and glistening, held back the man's sword. Time seemed to slow as she glanced toward the source. Michael stood staunchly by the railing, a glow emanating all around him. Had she gone mad? Was she already dead? But there was no time to ponder it as the man's cutlass continued to advance. Raising her sword, their blades rang together. Another sailor sliced her shoulder from the right. Blood trickled down her arm, but she felt no pain. No time for pain. She would feel that later. Abraham let out a yelp from her left, and she spun to see three men raising their blades to heave him in two.

"Stand down!" she yelled with all her might. Her breath came in rapid bursts and sweat stung her eyes, but oddly, the sailors froze.

Freddy looked her way. He had already left two more mutineers bloodied on the deck and was taking on the third. But a fourth, fifth, and sixth were already advancing behind him. Shoving his way past the sailors, Baines leapt onto the quarterdeck and sauntered toward Reena. "Do you surrender?"

Reena had no other choice. Either that or die here and now. Before she would have a chance to taste the waters of eternal life. *Bilge water!* If she had but drank her fill of the Fountain before now, she would fight this sniveling maggot to his death. Not hers. "You will not harm my friends, and you will not touch the boy. Not a thread of his clothes or a hair on his head. Do you hear me?"

Baines' beady eyes shifted to Michael, who to his credit, did not so much as blink as the brute of a sailor headed his way. Instead, he met his gaze head on and looked up at him as if he were the one in charge, not Baines.

"Those be yer only terms?" Baines laughed as he looked the boy up and down, a snarl on his face. "A tender heart is not befittin' a pirate cap'n. Good that we's replacin' ye."

Freddy snorted, blade still raised against his attackers. "You're a fool if you think you can rule this brig better than Captain Hyde, not to mention find these greedy men enough treasure to appease them. You might just find a knife in your gut whilst you sleep."

"And ye might jist find one in yers now." Plucking a blade from his belt, Baines charged Freddy.

Reena leapt in his path. "Do you accept my terms or not?"

"Terms, ye say?" He chuckled and a few of his men chuckled with him. "Yer in no position t' be dictatin' terms." He sheathed his blade and fingered the hair on his chin. "However, since ye saved me life, I accept yer offer. Yer friends and this lad will not die. D'ye surrender?"

Reena glanced at Freddy and saw his slight nod of acquiescence before she faced her enemy again. "I do." She said the words with strength, but 'twas a strength that defied the agony tumbling through her. With those two little words, she not only lost all her years of hard work, but most of her dreams along with it.

She dropped her sword and watched sunlight flicker over it as it fell slowly to the deck. It clanked onto the wood—a gong of defeat that sent a shiver through her. She looked away as Freddy and Abraham dropped their blades as well and raised their hands.

"Tie up the Negro," Baines ordered. "An' throw him, the lad, the lady gunner, and the surgeon in the hold."

Reena started toward the sailors who advanced upon Abraham and Michael, unsure what she would do, but desperate to do something to save her friends. "You said no harm would come to them."

Freddy gripped her arm and halted her, shaking his head.

"I'll keep me promise." Baines flashed her a row of yellow teeth. "No harm will come t' them as long as they behave. But as fer ye and yer lover"—a malicious gleam appeared in his eyes—"I have other plans."

CHAPTER TWELVE

Frederick stepped over the edge of the jolly boat into the incoming surf, the foamy spit and spew of the waves mimicking the cauldron of emotions broiling within him—some he couldn't even name. A sailor leapt in the water behind him and shoved him along. Waves struck his legs from behind, his boots sank into the soft mud. The sailor pushed him again, this time with the muzzle of his musket. Against every impulse, Frederick complied and sloshed onto the white beach.

On his left, Reena struggled in the hands of one of her mutineering sailors, uttering a dozen unladylike curses. She kicked and thrashed and even managed to free one of her hands, but another sailor came to his aid, and together they jerked her arms behind her. She whimpered in pain, and Frederick longed to charge the men and pummel them into the sand for treating a lady with such disrespect—their captain. But that cauldron of emotions held him back.

Anger, fear, guilt, sorrow, rage. Did he mention anger? Anger, not at these miscreants, but at Reena. 'Twas her fault he found himself in this predicament. Hers and hers alone.

Before him, a beach as white as a virgin sail stretched to his left and right and then up to a thick jungle that fluttered over the sand like the long green eyelashes of a beautiful woman.

Baines lumbered through the rolling waves and marched over to Reena, a mocking grin on his face. He handed her a pistol. Then gazing at them both, he opened his palm to reveal one shot and a small bag of powder.

Reena reached for them, but he jerked back his hand and tossed them into the sand some distance away. "One shot. One shot be all ye git, so ye'll 'ave t' decide which one gits t' die an' which one gits t' starve t' death."

Unable to control himself further, Frederick charged the worthless carp. Two sailors blocked him, taking the brunt of his assault. One of them toppled to the ground while the other was forced to draw his sword.

Baines smiled his way. "I be thinkin' ye might be the one t' die first. With that temper o' yers."

Reena lifted her chin, defeat clouding her eyes. "What's to become of my friends?"

"Would ye rather I leave 'em here t' die wit' ye? Naw." Baines shrugged. "I be droppin' them at the next port we make."

"And my parrot?"

He barreled over in laughter, holding his portly belly as if his blubber would come loose during the action. "Yer about t' die, an' ye worry 'bout a bird?" The other sailors joined in his mirth. "Another reason yer not suited t' be cap'n. Ye broke the articles we signed cause o' this pretty blitherhead." He nodded toward Frederick. "Ye deserve each other." He spit onto the sand and spun around to leave.

"I'll kill you for this, Baines!" Reena shouted after him. "I'll hunt you down and kill you."

He chuckled all the way to the boat, continued laughing as he leapt in. His sailors followed suit, and soon the craft was making its way back to the *Reckless,* anchored just offshore.

Frederick merely stood there with the warm water licking his boots and the hot sun spearing his face. He didn't know what else to do. He knew this island. He knew nearly every spit of land in the Caribbean. Even small ones like this one with no fresh water, no animals, and hence nothing to eat or drink. They wouldn't last long.

Beside him, Reena folded to the sand and dropped her head in her hands, a patch of blood growing on the sleeve of her shirt. It was the first time he'd seen her defeated, or at least accepting defeat. He had fully expected her to march up and down the shore, punching her fist in the air, continuing to shout obscenities at Baines, swearing to heaven that she would get him back for this. Instead, she wilted like a flower.

Moving to her side, Frederick plopped down beside her and eased his arm around her shoulders. Everything within him told him he should not be so close to her, should not comfort her. But he knew that her brig and the freedom it brought meant the world to her. And he knew exactly how it felt to lose something that meant everything—like your insides were being ripped out and swept away with the outgoing tide.

She leaned into him and sobbed. He could count the number of times on one hand this strong woman had ever cried in his presence. And every one of those times had been when he had told her he was leaving. He drew her close. "Shh. Shh, there now, Kitten. It will all work out."

Not that she didn't deserve this fate for the acts of thievery and violence she had perpetrated. But then again, so did he. He heaved a heavy sigh. Of all the people to be stranded on a deserted island with! He gazed across the foamy surf as the setting sun dappled waves with orange and yellow. *You must have a sense of humor, Father. Either that or this is the biggest temptation You have ever put before me, and You must think I'm strong enough.* But Frederick doubted that very much. He was his father's son, after all.

After several minutes, her sobbing spent, she glanced up at him. Her cheeks were moist and her eyes red, but there was a sparkle in them nonetheless. "You called me 'Kitten.' That's twice since I rescued you."

"It pains me this happened to you, Reena. I know how much the *Reckless* meant to you."

She batted tears from her face and stared at her brig growing smaller and smaller on the horizon. "I suppose 'tis what I get for trying to help the downtrodden, for saving people's lives, for feeding and giving them a job and a place to live."

He could feel her stiffen beside him, feel her grow warm with fury.

"Just like my parents," she continued. "They spend their lives helping those in need, telling them about God's love, and what do they get in return?" She leapt to her feet and took up a pace across the sand. "Nothing. Save insults, attacks, and poverty."

Digging his boots into the sand, Frederick leaned forward and placed elbows on his knees, unsure of what to say. His parents had endured the same. They endlessly served others and had naught to show for it—at least nothing this world valued. Frederick glanced once more at the *Reckless* sailing into the setting sun. A strange black cloud appeared around it, swirling and twisting, finally settling on the brig. Yet nary another cloud could be seen in the sky. He rubbed his eyes, but when he opened them again, it was still there even as the ship lowered out of sight. Another vision he supposed. Darkness had taken over the *Reckless,* and Satan's minions were celebrating. He quickly said a prayer for Michael, Abraham, Brodie, and Jo.

"There's more to this life than possessions and happiness," he said.

Reena halted in her tracks and swerved to stare at him, "And you think *me* mad. What could be more important than happiness? Isn't that what everyone craves, whether by wealth or pleasure?"

"Our lives are too short and too valuable to be spent on ourselves, Reena. There is so much more beyond this world."

Frowning, she took up a pace again and huffed. "Our lives will indeed be short unless we can find a way off of this island." Kicking up sand, she stared at the horizon where the sun slowly sank. The *Reckless* was no longer in sight.

And Frederick knew she was right. They would both die here unless God intervened.

Reena knew how to captain a tall ship at sea. She knew the name and function of each sail, mast, yard, line, halyard, and tackle. She knew how to navigate by the sun, moon, and stars. She could handle a ship in a storm and do even better in battle. She could load, prime, and fire a cannon with precise accuracy, and she could beat any man at swordplay and pistols.

But she had no idea how to survive on her own in the wilderness.

Apparently, however, Freddy had picked up that skill somewhere along the way. She followed him into the jungle, sparse as it was on this tiny island, as he selected certain pieces of wood, fronds, and vines, and brought them to the edge of the beach where he wove together the frame for a small enclosure. On top of the frame, he placed layer upon layer of fronds, tying them down with vines. Afterward, they searched for the largest leaves they could find, which took no time at all, for the island was one of the smallest Reena had seen. However, in the process, she discovered that, indeed, there was no fresh water to be had—not a trickle or spring anywhere. The greenery was no doubt watered purely by rainfall, which, by the lush variety, fell upon the island with great frequency.

Freddy must have assumed the same, for when they returned to the beach, he built several small wooden frames with sticks and twine and then used the leaves to form bowls within them. He did all this without saying much to her, of which she was grateful. She had not been able to calm either her fury or her fear. If she ever saw Baines and those traitorous crewmen again…well, they would regret the moment they had met her.

Regardless, her fear began to overcome her fury. Hence, following Freddy around with his confident gait and keeping busy helping him gather the things they needed was helping relieve both. If there was anyone she would have chosen to be stranded on an island with, 'twas Frederick Carlton. At least if she were to die, she would die in his arms. Which was the best place of all to be.

They finished the rain catchers just as the last vestiges of sunlight disappeared beyond the horizon and stars poked through the velvet curtain of the night. She wondered how many sunsets she had left to enjoy before starvation and thirst leeched away her life.

Freddy emerged from the jungle and dropped a bundle of dried sticks and wood onto the sand as if he could somehow make a fire appear from it. But she knew they had neither flint nor steel. What did it matter if they had fire anyway? How could they catch fish without a knife? Or pry open clams or crabs if they could find them? And it was plenty warm here in the tropics.

Still, he sat down, took off his neckerchief, looped it around a stick and used it to spin the wood atop another piece, where he had bundled dry kindling.

After what seemed like forever, a spark shot from the kindling, and Freddy leaned over the wood and blew. Within minutes, he had a fire blazing. He gazed up at her and smiled, that sensuous, yet boyish smile that always sent her senses reeling. Wind tossed his hair behind him as the firelight angled over his handsome face, and he patted the ground next to him in invitation as if they were simply on another adventure and not facing a long, painful death.

"You are amazing," she said as she lowered to sit beside him. "Within a few hours you have provided shelter, fire, and the possibility of collecting water."

"Not difficult. Though I do see why God had my father teach me such skills when I was young. I remember not wanting to do any of it, wanting instead to go back on the ship and learn more about sailing and swordplay."

"Mayhap he was not as bad a father as you think." Which reminded her of her own father—the infamous Captain Merrick Edmund Hyde. If anyone could have a decent father…if there was ever a father on this earth who was the best example of honor, integrity, decency, morality, and love, 'twas him. He had not coddled her, spoiled her, nor berated or belittled her. He had instructed, advised, taught, protected, and loved her. Even cherished her, if she admitted it. But he had not done those things very often, for he and mother were frequently gone on their missions at sea. Even so, she had adored him as a child. Still did, in fact. Though she was quite sure he was beyond disappointed in her now, as he'd been the last few years she had lived under his protection. She'd begun to get restless, tired of giving so much and getting so little in return. She sought adventure and romance and could not see that happening in her life as a missionary.

Freddy was the one who had prompted her to sail away with him. She spun to look at him again, wondering if he even remembered that.

He winced and she noticed the blood on his sleeve, which reminded her of her own wound. So fearful of her future, she'd not felt the pain, though now that she examined her arm, the wound was not deep and the bleeding had stopped.

"We should patch that up," Freddy said.

"And yours as well." It had not escaped her notice that he still limped slightly, that his expression pained when he'd picked up a heavy log—no doubt from his bullet wound and bruised rib. And now, this injury to his arm. Yet another wound she caused. She wanted to slide her hand in his. She wanted to lean on his shoulder, but she also didn't want to be rejected. Again.

As if he could sense her desire, he rose and headed toward the surf. "Stay here."

His shadow stooped over the waves, and he soon returned, wet neckerchief in hand.

"This may sting a bit." Kneeling, he separated the opening in her shirt and dabbed the cloth over her wound. Sting, it did. But she didn't cry out, so thrilled that he cared.

"The salt will help it heal."

"Another bit of wisdom you learned from your father?"

He didn't answer. Instead he finished his ministrations and sat back. Grabbing the neckerchief, Reena made a trip to the water as well and returned to care for his wound. "I'm truly sorry, Freddy, that I got you involved in all this." She patted his injury, which was slightly deeper than hers. "'Tis my fault all this has happened to you. Not exactly how I planned things after I found you again."

He stayed her hand. "Things never go as you plan, Reena. You are too much of a dreamer." He took the neckerchief.

Frowning, Reena sat back. "Was it too much to dream…to hope you would come back to me?"

A gust of wind stirred the sand at their feet and quivered through the leaves in the jungle behind them. Freddy didn't answer. She supposed that was better than him saying no. The fire crackled and the smell of smoke, salt, and earthy loam filled her nose.

Freddy stared out over the black waters as the moon poked its gleaming eye above the horizon. "Tomorrow I will catch fish," he announced with no hint of doubt in his deep voice.

"With what? You don't even have a spear."

"I can make a spear easily enough. 'Tis the fish that must cooperate." He smiled.

"How can you be so cheerful?" Reena laid back in the sand and gazed up at the stars—myriads of them glistening like morning dew on a field of dark grass.

"Because I know the God I serve. And I have been praying all afternoon. If He wishes us to die here, then so be it. If not, He will find a way to rescue us."

Reena gave a ladylike snort. Such misplaced faith. "No one knows where we are. No one save Baines."

Freddy leaned back on the sand beside her. "God knows."

Reena thought to change the subject. She never won when Freddy spoke of his God. Though she supposed He was her God as well. "Do you remember the time old Captain Blane Snaketoes made me walk the plank?"

Freddy laughed. "How could I forget? The look on your face was priceless."

She slapped his arm. "That was before I learned how to swim. Anyone would be afraid." She chuckled. "Little did I know, you were waiting below in a boat."

"'Twas not easy to escape their detection. Save for it being night, I would not have been able to."

"When you fetched me from the sea, I could hardly believe it. Plus the ten muskets you had at the ready to fire upon their ship so we could get away."

Freddy smiled and put one hand behind his head. "They weren't expecting it or they would've had their cannons loaded. We were lucky to escape from old Snaketoes."

"Heard his ship was sunk by the Spanish Navy."

Freddy nodded.

Reena smiled. "And what about the time we absconded with the governor's treasure right beneath his nose on Saint Martin?"

"Aye," Freddy said. "He thought he was giving us bags of grain. And we simply drove off in a wagon loaded with everything he had of value as he waved goodbye from his porch."

Reena laughed. It felt good to laugh with this man—to remember their wild adventures. "Since he had robbed his people with extra taxes, in truth, the gold was not his."

"But we should have given it to those very people," Freddy interjected soberly.

Not wanting to sour the mood, Reena propped up on her elbow and stared at Freddy. Flickers of firelight danced over his strong jaw as he gazed at the stars. But they also accentuated the bruises on his face from his fight with Antoine. Before guilt took hold once again, she said, "We had many delightful times, you and I, did we not?"

It took several minutes before Freddy answered, but finally he said, "Aye, we did." And his agreement sent a river of warmth through her.

She laid back down and dared to slide her hand in his. He took it and gave it a squeeze. And as she lay there, watching the parade of stars flinging pearly light down upon them, she could die right there and be eternally happy.

"So beautiful."

"Aye. God's creation always is."

Several minutes passed before Reena asked, "Are we going to die?"

"Not if I can help it, Kitten. Don't fret." He leaned up on one arm and gazed down at her, but his expression was lost in the shadows. He eased a lock of hair from her face.

"I don't know what I'd do without you, Freddy."

"I am not your savior, Kitten. I can't be."

His scent of leather, oak, and moss swirled about her, igniting her senses. His touch, so gentle, his body so close.

Memories of all their intimate moments came spiraling back, giving her hope.

She reached up and rubbed the stubble on his jaw, caressing his cheek. "Then just love me."

He lowered to hover his lips above hers, so close she could hardly breathe.

CHAPTER THIRTEEN

*F*rederick's lips touched Reena's ever so gently—a mere graze—but that's all it took to remember how soft they were, how sweet her taste, how heady her scent. So heady, he felt himself hovering in a chasm of indecision between right and wrong, good and evil, love and lust. With the sound of waves lapping against the shore and a soft breeze as sensual accompaniment, he knew she would give herself to him just like she always had. It was her way of luring him into her trap—the most pleasurable trap he'd ever been caught in. A bottomless pit from which a man might never find his way out.

With every ounce of strength within him, he pushed from her and sat up, turning to stare at the sea, an endless blanket of ink, sprinkled with ribbons of pearly waves.

"What's wrong?" she asked.

"We should retire. Tomorrow will be a long day."

She stood and held out her hand. "Then shall we?"

Against his will, Frederick's body reacted to the invitation. He averted his gaze from her. "The shelter is for you, Reena. I will sleep out here."

He was glad he could not see her expression, for he was sure both his words and harsh tone had hurt her yet again. In fact, instead of retiring, she spun on her heels and marched to the water, where she dragged her bare feet in the incoming wavelets. He didn't follow her. She was safe here where nary a man or animal dared roam.

Drawing a deep breath of the sea air, Frederick glanced across the wide expanse of dark sky. "Lord, what am I to do? Please save us. Please get us off the island. Please help me take care of this precious creature without crossing boundaries I should not."

Easing back down on the sand, he crossed his arms over his chest and closed his eyes, hoping to fall asleep before she returned. But though he was as tired as he had ever been, sleep eluded him until he heard her return safely and enter the shelter.

Sometime in the middle of night, a dream invaded his peace. Nay, 'twas more a nightmare. One by one, spiders, larger than any ship, slowly emerged from the sea. Their massive legs shook the sand as they crawled onto the beach and formed a circle around him and Reena. Covered with hairy spikes, the snap of their sharp jaws echoed ominously across the island like an orchestra of demonic cymbals. Their hollow eyes stared at Frederick, their large rounded bodies blocked the sun. Yet instead of pouncing on them, they waited, their bodies gyrating with anticipation, waiting…waiting…for Reena or Freddy to make one wrong move. One wrong move that would give the hideous creatures the permission they needed to devour them. But then a light appeared—not from the fire—but from beneath where Frederick sat, from deep within the ground itself. It rose, growing brighter and brighter, turning the sand into gold and raising a shield of transparent light around them.

Reena screamed. But, nay. She was sitting beside him, smiling. She screamed again and then shouted for him, her tone one of terror.

Finally, shaking off his slumber, he jerked himself awake. Another scream had him leaping up and dashing to the makeshift shelter just as she bolted out.

She dove into his arms, nearly knocking him over. "Freddy…Freddy…." She caught her breath. "'Twas the biggest spider I've ever seen. It crawled all over me, even onto my face." She gripped his shirt and clung to it as if doing so would keep all other spiders away.

Frederick laughed. He laughed so hard, he fell back onto the sand, toppling her with him.

"Are you still afraid of spiders?" he managed to say in between chuckling. "The fearsome lady pirate, Reena Hyde?"

She pushed from him and leapt away. "'Tis no shame in it." She backed into the darkness, hugging herself. "We all have our fears."

Frederick reached for her, still trying to control his laughter. "My apologies, Reena. You are truly a baffling woman."

She was a shadow in the darkness, but he saw that shadow spin to glance around on the sand, heard the terror in her voice. "I suppose there to be a ton of these dreadful creatures on this island. How will I ever sleep?"

Frederick was not about to invite her to join him. A man could only tolerate so much. "You'll survive Reena. You always do. Go back to bed."

He could tell that she did naught of the kind after she returned to the shelter. She tossed and turned across the sand and uttered groan after groan, no doubt keeping a weather eye out for any creeping creatures. Frederick felt a measure of sympathy for her, for he had trouble sleeping as well. The nightmare kept infesting his thoughts. Odd, that he'd been dreaming of spiders when one had crawled over Reena. What did they represent? And the light? The light that had surrounded him and Reena and kept them safe. It had to be angelic, of course.

He'd not had many dreams since he had left Reena over a year ago. Before that time, they had come more and more frequently. Until that final one that prompted him to return to God. He shivered even now at the thought of it. At the time, he'd told Reena the entire dream, hoping it would affect her as it had him and bring her running back into God's arms.

But not Reena. She had always been as stubborn and thick as the mighty hull of a navy frigate. It broke his heart to leave her. But he'd had no choice. And then the dreams had all but stopped. He often wondered why. If the visions came from God, shouldn't they increase when he, the prodigal son, returned? And now, when he was back with Reena, they started up again. He could make no sense of it.

As it was, he greeted the dawn with more questions than answers, but also with a prayer on his lips for their soon rescue. In the meantime, he must catch something to eat, or they would die sooner than expected. He gathered a large stick and sharpened it with his knife—the small knife he always kept hidden in his right boot—and prayed for rain as well. They would need water faster than they would need food. But God had not abandoned them. Frederick still felt His presence.

As he whittled, light snoring rumbled from within the shelter. Which, of course, brought back memories of sleeping beside Reena on so many nights. Shame assailed him yet again. Still, instead of a frown, a smile formed on his lips, only increasing his shame. He should find no pleasure in these memories…so many he shared with this woman. She had brought to mind a few of them last evening, and yet, there were so many more. He'd spent the last year doing his best to forget them all—adventures, sword fights, ship battles, treasure, outwitting the navy, the East India company, and of course, notorious pirates. How many times had they left their enemies on islands such as this? Of course, Reena had always insisted they send help after they left. She had a tender heart, though she tried to hide it. Last night, she had let down her defenses and allowed her insecurities and fear to break through her shield. Something she could never do on board the *Reckless*. How hard it must be for her to keep up such pretenses, to always be the strong one, the one in command.

Sighing, Frederick gave his hand a rest and glanced over the beach. The arc of a golden sun greeted the day above the gray horizon, sending out ribbons of glittering amber over rippling waves. Above him, stars faded as the light pushed the darkness away. A gust of wind struck him and spun an eddy of sand a few yards off. He and Reena had spent many a night on islands such as this, though with plenty of water and food—romantic interludes, a break from the pressures of captaining a pirate ship. Memories of their lovemaking, of impassioned, yet sincere words of love and promises made in the middle of the night, came crashing down on him.

Movement sounded from within the shelter, shattering the memories. He needed to keep his wits about him—had to remember his commitment to God. And right now, he needed to finish this spear. Frederick had never caught a fish with only a spear, but God said in His Word that He would provide for His children.

Time to step out in faith.

With that, he leapt up and headed toward the ocean.

Reena had never seen anything so magnificent. Not even her sleepless night, the bug bites all over her skin, her ravenous stomach, or her raging thirst could take away from the vision of Freddy, bare chested and wearing only his breeches, standing on a rock several yards offshore, spear in hand.

Sunlight spun a golden hue over his rippling muscles and mighty arms as his gaze was locked upon the poor unsuspecting creatures below. His dark hair hung around his face, occasionally tossed by a strong wind that turned waves into foam. Yet, he stood still, a Greek statue of a god from long ago. Her hero, her prince, her rescuer. And soon to be her lover again. She was sure of it. He'd almost kissed her last night. Her body still thrilled at the memory.

She bit her lip. She had made a fool of herself with the spider incident, but that couldn't be helped. Freddy would forgive her. He was not one to judge. He'd never been one to judge. Until he returned to his God, of course.

She lowered to sit on the sand beside the simmering coals of a dying fire. Tossing a log onto them to keep it going, she suddenly realized how horrid she must look. She tried to run her fingers through her hair, but she had no comb, no pins, and no water with which to wash. Ugh. Perhaps this was not so romantic, after all.

Birds warbled in the trees behind her, tweeting a happy melody to greet the day. Why not? They hadn't a care in the world, for they could fly away to the nearest island and get water and food whenever they wished. She glanced up at them as they pranced proudly over branches in all their glorious colors. Still, their happiness seemed to mock her, for she had not secured her own.

Her eyes latched on Freddy again. How could he stand still for so long? Especially under the hot sun. Waves crashed on the rock on which he stood, gurgling and foaming, and showering him with sea spray that made his muscles glisten as if they were made of steel. She smiled, amazed that she could still blush at the sight of him. Still, he remained, his spear hovering over a small pool of calm water formed behind a barricade of rocks. She wondered how long he'd been out there and was suddenly embarrassed that she'd slept so long. Taking her headscarf, she dabbed the sweat on her brow and neck, longing for a bath, longing to dive into a pool of cool water.

Freddy flung the spear into the water so rapidly she barely saw it go. When he lifted it back up, a fish flapped on its tip, shimmering in the sunlight. He glanced toward shore, saw her sitting there, and smiled. Then leaping on a trail of rocks, he plunged into the surf, and headed her way. If she hadn't loved him before, she would certainly have fallen in love with him now, seeing how capable he was of doing anything he put his mind to.

"You are awake," he said as he approached, kicking up sand with his bare feet. He knelt to stir the coals to life, then laid the fish on a rock, drew a knife from his pocket, and sliced it open. After gutting it, he stabbed another stick through it and laid it upon the coals. That infernal cross of his dangled in the sunlight, mocking her.

"Breakfast, Milady." The wink and smile he gave her were her undoing. She could only stare at him as he stooped by the fire, all man and muscle and wildness, the dark stubble on his jaw such a contrast to his deep green eyes.

And for the first time in her recollection, Captain Reena Hyde found she couldn't utter a word.

"Watch over it, and I will be back with more."

He walked away, confident and strong, the muscles on his back rolling with each movement. She would have continued to stare at him, save a crackle and spit from the fire drew her gaze to the fish. Freddy returned with one after the other of the little slippery creatures, and when he finally sat down to eat, they had five fish altogether. A feast!

Freddy gave thanks, and they both began eating. Reena attempted to behave like a lady, but in truth, she found it hard not to stuff pieces of the fish in her mouth. Freddy did the same, and they laughed at each other's boorish manners. She wanted to thank him again, to tell him how wonderful he was, but she dared not compliment him overmuch for fear it would go to his head and he'd seek someone out better than she. "This is so good, Freddy."

He smiled and plopped another piece into his mouth. "Anything for my lady."

"Would that that were true," she replied sarcastically. Taking another bite, she gazed over the turquoise waters, spanning in glittering waves as far as she could see. How could something so beautiful be naught but a prison, surrounding them on all sides? She scanned the horizon for any sign of her precious *Reckless,* the reminder of its loss causing her stomach to cramp. She set down her fish.

"Mayhap you realize now," Freddy said, "that there are far more important things than ships and treasure, things which can easily be taken away."

"I cannot imagine what," she answered playfully.

"Not even…wait. Your map! They've got your precious map." Freddy seemed almost gleeful. "I guess you'll have to give up your hunt for eternal youth." He took another bite of fish and spit out a bone, cocking one brow her way.

Wind tossed her hair into her face. Snapping it away, she reached in the pocket of her waistcoat and pulled out the crinkled piece of paper. "Nay. I still have it." She gave him a victorious grin.

Freddy's lips flattened. "Of course."

"Now, we must find a way off this island so I can recover the rest of the pieces." Stretching her legs out before her, she leaned back on her hands. "Baines may have my treasure, but I have the real treasure in my hand."

"Reena, you're already going to live forever. Why would you want to spend that eternity in this fallen world?"

"I don't have your faith, Freddy. I wish I did. But right now, whether there be a heaven or hell, this world is all I know. Besides, heaven doesn't sound very exciting to me. Can't imagine spending eternity singing in some choir or fluttering about playing harps, can you? Why, I bet there aren't even any ships or seas to sail."

Oddly, Freddy only smiled at her. "I don't believe heaven is anything like that. I believe 'tis far better than we could ever imagine, far more wonderful and adventurous."

Frustration bubbled up within her, and she turned to gaze at the sea. "I have no wish to take the chance on what some ancient book says. My life is here and now. And I intend to make the most of it. With eternal youth, I can do that." She sat up and leaned toward him, reaching for his hand. "And you can do it with me, Freddy. Can you imagine the adventures we could have?"

Freddy studied her, his green eyes shifting between hers. And for one brief moment, she thought she had convinced him. But the longing she saw in his gaze transformed to pity as he breathed a heavy sigh. "You may live forever here if you wish, Reena. But one life in enemy territory is enough for me."

Bilge water! Her anger rose. "Then you will grow old— old and feeble and gray-haired—and your skin will start to fall off your body and every muscle will shrivel and every joint will creak and ache like an old ship. Is that what you want? Is that how you wish to end your life? Like Dinah?"

The name caused a shadow to creep over Freddy's face, stealing all joy. "Your nanny. I'm sorry, Reena. I heard she died."

"Aye. Six months ago." Reena stared at the sand and forced back tears. "She was a second mother to me. Always there, taking care of me, teaching me, loving me when my parents were off saving the Caribbean." She picked up a handful of sand, hating the bitterness in her tone. "Even after I grew past childhood, she joined us on the *Redemption*."

"I remember. She was a wonderful, godly woman."

"She was a part of our family." Reena swiped at a tear that had managed to slip past her lashes. "She died in my arms."

"I'm sorry, Reena. But she was old. 'Twas time for her to go."

Reena looked up at him, cursing the tears blurring her vision. "Why?" she snapped. "Why does it have to be like that?"

Freddy opened his mouth to answer, but her anger cut him off. "Do you know her husband left her? Ran off with another woman—a younger woman—before she even came to us?"

"I didn't." Freddy tossed another stick into the fire. "Not all men are like her husband, Reena."

Ignoring him, she continued. "Leaving her alone in her old age. And after living such a good life, a life of kindness toward others, she shriveled up like an old rotted piece of fruit and breathed her last." Reena released the sand in a stream to the ground. "A good person gone, while so many evil live."

"Aging and death were caused by our enemy, Reena. God did not plan for that from the beginning. But we all must suffer through it. I do not relish it nor look forward to it, but in a way, I welcome it, because then I'll depart from this place. I assure you, Dinah would never wish to return here."

Reena wiped her eyes and swallowed down her pain. "You make no sense, Freddy. I never met any preacher like you. Well, save our parents. Seems our families have been infected with some strange sense of life beyond our own. When all I want to do is live this one. Is that so wrong?"

Freddy gathered the bones from their fish and tossed them in the fire. "Why does aging bother you so, Kitten? 'Tis the natural progression of the carnal life."

She looked at him dumbfounded. Did he truly not understand? "Because I do not wish to become feeble. What pleasure is there in that? Alack, you will find me disgusting and leave me."

He laughed. "You believe your only value is in your youth and appearance?"

She shot him a pointed stare. "Nay, I believe 'tis what the world views of women. And I must play within its rules."

A breeze whipped over them, cooling the perspiration on her face. Gathering her hair, she held it up and allowed the back of her neck to cool.

"Have you forgotten that God has marked you from birth?" He gestured toward her birthmark.

Reena dropped her hair. "'Tis not a cross. It simply looks like one." She glared at him. "And if so, why do *you* not have one?" She arched a brow.

"I need no reminder of whom I serve." He smiled.

She snapped her gaze away.

Freddy cleared his throat. "Reena, true love cares not for appearances. Look at your parents. They are well past their prime and yet still deeply in love. Has your father left your mother because she has wrinkles and gray hair?"

Indeed, Reena knew they were very happy, but she had seen enough couples in which that was not the case. Her parents were an exception in more ways than one. "Regardless, they will continue to age until they can barely walk and feed themselves. And then they will die. Just like Dinah. I don't want that for them! For any of our family. In truth, for anyone in this world, save mayhap those who are evil."

"So you wish to play God, is it?" Freddy cocked his head.

Reena frowned. "Nay. I simply wish *He* would." Sighing, she stared up at him, searching his eyes, even as her determination rose. "If we are to live forever as you say, why not do it here? Why be forced to face such a horrid ending? Nay, I will find this Fountain of Youth, and I will bring its waters to our families and to all those deserving. If only I could have found it soon enough for Dinah." Picking up a shell, she rubbed it between two fingers as if she could scrub the memories away. "I will not watch anyone else I love die. I will not!"

Shrugging off the morbid thought, she smiled up at Freddy. "Think of it Freddy, we will always be young and strong. Every day will bring a new adventure, and together we will sail the seas forever. If we ever escape this infernal island." She tossed the shell toward the water, expecting some retort from Freddy, some criticism of her wayward religion, but he remained silent, his intense gaze enough to incriminate the innocent.

"I'm thirsty," she said, hoping to change the topic.

Freddy nodded his agreement and squinted at the cerulean sky where only a few white puffy clouds drifted. Then grabbing the cross around his neck, he bowed his head and closed his eyes. He sat like that for so long, Reena was beginning to think he'd fallen asleep.

Just when she was about to nudge him, he lifted his head, his green eyes shimmering, and said, "The Lord provided food, Reena. He will provide water. If we seek Him and His Kingdom with all our heart, He promises to provide for all our needs." He lifted his head to the sky. "Thank you, Father. I thank you in advance."

Reena wanted to snort in disbelief. Instead, she drew a deep breath and gazed over the endless sea of white-capped waves. She longed to beg him to give up this ridiculous hope that God actually cared about their mundane needs. She longed to help him see that this present life was here and now and all they should be concerned with. But she supposed this faith, this religion of his, helped him cope with the fact that they were most likely going to die on this island. So, she stilled her tongue.

Minutes passed as they sat in silence, listening to the waves crashing and the leaves fluttering, both lost in their own thoughts. But then a dark shadow on the horizon caught Reena's gaze. A ship? Nay. Not a ship, a cloud. Too far away to do them any good, she ignored it. It grew bigger. Then another cloud appeared, and that one grew larger as well.

The wind heightened, and she glanced at Freddy. His gaze was locked on the clouds as well, a smile on his face.

By the time she looked back at the horizon, the clouds had grown so large and moved so close, they swallowed up the sun and cast a shadow over their little island. That's when the rain began. Not a light drizzle. Not a mist. But a pounding rain that seemed to pour from the skies as if angels moved in a line, dumping bucket after bucket on them.

Hardly believing what she was seeing, but suddenly not caring, Reena leapt to her feet and raised her hands into the deluge, allowing the water to wash over her. Freddy appeared beside her, his arms also lifted to the sky, his expression was one of worship.

"I can't believe it!" she said twirling around, lifting her face and opening her mouth to the fresh water, allowing it to trickle down her throat and saturate her hair and clothing. Ripping off her waistcoat, she tossed it to the ground, wishing she could do the same with the rest of her attire. Instead, she laughed and danced and skipped through the rain, urging Freddy to join her.

CHAPTER FOURTEEN

*F*rederick could hardly believe that God had answered his prayer so quickly. One minute, the sun was burning down in a clear blue sky, the next, it was hidden behind a bank of incoming gray billows. One minute, hot rays seared his skin, the next, cool rain was pouring upon it. All he thought to do was lift his face to the refreshing water and his hands to the God who answered all the prayers of His saints. Frederick allowed the water to wash over him—washing away his guilt and shame, washing away his unworthiness, his doubts. Though he bore the disgrace of illegitimacy…though he bore the shame of being unwanted from his very conception, though he bore the heart of his father—a pirate's heart—God still answered his prayers.

Laughter accompanied the rumble of thunder, and he glanced down to see Reena dancing in the rain, a frolicking sprite of beauty and grace—a vision from which he could hardly tear his gaze. She stopped and looked his way, wonder in her golden eyes and a smile on her face.

"Oh, Freddy. I can hardly believe it!"

His gaze dropped to her chest where the rain had plastered her shirt to her curves. And though he snapped his eyes away as fast as he could, it was too late, for his desire rose until it became all but unbearable. Shifting his thoughts back to God, he closed his eyes and begged God's forgiveness as the cool water continued to slide down his body.

Thunder roared so loud and close, the ground shook beneath him. A spire of jagged lightning stabbed the sky as if God were warning him for his lust. He glanced back at the makeshift bowls he had made and realized he should have made more.

Grabbing Reena's hand, he led her into the thicket of trees, shouting, "More leaves!" And together they scoured the jungle, gathering as many as they could. Still, the rain continued to pour over their tiny island as if the storm clouds had been instructed to remain above them. Hence, they were able to create two more bowls before the deluge slowed to a trickle, then to a drizzle, and finally stopped.

Their clothes and bodies drenched, their hair dripping, they both dropped to the sodden sand by the first bowl and brought handfuls of the fresh water to their mouths. Frederick had never tasted anything so good. He could have consumed the entire bowl, but he forced himself to stop and stayed Reena's hand as well. "Easy, Kitten, we need to conserve. Who knows when it will rain again."

She sat back and smiled his way.

The clouds moved, giving the sun reign once again. Its golden rays transformed droplets on the leaves and sand into sparkling diamonds and set Reena's moist skin glistening. Water dripped from her hair that tumbled to her waist in a cascade of sparkling mahogany. Her eyes, the color of a sunrise, gazed at him in love.

And yet again, his eyes lowered to her sodden shirt.

Thunderation! Growling, he shoved to his feet and stormed away. Her footsteps followed.

"You turn from me as if I am hideous. Yet, there is naught of me you have not seen before, Freddy." Her tone was pleading.

Freddy swallowed down a burst of desire and shame. "You are beautiful, Reena, but you already know that. You use your beauty and charm to get what you want."

"But it bears no effect on the one man I want above all."

He huffed, hating the sorrow in her voice. "Not true. I'd have to be a tree stump to not want you."

She eased in front of him, drawing his gaze her way. "Then what holds you back?"

Frederick turned to stare out to sea. "Have some modesty, Reena. You are no trollop and should not behave as one."

When he faced her again, the pain of his comment lashed at him from her face. Against his will, he ran a thumb over her cheek. "Apologies, Reena. I meant no insult. But I beg you to cover yourself. We no longer have an intimate relationship and cannot do so in the sight of God."

Her eyes misted and she moved back from him. "I cannot see why God disapproves of love."

"God *is* love. He does not disapprove of it. In good sooth, He encourages it. But sex is a different matter which He reserves for marriage. Without that commitment, it causes harm, illness, and heartache."

"It never caused *us* harm." She tried to smile, but it faltered on her lips. "I am committed to you, Freddy. You know that."

Aye, Frederick did. And that was part of the problem. "Come now, Kitten. No more talk of this. Let us be grateful for God's provision. He has given us more than enough water for several days."

"Whether 'twas God or nature, I am grateful," she said, her tone turning harsh. Then grabbing her waistcoat from the sand, she turned on her heels and marched into the jungle.

"Where are you going?"

"To the other side of the island to remove my clothing and allow it to dry in the sun. Hence, I will offend you no further," she yelled over her shoulder.

Sighing, Frederick watched her until the greenery swallowed her whole. He knew he was doing the right thing by remaining pure, but why did he feel like the most miserable wretch on the planet?

Hours passed, during which time he did his best not to envision Reena's bare body lying on a beach a short walk from him. Instead, he prayed and fished and then prayed some more.

He also repented. He had looked at Reena with lust, and Jesus had said doing so was as bad as adultery. Would he ever be free of his debased nature?

He waded onto the shore and placed the last of three fish on a rock near what remained of their fire and then went in search of dry kindling. Still, he could not get Reena out of his mind. Memories assailed him of their intimate moments—how she had made him feel, how perfectly her curves fit snuggly against him.

He angrily shook away the vision. He had destroyed his own life and hers as well. And broken both their parents' hearts in the process. He knew God had forgiven him. But how could he forgive himself? He had taken a young innocent Reena, only eighteen years of age, and he had ruined her for his own pleasure. He *had* loved her, but that was no excuse.

Gathering kindling, he found some dry wood under leaves and headed back to the beach. So consumed with his thoughts, he barely saw the figure before it leapt in his path. Frederick jumped back, dropping the wood. His heart seized. Not a figure…a dark shadow, no taller than a barrel, but just as wide. It shifted back and forth in front of him, blocking his path. Its wide mouth was agape and hollow, its eyes yellow and cold. The demon stared at him and laughed—the sound of metal scraping on metal that sliced down Frederick's back.

He knew what it was, and suddenly all fear fled him. This was the demon that was bringing back memories, taunting him with sins of his past. And somehow he had opened the door for it. He had allowed its torment.

"I command you to leave me at once in the name of Jesus!" he shouted, and instantly the shadow dissipated.

Amazed that God had given him this peek into the spirit realm, Frederick gathered the wood, emerged from the jungle, and knelt to build another fire, still shaking from the experience. His recent dream of gigantic spiders filled his thoughts—also demonic creatures. They had to be. But why was God showing these things to him?

Warfare.

The word bubbled up from within his spirit. Warfare, indeed. Perhaps 'tis why God put him here with Reena alone. To test him…to train Frederick to resist temptation. Something he had never conquered as a youth. But also for another reason—to lead Reena toward the light.

He bowed his head. "Help me, Father. Help me keep my thoughts toward Reena pure. Help me look upon her with only love for her soul. Help me to love her as You love her."

Pirates didn't cry. Reena kept trying to remind herself of that as she sat on the warm sands of the beach.

Her clothing hung from a branch of a nearby tree, waving in the breeze. It would be dry soon, and she would have to return. But she could not stop crying. She dug her feet into the sand and allowed waves to caress them, but it still was not enough to soothe her. Freddy had not meant to hurt her, but each time he rejected her, it felt as though a knife carved out another piece of her heart and tossed it into the sea. Stranded alone on a deserted island should be all they needed to rekindle their love, their intimacy. But he was so defiant—so stuck on obeying the rules of his distant God.

She sighed, brought her hair over her shoulder, and ran her fingers through the endless tangles. At least the rain had washed away the salt, and it had regained its silky feel. Reena felt clean and fresh for the first time in a long time. In addition, her stomach was full, and her thirst quenched—thanks to Freddy's skill and provision. Or, in the case of the rain, God's favor on Freddy. Reena still could not believe it had come upon them so fast after Freddy had prayed.

Sunlight winked at her from the pearl ring Freddy had given her. She twirled it around her finger. What an incredible man. Truly, there was none to match him.

A little crab popped out of a hole in the sand and skittered her way.

"Well, hello, little one. What makes you so brave to come out of your hiding place?" Mayhap the same thing that had made Reena brave enough to pursue the one man on earth who had the power to destroy her. Mayhap this little crab sought love and adventure as Reena did and was tired of hiding in a hole.

In truth, Reena had never hidden in a hole. She was not the type. Nor one to keep her mouth shut or her feelings to herself. Which was most likely why she found herself sitting alone on a beach, sobbing from a broken heart. Mayhap she embraced life a little too tightly, wanted more of it than was allotted for her to have. She glanced up at the blue sky, now speckled with white puffy clouds and wondered if God thought of her at all. And if He did, *what* did He think of her? Did He hate her for her sins, turn His back at the sight of her as Freddy so often did? Or did He take pity on her…understanding her weakness, even wanting her to come back to Him? She wished she knew. Her parents heard from God—or so they said—but God had never spoken to Reena. She was not worthy. She had taken a different path.

The crab skittered beneath her knees and ran down the beach, diving into a hole in the sand before the next wave swept him away. She smiled. Perhaps she should give up her quest for Freddy and dive back into a hole somewhere—at least for a while to lick her wounds.

Eddies of wind twirled her hair and caressed her face as a serenade of lapping waves and an orchestra of birds filled the air. She tossed her head. She was not one to lick wounds either. She was Reena Charlisse Hyde, infamous lady pirate. And not even the loss of her brig or the loss of her love could stop her from her goal.

She clenched her jaw. Nay, she would never give up. Besides, they were stuck on this island for who knew how long. She had plenty of time to make Freddy love her again. And she intended to do just that.

She'd simply have to try a different tactic.

CHAPTER FIFTEEN

Frederick felt Reena approach long before he saw her. Something in the atmosphere changed. If he were honest, something in his heart changed, and he looked up from the fire to see a vision of beauty floating his way over the sand. Her long, unbound hair fluttered in silk waves in the breeze, dancing over her rounded curves and feminine lines. The creamy skin of her face and neck, her rosy lips and stark golden eyes coming clearer into view with every step. Thank God she had dressed, even secured the top button of her shirt. She gave him a brief smile before she sat down by the fire and stared over the sea.

"You look refreshed." He could think of nothing else to say.

She didn't respond. Just continued staring at the waves as if she were hundreds of miles away. He longed to apologize for hurting her, but that would only offer encouragement he didn't wish to convey. So, instead, he finished cooking the fish, set one on a leaf, and handed it to her. Together, they ate and enjoyed the beauty of the setting sun—waves of crimson, lemon, and coral frolicking across the horizon as if they hadn't a care in the world.

Frederick broke the silence. "This is our second night. God has certainly provided all that we need."

She swallowed her bite of fish and winked at him. "Indeed. No doubt because you are here, *Preach*."

"I beg you, don't call me that. I struggle like everyone."

She had no answer to that. Nor did she say much in the ensuing moments. Most odd for Reena. They continued thus in silence, finishing their meal, both lost in their thoughts and the pain in their hearts. Soon, the darkness pushed the sun behind the horizon, and a fierce wind rose. It brought a chill that penetrated deep into Frederick's bones, even as it spun sand into cyclones that stung their faces. He glanced at Reena and found her hugging herself with her head dipped to her chin. She had not asked him to hold her, cover her, or protect her as he would have expected. Mayhap he had hurt her more deeply than he realized. The wind increased, absconding with their fire, and leaving them in a darkness so thick, Frederick could hardly see.

He groped over the sand for Reena's hand, found it, and lifted her to her feet. "Get in the shelter, Reena. Seems we are to endure another storm."

She nodded, and he wrapped his arm around her shoulder and felt her trembling. Kneeling, she crawled into the shelter, and much to his own surprise, he crawled in after her, laid down beside her and encased her in his arms.

"Will this not be far too much temptation for you?" she asked with sarcasm.

Frederick chuckled. "I will suffer through it in order to keep you warm."

He felt her smile as she snuggled back against him, her every movement causing him discomfort in more ways than one.

Was he to be tested so soon after his declaration to overcome his weaknesses? Yet mayhap it needed to be thus, in order to prove to God he was worthy to be a preacher in these godforsaken waters of the Caribbean.

He had to distract himself. He had to get his thoughts off the soft, warm lady in his arms. Nor did he wish to invite that hideous demon to return. Wind howled against the rickety shelter, and he wondered if it would stand the onslaught. Waves crashed ashore, fronds screeched. And her unique scent that was all Reena swirled beneath his nose.

Lord, help!

"Pray, tell me what you've been doing for over a year, Reena."

Laughing, she wriggled again, and he longed to tell her to stop—*for the love of all that was holy, stop moving*. But then she responded. "I doubt you would find much favor in my activities, Freddy."

"Surely you engaged in an endeavor or two of a more redeeming nature than pirating?"

"If you must know, I rescued several people from a slave insurrection on Saint Lucia and brought them on my brig. Oh, and I also saved a little girl who had been kidnapped by Captain Every."

"The vicious pirate Every?"

"Aye, the very one. My plan was merely to steal his treasure whilst his ship was at port and all his men were either ashore or cupshodden. We snuck aboard under cover of night and had nearly gathered all the treasure we could carry when I found a young girl no older than six locked in the hold. God only knew what they intended to do with her."

"You have a kind heart, Reena." He wanted to rub her arm but didn't.

Wind quivered through their shelter, blasting them with sand. Surprisingly, Reena didn't complain.

"Turns out she was the daughter of the governor of Grenada, Louis Ancelin de Gemostat," Reena continued, shouting over the storm. "Of course I returned her forthwith."

Frederick gave her a squeeze. "You spoke with the governor himself, and he didn't arrest you for piracy?"

"Nay, so overcome with joy at having his daughter back, he not only refused to arrest me, but he offered me a reward." Chuckling, she turned her head slightly his way. "You'll be much pleased to know I did not accept it. For I rather enjoy restoring the helpless back to safety."

Without thinking, Frederick brushed hair from her face and caressed her cheek with the back of his hand. "You would make a better Christian than most."

She gave a ladylike snort. "One good deed does not cover a multitude of sins."

Freddy was silent for a moment, his thoughts skipping from the helpless girl to his own helplessness as a babe. "Would that someone like you had been around when I was kidnapped."

She nodded. "'Twas John Morris who stole you from your mother. Wasn't that how your father found her, and together they sought you out?" She sighed. "And fell in love again." Her words held hope that the same would happen between them.

But their situation was quite different from his father and mother. He still could not understand how his mother could have possibly fallen in love with the man who ravished her.

"I would have never been kidnapped if my father had been present, but he was off pirating the seas, leaving my mother to give birth to me alone, poor, desolate, and abandoned by her own family."

"Have a care, Preacher. I hear bitterness in your voice. What of the forgiveness of which your Bible speaks?"

Frederick ground his teeth together. *Thunderation*, but the woman was right, of course. A blast of wind pummeled their tiny shelter, nearly toppling it, and she moved closer to him, if that were possible.

"How long do you think we will be here?" Oddly, he heard no fear in her voice.

"As long as God deems."

Shifting, she turned to lay on her back and looked up at him. He could not make out her face in the darkness, but he could smell her sweet breath fill the air between them and yearning welled up within him.

"I wish we could stay here forever. Just you and me, Freddy."

And he knew she meant it.

He longed to say how wonderful that sounded, but he should keep such sentiments to himself. He was in a battle here—one that, at the moment, he felt he was losing as her lips were just inches from his.

Yet, she didn't try to steal a kiss as she so often had attempted in the past. Instead, she laid there innocent and sweet, hoping and expecting….

And Frederick suddenly found his lips on hers.

Ah, such sweet delight! He caressed her lips with his… gentle, soft, but then he deepened the kiss and drank her in like a fine wine. A heady wine, for his senses took their leave as she responded with as much passion as he remembered. Suddenly his arms were around her, and she clung to him as if she were drowning and he her only hope. They pressed harder and harder together as if they couldn't get close enough. Still, he kissed her…desperately…hungrily. He had missed her so much. He'd missed her caresses, the feel of her silky skin, her passion, and her need for him as if he were her only reason for living.

You can have that sensation again…you can have it right now.

Wait! Nay! He had changed. He was different now, his spirit renewed. He'd experienced too much of heaven, seen too much of the spirit realm, spent too much time in the presence of God. He could never go back.

He pulled away, leaving them both breathless. "Forgive me, Reena. This has naught to do with you." Then rising, he raced from the shelter, relishing the cold slap of wind and sting of sand on his face. He deserved it and more. Still, he felt lighter, freer, as if a heavy presence had fled him. He curled up in a ball beneath a tree and prayed for God's forgiveness, even as he thanked Him for His strength.

Sometime during the long night, the wind yet howling in his ears and the sand whipping his face, he fell into a deep sleep. He dreamed of an angel standing on the beach as tall as the tallest tree. Brown hair hung to his shoulders that were covered with plates of brilliant armor extending down over his chest and thighs. It shimmered like no metal he had ever seen. An enormous blade hung by his side, pointing toward golden boots that rose to his knees. Around him, glittering light swirled and spun in every direction as if it had a life of its own. Then suddenly, the angel drew his sword, the mighty sound of it reverberating like a cannon shot.

Frederick shrank back, fearing for his life, but the angel turned and pointed his blade toward the horizon. Instantly, a path of light sliced through the darkness, cutting a bright chasm through sky and sea. Though stars still hung in the night sky and the sea was black on either side of the path, dry land appeared, covered with reefs and small sea creatures.

The light stopped in the distance on a ship out at sea. Though he could not make out its details, Frederick knew it was the *Reckless*. Before he could ask about it, the angel withdrew his sword, drawing all light back with it, and sheathed it at his side. The dream ended and Frederick woke with a start. The wind had died down and the chill had dissipated, but all was still dark, the night stars winking at him from the sky. Snores rose from the shelter and he was glad for it. Reena had finally fallen asleep.

Rising, he shook off the sand, and wandered down to the dark waves, lit only by the glow of a cloud-covered moon. What a strange dream. What did it mean? Could it be an expression of God's pleasure with him? For he *had* resisted Reena. He'd kissed her, but he'd not allowed it to go farther. A huge victory. He knelt in the sand and stared above at the wonder of God's creation, seeking answers from the only One who knew.

And suddenly the thought came to him. He knew exactly what the dream meant. They were to be rescued soon—by the *Reckless*.

⚓

Reena woke with the feel of Freddy's lips on hers and a pain in her heart that would not go away. Once again, she had cried herself to sleep, cursing herself for her weakness. She had shivered through most of the night, the cold wind a reminder of the absence of his arms around her. But finally, the wind ceased, her tears dried, and she must have drifted into slumber.

A ray of sunlight wavered over her, stirring her awake, but her heavy eyelids prodded her to go back to sleep—to sleep away the days until Freddy would love her again. The warble of birds, smack of waves, and the bright sun easing through the cracks of her shelter forbade her that luxury.

Something crawled on her leg. The wind? *Bilge water*, it had to be the wind, right? There, it moved again. She leapt up, darted out of the shelter faster than she intended, tripped over a log, and fell flat on her face in the sand.

"Sleep well, Kitten?"

Growling, Reena pushed herself to sit and spit sand from her mouth. Freddy's hand appeared in her vision, and she clasped it and stood, brushing sand from her breeches and waistcoat. She dared to glance up at him and found him smiling at her, but there was a new light in his eyes as if he knew a grand secret.

Whatever it was, she didn't want to know. Her stomach growled, and she was thirsty. More than that, she was tired of being rejected by this man. Spinning away from him, she held her head high and marched to their remaining bowls of water. Unfortunately most of them had been destroyed in the storm, but she found enough to get a good long drink.

"I would spend the day making more of those if it mattered," Freddy said. "But we won't be here that long."

She glanced at him, thinking he'd gone mad overnight. But she saw the usual confidence and intelligence in his eyes— those eyes that used to look at her with such love. Last night had reminded her of days gone by, their bodies melding together, kissing…loving…caressing. Another minute, and she knew he would have made her his all over again. But then he had left so abruptly. Pain cut through her even now at the memory.

Putting on an expression of indifference, she perched a hand on her hip. "Do say? And how have you come by this information?"

He flashed his brows and grabbed his spear. "I had a dream last night we were rescued."

"Rescued?"

"By the *Reckless*."

Reena laughed. "Too much sun has befuddled your brain, Freddy. Baines will never return to get us." She paused and patted her waistcoat pocket. "Yet…if he knew what map I possess. But how could he?"

"I didn't say it would be Baines, did I?" He winked and made his way to the surf, spear in hand.

Mumbling curses to herself, Reena gathered wood for the fire. Yet, despite her every attempt otherwise, her gaze always wandered back to Freddy perched on that rock in the surf, spear raised and ready, his bronze skin glowing in the sun, and that cross winking at her from around his neck.

By the time he headed back with two fish, the sun was halfway to its zenith and a shadow appeared on the horizon. Shielding her eyes, Reena studied it, wondering if it was another cloud sent to gift them with fresh water again. Freddy followed her gaze. But after a few minutes, they both knew it was a ship.

Reena humphed, hiding a twinge of fear. "If 'tis the *Reckless*, I'll be a slimy octopus."

Freddy squirmed and made a face. "Almost hope it isn't, then."

"Ah ha! You *do* care what I look like." She gave him a sarcastic smile.

"Nay. I just don't think you'd be happy as an octopus." He winked.

Shaking her head, Reena returned her gaze to the ship that was growing larger and larger on the horizon, heading their way. In truth, she hoped with everything in her that Freddy's dream had been real and this was her precious brig. But that would be a miracle, and she had long since given up on those.

Indeed, 'twas no ship at all, but a schooner, flapping a pirate ensign, and loaded with armed men from prow to stern.

"Get the gun," Freddy said as he tossed sand on the fire with his foot and then scattered the coals. Reena gathered the pistol Baines had left them and turned to find Freddy tearing her shelter apart and tossing the wood into the jungle. Even more upsetting was watching him spill what remained of their precious water. She felt like crying… like screaming, but when she glanced up and saw the schooner anchoring just off shore, she put aside those female emotions, threw back her shoulders, gathered her courage, and became Captain Hyde once again.

Taking her hand in his, Freddy led her a few yards into the jungle where he stopped and knelt before a thick fern. Reena peered through the fronds. A boat had been lowered, filled with a raucous group of men, and they were rowing toward shore.

Pirates. With only one bullet, nowhere to hide, and no way off the island, Reena knew they'd soon be captured. With the likes of these, she'd be ravished and Freddy killed. Not good prospects.

"What could they be looking for?" she whispered. "There's naught on this island of interest or value." She reached in her pocket and felt her map. Still there. Though what difference did it make now?

Freddy remained silent beside her. His eyes were closed and his lips moving as if he were praying. At a time like this! Surely the man could think of something better to do. Seek a place to hide, gather sticks for weapons. Not that she was afraid of dying. She'd faced death well enough. But being ravished? That she could not handle.

She peered once again toward shore as the men leapt from the boat, pistols and swords in hand, and marched across the beach.

Within minutes, they found the hot coals of their fire and examined the remains of their shelter. One of them spit into the sand and stared into the jungle, a leer forming on his lips.

Freddy squeezed her hand. "Never fear, Reena. God will protect us."

She was about to laugh, to chide him for wasting time on useless prayers, when all of a sudden, the men on shore darted back to their boat, leapt in, and rowed in haste back to their schooner.

The loud *boom* of a ship's gun thundered across the sky.

CHAPTER SIXTEEN

*R*eena and Freddy crept toward the edge of the jungle for a better look as another cannon blast battered the sky. A mighty splash spit up water just off the pirate schooner's bow. A warning shot, no doubt. And it appeared they were taking that warning seriously as their captain's voice echoed over the bay, spewing orders to raise all sail and get the craft underway.

Reena scanned the horizon. Where was the attacking ship? More importantly, were they friend or foe? For she feared she and Freddy had traded one menace for an even larger one.

Freddy took her hand in his and gave it a squeeze as if he already knew the answer. The schooner's sails caught the wind and the craft moved, each inch revealing a ship looming behind them. Squinting in the bright light, Reena studied the craft, the lines of her hull, the angle of her yards and canvas, the flag fluttering at her masthead. And her heart took up a dance in her chest.

The *Reckless*!

Freddy laughed and smiled her way.

Reena had no words. How could Freddy have known this would happen? Yet two thoughts shoved all others from her mind. Had Baines come to finish them off or was Abraham at the helm? And if 'twas Abraham, aye, she would get her precious brig back! But that also meant her time alone with Freddy would come to an end.

Within minutes the *Reckless* dropped anchor, lowered a cockboat, and headed toward shore. Breath crowded her throat as she waited to see who was in it, but she quickly recognized Abraham and a few of her loyal crew. She and Freddy broke from their cover.

No sooner did her quartermaster's feet land on the sand then he dashed toward her. "Good t' see yuh, Cap'n!" Against protocol, he gripped her shoulders, his face beaming. Then clearing his throat, he stepped back and glanced at Freddy. "Captain Carlton, an' yuh too."

Freddy gripped the man's hand and shook it firmly. "You are a welcome sight, my friend. We thought we'd be here awhile."

Reena glanced over the two sailors holding the craft ashore. "But how? What of Baines?"

"Dat's a long tale, Cap'n. Let's get yuh back on board first."

Reena glanced at the fading silhouette of the schooner and winked at her quartermaster. "Friends of yours?"

Chuckling, he scratched his graying hair. "We was comin' t' get yuh an' saw dem rowin' ashore. Figured dey wasn't here t' help."

She nodded her approval.

His dark eyes scanned the beach, then shifted between her and Freddy, a knowing grin on his lips. "Seems yuh's not suffered too much."

She glanced at Freddy, longing to say how well he had taken care of her, but that wouldn't be very captain-like.

"Let's be off. I'm anxious to leave this place." Even as she said it, she knew it wasn't the whole truth. But they couldn't stay here forever. At least not yet. Not until they both drank of the Fountain.

The minute Reena's boots landed on the deck of the *Reckless*, she felt home again. Somehow a miracle had occurred, and she had gotten her brig back—an impossible task with so large and successful a mutiny.

From within a crowd of hesitant faces, young Michael burst and dashed into her arms.

"You should have seen it, Captain Reena." He stepped back from her, his blue eyes twinkling. "'Twas all Abraham's doing. He talked ol' Clay, who was bringing us our food, to gather as many loyal to you as he could."

"Tha' be most o' the crew," Jo said, approaching from Reena's left, a welcoming smile on her face.

Abraham nodded. "Dey armed demselves, let us out, an—"

"We fought them!" Michael slashed his hand through the air.

Reena drew him close, suddenly remembering the strange light that had enveloped him during the mutiny. "I hope 'twas not you who fought?" Movement brought her gaze to Brodie, emerging from a hatch, blood splattered on his apron.

"He helped a wee bit." He wiped his hands on a cloth. "Didna take long tae subdue them."

Abraham crossed arms over his chest. "Yuh woulda been proud o' yer crew."

"I *am* proud." She raised her voice for all to hear as she glanced over her friends and the rest of the crew gathered behind them, forcing back tears. Sedley shifted from foot to foot at the head of the pirates, alternating between glancing at her and then down at the deck. "You will all be rewarded for your loyalty!"

Freddy moved to stand beside her, an odd sorrow claiming his expression. Sorrow? Could he be as sad as she that their time alone had come to an end?

She gestured toward Brodie's stained apron. "Whose blood?"

"Some were injured durin' the battle."

"Deaths?"

"Jist Baines and ten of his men."

Freddy huffed. "Where are the rest of the scoundrels?"

"Locked below." Jo spat a curse.

The brig teetered over an incoming wave as a gust of wind flapped the loose sails. "My weapons, Michael."

The lad darted off, returning in minutes with her pistols, knives, and cutlass. She had felt naked without them. Or had she? She couldn't recall thinking about them or her brig most of the time on the island.

"Bring up the rest of the mutineers."

With a nod, Abraham gathered five sailors and went below. Soon, twenty men lumbered above, squinting at the sun, shackled and bedraggled. The rest of her crew flung curses at them, hissing and booing and spitting.

The mutineers refused to meet Reena's gaze as she ordered them into the waiting cockboat. Standing staunchly at the railing, she looked down upon them. "You'll have one pistol and one shot for the lot of you. I left it on shore. That's all you left me, and that's all you'll be getting. This will teach you to cross Captain Reena Hyde."

Her crew cheered behind her. "Huzzah! Huzzah! To the devil wit' ye!" Their shouts drowned out the villains' curses as her men rowed them ashore.

Then taking the ladder to the quarterdeck, Reena approached the railing and glanced down at her crew. Some refused to look her way, others gazed at her with fear. Freddy came to stand by her side, while Abraham remained on the main deck below.

Before she had a chance to speak, one of the men—Cooper, if she remembered his name, a hard-working linesman—approached and gazed up at her. "We had no choice, Cap'n. He would've killed all o' us. We didn't want t' go wit' him. We"—he glanced behind him at the sailors amassing on deck. "We didn't want him as Cap'n. Weren't none o' us a part o' this. An' we all fought t' get rid o' him. Ye can ask Abraham." He fumbled with his hat and stared up at her, fear twisting the corners of his mouth.

But she knew he told the truth. They had been unarmed and unable to resist the mutiny and would've died trying. How could she blame them?

She scanned the mob. "I believe you. Baines was a vile sort, but he is gone now. However, I expect loyalty on this ship. If I even suspect a hint of mutiny, you'll find yourself in worse straits than Baines."

She used her sternest voice, her most vicious tone, and it bore the effect she desired as a tremble seemed to pass over the men.

"Aye, Cap'n!" a few sailors shouted. "Let's hear it fer Cap'n Hyde!" And they all cheered together, their shouts of loyalty rising to the wind.

"Now back to work!" she bellowed, placing hands at her hips. "Abraham, when the men return with the cockboat, take us out full and by." She turned to Fletcher standing at the tiller. "Point her south-southwest."

"Aye, aye, Cap'n."

Reena entered her cabin, more tired than she'd been in a long while. Fred squawked at her from his perch, and she grabbed a peanut from a bowl on her desk and tossed it his way. He caught it and cracked its shell with his beak.

"I missed you." She stroked his feathers as he quickly consumed the peanut and then leaned his head against her cheek.

"I didn't mean to intrude." Freddy laughed from the doorway.

Reena stepped back from the bird and arched a brow at him. "I must seek affection where I can."

She hadn't been sure he would follow her, but his presence suddenly filled the room. In this brief moment alone, their eyes latched onto each other and understanding flowed between them. They had shared much together over the past few days…had grown closer. At least that's how she felt. But she was no longer a maiden dependent on his care. She was a pirate captain once again. And she was determined to find the rest of the map.

It would come between them, for he would not approve.

Behind him, Brodie and Jo entered, followed by Michael, who darted toward her and embraced her again.

"I missed you," he said. "How did you survive for three days?"

Fred squawked. "Burn an' sink me. Burn an' sink me."

Ignoring the bird, Reena glanced at Freddy. "Captain Carlton is quite resourceful."

Abraham's commanding voice echoed from above. Footsteps pounded, and the thunderous snap of sails catching the wind reverberated through the brig.

Reena gestured to the blood staining Brodie's hands. "Are there any sailors severely injured?"

"Nay." Brodie glanced at Jo. "Couple of scrapes is all."

Jo? Reena moved toward her master gunner. "You were injured?"

"Aye, Cap'n. Is nothin'. An' Brodie fixed me up right quick." She smiled at him.

Fred skittered back and forth on his perch. "Old sawbones is he, is he, is he."

Shaking his head at the parrot, Freddy sank into a chair and sat back, no doubt as exhausted as she was.

The brig jerked, and water gushed against the hull as the *Reckless* picked up speed.

Reena circled her desk and leaned back on the stern window seat. "Regardless, I can't thank you all enough for risking your lives for me. For your loyalty."

"Loyalty!" Michael fingered a chalice atop her desk. "We're friends. And friends help each other, right?" He beamed.

Brodie poured himself a sip of rum from an open bottle. "Ach now, I ne'er woulda answered to that chimp-faced cockroach, Baines. Nae fer all the money in the world."

"Not fer all the treasure in the seas!" Fred chirped.

They all laughed.

"You don't intend to leave them on that island?" Freddy finally spoke up.

"Nay. When we make port, I'll send a ship to get them."

He nodded his approval.

Sunlight stroked Reena's back through the windows, up and down with the movement of the brig, relaxing her weary bones.

Brodie went to pour himself another drink, but Jo stayed his hand and gave him a look of censure before she faced Reena. "Ye must be tired, Cap'n. Let's leave ye t' yer rest."

And with that, the three of them headed for the door. Michael cast a final grin at her over his shoulder.

"Have cook prepare anything but fish for supper," she shouted after him. "And have some of my chocolate sent up."

"Aye, aye." He gave a mock salute and was gone.

One side of Freddy's lips curved upward. "I thought you liked my fish."

"Best fish I ever ate." Reena gripped the window seat, relishing the feel of solid oak beneath her fingers. "I never thought to see this cabin again."

"You're still going after the other map, aren't you?" Freddy's voice harbored the disappointment she'd expected.

"Aye."

Sorrow dragged his expression down as he leaned forward on his knees and gripped the cross around his neck.

"But I will take you to Jamaica first. I owe you at least that. And more for all you've done for me."

"I heard your directions to Fletcher. Thank you." He rose and headed toward the door.

"Freddy, don't leave." She hated her pleading tone.

He faced her, and she could tell he was doing his best to keep emotion from his face. She knew him too well.

"I need you," she said. "I want to be with you. Let's not return to the way things were before the island."

"I'm tired, Reena," was all he said before he left and shut the door behind him.

She didn't see him the rest of that day, nor even at dinner with all her friends around her. Nor the next morning when she'd come above to check the direction of the brig. Finally, in the mid-afternoon, she found him on the foredeck teaching Michael how to sword fight. The sight warmed her even more than the hot sun.

He was gentle with the lad. Yet, at the same time, he did not hold back using his skill. She stood there, mesmerized by their swordplay. First Freddy would demonstrate a move to Michael and then he would allow the lad to practice it in a mock fight between them. When Michael did well, Freddy praised him. When he failed, Freddy did not yell or chastise him. He merely demonstrated the move again, offered further suggestions and allowed him to attempt it once more. A few sailors stopped to watch. What a wonderful father he would make—much like her own who'd been more than patient. When he'd been around. In fact, 'twas her father who had first taught her to sword fight, with Freddy picking up her instruction later. Captain Merrick was the best of the best on the Caribbean.

She frowned. Now that she thought about it, she had never thanked him. If she ever saw him again…if he ever wanted to see *her* again, she would correct that.

Freddy stopped and glanced her way before quickly shifting his attention back to Michael.

A palpable pain scraped across her heart. Every gain she'd made on the island seemed to have vanished with the trade winds.

"Him's good wit' de lad," Abraham commented as he took a stance beside her.

"He's a good man."

"A godly man I was happy t' hear."

"Aye. They called him Preach on HMS *Viper*." She chuckled.

Brodie stumbled across the deck and made his way to the railing, bottle in hand. Just two in the afternoon, and the man was already inebriated. She would have to speak to him. Though she allowed her men to drink whenever they wished, who knew when they might encounter an enemy?

Jo noticed him and went to stand by his side. He offered her a drink, but she turned him down, instead berating him with harsh words that dissipated in the wind before they reached Reena's ears. Then Brodie did the oddest thing. He threw his bottle overboard as if it suddenly repulsed him, took Jo's hand in his, and kissed it.

Odd. Was a romance brewing between these two? She turned to ask Abraham, but he had plucked out the scope and was staring at something on the horizon.

She raised her own spyglass and followed the direction of his gaze. A ship came into view—a large ship from the looks of her.

"A set of sails!" the lookout shouted from the crosstrees.

"Two sets of sails!" he added, and Reena adjusted her scope once again and focused on the white canvas floating along the horizon. Just one ship as far as she could tell. Then another sail appeared to its left. And still another as a second ship slipped out from behind it.

"Bilge water! Can you make out her colors?"

"Not yet, but dey's headin' straight fer us."

CHAPTER SEVENTEEN

*F*rederick had spotted the oncoming ships before the lookout shouted the warning. More like sensed them. He'd been able to sense enemies at sea ever since he first sailed with his parents. His father had told him he had a unique gift of discernment and had called Frederick his "little seer." The memory brought a smile to his face, but it instantly faded when he realized he'd taken that gift and lived a life of debauchery. Guilt prickled down his back, and excusing himself from Michael, he sheathed his sword and made his way up the quarterdeck to Reena. Would his past ever leave him be?

"French," Frederick said as he took a stance beside Reena and Abraham.

"By Neptune's blood, how do you know that?" Reena leveled the scope once again on the intruders and brought them into focus.

"He's right." Abraham lowered his spyglass and slapped it against his palm. "Dey be frogs."

Reena flattened her lips. "What do they want?"

"We are at war with France, in case you don't remember," Frederick offered. "Any ship, merchant, naval, or privateer is a target." Then marching forward, he gripped the railing and glanced at the main deck below where the crew was amassing, staring at the oncoming ships.

"Beat to quarters! Ready the guns!" Frederick addressed the last command to Jo, who was still talking with Brodie by the starboard railing. She glanced up at him with a nod and brayed a string of orders for her gun crew to assemble around the guns fore and aft and the ones below deck.

When he turned around, he found Reena staring at him, and he realized what he'd done. "I apologize, Captain. Old habits."

But instead of chastising him for taking command, she smiled, though he thought he saw her bristle slightly. "I made you co-captain. You have every right."

The men swarmed across deck like flies scattered by a whip. Turning, he studied the ships, longing to take the spyglass from Reena, but she raised it to her eye again.

"Extinguish the galley fire!" she shouted, then she turned to Fletcher at the tiller.

"Wear round to a starboard tack. And watch your luff! Let's see if we can outrun these frogs." She nodded to Abraham, and he ordered the topmen as Fletcher veered to starboard.

Itching to issue further commands, Frederick went to assist the gun crew, hoping to keep from infringing on Reena's authority. He'd never been good at standing down, but his time aboard HMS *Viper* had taught him to keep his thoughts to himself and his mouth shut. Most of the time.

He made his way to a five-pounder positioned on the larboard quarter of the brig around which a gun crew furiously worked. Michael sped by, depositing shot and powder cartridges for the guns. He offered Frederick a smile before he sped on his way. But the crew didn't need Frederick's help. In truth, they were doing exactly as they should. Why should he expect any less? Reena had told him Jo was an excellent master gunner who had trained her crew well.

The brig made a sharp turn. Sails floundered, seeking new wind. Finally, they glutted themselves with a fresh breeze, snapping to attention. The deck canted, and Frederick balanced himself as he passed by the other guns, ensuring each was primed, loaded, and ready to fire should a battle ensue. He hoped not. Especially not against two French warships, which—as he glanced their way—appeared to be better gunned than the *Reckless*. At least the larger one.

Even if they weren't, they'd have the advantage of maneuverability with two of them. Reena was good in battle. She'd inherited both the wits and skill of her father and her mother. But none of that would matter if either of these two captains possessed any skill at all.

Halting, Frederick gripped the railing and closed his eyes for a moment. What was he thinking? He must remember God was on their side, and that nothing happened without His permission. At least for those who truly followed Him. He offered a silent prayer, then continued onward.

With every stitch of canvas stretched to the wind, the *Reckless* shouldered the sea high and wide, leaping over rollers as if she owned the Caribbean. The brig creaked and groaned and heaved, laughing in delight as the sea charged against the hull and came flying over the bow, sending spray over the deck in glittering rainbows. Frederick halted at the prow, allowing the wind to blast over him, drowning out all sound, save the mad dash of the sea. Before him, the Caribbean spread out like a turquoise jewel, studded with diamonds.

In truth, he had missed this—the exhilaration of impending battle, the chase, with the sea his footstool and the sky his limit. And he hated himself for it.

The sound of Jo's commands spun him around to see her barking at one of the men assisting with a swivel at the bow. The rest of the sailors who weren't in the tops adjusting sail were arming themselves with swords, axes, and pistols.

Making his way to the main deck, he glanced up at Reena, her feet spread on the heaving planks, wind tossing her hair behind her, her chin raised as though she hadn't a care in the world. She was a pillar of strength, oscillating between gazing at the oncoming enemy through her scope and giving orders to Abraham to adjust sail in order to get the most speed out of the brig.

Frederick was impressed. 'Twas no wonder she and her crew had garnered a reputation across the West Indies, along with much treasure.

What an incredible woman. *Father, if only she belonged to You, I would marry her on the spot.* Thunderation, where had that come from?

The brig struck a wave and took flight. Frederick clung to the capstan as a sailor tumbled across the deck in front of him. Extending his hand, he assisted him up, then made his way to the larboard railing and studied the ships fast on their tail. No need for a spyglass to see them now. One was a smaller ship—a two-masted sloop, from the looks of it—and the other was at least a 40-gun frigate. *Reckless* could outrun the frigate, but not the sloop. Problem was, the smaller craft would engage them first, and they'd be forced to slow down to return fire, which would allow the more heavily armed frigate to catch up. 'Twas a tactic used by the French. And quite an effective one.

When he leapt on the quarterdeck, he could see in Reena's eyes that she'd reached the same conclusion.

"Dey within firin' range, Cap'n, an' comin' across our stern!" Abraham shouted over the wind.

"Recommendations, Captain Carlton?" she asked.

"Pray." No sooner did the word leave his mouth then the thunderous boom of a cannon pounded the air.

"All hands down!" Reena shouted, fully intending to remain upright as a captain should, but Freddy forced her to the deck and covered her with his body—a shield of warmth and love that caused her heart to swell.

She pushed him aside. "Let me up. I'm the captain."

"So am I, and I'm not about to let you get blown to bits." He leapt to his feet, scanned the situation, and added, "It fell into the sea off the port side. Too close."

Reena rose and glanced at the advancing sloop, white smoke curling from the swivel at her prow. Another shot would certainly hit them dead on. She was about to issue orders to veer to larboard and bring all her guns to bear when Freddy shouted the exact same commands. She didn't have time to argue who was in command during battle. And in truth, she was glad to have him by her side. Yet, she added a few of her own orders, lest her crew find her weak.

"Reduce to battle sails! Mizzen and Sprit!"

The buccaneers sprang to the ratlines as the *Reckless* veered to larboard, slanting the deck between sky and sea. Foamy claws reached over the railing, and for a moment, it seemed they would capsize. But then the sails snapped and the brig eased back down.

Their larboard guns were now aimed at the oncoming sloop.

Reena leapt down the quarterdeck ladder to the main deck, glanced quickly at the position of the sloop, then turned to Jo. "Fire as you bear!"

"Fire as you bear!" the master gunner repeated.

The cannons belched black smoke and ricocheted backward from the force of the blast, sending the air aquiver with their thunder. Smoke stung Reena's nose. Coughing, she batted it away, peering through the fog. Their shots had done minimal damage.

"Bilge water!"

Flames shot into the sky from the sloop's guns. *Boom! Boom! Boom!* pulsated over the waves.

"Hit the deck!" Abraham shouted.

This time, Freddy was not nearby. Hence, she remained standing, defying all odds, waiting to see where the blasts would hit. One shot shivered main and mizzen topsails. The other went whistling through the shrouds, slicing the mainmast. The third struck the railing, firing splinters in every direction. Screams filled the air from sailors pierced by the flying spears.

She turned to look for Abraham, but he was climbing up the shrouds to assist sailors with a tangled line. "Helm, hard to starboard!" she shouted, not wanting to give the sloop another chance to broadside her. "Bellamy, James," she gestured to two men. "Take the injured below to Brodie." They stared at her for a moment, wide eyes lowering to her side. "Now!" she bellowed, and they scrambled to do her bidding.

Something warm saturated her waistcoat. The sky spun. The brig bolted over a wave, and she stumbled to grip the railing.

"Reena!" Freddy appeared in her vision. He gripped her shoulders and called to Sedley for help.

Reena glanced down to see blood bubbling around a large splinter stuck in her side.

"Take her below, Sedley."

"Nay!" Reena gripped the splinter and yanked it out, barely feeling the pain. Then reaching up, she ripped Sedley's neckerchief from his neck.

"I will not abandon my crew during battle!" She stuffed the cloth beneath her shirt. Then yanking off her bandanna, she tied it around the wound. Tight. "I'm all right." Blinking back stars, she nodded at Freddy. "Really."

He growled, but another gun exploded with a mighty roar, and he swerved to assess its aim. Holding her side, Reena climbed the ladder and once again took her spot at the quarterdeck. The shot fell impotently in the sea two yards from the *Reckless*. Freddy glanced her way and she gave him a nod she hoped he understood.

He did. He took command, firing orders fore and aft, sending her crew up ratlines and over the deck to assist the gunners.

The sloop made a quick tack and was coming up on their stern, no doubt intending to rake them—a bloody prospect that would kill many and cripple their sails.

She opened her mouth to issue commands, but nothing came out. Instead, she leaned against the railing and blinked back the darkness that threatened to swallow her whole.

"Hard to starboard! Stern chasers, prepare to fire!" Freddy continued shouting commands as the ship canted, and her sails flapped before catching the wind yet again.

"Fire!" The stern chasers exploded, sweeping the sloop with deadly shot just as a volcano of cannons returned fire. But the *Reckless* had tacked just in time and only one shot struck the stern railing.

Frederick marched across the deck, leapt onto the bulwarks, grabbed the backstay, and leaned into the wind as he studied their enemy. His hair splayed around him in wild abandon, his shirt flapped in the wind, his jaw was firm, his eyes steely. This was the Freddy she knew. In command. One of the best pirate captains she'd ever seen. This was what he was made for, his destiny, despite what his God said.

Leaping from the bulwarks, he spit out a string of commands that turned the brig, adjusted the sails to the perfect position, and reloaded and aimed the guns at the sloop for a damaging broadside. Brilliant. If they could only cripple the tiny menace, they may have time to escape the frigate.

The sloop floundered to catch the wind, Freddy expertly lined up the broadside and eased the *Reckless* across the sloop's port side.

"Fire!" He shouted at the perfect downswing of a wave. Five culverines vomited fire and fury upon the sloop, barreling back a good two feet against the straining ropes of the tackle. The *Reckless* shook from stem to stern as gray smoke flooded the deck. Coughing, sailors swatted it away, anxious for a look at the damage they'd inflicted. A charred and gaping hole smoked from the sloop's bulwarks, her foremast was shattered, and fragments of yards hung to the deck.

"Huzzahs" flung into the air.

Reena smiled. He'd done it. Freddy had done it!

But the cheering slowly faded, and Reena dragged her gaze to the horizon.

The frigate was coming up on their starboard quarter…slowly…methodically—the dark muzzles of twenty guns poking through their hull like the hissing tongues of a snake. They had taken too long to cripple the sloop and now were in gun range of this monster. One command from their captain would pulverize the *Reckless* and sink them to the depths. Reena pressed her bloody side and leaned on the railing. What was he waiting for?

No doubt assessing the futility of an engagement, Freddy mounted the quarterdeck and reached for her. She pushed him away. She could not accept she was about to lose her brig once again. And to the French!

The frigate eased beside them, hull to hull, and a man sporting a blue-plumed hat appeared on their deck. He lifted a speaking cone to his mouth. "*Reckless*, you will be given quarter if you lay down your arms and surrender."

Rage boiled deep within Reena's belly, along with fear, hatred, and despair. She knew that voice!

"'Tis Antoine du Casse. He wants his treasure back."

Freddy gripped the hilt of the sword. "I believe he wants more than that. Revenge is my guess, which does not bode well for us."

Reena fisted hands at her waist. She could not lose to that thumb-sucking coxswain. She could not. There had to be a way out of this. She glanced at the frigate ready to loose a broadside that would send them all to hell. Save for Freddy, of course. She punched the railing. Pain throbbed through her hand, matching the one in her side. She had lost this battle. Her first one. Nay, she would not lose! There must be a way…

Freddy clutched her hand and gave it a squeeze of consolation.

She tugged it back.

"Reena, I know that look." His brow rose above narrowed eyes. "You're a great captain, but part of being a great captain is knowing when you've lost. You're injured. To fight now would be certain death."

"I would rather die fighting than hang from that Frenchman's yardarm."

"Nay, he would've already blown us to the depths if that was his goal. He wants something."

"His treasure an' yer ship," Abraham offered as if they were discussing what to have for dinner.

"Well, he's not going to get either!" Reena drew her blade.

Freddy shook his head, and she knew he was right. "Let's find out what he wants first."

"Mademoiselle Pirate." The taunting voice made her want to fire on him no matter the cost. She glared his way, could make him out now, all feather and lace standing there with one hand on his hip. "By now you know 'tis me, *ma chérie*. I wish you no harm. I wish merely to have a parlay. Raise your flag of surrender, and I'll send a boat for you."

"Bilge water! A parlay?" Reena had never surrendered to anyone. But as always, Freddy was the voice of reason. His calm, rational thinking had saved her life on many occasions when she had wanted to charge, guns blazing, into a situation where she would have surely been killed. Besides, she didn't want Freddy to die. She turned to Abraham who looked at her with the sorrow she was feeling inside. "Raise the white flag."

And so, white flag flapping from the masthead, the great pirate Reena Hyde affected her first surrender. Within minutes, a boat was lowered from the frigate and rowed toward them, and despite Freddy's insistence she stay on board the *Reckless* and have her wound tended, Reena refused. Antoine had requested her presence, and she would not appear weak in front of her enemy.

Hence, while she and Freddy waited to depart, Brodie tended her wound—which he proclaimed was shallow—and bandaged it up as best he could. "I wull hae to examine it later."

She thanked him. "Tend to the rest of the wounded, if you please."

Michael darted toward her, an unusual light in his eyes and a peaceful look on his face. "You'll come back, Captain Reena. You'll come back. That man will not hurt you. I know it." He lifted his hand and briefly touched her side where she'd been wounded, as if he could take her pain away.

Ah, the foolishness of innocence. She cupped his chin and smiled. "Until I do, take care of Abraham, will you?" She looked up at the large man. "You have the helm."

He gave her a quick nod of assurance.

Jo glared at the French frigate. "We should 'ave fought 'em, Cap'n."

Regret swamped Reena, along with guilt, for she had wanted to fight with all she had. "You did excellent work, Jo. And your crew."

"Wha' I want t' know," Abraham said, glaring at the frigate. "Is how he found us. How did he know where we be?"

"Good question." Freddy huffed. "'Tis too large a sea to be a coincidence."

Reena had wondered the same thing. She scanned her crew, noting Sedley fidgeting as usual over by the capstan. The rest of the men looked as if they'd been sentenced to death.

She opened her mouth to address them, wanting to encourage them, but her words would not come.

Freddy stepped before her. "This is not over. We shall return to fight another day. Stand your ground, men."

This caused a surge of "ayes" and "huzzah" from the pirates. Reena was glad for Freddy's confident tone, for she doubted she could express such hope at the moment. In truth, as she climbed down the rope ladder and took a spot in the boat where ten of Antoine's armed sailors waited, she couldn't help but wonder if she would ever set foot on the *Reckless* again, or if Antoine would have them both executed on the spot.

CHAPTER EIGHTEEN

*F*rederick still bore the bruises from his last meeting with Antoine du Casse. Now, as he climbed the ladder and set foot on the main deck of the blackguard's ship, *Conquérant,* he found his anger and disdain returning. Dressed in all the regalia and pomp of a formal captain—though Freddy knew Antoine had never been in the French Navy—he sauntered up to them, a triumphant grin on his thin lips. Sunlight gleamed off the gold buttons and fringed braid lining his blue coat and shimmered off his pantaloons and white silk stockings tucked into black shoes. A blue plume waved in the breeze from his cocked hat that sat upon hair that had been curled and powdered. He circled them, fingering his chin, as if assessing their value.

Halting before Reena, he smiled. "*Ma chérie,* even dressed as a pirate, you enchant me."

Without faltering, Reena gave a tight smile, withdrew her cutlass and handed it—hilt end—to him.

"Ah, *non, non.*" He waved a finger back and forth. "I will not accept your blade, mademoiselle. We are friends, *non?*"

"Friends do not fire on friends," Frederick said, drawing the man's narrowed gaze.

Antoine cocked his head and scanned Frederick with disdain. "Ah, you again, I see. Hmm. So, you are not a common sailor… but perhaps the lady's *amant?*" He winked at Reena.

"I am not, monsieur."

"This is Captain Frederick Carlton, Antoine." Reena gestured toward him.

Antoine chuckled. "A captain?"

Frederick released a sigh, bored with the man's theatrics. "The lady is merely taking me to Kingston."

"So, you take on passengers now, *ma chérie?*" He laughed. "*Mais,* no matter. Join me in my cabin." Antoine gestured toward a set of ornate double doors, which two of his men opened as he approached.

Seeing that he had no choice, Frederick ducked beneath the beam and followed Reena inside. Two of Antoine's officers joined them, closing the door.

The first thing Frederick noticed was the odd scent of bergamot cologne, beeswax, and alcohol permeating the room. The next thing was that the cabin was an exact reflection of its master—pompous and extravagant.

Three Louis XIV red velvet chairs perched before a massive wooden desk that was covered in silver and gold trinkets, bowls of jewels and pearls, navigational instruments, and quill pens. Matching velvet curtains framed an elaborate stained-glass window that spread across the stern. A plush Turkish carpet centered the room, extending to the sides where an assortment of weapons were strewn across a gilded cabinet. Tapestries lined the bulkheads. Sideboards and shelves contained books, crystalline glasses and pewter tumblers, while a four-poster bed covered in white lace stood off to the side.

Removing his plumed hat, Antoine proceeded to a sideboard where he laid out three glasses and poured amber liquid into each. Grabbing two, he offered one to Reena and the other to Frederick.

Frederick held up a hand of refusal and met the man's gaze. He could no longer see the demons slithering about him, but he knew they were there, felt them deep in his spirit, their loathing, their threats. He must find a way to get Reena away from this man.

Antoine blinked. "A pirate captain who does not drink. Hmm. Such a man is not to be trusted."

Reena sipped her port. "He fancies himself a preacher."

"Ah. *Oui.*" Antoine picked up his glass. "Now I know where I heard the name before. Your father is a pirate turned preacher, *non*?"

Frederick made no answer.

Reena glanced his way. "Aye. And he hopes to follow in his father's footsteps."

"Then what is he doing with you?" Antoine's eyes gleamed with a devilish twinkle.

Reena stepped forward. "Enough of this. I can explain about the treasure, Antoine."

He chuckled and waved a jeweled hand through the air. "Do you think that is what this is about? *Vraiment*, I would have been surprised if you had not attempted to steal the treasure. However, had I known you were aware of its presence, I would have assigned more men to guard it. It is not every day I host a notorious pirate in my house." He smiled. "*Non, non, non*, I have not chased you across the West Indies for treasure I can easily replace." He leaned toward her and raised one cultured brow. "However, now that I have caught you, I *will* take it back."

"Of course." She sipped her port and gave him a coy grin. "On the condition that you allow me and my crew to leave unhindered and unharmed."

He chuckled and his officers joined him. "Mademoiselle Pirate, you are in no position to barter with me. *Très adorable*." He set down his drink and fingered the lace of his cuffs. "As I said, I did not come for the treasure."

"Then what?" Frederick asked.

He grinned. "Why, the map, *bien sûr*."

Though most people would not have noticed, Frederick saw the slight flinch on Reena's lips.

"What map?" She lowered to sit in one of the velvet chairs and spun a strand of her hair tighter around her finger.

Plucking a cheroot from a wooden box on his desk, Antoine lit it in a candle, then leaned back on his desk and took a puff. "Let us cease lying to each other, *ma chérie*. There was a map in the treasure chest. A map I'm sure you discovered or perhaps you knew about, which is why you went after the treasure."

"Truly, Antoine, I have no idea what you are talking about."

Frederick bristled at the ease with which she lied.

"There was nothing in that chest save a vast amount of treasure of which I have told you I will return." She set her glass on the table, pushed to her feet, and Frederick joined her as they made their way to the door.

Antoine snapped his fingers, and his two officers stepped in their path. Frederick gripped the hilt of his cutlass, examining them. He could probably engage them both and win, but then what?

"The thing is, Mademoiselle Pirate, I insist you give me the map, or I will be forced to broadside your pathetic little brig and sink it and everyone on it to the depths."

Reena slowly turned to face him. "You would kill innocents for some mythical map?"

He shrugged. "I have killed for less. But I did not say it was mythical." He grinned.

Reena groaned.

"Let me make this easy for you, *ma chouette*." Antoine puffed on his cheroot, then lifted his head and exhaled smoke into the air above him. "I do not wish to steal the map, I wish to share it with you. It is my understanding that it is only a part of the puzzle which must be solved. I know you to be in possession of great intellect, and with your wit and my…hmm"—his devious brows arched—"connections and abilities, I believe we can solve this puzzle and find the prize of eternal life."

"There is only one way to find such a prize, and it has naught to do with a map," Frederick said with authority. No sooner did the words leave his mouth than a hideous face with red eyes and yellow fangs shot out from Antoine toward Frederick. It came within an inch of his face, dripping hatred and malevolence. But Frederick held his ground and uttered the only name with the power to defeat such evil. "Jesus." The shadow melted away.

"Ah, you were right about him." Antoine chuckled, then sipped his drink, the jewels on his hand sparkling in the lantern light as he lustfully assessed her. "I have always had a place for you in my heart, *ma chouette*. Please do not break it again.

Why not join forces with the great Antoine du Casse? Think of the adventures we will have." He winked.

Apparently Antoine knew Reena well, for if anything would break down her resolve, 'twas the lure of adventure and treasure. He longed to take her aside and tell her to give the map to this fiend and let them be on their way. But he knew Reena. She would never give up her dream of eternal youth. And if such a fount existed, there would be plenty for both her and Antoine and a host of other people.

"Do we have a bargain, mademoiselle?"

"Do I have a choice?" Reena said.

"*Non.*" He chuckled. "If you decline, I will simply take the map and be on my way."

Tugging her close, Frederick leaned to whisper, "Reena, don't. This will only end in failure."

"I must," she shot back. "Please try to understand." Then jerking from him, she approached du Casse.

"Very well, Antoine. We have an agreement."

Antoine's eyes lit up like the fires of hell. He set down his glass and took Reena's hands in his. Then, bowing, he placed a kiss upon each one—slobbery kisses from the look of disgust on Reena's face. Frederick wanted to vomit. How stupid could she be, aligning herself with this deviant? This would only lead to trouble and disappointment—or worse, her death.

"Then let us see this map. I assume you have it on your person since that is what I would do."

Hesitating, Reena glanced at Frederick as if seeking his understanding, but 'twas too late for that. She would do what she would do, regardless of his disapproval. Which she must have seen on his face. Antoine was quick to regain her attention when he said. "I give you my word, *ma chérie*. We will share the map, and I will not destroy your brig. Let us see it and then we can plot our course."

Time seeped by like the slow drip of water through rotted wood as Frederick stood in this buffoon's cabin and watched him and Reena pore over the map, exchanging ideas. 'Twas Antoine's opinion the tavern in question must be the Hairless

Snout, for it was the oldest tavern on Saint Lucia. Reena agreed.

Regardless, Freddy could tell the man had affections for Reena—though affections might be too strong a word. 'Twas more a desire to conquer her. If Reena couldn't see that, if she couldn't see past her own lust for eternal youth, then she was truly abiding in the dark.

Finally, they settled on a course of action to find the first missing piece of the map, and as promised, Antoine sent them safely back to the *Reckless*. But what did it matter? They could not escape him now. Not that Reena would even consider it. She may be a pirate, but she was a woman of her word.

Reena stormed into her cabin, surprised to find Brodie and Jo there. But once she saw the surgeon patching up a wound on Jo's arm, she remembered she had insisted that any of Jo's injuries be treated in her cabin, where the woman would find privacy.

"I didn't realize you were hurt, Jo." Reena chastised herself for not paying attention to her crew after they'd been so easily defeated. She'd only thought of her own anger and shame and hadn't made sure that her friends were not injured.

"'Tis nothin', Cap'n, jist a few scratches. But Brodie insisted."

Brodie continued his ministrations, gently applying salve to a wound he had just stitched as if Jo were a delicate flower. "Ach now, more than scratches, I'd say, lass."

Now that he mentioned it, Reena's own wound no longer pained her. She lightly pressed against the bandage beneath her shirt and felt nothing. Strange.

Frederick, Abraham, and Sedley burst into the cabin, Michael dashing in behind them. The lad rushed up to her. "I can't believe you're joining that…that vicious, pirate captain. What'd ya do that for?" Though innocence plagued his eyes, there was also fear resident there.

"Humph," Abraham said. "Nuttin' good t' come out o' de likes of dat vermin, Antoine du Casse."

Fred screeched from his perch. "Devil's blood be in his veins…devil's blood, says I."

"Hush your feathers, Fred." Reena circled her desk and stared out the stern windows. "We would all be at the bottom of the sea if I hadn't agreed to his proposition."

Abraham humphed yet again. "I agree wit' de bird. A deal wit' de devil's more like it."

"Precisely," Freddy added. "Though I'm sure you already know that."

She swung about and glared at him. "What I know is that all you care about is getting to Kingston." She swallowed down a lump of sorrow. "And I still plan on taking you. But now I have an obligation to Antoine. I gave him my word."

Freddy crossed arms over his chest. "You didn't give him your word that you would not take me to Kingston. I want no part of this crazy adventure."

The parrot flapped his feathers. "Split me skull, madder than a beached shark!"

"'Tis not crazy. You'll see, Freddy. And I *will* take you to Kingston. But I can hardly allow Antoine to retrieve the remainder of the map. Indeed, 'tis my plan to beat him to it."

Freddy huffed. "Surely he knows you would try such a thing, having the faster ship."

"Wit' a couple ripped sails, we ain't that fast," Abraham offered.

She shrugged. "Easy repairs, and his sloop sustained far more damage."

Freddy rubbed the back of his neck. "He may be a craven-souled knave, but he's no fluffhead. You think he has not considered that you would make all haste to beat him?"

"He be right," Abraham interjected with a scowl.

Grabbing a strand of her hair, Reena twisted it around her finger. "What choice do I have?"

Brodie tightened the bandage around Jo's arm. Wincing, she looked up. "We should at least try, Cap'n."

Sedley shifted his stance, more twitchy than usual. "I'm wit' ye, Cap'n. An' so is the crew."

Michael scratched his head. "What sort of treasure is at the end of this map?"

Reena chuckled. "The best treasure of all—a fountain which brings eternal youth."

Michael's eyes widened at first, but then he shook his head. "I have no need of that. I'm young already."

"You will not always remain so." Reena smiled and cupped his chin. "Wouldn't you like to live forever?"

"Don't sully the lad with your foolish ideas," Freddy said, and she wished he would stop ruining her good mood. When Antoine had summoned her to his ship, she thought her life had come to an end. But she'd been given another chance to find the Fountain, and she didn't intend to squander it.

Brodie hummed a pretty tune as he tied the final bandage and smiled at Jo. But 'twas the look in Jo's eyes as she returned his gaze that set Reena aback.

She faced Abraham. "Repair the damaged sails and then raise all canvas. Tell Fletcher to head east-southeast. We can make the other repairs as we sail."

Shaking his head, Freddy turned and marched from the room, chipping off yet another piece of her heart with him.

But it couldn't be helped. He'd see reason soon enough. Turning about, she watched the last vestiges of sunlight sink to the depths and a dark curtain of twinkling stars descend. "We're heading to Saint Lucia to find the next piece of this map, and I'll not hear another word about it."

"Shiver me timbers, Cap'n's orders!" Fred squawked.

CHAPTER NINETEEN

*F*rederick sat on a barrel by the foredeck, sipping a strong cup of coffee that Michael had brought him. He'd had a restless night, fraught with nightmarish dreams. Only one in particular stuck in his mind—a dream of Reena onshore with Abraham, Brodie, and Sedley, searching for something in the dark corners of a boisterous tavern. The dream had seemed so real. Even in the light of day, he remembered the words to the bawdy tunes the men sang and the discordant twang of an off-key fiddle, the raucous laughter of the patrons, and the stench of sweat, smoke, and ale. Every detail of the tavern remained stark in his mind's eye—the long wooden stained bar, from which the owner served mugs of kill-devil rum and jugs of foamy ale, the lanterns swinging from rafters every time the door opened, allowing a fresh breeze to enter, the candles atop tables, casting malevolent shadows upon the patrons. He even felt the crunch of dirt and squish of spittle beneath his boots as he had walked in.

He scrubbed a hand over his face. But that hadn't been the worst of it. Four large, well-armed men had risen from one of the tables and slunk toward Reena and Abraham as they headed toward the back corner. Spotting them first, Abraham spun and quarreled with them, but to no avail. Swords were drawn, and Reena turned to engage the attackers as well. All Frederick could do was stand there and watch as the battle ensued. Brodie, who'd gone to the bar for a drink finally came to their aid, but 'twas still three to four, and the brutes were getting the best of them. Sedley was nowhere in sight. Patrons leapt to their feet, shoving fists and mugs in the air, thrilled to watch the slaughter in their midst. Then, without warning, and while Frederick stood by, unable to even move, one of the men thrust his sword into Reena's belly. She collapsed to the filthy floor in a pool of gurgling blood. Frederick had woken up in a cold sweat, his heart pounding.

Hence, he'd come up on deck to pray. 'Twas before dawn, that wondrous time between complete and utter darkness and the glorious emergence of light, that peaceful time when the earth whispers its prayers to the Creator for the coming day. There, he'd met with God and whispered his own prayers, receiving the peace and joy that always came from the presence of the Almighty.

Afterward, he'd spent most of the day avoiding Reena. He understood the urgency of beating Antoine to Saint Lucia, but he was still angry his journey to Kingston had been delayed yet again. Hence, whenever she'd come above decks, Frederick went below. Whenever she went below, he came above to help with sails and lines. Finally, as the sun sat heavy on the horizon and the island of Saint Lucia rose from the sea in the distance, Reena emerged from the companionway and navigated the *Reckless* into a small cove a few miles from Castries Harbor. Saint Lucia was, at the moment, a French port, though it had been claimed by the British in the past. People of all nationalities inhabited the island, including some pirates who frequented the main port. Regardless, she would have to be cautious when she went ashore.

Frederick's stomach twisted at the thought, but he quickly shoved his anxiety away as Reena gave orders for sails to be furled and the anchor tossed. Her men quickly obeyed, and the brig soon came to rest among the sapphire waters of the hidden inlet. Her gaze latched upon him then—the first time since she'd come above—and he saw pain and determination in her eyes before she whirled about and descended to her cabin once again.

Shrugging off the nightmare, Frederick sipped his coffee and glanced down at Michael sitting at his feet. After all, Reena would never take Sedley with her onshore. She had already divulged that she didn't trust the man. Thus, 'twas only a silly dream conjured up by Frederick's own fear that the stubborn woman was racing down a path that would end in her demise.

Michael looked up at him with eyes of innocence. "Tell me more, Captain Carlton. I want to hear more about Daniel being tossed into a den of lions and how the angel protected him!"

Frederick loved the boy's enthusiasm. He could relate. When he'd come back to the Lord, all the stories in the Bible had come to life. No longer were they just boring tales from his youth, but living, breathing tales imbued with power and love.

He opened the Bible on his lap and searched through the book of Daniel. He stopped on the chapter about Shadrach, Meshach, and Abednego. "Ah, you're going to love this story. Three of Daniel's friends are thrown into a fiery furnace for not bowing down to the king's statue. And they were not much older than you."

Michael's eyes widened. "Did they burn?"

"Just listen." Frederick began to read. He became so engrossed in the story, he didn't hear Reena march up until he saw the leather of her boots appear beneath the top of the Bible.

"What is the meaning of this?"

Blinking from the setting sun, he gazed up at her, hands on her hips, her braided hair tossed over the front of her shoulder, her eyes alight with fervor, and the ring he had given her winking in the sunlight. Thunderation, but she was beautiful. Especially when she was mad. "I am reading the Bible to the lad, as you can plainly see."

She flattened her lips. "I won't have you turning him into a duck-kneed barnacle, tossed by every wave of the sea and good for naught but clinging to the keel. Michael shows promise to be among the greatest pirates in the West Indies."

Abraham chuckled as he walked up behind her, shoving sword and pistol into his baldric. "De Scripture can only make him stronger an' wiser. No harm in dat."

Wind tossed Michael's light hair as he looked up at her. "You wouldn't believe the stories in here, Captain. They're better than anything that's ever happened to me or you. God's power is exciting."

Frederick cocked a brow at her. "The lad has a zeal for God that will not be extinguished."

"All a zeal for God will do is take you to the poor house." She glanced off the port railing at the shadows creeping out from a row of trees lining the shore.

"Abraham. Lower the boat."

"Aye, Cap'n." Abraham marched off, shouting commands.

Closing the Bible, Frederick stood. "I see you still intend on proceeding with this madness."

"I do. And when I return with the rest of the map or at least another piece, we'll be that much closer to the Fount." She cocked her pretty head and smiled.

Brodie came up behind her, strapping on a baldric lined with knives and pistols. Without the haze of alcohol, his eyes were as blue as the sea.

"I didn't expect the surgeon to be going with you."

Brodie smiled. "Weel, I used tae be quite the fighter in me day. And I'm tired of stayin' on this brig."

"I wish you'd come with us, Freddy. I could use another man in case something surprising happens."

"You mean in case Antoine predicted your duplicity?"

She flattened her lips. "Predicted or not, his frigate is slow, his schooner damaged, and we made all haste." She sighed. "Say you'll join me."

"Nay. I'll leave you to your adventure, Reena."

Michael leapt to his feet. "Can I come, Captain? I promise I won't be any trouble."

She tousled his hair. "Not this time. 'Tis a French port. Could be dangerous, and I don't want you hurt."

The boy frowned, and the innocence fled his expression, replaced by sober reflection. Odd.

The rattle of tackle and whine of straining cordage brought Frederick's gaze to the boat being lowered into the water with a splash.

Uneasiness stirred within him as the sun bid its final adieu in waves of maroon and saffron. Was it him, or did the night descend quicker than it should?

A gust of wind spun around them, bringing the smell of fish and the loamy scent of the jungle—and a chill raked down Frederick's back, though the night was warm.

Reena's eyes met his. "You have the helm, Captain." She swept her hat out before her in a mock bow. "Just don't think you can sail off with my brig and leave me stranded."

He wanted to embrace her for some odd reason. He wanted to run a thumb over her cheek. Instead, he merely smiled. "I wouldn't dream of it."

She gave him a playful look. "Remember, preachers aren't supposed to lie."

"Oh, now I'm a preacher?"

Abraham chuckled just as Sedley popped through the hatch onto the deck, hurrying to Reena as he slipped the last knife into its sheath. "Sorry t' be late, Cap'n."

"You're taking Sedley?" Frederick asked, alarm crowding in his throat.

"What is it to you?"

It meant that she expected trouble. "Surely you have beaten Antoine here. Alas, leave Sedley, go get your map, and let's quit this place." A sense of danger raised the hairs on Fredericks neck and he gripped his cross. Everything in his dream was coming true. How could he allow her to go without him now?

She arched a brow. "Egad, is the preacher worried? Isn't that a sin?" But then she grew stern and waved a hand through the air. "I'll take whomever I please."

Closing his eyes, he growled out, "Very well, I'll accompany you."

A victorious smile curved her lips. "Make haste, then, and get your weapons. I'll leave Jo in charge."

Frederick stormed back to his cabin, wondering with each step if he'd finally lost his mind.

The town of Castries was nothing like Reena remembered. She had come here with her and Freddy's parents some years ago, and the place had been a sewer of poverty and debauchery. It had reminded her of Tortuga in the old days when both men and women of ill repute wandered the streets and beggars lined the avenues, palms open, pleading for a speck of food or a small coin. As a young girl of fifteen, it had broken her heart. She remembered her parents arguing whether they should bring her…whether she was old enough to witness such wickedness. But now, even as darkness descended and the evil shadows of night should be emerging for their play, the town appeared to be thriving. Instead of brothels and taverns marring the main street, shops had taken their place—a millinery, chandler, a tailor, even a church! Instead of beggars scattered throughout, vendors sold fresh fruit and fish from traveling carts. Instead of drunken mobs of seafaring freebooters threatening the innocent, modestly-dressed citizens rode in carriages and upon horseback.

Stunned by the transformation, she halted to stare as Freddy came up on her right and Abraham on her left. Brodie and Sedley brought up the rear.

"What's wrong?" Freddy asked.

"Don't you remember coming here?"

"Aye, many years ago. 'Tis very different, eh?"

"I hardly recognize the place."

Placing his fists at his waist, Freddy scanned the street. Dressed in jackboots, tan breeches, leather waistcoat, with a sword at his hip and a brace of pistols, he looked more pirate than preacher. Until he opened his mouth. "The Gospel of truth can do marvelous things to a city and its people."

Ridiculous. Reena started walking again. "So, you think this is because of our parents' preaching here?"

"I have no doubt. You saw it with your own eyes. They preached love to these people—God's love. They brought ships full of supplies for the poor, helped people get established in businesses, built homes, mended families, and even healed the sick and delivered those oppressed by demons."

Indeed. Reena had been awestruck at some of the miracles of healing and deliverance she had witnessed. But she also remembered longing for a life of adventure of her own. Not one where she followed her parents around like a sniveling dog. They had worked tirelessly day after day from dawn until the late hours of the night, giving up their wealth, sleep, strength, time, and food to "set these people free" as they had so often proclaimed. But when they finally left Saint Lucia, they were tired, sick, and far poorer than when they had arrived.

Still, as she glanced around at the fancy phaetons and well-dressed citizens strolling down the street with no fear of marauders, she could not deny that something *had* transformed the city. There was even a different feeling in the air. 'Twas like the atmosphere had changed from one of darkness to one that was sprinkled with light.

Which caused her sudden alarm. Would the Hairless Snout still be standing? For without it, she had no idea where to find the rest of the map.

"Look what God has done through your parents and mine," Freddy continued, beaming as if he had performed the miracle himself. "Can't you feel the difference?" His green eyes met hers, a new sparkle within them.

All she felt was anger and frustration. Scowling, she offered no response.

But the infernal man wouldn't stop talking. "You think your parents are poor and old and have wasted their life, but witness the power God has given them—to all of us—to change people's lives. That is true treasure, Reena, not gold or silver or some fabled fountain."

"Dems good words, Cap'n Carlton," Abraham said, offering him a grin.

Brodie laughed and licked his lips. "But did they hae tae get rid o' *all* the ale-houses?"

Ignoring them, Reena picked up her pace. A brisk wind spun eddies of sand before her as boys climbed ladders to light street lamps. Soon, cones of golden light lit their way like bread crumbs to a prize. At least she hoped it was a prize. Music sounded in the distance, along with the lap of waves and rattle of carriage wheels. The smell of roasted meat and horse dung bit her nose. And something else, the sting of alcohol as she turned onto Lewis street. A good sign.

Finally, here was a small section of town which had not surrendered to the purity of her parents, for as she proceeded, taverns and brothels littered the side of the road where scantily-clad women stared down from balconies, cooing their siren's call to men below. Off-key music and angry fisticuffs blared from various buildings as packs of sailors roamed about in search of rum and women.

There. Reena spotted the Hairless Snout up ahead and breathed a sigh of relief.

That sigh halted in her throat as her heart leapt to join it. Antoine and two of his men stood before the tavern. Before Reena could turn and run, the grin curling his lips told her he'd already seen her.

Bilge Water! How had he gotten here before her? Pasting on a smile of delight, she sauntered up to him. "Bien. You're here already."

"Did not expect me so soon, Mademoiselle Pirate?" Winking, he drew her hand to his lips for yet another overly moist kiss.

"Indeed, I did not. But I thought it best to inspect the tavern to ensure it still remained standing and the walls were intact."

Freddy cleared his throat.

The look in Antoine's dark eyes said he didn't believe a word she said. "Once a pirate always a pirate, eh?"

"You have the map, Antoine. What could I do without it?" A lot, for she had memorized the rhyme.

"Ah, *c'est vrai*." He plucked it from his coat and waved it before her nose. "*Mais non*, I will not be fooled again by one so beautiful." He reached to caress her cheek, but Freddy moved to stand before her.

Antoine glared at him. "I see you have brought your dog."

Freddy grabbed the man by his bounteous neckerchief.

Reena nudged him back. "Since we are all here, shall we?" She gestured toward the Hairless Snout, already bursting with patrons.

Smiling, Antoine placed her hand in the crook of his elbow and escorted her up the stairs.

Now, how was she ever to get this map and lose him?

CHAPTER TWENTY

*F*rederick gave a nod to Abraham walking beside him as they mounted the steps to the Hairless Snout—an unspoken admonition to keep a weather eye open and protect Reena at all costs. Abraham nodded his understanding as Antoine's men opened the door and the fiend escorted Reena into the befouled den as if he were royalty.

Before Frederick even stepped inside, the stench of tobacco, rum, unwashed men, and some other putrid smell he could not identify filled his lungs and made him cough. The same odor that had permeated his dreams. In truth, as his eyes adjusted to the darkness, the scene before him was an exact image of his nightmare.

Frederick was not one to fear many things—not even before he'd given his life to God. And especially not afterward when he knew the Almighty protected him. But he could not deny the sudden terror that snaked up his legs and shot up his spine. That dream might not have been a dream at all, but a vision of the future—an unalterable future.

Or could he change it?

Detaching herself from Antoine, Reena snagged the map from his hand and forged through the drunken mob, unaware of the lecherous eyes that followed her from those who'd noticed she was a woman. Which was not hard to do, despite her male attire.

Pushing past Frederick, Sedley pulled Antoine aside and leaned toward his ear. Odd. What did the pimpish ruffian have to say to Antoine du Casse? More importantly, why did du Casse look rather interested in whatever it was? The exchange was over quickly, and du Casse nodded and headed on his way, but there was something in his pompous gait that caused Frederick alarm.

No matter. Frederick's only job this night was to keep Reena alive. He stepped further into the tavern and scanned the patrons. To his left, a group of sailors, mugs of ale in hand, belted out a ditty around a pianoforte. Card games consumed most of the tables. Doxies wove trails of cheap perfume through the mob, while others sat on men's laps. Servants carried mugs of liquor to shifty-eyed sailors. And yet, beyond it all, and apparently unseen by everyone but Frederick, shadowy figures of every shape and size hovered near the rafters above and slithered around every person present. *Demons.* Why Frederick was permitted to see them on some occasions and not others, he had no idea, but he assumed God had a purpose. Though in truth, Frederick had often prayed for his gift to be revoked. He had no need to see these evil beings, he could feel their presence well enough.

One particularly large spirit advanced toward him, his pale-yellow eyes large and vacuous. Frederick held up a hand and whispered, "Jesus." The creature shrieked to a halt. Sheer terror twisted his features, but he quickly shrank back. In fact, none of the demons seemed able to break an invisible barrier around Frederick. God was with him. He offered his silent thanks even as his confidence rose. Mayhap God was not so displeased with him after all. Mayhap he was allowed to see these evil spirits for that very reason.

He scanned the room again, seeking Reena, and found Abraham instead. The barest shimmer of light surrounded the large Negro. Three demons flung their bodies against it but were unable to break through. Frederick smiled. Darkness could never defeat the light. As long as a person stayed in the light, of course. 'Twas their choice. And one he prayed he made every day.

He started forward when one of those dark shadows dove from the rafters onto a portly man playing cards at a table to Frederick's right. Pushing his chair to the ground, the man shot to his feet, raised his fist, and punched the man beside him, sending him careening to the floor. Ahead of Frederick, another spirit tugged on Brodie's arm, and the Scot followed him to the bar where he ordered a drink.

Closing his eyes, Frederick wished the visions away. He could not help everyone. He was here for Reena. When he opened his eyes, he could no longer see them, though he knew they remained. Shoving his way through the crowd, he headed toward the back of the tavern, where he found Reena staring at the map and Antoine salivating over her shoulder. His two men stood behind him, Abraham to her right.

"Whistle, whistle on the clock
Treasure is behind a rock
Two steps back and five steps east
Eight toward the south, beware the beasts"

Reena looked up, spun around, and nearly bumped into Frederick. "Look for a clock," she ordered, scanning the tavern.

Antoine held out a jeweled finger. "I'll take that map, *si vous plait.*"

She quickly folded it again. "'Twill do you no good if we can't find a clock."

He grinned, turned, and snapped his fingers. "You heard the mademoiselle. We seek a clock." His men darted through the mob. Unfortunately, both the sight of Antoine in his posh attire and Reena all curvy and soft beneath her breeches and waistcoat was drawing a bit of attention. They needed to find this ridiculous map and leave.

Frederick needed to protect Reena. But how could he when she kept running off? He found her weaving through the throng, her gaze traveling over tables, walls, posts, even the rafters—anywhere where a clock might be placed. Hands groped for her, but she slapped them away as if they were annoying bugs.

Growling at her naivety, Frederick started for her when a whistle came from the other side of the room. As she passed him, he grabbed her hand and led her onward, glaring at the men who ogled her. Better to relay the message that the lady had a capable escort.

They found Brodie pointing upward, a grin on his face, and a drink in his hand.

'Twas a round clock, the size of the muzzle of a twenty-pounder. The hands were made from bosun's whistles, the large one pointing to the twelve and the small one at three.

"*Voilà!*" Antoine clapped his hands and pointed toward it, but Reena shoved them down.

"We don't want to draw attention, Antoine," she seethed.

Frederick shook his head at the man's ignorance. But it was too late. Too many greedy eyes had found their way to them.

"We must hurry," Frederick grabbed the map from Reena's hand, unfolded it, and read the first words. "Two steps back. Five steps east."

Reena leapt beneath the clock and took two steps back. Then pulling a compass from her pocket, she examined it and walked another five steps to the right. Before Frederick read the next directions, she was already moving eight steps toward the back of the tavern. *Beware the beasts*. Freddy stared at the last phrase before he folded the map and followed her. Abraham was by her side, but where was Sedley? A quick glance revealed the man was nowhere in sight.

Curses flew from the other side of the tavern where another brawl had sprung up. A besotted sailor banged a jarring tune on the pianoforte.

Reena now stood before a wall of stones that made up the back of the tavern. A group of sailors sat around a table beside her, their eyes stripping off her garments. Frederick drew his cutlass while Antoine rushed to the wall, paying them no mind.

"Disappear," Frederick ordered the sailors, waving the tip of his blade over the group. Only one was hesitant, returning his stare, but the rest grabbed their mugs and scampered away like rats. The last man finally left as well, muttering curses beneath his breath. Pushing the table aside, Frederick advanced to the wall while Antoine gave an order for his men to guard them from behind.

"I don't see anything," the French swine complained. "It is just a wall of stones."

Reena moved her hands over the rough brick as if she could feel the answer. Her shoulders slumped, and she glanced at Frederick. "All the stones look alike. None of them appear loose."

"Mayhap the time on the clock is a clue," he offered, brows raised. Though he hated to aid this fruitless quest, neither did he wish to stay in this tavern another minute.

Her eyes lit, and she returned her attention to the wall, counting twelve stones from the ceiling and then three to the right. There, she fingered a single stone. It moved slightly. Plucking her knife from her belt, she chipped away the mortar.

"*Sacré bleu*, is that it?" Antoine leaned toward her. "Is the map behind it? What else does the rhyme say?"

"Beware the Beasts," Frederick offered with a chuckle, wondering whether it referred to Antoine and his men. 'Twould seem fitting.

Before he had even completed the thought, a foreboding prickled the hair down his arms. Drawing his sword yet again, he swung about to see two men the size of masts, their blades drawn, advancing straight for them. Abraham spun just in time to catch the thrust of the first man, while Frederick met swords with the second. Metal on metal rang through the riotous mob, jarring them from their rum-induced stupor and raising them to their feet. From the corner of his eye, Frederick saw Brodie slam a drink to the back of his throat, draw his cutlass, and join them as Antoine's men came alongside. Five to two. Good odds. That was before he saw three more men coming at them from the side, fully-armed and baring their teeth like a pack of hungry wolves.

⚓

Reena was sure the map was somewhere behind this blasted stone. If only she could pry it loose. Freddy's idea of matching the time on the clock was brilliant, absolutely brilliant. If only she'd thought of it herself—and if only she could assist with the battle she heard behind her. She shot a quick glance over her shoulder to see that Freddy, Abraham, Brodie, and Antoine's men had it well in hand. Or did they? Two of the attackers were as tall as the rafters and had biceps as big as powder kegs, while another one looked as though he'd been keelhauled more than once—and survived. The last two were smaller but quick on their feet and skilled with their blades.

A flash of concern for Freddy halted her efforts and prompted her to join the fray, but Antoine urged her onward. Besides, she couldn't very well leave him alone to retrieve the map and then run off—*like she planned to do*. Nay, she'd not come this far to lose it all. In truth, the fight was a good distraction—a distraction which might even provide a way for her to escape Antoine and his men.

Scraping away the final pieces of stone, she pulled it slowly from its spot, the grinding of stone-on-stone barely audible above the clamor of the fight. She peered inside. Nothing but darkness stared back at her. Grabbing a lantern from a table, Antoine held it up and attempted to nudge her aside. But she held her ground and reached inside the cavern. Her fingers touched something smooth and hard. She pulled it out and examined it in the light. 'Twas a small wooden box.

"*Qu'est-ce que c'est?*" Antoine reached for it.

Turning away from him, Reena opened it to discover a small scroll tied with a red ribbon. "This has to be the map." The tumult behind them increased, and she looked up to see that more men had joined the fray, and Freddy and the others were having a difficult time containing them.

Quickly untying the ribbon, she carefully unrolled the aged parchment. Y*es*! 'Twas indeed the map, or at least another part of it.

"Give it to me!" Antoine reached for it.

Retreating a step, she rolled it and stuffed it down her shirt. Then giving him a quick smile, she gestured toward the fight. "Mayhap we ought to help our friends first, eh?"

Drawing her sword, she dashed into the melee and engaged one of the attackers.

Freddy, embattled with another man, glanced toward her. "Get what you came for?" he shouted.

"Aye." She dove beneath the man's huge arm. He was skilled, she'd give him that. But he was big and too slow for her.

A quick glance revealed Brodie and Abraham parrying with one of the largest men, while Freddy now had another man in a headlock. Antoine's men battled three others near the bar.

No sign of Sedley or Antoine himself. Cowards. Surely Antoine wouldn't leave the map in her possession. A blade cleaved the smoky air toward her, and she met it with a mighty clang of her own.

The crowd stirred into a frenzy, placing bets on projected winners and tossing encouragements and curses into the air. Some of them joined the fight. Others started fighting amongst themselves. Utter chaos ensued, so much so, that it became impossible to know which men were enemies and which were friends. Reena, cutlass held high in one hand, pistol in the other, ducked, dashed, and lunged, keeping her eye on the five men who had originally attacked. What was their intent? Did they know about the hidden map?

"Behind you!" Freddy yelled, and Reena spun to see a knife thrusting toward her heart. With a flick of her sword, she sent it flying, and the man who held it scampered away after it. No doubt they thought because she was a woman, she would be easy prey.

A flash of metal blinded her from the left, and she hefted her cutlass and met her attacker head on. 'Twas one of the smaller men. He snarled and sidestepped her next thrust. His eyes snapped to her right ever so briefly, and he smiled, but she didn't have time to turn. A man flew across her vision, sword dropping from his hand, and a look of terror on his face. His head struck a wooden pole, and he slumped to the ground. She glanced over to see Freddy, breath heaving, but a smile on his lips. He'd just saved her life.

She had no time to thank him as the tip of a blade advanced from the smaller man. She dove to the side, knelt to avoid his second attack, and then slashed him across the legs. Blood soaked his breeches. He dropped to the floor. To her right, the largest two of their attackers also lay on the ground, unmoving, while Abraham engaged a third. Freddy pounded yet another with the hilt of his sword, while Brodie chased off the last. Antoine's men were nowhere in sight.

Breath coming fast and hard, Reena sheathed her cutlass and glanced around to make sure Abraham and Brodie were unharmed. The crowd stood stunned, mumbling and cursing and lumbering back to their tables where fresh ale awaited them.

"Let's be gone." Freddy grabbed her arm, and together with Abraham and Brodie they dashed out the front door and into the night.

"Where's Sedley?" Reena asked as they hurried down the street.

Brodie sheathed his sword and ran a sleeve over his forehead. "Nae doot run off when the fightin' started."

"Anyone hurt?" Amazingly she had not even suffered a cut, though the pain in her side renewed from the exertion. She could only imagine what Freddy suffered with all his prior injuries. Yet he made no complaint.

"Nodin to speak o'," Abraham grunted.

"Where's Antoine?" She still could not believe he would leave the map.

"After you joined the fight, he dove into the crowd and disappeared." Freddy huffed beside her as they turned a corner. "Never saw him after that."

Reena allowed herself a smile. Mayhap one of the beasts subdued him and dragged him off to rob him. "Excellent. Come, let us be off to the *Reckless* before he realizes we are gone."

Sedley materialized out of the darkness and rushed toward them.

"Where were you? We needed your help!" Reena shouted as he fell in line behind them. "You know what I do with cowards."

"No, Cap'n." His voice quavered. "I weren't no coward. When those vermin attacked, I fought one o' them, forced him outside. Finally got the best o' him an' he ran. Sos I chased after him, hopin' t' find out who he were."

"Humph," Abraham said.

Freddy said nothing, while Brodie took a sip from a bottle he had grabbed from one of the tables as they'd left.

True or not, she would deal with Sedley later. Right now, she had more important things on her mind.

Once they exited Lewis Street, they found the rest of the city in quiet slumber. At close to ten in the evening, most decent people were home with their families. The shops were shut down, and only the street lamps lit their way down the sandy street. They plunged into the jungle lining the edge of town and made their way to the beach where they'd left their boat.

Heart thumping against her ribs, Reena leapt into the dinghy with her men. Shoving off, they headed toward the *Reckless*. Antoine was not the type of man she could deceive more than once and get away with it. She knew she was making an enemy for life. One who would certainly find it worth his while to hunt her down. But how could she share eternal life with the likes of him? 'Twas one thing if she lived eternally young and beautiful, and quite another if someone as evil as Antoine had an eternity to enact his wicked plans.

Yet no sooner did their boat thud against the hull and she climbed the rope ladder, then an icy chill permeated her skin. Trying to shake it off, she planted her boots on the main deck of the *Reckless*. Freddy and the others came up behind her. But something was wrong. Where was everyone? At least her watchmen should be on deck. A figure stepped from beneath the quarterdeck and into the light of a lantern hanging at the main mast. The blue plume of his hat fluttered in the breeze as a malevolent grin twisted his lips.

"You weren't thinking of leaving without me, *ma chèrie?*"

CHAPTER TWENTY-ONE

Frederick leaned back in his chair, refusing the flagon of rum Brodie passed his way. He'd had a few sips from his cup already and that was enough. He needed his wits about him. Especially with Antoine and his men present. *Thunderation*! They had nearly escaped the braggart. But Antoine seemed to know not only what they were planning every moment, but where the *Reckless* was anchored. How?

Frederick rubbed his chin and glanced around the dinner table in Reena's cabin. Antoine sat across from him, swigging his fourth glass of rum, leaning toward Reena, a salacious leer on his face. Two of his men stood behind him, stiff as statues. Beside Antoine, Abraham ate and surveyed the festivities with a suspicious glare. Sedley sat at the end, guzzling down rum and becoming far too loud and loose in his ignorant speech.

Beside him, Michael shoveled food into his mouth. Next, Jo sat beside Brodie, and Frederick was at Reena's right. His gaze traveled back to Sedley. Though Frederick suspected he was the one who'd told Antoine of their plans, he couldn't prove it. Not yet, at least. But he would keep an eye on the little snake.

The deck tilted, sending bowls of peas and platters of roasted duck, plum cake, and breadfruit toast sliding over the table. A crisp breeze whistled against the stern windows and sent the lanterns sputtering. Past those windows, stars proclaimed the glory of God with every brilliant twinkle.

Frederick took a bite of roasted duck. It soured in his mouth. He shouldn't be here. He wanted off this brig and away from the darkness he felt threatening him from all sides. And most of all, the temptation. He gazed at Reena. Candlelight brought out the streaks of ruby in her hair and sent her golden eyes glittering. He took in her forest of sooty lashes, soft creamy cheeks, pert little nose, and that strong chin she so oft lifted at him in defiance. But more than her beauty, 'twas her spirit that attracted him, her determination, intellect, zest for life, *and* her compassion.

If Antoine continued staring at her like that—like he was imagining every curve beneath her waistcoat, Frederick would give him something to stare at—the tip of his cutlass!

"*Ma chérie,*" Antoine broke his wanton gaze to pour more rum in his glass. "Though I appreciate a good feast, let us see the map again. We must plot our next course, *non?*"

Planting her elbow on the table, Reena placed her chin in her hand. "Why the rush? I cannot escape you for you've taken residence upon my brig."

He chuckled. "*Tsk tsk*, Mademoiselle Pirate, you were trying to rid yourself of my charming company, *non*? And I thought you were a woman of your word." He gave a sigh of feigned disappointment.

"I am." She sat back and scooped more peas onto her plate. "However, I only promised I'd let you accompany me to Saint Lucia to retrieve the rest of the map. Not that I would share it with you."

Antoine jerked his head back in shock, his forehead crinkling. But then grinning, he leaned forward on his elbow. "You are clever, *ma chérie*. I must remember that no matter how *belle* you are, you still harbor a pirate's heart in that"—his glassy gaze lowered to her chest—"enchanting bosom."

"Dangle 'im from the foreyard!" Fred chirped from his perch.

Frederick's sentiments exactly. He gripped the pommel of his sword beneath the table.

But Reena only lifted her glass to the fiend in a salute.

"However," Antoine sat back and adjusted his silk cravat. "*Promesse* or not, I can still blow your *petite* brig out of the water."

Frederick stood, his chair scraping a warning. "I challenge you to try, Monsieur du Casse."

The man was unmoved. "*Caiptaine* du Casse to you." His insolent grin threatened to destroy Frederick's resolve to control his temper. "I perceive there's a bit of your father in you, *après tout*."

Though Frederick gave no outward indication, the insult struck him hard in the gut. Precisely what he didn't want to be—like his father.

"Do not think, monsieur," Antoine continued, "that you can overpower me on this vessel. If the *Conquérant* does not get my signal every hour, they have orders to cripple the *Reckless*." He dabbed a handkerchief over his lips as if he hadn't just threatened to sink them all.

Fred flapped his wings. "Split me skull, he be a scabrous toad!"

Silence stole all sound from the cabin as Antoine's face hardened. Frederick remained standing, preparing for the man's outburst. Seconds ticked by with naught but the sound of the sea sloshing against the hull and the grind of wood. But then Reena and Brodie laughed, and the indignance on Antoine's face faded to humor before he joined them.

Brodie grabbed another piece of breadfruit toast from a platter. "The men who attacked us wir bigger than Abraham. What was that aboot?"

"Indeed." Reena slipped a bite of duck into her mouth, her suspicious gaze wandering to Antoine.

But the miscreant took no note.

Frederick lowered to his seat. "'Twould appear someone sent them to thwart our mission. Or mayhap steal the map?"

Fred bobbed his head up and down. "Devil a doubt, thar be a traitor about."

This seemed to draw Antoine's gaze away from his meal, first to the parrot and then to Frederick, but he merely shrugged.

Jo sipped her port, her eyes on Brodie. "An' ye 'ad no trouble dispatchin' the lot o' them."

"A wee bit o' trouble," he returned with a smile.

Frederick sat back in his chair. "No thanks to you Antoine, or Sedley there."

Antoine sipped his rum, smiling at Reena. "I am more of a—how do you say *amoureux*—ahh…*oui*, I am more of a lover than a fighter. This is why I have my men with me." He flicked a hand at them over his shoulder as if they were made of wood and not human beings.

Frederick glared at Sedley as the little runt gulped down his last bite and fidgeted in his seat. "Ye know me, Cap'n, I ne'er shy away from a fight. I swears it. I'm loyal t' ye, as ye knows."

Reena assessed him with a heavy glare, offering no response. At least she didn't seem duped by the fool.

Michael finished his plate. "I knew you'd come back safe," he addressed Reena, excitement in his eyes. "You weren't alone."

An odd thing for the lad to say.

Reena smiled. "Of course I wasn't alone, Michael. I had three men with me." She glanced at Frederick.

"You had more than that," he said with such authority that everyone looked his way.

Brodie slammed the last of his drink into his mouth. "No doot the lad means Antoine's men."

But Frederick didn't think so, and neither did Michael from the look on his face—a look he shared with Frederick before a boyish innocence reclaimed his features.

Abraham finished his plum cake and leaned back, hands on his belly. "Yuh got de map, Cap'n, now wha'? Even if dis Fountain of Youth be real, does no good t' live forever in dis condition."

"What condition is that?" Antoine turned his nose up at the quartermaster.

Frederick sighed. "You of all people should know, Antoine. Our fallen nature, our sin—our hatred, greed, violence, selfishness, and vanity." His eyes found Reena. "Who wants to live in that condition forever when you have a chance to live without all of those failings after you die?"

Antoine chuckled as he glanced around the table. "You were telling the truth, *ma chouette*, when you said he fancies himself a preacher."

"He speaks de truth," Abraham said. "It be vanity an' sheer folly t' want t' live forever in dis fallen state."

"Vanity, vanity, all is vanity!" Fred added.

Frederick was starting to like this bird.

"Michael," Reena glanced at the boy. "You are the youngest one here. Would you not like to keep your youth forever?"

"I can't say, Captain, seeing as I don't know what it is like to grow old. But I like what Abraham and Captain Carlton say about living forever without all this evil around me."

Brodie poured more rum in his mug. "What dae ye know aboot evil, lad? Yer far tae young."

Tossing back his shoulders, Michael sat up straight. "I'm old enough to know selfishness, anger, pain, and hatred when I see it." He stared at them all with eyes wiser than his years. "Plenty of it on board this brig."

Antoine snorted. "*Sacré bleu*! We are surrounded by preachers, mademoiselle. If you aren't careful, they will take over your ship!"

"One can only hope," Frederick added with a wink.

Antoine's features twisted in a knot. "Mademoiselle Pirate, you have a most unusual crew—a former slave, a besotted, indentured servant, an orphan, a pirate turned preacher, and, lest we forget, a trollop to run your guns."

Reena opened her mouth to say something, but Brodie punched to his feet, wavered a bit, and glared at Antoine. "Ye should know that Jo is the best gunner that e'er sailed the seas. Lass or no."

Jo gave Antoine a curt smile. "If ye'd like a demonstration t'ward yer ship, I'd be 'appy to oblige."

"The captain rescued Jo," Michael interjected proudly, no doubt by way of defusing the situation.

"The captain rescued all o' us," Abraham added.

Fred paced over his perch. "Saved from hellfire!"

Brodie fell back into his seat.

Antoine inched his hand toward hers on the table. "That is why I love you so much, *ma chouette*. You have a heart of gold. And you know how pirates love gold." He flashed a salacious eyebrow.

The food in Frederick's stomach soured. "Monsieur du Casse, tell me of your father. He is Admiral du Casse's brother?"

His question had the desired effect of jerking Antoine's attention off Reena and putting a frown on the man's face.

"That he is, monsieur. But what is it to you?"

"Just curious how you came to be a pirate. Does your mother approve? I heard she is a noblewoman, a baroness is it?"

Antoine snapped the remainder of his rum to the back of his throat. "Mademoiselle Sophia de Bourbon is not my mother," he said between tight teeth. "My mother was one of my father's mistresses whom he paid to leave us be. I never met her." He poured himself more rum.

"No doubt Lady Sophia cared for you as her own?" Frederick knew he shouldn't poke this volatile man's wounds. He knew 'twas but the rum which bade Antoine speak so freely of his past. But curiosity overcame his better judgment.

Antoine adjusted the lace at his neck as if it had suddenly become too tight. Frederick felt a measure of pity for him.

"She loathed me, if you must know." He glanced up at Frederick with a tight smile. "She and my father were oft gone, leaving me to be raised by *les nounous*—nannies and tutors. And"—he arched an arrogant brow—"my uncle. Which is how I came to be a great pirate."

Great pirate or not, Frederick saw the agony in the man's eyes. Even beyond the haze of alcohol. Antoine had grown up unloved and unwanted. No wonder he searched for value and meaning for his life. The only problem? Like most, he searched for it in the wrong place.

Thank heavens Reena changed the subject, and they soon talked about winds and waves and where they could find the best rum and pearls. Frederick sat back and took a moment to utter a prayer of thanks for their safety and to gaze around the room yet again. Shadows slunk in the corners, but he paid them no mind.

Antoine returned to leaning on the table, gazing at Reena as if she were a treasure chest he'd yet to open. The same chains Frederick had seen before on the man appeared yet again—thick and heavy as an anchor chain—and Frederick wondered how the man could even walk. Yet when he shifted his gaze to Reena, shadows also slithered about her. Instead of chains, however, boulders sat upon her shoulders and lined across the back of her neck, causing her to slump beneath the weight.

Fearing he'd gone mad, he glanced at the other people present. Light glittered around Abraham. Michael too, but a different kind of light—brighter than he'd seen on a person before. Sedley was so deep in shadows, Frederick could barely make out his face. Beside him, a large chain wrapped around Jo's chest, clasped in front with an iron lock. Brodie was also encased in shadows and chains.

Why are you showing this to me, Lord? Closing his eyes again, Frederick rubbed them, begging the visions to disappear. When he glanced around the cabin again, they were gone, but the sense of their meaning on each individual rose in his spirit. Antoine du Casse was bound in chains of rejection, greed, lust, and pride. Reena was weighted with fears of growing old and not being loved. Sedley was in a thick cloud of lies, fear, and deception. Jo had been hurt so deeply that she locked her heart away where no one could reach it. Brodie harbored unforgiveness, along with the weight of despair, depression, and alcoholism.

Frederick's heart sank in its own despair—despair for these people who bore such burdens and didn't even know it. Oh, how clever the enemy was to hide himself thus. But why was God revealing this to him? What could he do, save pray? He was most often a failure in his own efforts to do the right thing and be a better man than his father. Lord knew, he wished more than anything he could remove those weights from Reena's shoulders, set her free! But she knew the truth. She had the means to remove them herself if she would but turn to God.

Frederick found her staring at him—her stunning golden eyes filled with such intensity and affection, he nearly fell off the chair.

"Are you quite all right, Freddy?"

He nodded, not wishing to break the bond between them.

Antoine noticed the exchange and was quick to draw Reena's attention back to him. "Mademoiselle, you may be interested in some plans of my uncle which I recently overheard."

She tore her gaze from Frederick. "Only if they have something to do with the Fountain of Youth."

"*Non*, but I do believe you will find them of interest. I overheard my uncle last month when I was at his estate for a...how do you say *fête*...party. He intends to attack Kingston."

Frederick was afraid to move, afraid to say anything that would alert the drunken fool not to reveal such things. Especially among British subjects. *Attack Kingston*! That's where his family lived, his siblings, uncle, aunt, and their families. Where Reena's family lived.

"He plans to anchor at Cow Bay, just north of the mouth of the Yallahs River and ravage the eastern parishes before regrouping and heading to Clarendon."

"Indeed?" For the first time that night, Reena allowed the man to touch her hand. She offered him a sweet smile. "And when does he plan this great attack?"

"Late this month, I believe. Or perhaps next."

"Why tell me this?" Snagging back her hand, Reena shrugged.

But Frederick wasn't listening anymore. Could this be true? Antoine was no fool. But he was quite drunk at the moment. He must have realized his condition—*and* what he'd disclosed—for he finished his drink, rose, tried to kiss Reena's hand but stumbled when the deck tilted. Laughing, he quickly excused himself, snapped at his men to follow, and left.

"De devil be gone now," Abraham stood up. "I's goin' t' get some rest."

Brodie slammed his cup on the table. "Aye, we all need rest tae face the morn."

Michael ran over to hug Reena before they all stood and sauntered out, leaving Frederick and Reena alone.

Which did not bode well for his resistance to her charm. Standing, he dipped his head toward her, avoiding eye contact, and made for the door. He had much to ponder and pray about that night. But before he took two steps, she grabbed his hand and held him back. Frederick would be a liar if he denied that her touch didn't send a thrill through him.

"'Twas just like old times today, Freddy, was it not? I know you felt the adventure of it all, the fun, the victory!"

He turned to face her. "Reena, I am not part of this quest of yours. I merely came along to protect you."

"But that means more than you can know." Her pleading eyes searched his. "You saved my life, Freddy. If not for you, I'd be dead in that tavern right now, and Antoine would have my brig and crew."

He took her hand and placed a kiss upon it. A mist covered her eyes, and his gaze dropped to her lips, full and moist. Snapping his eyes back to her face, and unable to control himself, he eased a thumb over her cheek. She leaned into his hand and sighed, her sweet breath filling the air between them while her scent of coconut and lavender drove him to distraction. At one time, he had vowed to always protect her. But how could he do so when she ventured down a path he could not travel?

Releasing her hand, he backed away, and crossed his arms over his chest. "Did you hear what Antoine said? His uncle intends to attack our home."

Pain darkened her expression. "He's drunk and most likely bragging."

"And what if he isn't? Do you not feel some obligation to warn our families?"

"'Tis not for another month." She grabbed a lock of her hair and twirled it around her finger. "Besides, our parents are probably not even there. No doubt they are aiding the poor on some wretched island or preaching to the natives deep in the jungle."

Frederick cocked a brow, surprised at her callousness. "We have friends there, as well. These are our people, Reena. 'Tis our duty to warn them."

She fumbled with a spoon on the table. "And we shall. After I find the Fount."

"Nay. You will take me to Kingston forthwith so I can warn them. Then you and Antoine can sail away into eternity together."

"I said I would take you." She swallowed, anger flaring in her eyes. "Why do you mistrust me so?"

"Because I know you, Reena. You are doing everything in your power to keep me with you—to rekindle something that has long since died." He instantly regretted the words, for Reena's countenance fell and she lowered her gaze.

Turning, she walked toward the stern windows. "Dead, is it? Never to be resurrected?" He could hear the pain in her voice and hated himself for it.

"We are going down two very different paths, Reena. I cannot join you on yours, and you refuse to join me on mine."

She spun around, tears flowing down her cheeks. "How can you ask me to join you in a life of poverty and service to others where I will only grow weary and old with each passing day? Nay, I do not choose to join you."

"And that grieves me most of all."

She faced the windows again.

"Nevertheless," Frederick used his sternest tone. "You *will* drop me off near Kingston. I may be a preacher, but I still have pirate blood in my veins, and you do not want to test me, Reena."

Fred squawked from his perch. "Don't cross the son of a seadog!"

Reena said naught, though Frederick thought he saw a sob shudder down her back.

He didn't stay to find out.

Fallen fallen before his time
Ne'er remembered by his kind
What you seek is with the dead
If you dare to disturb the red

CHAPTER TWENTY-TWO

Reena stared at herself in the looking glass, the dark shadows under her eyes evidence of her restless night. A few years past, she could stay up all night and not appear worse for wear. But no longer. She was aging. She turned her head slightly and smiled. Tiny lines formed at the edge of her eyes and mouth. *Bilge water*! They seemed to have grown overnight. As did the slight droop of her right eyelid and the bland color of her skin. She pinched her cheeks, bringing forth a pinkish bloom that had always been present not long ago.

Leaning over, she splashed water on her face from the basin Michael had brought early that morning. She patted it with a towel then opened a jar and applied some lavender-scented cream she'd purchased from an apothecary on Barbados—a rather expensive cream that didn't appear to be doing any good. How long would her youthful beauty last? With the wind, sun, and salt of the Caribbean, she'd seen women twice as beautiful as she crinkle up like used parchment by the time they were thirty.

Which was precisely why she needed to find the Fountain of Youth. She had no intention of growing old…losing her comely face and eventually dying. Not that her beauty was doing any good with Freddy. Stubborn fool! She saw the desire and affection in his eyes. Blast his religion!

A knock preceded Jo entering with a freshly-cleaned shirt and breeches for Reena. Being the only other woman aboard, Reena counted on her to assist in cleaning her clothing, particularly her underthings. While Jo closed the door and laid the garments on the bed, Reena took the opportunity to study the woman. "How old are you, Jo?" Though Reena knew she had to be in her thirties.

Jo looked up at her curiously. "Let me think. 'Tis been ten years since my husband died an' two years since ye rescued me from that brothel. So my guess is three an' thirty."

Approaching the lady, Reena raised a hand to touch her cheek. "May I?"

Jo flinched at first, but then nodded, and Reena gently rubbed her thumb over the woman's soft skin. Wrinkles had formed around her eyes, and there was a slight indentation curving around the sides of her mouth, but otherwise, there was no indication of her age. With a round, but pleasant face and plain brown eyes, she was not uncomely, but no beauty either. In addition, she had neither name nor fortune, but 'twas obvious Brodie found her highly desirable.

"What is your opinion of this Fountain of Youth?" Reena made her way to her bed and took off her nightdress.

"I think it be a grand idea, Cap'n. After my husband were killed, the only way I could survive were by marrying agin, but I were not young or comely 'nough to git a man wit' wealth." She shrugged, but Reena heard the bitterness in her voice. "Ye knows the rest."

Indeed, Reena did, and 'twas not a pretty story. She tossed her shirt over her head, then stepped into her breeches and tucked it in. She could have helped Jo if she'd found the Fount sooner. She still could help the woman—and many others as well.

Jo crossed arms over her chest and leaned back against Reena's desk. "Men be sich brutes. Jist due to their physical strength, they think they can rule o'er us…tha' our softness makes us weaker than them. The only weapon we possess be beauty or…or…" She shuddered.

"Or piracy," Reena added with a smile as she put on her waistcoat and tied up the front.

Fred bobbed his head up and down. "A pirate's life fer me!"

Jo chuckled. "I 'ave ye to thank fer that power. I will not be used agin by any man thanks t' ye. And if ye allow it, I'd love to partake o' this Fountain of Youth. I may not be as comely as ye, Cap'n, but wit' youth an' strength, I can be independent an' make my own fortune."

Reena had not realized until this moment how bitter and angry Jo was. Not that she could blame her. She'd suffered under male dominance her entire life. As the eldest of ten, her father had used her to care for the other children, to cook and clean and slave away at home. Then her husband had used her in the same way. Jo had revealed theirs was not a happy match. And then, of course, the men on the street had used her to satisfy their lust.

The brig pitched and plunged over a wave, complaining with grates and groans.

Lowering to sit on her bed, Reena slipped on her boots, then rose and grabbed her baldric. When she looked back up, Jo stared into the cabin, her face a contortion of angst. Sorrow for the lady tugged at Reena's heart. What could living forever offer one so bitter? Wouldn't this world make Jo more and more angry as the years passed? Did bitterness have an end, or would it eventually destroy her soul and leave her naught but an empty carcass—forever? Mayhap, in that case, death would be a welcome reprieve.

She didn't have time to think about it further when a knock on the door and her "enter" brought in Antoine, his two lackeys, along with Abraham, Sedley, and Brodie.

"I wish to see the map again, *s'il vous plaît*." Antoine marched to her desk, halted, and rubbed his temples, where, no doubt, a headache brewed from his overindulgence in rum the night before. In truth, she was surprised he was awake this early. The reek of stale rum mixed with his lemon pomade in a rather putrid scent that wrinkled her nose.

"Death and damnation shall be yours!" Fred cackled.

"Hush your feathers, Fred." Grabbing a slice of melon from her desk, she flung it at the bird. Then smiling sweetly at Antoine, she plucked both maps from her waistcoat pocket. "Of course." Circling her desk, she spread them out in the sunlight spearing in through the windows.

Brodie moved to stand beside Jo while Abraham and Sedley inched closer.

She pointed to a land mass on the second map. "This is Montserrat. I'm sure of it." She spread out her chart of the Caribbean and laid it side by side. "See? And here is Saint Lucia where we just were. So, this must be Martinique."

Sedley scratched his head. "But that be French again."

"Thank you, Sedley. I am aware." She glared at the man, also aware he couldn't be trusted.

Antoine nodded, releasing a sigh. "*Oui, bien sûr.* It does appear to be one and the same." He dipped his head to the right and left as if trying to dislodge his headache. "*Mais,* this riddle. It makes no sense." He waved at it, then groaned as if the effort pained him.

Reena hid her smile at his discomfort.

"Fallen fallen before his time
Ne'er remembered by his kind
What you seek is with the dead
If you dare to disturb the red."

"No doubt it refers to someone who has died," Antoine offered.

"Precisely." Reena nodded. "I'm guessing we'll find what we seek in a graveyard."

A ray of sunlight oscillated over the map, spinning glittering dust in its path as if agreeing with her assessment.

Abraham humphed.

Reena looked up at him. "You wish to comment?"

"Der has t' be dozens of graveyards on dat island."

"Aye, but this small red X is on Fort Royal. How many graveyards could there be in one city?"

Fred bobbed his head up and down. "Dead men tell no tales."

Brodie crossed his arms over his chest. "But e'en if we dae fin' the right graveyard, who are we lookin' fer?"

Michael scurried in, cup of hot chocolate in hand and a smile on his face.

Taking it, Reena thanked him and took a sip. *Heaven.* Now, maybe she could deal with these naysayers.

The young lad leaned over her map as the brig angled to port. Her quill pen rolled across the desk, and he picked it up and gestured toward the riddle. "Weren't there a pirate who died long ago whose name was 'Red' something?"

"*Wasn't* there a pirate," Reena corrected him. But the lad had a point.

Brodie rubbed the back of his neck. "It haes to be Crimson Jack."

"Crimson Jacque?" Antoine seemed to suddenly wake up. "Oui, Heard many tales about him. A good French pirate!"

"Aye, he captured more prizes and gathered more treasure in the Caribbean in his day than any other pirate since." Reena had always been jealous of the man.

"Aye, 'eard 'e were a fearsome bloke," Sedley commented, sharing an odd glance with Antoine.

"But him died o'er sixty years back," Abraham said.

Jo shook her head. "The poor man ne'er reached 'is thirtieth year."

"A true shame." Reena sipped her chocolate, balancing on the shifting deck. "But 'tis his tomb we are seeking. Thank you, Michael."

The lad smiled but then shook his head. "Not a good idea to dig up a grave, Captain. Danger awaits you, I'm sure of it."

"Mere superstitions, lad." Reena batted his words away, but in truth, they disturbed her. The boy was rarely wrong, if ever.

"I don't understand," Jo pursed her lips. "Word was 'e were hung for piracy then chained in the gibbet on Martinique. Pirates don't get proper burials."

"Nay. 'Tis true." Reena let out a ragged sigh and placed one hand on her hip. "How are we to find him, then? And why would the man who hid these maps have visited a pirate's grave with his lady love?"

Antoine raised a cultured brow. "Do you not know, mademoiselle? Ah, non, you couldn't. He's French and we French love to pass on tales of our own. His wife begged the governor for her husband's bones. After the birds had pecked them clean, that is." He fingered the beard on his chin. "The story goes that she gave him a proper burial under the name Jacque Bonhomme, which was his real name."

Brodie lifted his flask in a mock toast. "Tha' haes to be it, then."

Reena stared at the map. "But it still doesn't explain why the pirate would visit such a place with his lady."

"Looks like we's come t' the end of yuh's quest." Abraham crossed his meaty arms over his chest and smiled.

Reena snorted. "Don't be ridiculous."

Jo leaned on the desk. "I say we should seek 'is grave. There may be another clue there."

"Agreed." Reena straightened and raised her shoulders.

Sedley grinned his approval.

Abraham frowned.

Michael's brow wrinkled. "I still don't think it's a good idea, Captain."

Antoine squeezed the bridge of his nose, sunlight glittering off the jewels on his fingers. "Shall we be about it, then? I'm anxious to find the next map, *ma chérie*."

"Never fear, Antoine. I have already set our course to Martinique. We shall be there by nightfall."

Fred let out a shrill twitter. "Cursed be them who disturb the dead."

⚓

Frederick turned the page in the Bible to Romans 8, one of his favorite chapters. Thus far, only Michael sat at his feet listening to the holy words, but it did not escape Frederick's notice that several of the sailors leaned their ear toward him on occasion.

The *Reckless* leapt over a wave, showering him with salty spray. Fitting, since the word of God was described as living water and its people as salt.

Frederick had spent a difficult night filled with nightmarish visions, most of which had been swept away by dawn's light. But one in particular would not leave him be. 'Twas a vision of Reena walking through a thick jungle along with several of her crew. She crept forward, shoving aside foliage, and stepped into a small clearing. Instantly she sank, the soft sand folding around her feet, then her legs, and finally her torso. A look of horror etched across her face as she yelled for help and reached for her crew standing around her. But they merely stared at her as if some natural thing were occurring and she wasn't about to be swallowed whole. In the vision, Frederick knew he was the only one who could help her, the only one who could grab ahold of her—that, somehow, he had been chosen for the task.

Gripping the thick branch of a nearby tree with one hand, he reached out for her with the other.

"Grab hold, Reena! Grab hold and let me draw you into the light." The "drawing into the light" made no sense, but she reached for him anyway. Her hand floated midair toward his, fingertip to fingertip…when he suddenly woke, heart spinning in his chest.

His first thought was that Reena was in immediate danger. But after he found Michael below deck and inquired about her, the lad said she was perfectly well. Abraham had left the cabin early so Frederick returned to pray. He prayed for the enemy to release this woman, for her safety and protection, prayed that if the dream had continued, and she had grabbed hold of him, that she wouldn't have dragged him beneath the sand along with her.

"I'm not strong enough, Lord. She has too tight a grasp on my heart. Please free me from her. Find someone else to rescue her. I am too much like my father."

After his prayer, several minutes passed in silence, save for the purl of water against the hull. No word from above, no inner voice, not even a sense of God's presence. But then, a beam of light struck his face from the porthole, shifting over it with the movement of the ship, and he heard in his spirit, *Indeed, you are just like your father…your heavenly Father*!

That one sentence had spurred him to grab his Bible and head on deck, where he now sat reading his Bible to a very excited Michael. He began reading Romans 8. "There is therefore now no condemnation to them which are in Christ Jesus."

One of the sailors—was his name Mack?—stopped reeling in the line he held and turned to face him. "Did ye say *no* condemnation? Like it don't matter that I killed people an' stole their goods?"

Sunlight tossed the man's dark hair around him as sails above thundered to catch the wind.

"That's exactly what it says." Frederick nodded, excitement stirring within him. "But only if you put your faith in Jesus and follow Him the rest of your days. He forgives every wrong thing you've ever done. God's Spirit comes to live inside of you, and you become a new person. And then when you die you are escorted into heaven."

The sailor chuckled and rubbed his sleeve over his mouth. "Me? Escorted into heaven? Now that's something I ne'er thought to see."

Another sailor beside him elbowed him "Ye ain't goin' t' no heaven, Mack. Ye'd ruin it fer all them saints up there." He laughed and others joined him.

But Michael was beaming. And Frederick felt as light as the foam atop the waves.

"Keep reading." Michael gestured toward the holy book.

Happy to oblige, Frederick raised his voice a little higher this time, hoping more sailors would hear. But by the time he finished reading the chapter, no one else had said a thing. No matter. Seeds were planted. He closed the Bible and looked up to find Abraham standing a short distance away, smiling at him.

Reena leapt on deck, scanned the brig, her gaze briefly landing on Frederick before calling Abraham to the quarterdeck. As usual, she was a vision of feminine ferocity, and he couldn't help but smile. Aye, he'd been angry at her last night. But 'twas hard to stay angry at someone when you prayed for them.

Michael scurried to his duties, leaving Frederick to put away the Bible, grip the railing, and stare across the wild turquoise sea. Antoine's two ships kept pace with them just off their starboard quarter. But aside from them, morning sun glittered gold atop waves as far as his eye could see.

Did he truly believe what he had just told Mack—that God's Spirit lived inside of him and made him a new creature? Then why did Frederick struggle with so many wrong desires? Why wasn't he getting any better? Yet…wasn't God giving him dreams and visions again? Would the Almighty do that for someone who wasn't His child, who hadn't at least changed a bit?

He thought of the city of Castries and all the good his and Reena's parents had done there. Transforming the place from a cesspool into one where families felt safe to roam the streets at night. He knew his father had changed, but for some reason Frederick could not get over the violence of his conception…the horror his mother must've suffered, and how he'd been brought into the world—not by two people who loved each other, who were committed to each other by the sacred covenant of marriage. He was an accident, born out of lust and violence.

Reena suddenly appeared beside him. Her unbound hair fluttered in the wind behind her, the long ribbons of her head scarf trickled—along with her hair—over the hilt of the sword at her side. Several knives and a pistol peeked at him from her baldric. But it was the alluring smile she cast his way that heated his insides.

"Good day, Freddy. I see you've been instructing my pirates in the ways of God. Have a care or they might join you in your missionary work, and I'll be left without a crew."

"That would please me greatly, Reena." He grinned at her, but all he longed to do was take her in his arms, embrace her, kiss her, shake some sense into her.

The *Reckless* crested a wave, white foam exploding over her bow. With every stitch of canvas spread, she flew through the sea on yet another grand adventure, without a care in the world. Or so it seemed from the excited look in Reena's eyes as she scanned the horizon. Finally she faced him.

"I'm surprised you're not angry at me for not taking you to Kingston right away." Wind snapped hair in her face, and she brushed it away. "I must say, in that regard, you're not like the old Freddy at all. That vicious temper of yours oft made an appearance, especially when you didn't get your way."

Frederick couldn't help but smile. Hadn't he just been wondering if he had changed? And here the Lord was giving him confirmation—from the most unlikely of sources. "I apologize for those moments, Reena. 'Twas not fair to you. But you may thank God for the change in me."

"Mayhap I will…when I get around to talking to Him again." She smiled. "So, have you resigned yourself to join me in my quest?"

Frederick tore his gaze from hers, not wanting to crush her hopeful tone, not wanting to see her pain when he said what he needed to say. "Nay, since you will not take me to Kingston, I will disembark at Martinique and find my own passage there." 'Twas the best solution he could come up with during the long night. Either that or take over the brig. And he couldn't do that to Reena.

"Surely you can't mean that." Her brow furrowed. "'Tis a French port and hence, dangerous."

"Then why are *you* going?" He raised a brow.

"You know why." Her lips flattened as the deck canted, and she gripped the railing. "If I find this map and then the next, I will know the location of the Fount."

"And what of Kingston?"

"I'll have plenty of time to get to the Fount and then to Kingston."

"'Tis a gamble, and you know it. How can you leave those people to suffer?"

She shrugged and stared across the sea. "I don't believe much of what Antoine says, and even if it were true, I have every intention of warning them. In truth"—her eyes met his again, and he balked at the pain he saw in them—"I simply don't wish to go there and have you leave me."

"I am going to leave you, regardless, Reena, as I have said."

Pain fizzled across her expression, and she lowered her gaze to the foamy water reaching for them up the hull. A single tear appeared beneath her long lashes, but the wind tore it away. Finally, she threw back her shoulders, and was about to say something when a shout came from the tops.

"A sail! A sail!"

"Where away?" Reena shouted, already heading toward the quarterdeck.

"One point off the larboard bow!"

"Two sets of sail!" Blared from above.

Plucking the scope from her belt, Reena held it to her eye and shifted it in that direction. A look of horror, followed by shock, turned her face white.

Frederick dashed up to her. "Who is it, Reena?"

"'Tis my father's ship, the *Redemption*."

Grabbing the spyglass, he lifted it to his eye. "A brig follows her. My father's. The *Restitution*."

CHAPTER TWENTY-THREE

"*L*ay aloft yardmen! Lay out and loose!" Reena's shout echoed across the deck, sending her men flying into the shrouds and scampering to the tops. "Make all sail! Man the royal halliards and sheets!"

Abraham shouted further orders as Reena spotted Freddy, his face red with fury, coming at her from her left.

"By all that is holy, what in thunderation are you doing, Reena? I'm sure they merely wish to talk."

"Precisely." She cast him a scathing glance. "Talk me into relinquishing my brig, my pirating, my quest. Talk me into a life of service and drudgery."

"And we cannot allow that to happen, Mademoiselle Pirate." Antoine's nasally voice grated over Reena's back as he approached, lifting a spyglass to his eye. "*En plus de…* my ship has orders to fire upon anyone who dares approach us. And, mark my words, they will do it."

Freddy huffed. "Then they are more stupid than brave, monsieur, for only a fool would engage in battle with Captain Edmund Merrick and his wife Lady Charlisse, nor my father."

The side of Antoine's thin lips twisted. "Captain Merrick is *âgé* and so is his wife. They should have retired long ago." He waved a hand through the air. "Their religion has made them weak."

Loose sails billowed in the wind above them as the *Reckless* sped on an eastern tack, the deck angling to larboard.

Reena gripped the binnacle. "Regardless, gentlemen, I have no intention of either engaging them or speaking with them."

Freddy faced her, a mixture of anger and urgency in his green eyes. "Bring the brig about, lower a boat, and allow me to join them. I'll tell them you do not wish to see them, but I must…"—he gestured with his head to Antoine who was staring once again through his spy glass—"warn them," he whispered the last words.

Reena sighed and stared at her father's ship and the *Restitution* just beyond its starboard quarter. The *Redemption* had sailed these waters for over thirty years and was still one of the fastest brigs around. Aye, Freddy wished to warn them about Kingston, but she could not allow that to happen for two reasons. One, she wasn't ready to lose him. And two, she knew her parents. They would never allow her to get so close without…

"Nay. They will insist on speaking with me. Besides, Antoine's ship will engage them, and I don't wish them any harm. 'Tis better for them *and* for us if we make all haste and escape."

Blocks creaked as sails hoisted, catching the wind in a thunderous snap. The *Reckless* slid into a trough. Reena balanced over the heaving deck as Abraham issued orders that brought the brig close-hauled and skimming rapidly over the sea.

Wind blasted over Freddy, freeing a strand of hair from his tie. "Signal your ship to stand down," he ordered Antoine.

But the Frenchman merely sneered in reply. "I take no orders from you, monsieur."

Jaw stiff and one hand gripping the pommel of his blade, Freddy scanned the deck as if contemplating inciting a mutiny. But instead, he marched away, leaving a wake of fury behind him. She hated to disappoint him, hated that he was always angry at her. Yet now, as she gazed toward the *Redemption*, a mustache of foam on her bow as she gave chase, a strange sense of longing enveloped her. She had not seen her parents or her siblings for two years, and she wondered how they fared. She'd seen evidence of their charity in ports she'd visited, heard they were doing well and still about God's work. She'd also learned her brother Alex had married. And that his wife's brother had married a strange female artist. Babies were on the way. The family was growing. And she was missing it all.

But she had tried that life and it had not suited her. She was born to be a pirate like her father was in the beginning. She could not allow them to convince her otherwise, especially not when she was on the most important quest of her life.

In truth, she could not bear, yet again, to look into their eyes and see nothing but disappointment.

Captain Edmund Merrick Hyde, Earl of Clarendon, stood with feet spread apart on the quarterdeck of the *Redemption*, spyglass to his eye. Wind spit a strand of his ebony hair into his face, and lowering the scope, he shook it aside. "She's running from us." His tone held a bit of surprise, but more sorrow than he intended. For he didn't wish to upset his precious bride.

Too late. He felt her arm loop through his as if she needed his strength to accept his words.

"Why is she always running?" Her tone lacked its usual hope.

Merrick turned toward his wife, amazed he found her as beautiful as the day he'd first discovered her on a deserted island nearly thirty years ago. Golden curls, tossed by the wind, circled her comely face, a fitting halo for such an angel. The lines etching the side of her luscious lips and across her forehead did naught to distract from the love and beauty pouring from her crystal-blue eyes—eyes that now held a bit of fear.

The brig leapt over a wave, showering them with sea spray, and Merrick drew her into a tight embrace. "She is still in the darkness, love. But she will soon find the light."

He felt her tremble. "My poor baby girl. I wish I had your faith."

He nudged her back. "You've always had more faith than I have, dearest. Always. Remember when you commanded this brig of pirates and went in search of me when I had fallen from grace?"

She smiled. "I do. Forsooth, you gave me quite a run for it, if I remember."

Jackson approached, his bald head shining like black onyx in the sunlight. "We've hoisted all sail, Cap'n. And milady"— he faced Charlisse—"I agree wit' de cap'n. Yer faith puts de rest o' us to shame."

Releasing a deep sigh, Charlisse turned and gripped the quarterdeck railing, staring after her daughter's brig and the two ships sailing by her side. "Yet somehow when it comes to my babies, that faith falters."

"'Tis the tenderness of your mother's heart," Merrick said. "But you know as well as I that God promises the descendants of the righteous will be delivered."

"Aye, I know that verse well." She returned his smile. "Now, I must stand on it and believe."

Captain Kent Carlton leapt on the quarterdeck and made his way to Merrick, spyglass in hand. "Who are those other ships with her?" Hard to believe the man had been Merrick's arch enemy for so many years—had even kidnapped his wife!—yet now, for even more years, they'd been the best of companions, fellow servants in the work of the Lord.

"They're French." Merrick said, feeling his jaw stiffen. "The *Conquérant*, though I am not sure who captains her."

"Antoine du Casse." Kent spit out the name in disdain as he lowered his scope.

"Du Casse?" Charlisse asked, sudden alarm in her voice.

Isabel Carlton approached the railing and slipped her hand into her husband's. "The nephew of Jean-Baptiste du Casse. We know of him." She glanced at her husband. "We've had dealings with him before." The deck canted as wind blasted over her, tossing a wayward lock of auburn hair over her neck.

Kent eased her hair behind her ear as he gazed affectionately at his wife. "He fancies himself a pirate."

"What is he doing with Reena?" Charlisse asked, glancing back at the ships. "Are we not at war with France?"

Merrick lifted his scope again. "'Twould seem *we* are, but not Reena, for the *Conquérant* opens her gun ports at our approach."

Kent glanced over his shoulder at his ship, *Restitution,* then cocked a playful brow at Merrick. "We could easily take them."

Merrick grinned. "Indeed. But at what cost?"

Charlisse grabbed a curl and spun it around her finger. "I won't see my daughter harmed." Grabbing the scope from Merrick, she lifted it to her eye, even as she balanced over the heaving deck. Below on the main deck, Jackson shouted orders to adjust sail to get the most speed out of the shifting trade winds.

Charlisse gasped, lowered the glass, and faced Kent. "You should take a closer look on deck." She handed her scope to Isabel as Kent raised his to his eye.

"Frederick!" he shouted.

"My son!" Isabel faltered, but Kent quickly grabbed her arm and bore her up. "What is he doing? I thought he was on the *Viper.*"

"My brother?" Lydia dashed toward them, looking more pirate than lady in her breeches and waistcoat. Levi followed close behind.

"Aye, 'tis your brother." Kent handed his scope to Lydia.

"Indeed, and there's Reena on the quarterdeck."

"In trouble again, I see." Levi smirked.

"We won't know until we speak with him." Merrick glanced at the mound of sails bloated with wind above them.

Gabrielle joined them, her skirts billowing in the breeze, and Charlisse swung an arm around her eldest daughter and drew her close. "We have found your sister."

Shielding her eyes from the sun, Gabrielle gazed toward the fleeing ships. "'Twould seem she doesn't wish to be found."

"Surely we can catch them," Lydia urged.

"We could," Merrick said. "But the French frigate's message is clear. We cannot risk a battle in which she and Freddy might get hurt."

"Agreed." Kent nodded with a sigh.

"Do you suppose she's a prisoner?" Gabrielle bit her lip.

"Nay." Isabel still had the scope to her eye. "She is unbound and unfettered."

The brig slammed down a wave, sending spray over them all. Frowning, Gabrielle wiped it away. "I am glad Alex and Juliana are not here to witness this. He loves Reena so."

"Indeed." Charlisse hugged her daughter tight. "'Twas best we left them at Kingston. She has most likely borne their child now."

Merrick noticed the longing in her tone. "Never fear, love, you will see your new grandchild soon." He caressed her cheek.

Tears glistened in her eyes as she gazed back at the *Reckless*. "If I could only hug Reena and tell her how much I love her."

"Me, as well." Merrick nodded, before he reluctantly turned to Jackson. "Let go the bowlines, in topgallants. Down jib and staysails."

"Aye, aye, Cap'n."

Kent faced them all. "We may not be able to catch them now, but we can pray."

"Indeed." Merrick nodded his approval as one by one, they took each other's' hands, forming a circle on the quarterdeck, and appealed to the only One who could help Reena and Freddy.

⚓

"Should we encounter anyone, allow me to do the talking, *ma chérie*. I have *les amis* on this island," Antoine whispered as the sailors rowed them to shore. Water as dark as Hades reflected a three-quarter moon and a host of sparkling stars above, but the beauty did naught to settle Frederick's nerves.

"Friends or fellow conspirators?" He snapped back. They had anchored in a hidden cove north of the capital city of Fort Royal, hoping to find the graveyard on the western side of town, do their sordid business, and leave without alerting the French authorities. Antoine had brought five of his men while Reena had brought five of her crew—Brodie, Jo, Abraham, Wilson, and himself. She'd left Fletcher in charge of the *Reckless*.

Regardless, Frederick's only longing at the moment was to push Antoine du Casse overboard. The man's arrogant manner, the lecherous glances he gave Reena when she wasn't looking, and his ostentatious attire created a perpetual sourness in Frederick's stomach. A wolf in sheep's clothing. But it would not be his problem much longer. As soon as they set foot on land, Frederick intended to make his way to Fort Royal and barter work on a ship heading anywhere close to Kingston. Being in a French port shouldn't be a problem, for he could disguise his voice, and he knew enough French to pass as an uneducated sailor.

Yet, even before they landed on shore and his boots sank into the sand, Frederick's heart sank as well. How could he leave Reena with this pustulant miscreant by her side? Under normal circumstances, he wouldn't. He'd stick with her until he ensured her safety. But he had a duty to warn Kingston and a family to protect, and he had learned long ago that he could not control Reena.

He assisted her out of the boat. "Alas, you hope to find ol' Crimson Jack in the main cemetery outside town?" He turned to help the sailors drag the boat ashore.

"'Tis my hope. If the tale Antoine told us was true."

Antoine brushed sand from his coat. "*Oui*, we must first get through this jungle."

Reena checked her pistol then stuffed it in her belt. "I don't see why we couldn't sail right into the harbor, since you are French, monsieur, and you *insist* you have friends here."

His grin was lost in the shadows. "I also have enemies, Mademoiselle Pirate."

But Frederick was still stuck on the word *jungle*. Memories of his nightmare rose to pinch his heart. At the time, he had thought it was merely an allegory of his efforts to save Reena from her dark path. But now it seemed more a warning of upcoming disaster. Dare he let her go into the jungle alone? Of course, she had loyal friends with her, but in his dream, none of them had raised a hand to help.

Thunderation!

"You are free, Freddy." She gestured into the darkness, the slight catch of grief in her voice, one only he would notice. "I thought you weren't interested in going to the tomb with us."

"'Tis on my way." Frederick grabbed the cross around his neck, seeking wisdom, strength…whatever gift the Lord would grant him. "I will accompany you there and then head into the city."

"No need to grace us with your presence, monsieur." The stench of Antoine's lemon pomade stung Frederick's nose as the man came alongside them. "I have things well in hand. Go tend your business, whatever that is."

Frederick did not respond. Instead, he drew his sword and plunged into the dark jungle. The sooner he got this over with, the sooner he could find a ship and get as far away as possible from Reena Hyde and her crazy schemes.

CHAPTER TWENTY-FOUR

Reena couldn't be more thrilled that Freddy was accompanying them to find the next map, though she did not fully understand why. Dare she hope that when it came down to it, he could not bear the thought of leaving her? Nay, there must be some other reason, for he had made his sentiments clear. Yet, now as they exited the jungle and spotted the flickering lights of Fort Royal in the distance, he sheathed his blade and made his way along the outskirts of the cemetery as if he had every intention of staying.

Reena would not have recognized the clearing as a graveyard if she had not stumbled over a cross perched before a recently dug mound of dirt. In fact, rows of graves—some marked with crosses, some marked with stones, some not marked at all—extended into the darkness in such a haphazard pattern, it seemed people merely tossed their loved ones about without respect or regard.

A chilled mist rose from the ground, and she hugged herself. She hated cemeteries. She hated death. So demeaning an end to one's life—no matter how insignificant that life was. Which was why she was here in the first place. To put an end to death once and for all.

Leaves fluttered in a breeze as if laughing at her resolve, even as a cloud stole what little light the moon afforded. At least the graveyard was a good distance from town and no one would be about at this hour.

Turning, she ordered her crew to split up and search for a grave marked with the name Jacque Bonhomme. No wonder the man didn't use his last name, for didn't it mean *good man*?

Reena followed behind Abraham, fully aware of Freddy's presence beside her. His scent of oak and leather surrounded her, taunting her with his impending departure. She longed to ask him why he remained but didn't want to prompt him to leave. Instead, she remained silent, listening to the crunch of dirt under their boots, the distant sound of waves, and the warble of a night heron.

Weeds and thorns had choked several of the graves, making it difficult to see the names of the dead on crosses and stones. Some of the headstones had tilted on their side, others had fallen over, still others had been swallowed whole by vines. Was this to be the end of man? After a life lived on this earth, were all men destined to be laid so carelessly about, cared for so little? Perhaps none of these people had anyone who truly loved them.

A frown pulled her brows together. Did anyone truly love her? She swallowed a lump of pain at the thought.

Surely Crimson Jack's grave was better attended. But when she heard the shout from Brodie and headed in that direction, she found his grave in much the same condition as the rest. Grabbing a lantern, she held it over the cracked and fallen stone on which his name was carved. It merely said

Here lies Jacque Bonhomme
1613-1641

No mention of the riches he had garnered, the battles he had won, the respect and fear he had invoked in everyone around him. But of course, there couldn't be since he'd been buried in secret. A mass of tangled weeds webbed across the ground where he lay as if trying to cover up his very existence. The others joined her, including Freddy, who crossed his arms over his chest and shook his head.

Reena sighed. "A shame to be laid to rest in such disgrace."

"He was naught but a pirate, Reena."

Freddy's words deflated her. "A good pirate—one of the best," she retorted. "He defeated over twenty Spanish merchant ships, five Spanish Galleons, six French, three Dutch, and two East Indiamen. He gathered more wealth than any pirate before him or since."

Antoine nodded, staring at the grave almost reverently. "*Oui*, we French make the best pirates."

Jo gave a ladylike snort. "So young."

"For what is your life? It is even a vapour, that appeareth for a little time, and then vanisheth away." Freddy quoted.

The Scripture hung in the air above the grave like an omen, a rather depressing omen.

"Enough of this." Reena shook off the chill spiraling down her back. "But what do we do now? Dig him up? I still don't understand why this would be a place the pirate would take his lady."

"I do." 'Twas Freddy's voice coming from the grave beside Jacque's. He held a lantern over another headstone. "Didn't you say the lady's name was Bauffremonts?"

"Aye." Reena circled Jacque's grave and approached, the words etched in the stone coming into view:

Delphine de Grenaille
Serviteur bien-aimé et ami des Bauffremonts
Mis au repos le 17 Octobre dans l'année de notre Seigneur
1649

"Translate please, Antoine."

The man drew close and cleared his throat. "Delphine de Grenaille, beloved servant and friend of the Bauffremonts. Laid to rest October 17th in the year of our Lord 1649."

"Ah ha!" Reena grinned. "That's it then."

"Aye." Freddy rubbed the back of his neck. "Seems the lady must have loved her servant as much as you did Dinah."

His words stole the grin from her face before she turned back to Jacque's grave and ordered her men to start digging. She hated to add further dishonor to poor Crimson Jack, but she assumed the map was on his person. Holding the lantern high, she lifted up a quick prayer of forgiveness for disturbing the dead, surprising herself in the process. But she supposed it couldn't hurt. The scent of earthy loam and decay pinched her nose as the cloud moved aside, showering the morbid scene in an eerie silver light.

Freddy gave her a look she knew all too well—a look of judgment and disappointment. "So, you intend to continue with this nonsense, dig up this man's bones?"

"There is no other way." She could not look at him. "The clue said he must be disturbed. This is no doubt where the pirate hid the map. Surely being a pirate and contemporary of Crimson Jacque, he would have known the stories of where the man's wife had buried him. Maybe he and his lady love had discussed it as they stood here honoring her servant."

Freddy hesitated and she thought she heard a low growl emanate from him over the sound of digging. "Then I shall leave you to your wretched task," he finally said.

The words muddled in Reena's mind, like an anchor slogging through a swamp. She didn't want to hear them, didn't want the anchor to take hold. Yet before she could accept them, before she could respond, Freddy turned, bid Brodie, Jo, and Abraham adieu, and walked away, dragging yet another piece of her heart in the mud behind him.

Unable to find her voice, she stared after him until the darkness obliterated all trace of him… longing to give chase, begging him to stay. But she'd already done that on board the *Reckless*—many times—and she could not appear weak in front of Antoine.

Forcing back tears, she shook off the terrifying thought that she would never see Freddy again. Of course, she would. She had found him on HMS *Viper*, and she would find him again. She had no choice. She couldn't live without him, and strangely, the maps, her quest, none of it seemed to have meaning without him.

But she couldn't think like that. Drawing a deep breath, she squared her shoulders and focused on the task at hand. Which seemed to go on interminably long as the men dug through weeds and soil and shoveled dirt onto a growing pile off to the side. Finally, the shovel hit something hard, and Wilson and Abraham leapt into the grave and brushed dirt aside. White bones appeared, poking through the soil like ghosts emerging from the darkness.

Stepping back, she pressed a hand over her stomach. "Check all around him," she ordered.

Antoine stood at the foot of the grave, grinning like a lion about to pounce on its prey.

Plucking a flask from his pocket, Brodie took another swig.

Wilson held up a corked bottle. "Here it be, Cap'n."

Antoine's man reached for it, but Abraham beat him to it. Climbing out of the hole, he handed it to Reena. Excitement trickled through her as she gave the lantern to Wilson, uncorked the bottle, and spilled the map into her hand. Antoine sped to her side.

Carefully unrolling the parchment, she scanned the contents, spotting familiar landmarks and reading the riddle written in the center.

So intrigued with the contents, she didn't notice movement around her until the cock of several pistols snapped in her ear.

The map disappeared from her hand. Antoine grinned. "I shall relieve you of that, *s'il vous plaît.*"

Reena seared him with a glare. "What are you doing Antoine? We had a deal."

"One which you would have gladly broken. *En fait*, you had plans to do just that."

It was a hard way to learn the truth. But now Reena knew with certainty. Sedley was a rat.

Antoine held out his hand. "The other two maps, *ma chérie.* I know you have them."

Reena stared at him, unmoving, wondering if she and her four crew could beat him and his five. Why did Freddy have to leave?

Antoine curled his fingers toward her. "Give them to me, mademoiselle, or I'll shoot you and your comrades on the spot."

Reaching into her waistcoat, she pulled out the other two maps and reluctantly handed them to the traitorous carp.

He folded them carefully and slipped them inside his doublet. Then with a snap of his fingers, a dozen men emerged from the shadows. "Arrest her at once. She's a British pirate!"

CHAPTER TWENTY-FIVE

Frederick stood at the docks of Fort Royal harbor, awaiting a dory to take him out to *La Sirène*, a three-masted merchant ship headed for Saint-Domingue—back to Antoine's home. But that couldn't be helped. It had been difficult enough to barter with the captain for passage in exchange for working on board. When he'd explained to the man—in Frederick's limited French—the extent of his sailing skills, Captain Agard, a man as thin as a rope and just as frayed, had plucked the pipe from his mouth, looked him up and down and grunted.

"If ye can't do the work, I'll toss you to the sharks," he had said in French, and Frederick knew he meant it.

But he *could* do the work and more. If the captain only knew. Though now as Frederick pressed his shoulder and ribs and felt how sore they still were, he wondered.

Despite that, with each passing minute as he watched the boat approach, his spirit grew more and more restless—as if a hot wind cycloned within him, tossing anything that made sense into chaos. What was wrong with him? He should be overjoyed to be leaving Reena and her motley crew. He should be thrilled to get as far away from her as possible and make his way back home. Especially since he had an even more urgent reason to return.

There had been no quicksand in the jungle, no dangers which had required his protection. When he left her, she was about to retrieve her precious map, and no doubt by now she and her band were heading back through the jungle to her brig.

Yet…something within him made him feel like he was making a huge mistake.

Frederick glanced up at the ebony sky, where stars winked at him as if they held a grand secret. *Surely it cannot be Your will that I remain in such debased company. Better to join my parents and do Your work than face such overwhelming temptation every day.*

I am...your strength. The words filled his soul to near bursting as if he'd swallowed a hallowed wind. A gust tore over him, whipping his shirt and fingering his hair. Nay, merely the wind playing tricks on him. Of course he must leave. 'Twas the right thing to do.

A sailor at the head of the dory held up a lantern as it approached the wharf, where Frederick and two more sailors awaited transport to the merchant ship.

Footsteps thundered behind him, quaking the planks beneath Frederick's boots. But he didn't want to know who it was. He didn't want anything to prevent him from doing what he must.

Hands grabbed his arm and twirled him about. A familiar voice, frantic faces—Brodie, Jo, Abraham, and Wilson.

Brodie was shouting, but his accent was too thick, his words too fast. "Slow down, Brodie." Frederick grabbed him and drew them all aside. "What's happened?"

"Dat scoundrel, Antoine," Abraham said, breathing heavy. "He double-crossed us. Took Reena's map an' handed her ov'r to de French."

Jo pushed her way forward, her eyes shifting between his in terror. "They whipped 'er, Cap'n Carlton. Put 'er in stocks in the public square fer all t' see, claimin' she's a pirate."

Frederick's heart shriveled until he could barely feel it beat. The French were notoriously ruthless to British pirates. After her whipping, they'd break her bones, then leave her in the square to rot.

Thunderation! Raking back his hair, he took up a pace. "I knew we couldn't trust that snake!" Halting, he scanned their faces, barely making them out in the moonlight. "How did you get away?"

"They didna care aboot us," Brodie had finally settled down. "They jist wanted *her.*"

Anger rising, Frederick glanced toward the peninsula, beyond which both Reena's and Antoine's ships were anchored. "No doubt he'll try to take her brig as well. Abraham, you must return to the *Reckless*."

"But what aboot the cockboat?" Brodie asked. "Ach now, Antoine's likely already got to it."

"Nay." Abraham said with authority. "The cap'n tol' dem to move it to a dif'rent spot."

"Smart lady." But then, Frederick already knew that. "Then go, Abraham, and be quick about it."

"But wha' about de Cap'n?"

"We'll save her." Frederick's tone bore more confidence than he felt.

"How?" Brodie huffed. "There be only four of us aginst an army of French soldiers."

Abraham darted off, and Frederick gripped the Scot's shoulders. "You forget. I am my father's son."

The French officers shoved Reena into the open square. The irons around her ankles clanked and rubbed her tender skin. Tumbling forward, she tripped and fell on the cobblestones. Pain spiraled up her knees and elbows. Vicious hands yanked her up by both arms, nearly pulling them from their sockets. The barrel of a musket pushed against her back. Ankles burning, ropes grinding the skin at her wrists, she stumbled forward. The officers chattered amongst themselves in French, obviously thrilled to have captured a British pirate— and a female at that. She wondered how much Antoine had collected for her, the viper! She had not trusted him, but she had not expected such a hateful betrayal.

The soldiers spewed more French slurs upon her as they advanced toward an empty pillory in the middle of the square. An occupied one stood to its left. At least she thought 'twas occupied. Hard to tell in the misty shadows. What she *could* tell were morsels of what the Frenchmen were saying— something about a trial in the morning and an appointment with the noose in the afternoon. One of the officers—the one who stared at her, licking his lips as if she were a pint of ale—

suggested they take their pleasure with her before they put her in the pillory. But thank the Lord, the lieutenant in charge refused.

She shivered at the thought and was grateful the man seemed to have a modicum of honor. Though, aside from not being ravished, her future prospects appeared bleak.

She cursed Antoine under her breath. The lecherous swine had professed his love to her over and over, but 'twould seem his love of eternal youth and fortune far outweighed his love for her. And Sedley. If she ever got out of this…she'd have him keelhauled or worse. He was the only one who knew she had the other two maps with her. As she had planned. To test his loyalty.

To test Antoine's loyalty.

But hadn't she been willing to betray him as well? Aye, but not to turn him over to be hung. She would never do that, tenderhearted fool that she was! She was as gullible as Freddy said. Far too gullible. The musket struck her back again, and she tumbled to the hard ground at the base of the pillory.

Dust from the street rose to fill her nose. Coughing, she scanned the square. At least six armed men stood guard around the outskirts. For her? Or for the other poor soul in the next pillory?

The officer was saying something about a whip as a salty breeze blew in from the harbor. Reena glanced up to see twenty or so ships at anchor and the moon dabbing silver paint on rippling black wavelets. A scene far too beautiful for the proceedings onshore. Not many were about at this hour. Light and music poured from a few taverns and punch houses lining the street, and some men stumbled about, but most of the good townsfolk would be asleep as it was no doubt past midnight. Why whip her then?

Against her will, fear trickled up her spine and gripped her heart. *Bilge water*! She was a pirate captain and should not be afraid. Yet, she couldn't help the slight tremble as they tore the ropes from her hands. She had but a moment to rub her raw skin during which the man in charge, the lieutenant who'd saved her from being ravished, knelt and finally looked her in the eyes. She thought she saw pity in his, but they quickly hardened and he rose, yanked off her waistcoat, and ripped her shirt open in the back. A gentle breeze caressed her skin, as if giving her one last moment of pleasure before the coming agony.

A command was given and two men laid her head and hands on the block and then slammed down the top piece of wood. The strike echoed down the street, sealing her fate.

If she were a praying woman, she would beg the Almighty for a chance to escape. Or at the very least, for release from the pain that was sure to come. Instead, she squeezed her eyes shut and forced back womanly tears that threatened to break free.

She barely heard the sound of the whip before her back split open in agonizing pain.

"This is what we do to British pirates," one of the men said in English before another blow ripped across her back. She clenched her jaw, refusing to scream, determined to show these men that a woman pirate was as tough as any man.

She heard the whip snap in the air again and braced for the impact.

"*Assez*!" the lieutenant shouted.

It never struck.

The Frenchman who'd wanted to ravish her stooped before her face. "Two stripes tonight, *ma chérie*, and another thirty-eight tomorrow before you are hung." He smiled and slid a finger down her cheek. She longed to spit on him, but she could not lift her head high enough.

"*Allons-y*!" the lieutenant barked, and the men scattered to one of the taverns across the way.

Reena hung her head, unable to think, unable to cry, unable to do much of anything but feel the pain throbbing through her. She struggled to free herself, but to no avail. Alas, this was to be her fate, then. Did her parents not warn her that the end of every pirate was the noose or Davy Jones' Locker?

But she had not listened. She thought herself too wise, too skilled to ever be caught. Yet should such a disaster occur, she had hoped one drink from the Fount would release her from any such fate.

And she'd been so close to finding it...so close.

"Save me," she whispered a prayer, harboring no hope that God would listen. Why would He? She had turned her back on Him long ago.

"Whaddya do t' make 'em so mad at a lady?" A voice, bearing a British accent, emerged from the darkness, and Reena turned her head with difficulty to the pillory beside hers.

She made no reply.

The man sighed. "They caught me stealing from one o' their merchant ships. My family were starvin'."

Pain seared through her, and she struggled to find her voice.

"Are you really a pirate?" he asked.

"Not just a pirate," Reena breathed out, finally. "But the captain of a pirate ship."

"Lud! I ne'er saw no woman pirate afore."

"It pains me to hear about your family, if 'tis true," she managed.

"Why would I lie? What good can I do them now? We're t' be hung on the morrow."

Not if she could help it, though she had no idea at the moment how to escape.

"I'm Captain Reena Hyde."

"Henry Florence. A pleasure, Miss…I mean, Captain."

They both fell into silence, for what else was there to say? They had nothing but agony to look forward to and neither of them could help the other.

Reena hung her head again, her chin scraping over the rough wood, where, no doubt, hundreds of poor victims had drooled, bled, and cried. Flies landed on her open flesh, biting and stinging. She tried to move, to fling them away, but it was no use. Instead, she tried to think of happier times—sailing the seas with Freddy, desperately in love with life and with each other.

Did he even know where she was? Or had he already embarked on a ship in the harbor behind her? Had her friends made it back to the *Reckless,* or had Antoine captured them? It was all too horrible to consider.

After what seemed like forever, but could only have been an hour, the music from the taverns died down. Laughter dwindled as well, along with flickering lights, and the city fell into a deadly silence. Even the moon slipped behind horizon, leaving Reena and Henry in such darkness she could taste it.

The peaceful sound of lapping waves brought her little comfort as she tried to not give into the pain. She must use her agony to remain conscious. If these were to be her last moments on earth, she wanted to use them to fight, to plan an escape…not to curl up and die.

Jerking her head up, she drew in several deep breaths and fought to keep her eyes open. A light drew her gaze to the right. A glowing figure formed in the brightness. A tall, thickly-muscled man, bearing sword and shield stood near her, saying nothing, doing nothing.

Freddy?

Then he was gone. She closed her eyes, feeling her strength leech away, her pain overwhelming her. She could hear her own breathing, feel herself drifting…drifting…

A thunderous blast shook the ground beneath her and roared across the square.

CHAPTER TWENTY-SIX

"Hae ye ever made these before?" Brodie asked Frederick as they sat in the shadows behind a blacksmith's shop, assembling the powder flasks—or grenades—that his father had taught him to make when he was young.

"Aye, but I've never had occasion to use them." Now that he thought about it, his father had taught him many useful things, some of which had already saved his life. He had also taught him many unhelpful things, such as how to spew a barrage of unyielding criticism, a skill he'd learned from the many times he'd made a mistake. Captain Kent Carlton was a hard man to please, and for all of Frederick's efforts, he had consistently failed to do so.

"Nay. Here. Like this," Frederick took the hollow ceramic ball from Brodie. "First pour in the tar, then the gunpowder, then you stick the fuse in like this." He coated more tar over the top around the fuse, then gently laid it aside. "The tar will make a great smoke screen," he added, examining the one Jo had just assembled. When he'd first explained what they were making, the master gunner could hardly contain her excitement. As it was, she caught on quickly and had already made more than either Brodie or Wilson.

He smiled her way before rising and stretching his sore rib and shoulder. They'd had to "borrow" the required supplies from several shops in Fort Royal. Frederick had left enough coins in each to cover the cost. Still, guilt assailed him. But what else could he have done?

Inching around the back of the blacksmith's shop, he peered toward the town square across the street where Reena and another prisoner hung in pillories. Three guards stood on either side of them, muskets slung across their chests, ready to fire, though he could hardly make them out now in the darkness. The moon had slunk away as if disgusted by the gruesome scene. Frederick couldn't blame it, but he could no longer see Reena. He heard her shifting in the pillory, heard her chains rattle, her tiny moans of pain. And it took everything within him to wait, to plan, and to do things right so he'd have the best chance of rescuing her without further injury—to any of them. Yet his heart bore a palpable ache knowing she was suffering so much within his reach. He longed to tell her that he was near…to hang on, that he was coming. But he dared not. Instead, he had spent the past two hours forming a plan, gathering supplies, and making grenades.

In the meantime, the town had grown quiet as well, which was perfect for his plan.

He wandered back to the group. Wilson glanced up at him. "Cap'n, if we toss these toward those guards, won't that bring others into the square?"

"Precisely why we aren't going to do that. At least not at first. How many do we have?" He stooped to examine the pile.

"At least a dozen," Jo said.

"That's enough. Brodie, you and Jo take six and set them off as I instructed near the governor's house two miles north, then hurry back here."

Nodding, Brodie and Jo carefully gathered the grenades and started away.

"And don't get caught," Frederick whispered after them.

"Never," Jo responded before they disappeared around the corner.

"Follow me," Frederick ordered Wilson as they gathered the rest of the grenades and crept along the back of the blacksmith's shop, then past the chandler, the tailor…and finally across the main street where the guards wouldn't see them.

Oh Lord, I need your help. Help me to rescue Reena. He knew this must be God's plan or else Frederick would be on *La Sirène* right now, preparing to set sail at dawn to Saint-Domingue. And that gave him courage to proceed.

Halting in the shadows beside a warehouse, Frederick peeked around the corner. Naught but darkness and shifting shadows met his gaze, but then a strange light appeared—a tiny spark that grew into a glowing column. It showered over Reena in the pillory, and she looked up as if she saw it as well. Frederick couldn't be sure what it was, but the sight gave him hope that God was, indeed, on their side. And so he waited…and waited… for the expected explosions.

Retrieving flint and steel from his pocket, he gestured for Wilson to hold one of the grenades.

And still they waited. Minutes ticked past like hours. The column of light was still there, but Reena had hung her head again.

Boom! Boom! Boom! Air and ground reverberated with the blasts. The guards dashed from their spots into the square, muskets at the ready. Their frenzied voices filled the air with French expletives. One of them pointed down the street, exclaiming, "*la maison du gouverneur!*" Three more explosions punched the sky, and one of the men brayed orders that sent four of them barreling down the street.

Two remained. Good. Smiling, Frederick struck flint to steel, lit the grenade, then tossed it into the square, far enough from the guards so as not to hurt them, but close enough to flood them with smoke. The blast thundered louder than he expected. Ears ringing, he lit another and another and tossed them after the first.

Explosion after explosion rocked the night. French curses whipped the air, along with the sound of boots scrambling to and fro. A musket fired. Thick, black smoke bloated the plaza.

Drawing his cutlass, Frederick gave a nod to Wilson, and together they charged forward. He couldn't see Reena but headed straight for her pillory. A glimmer caught his eye. A blade sliced the smoke toward his head. He lifted his cutlass just in time and met it with equal intensity. A Frenchman emerged from the fog, his face lined with soot and sweat. He whirled about and sliced at Frederick from the left.

Thunderation. He had hoped the smoke would hide him until he could free Reena.

Swooping down, Frederick rushed blindly at the man. The steel of their blades hissed in the night. Another clang in the distance told him Wilson was equally engaged.

A horn rang through the city, sounding the alarm. They hadn't much time. Where were Jo and Brodie? Lifting up a prayer for their safety, he tilted his cutlass down in defense, then swung it back up, caught his opponent's hilt with his tip, and snapped it from the man's hands. Shock widened the Frenchman's eyes as he plucked the pistol from his belt, but before he could cock it, Frederick slammed his pommel on the man's hand. The pistol fell to the ground and the Frenchman darted away.

The smoke began to clear. Wilson shrank back from his opponent, obviously outmatched. Frederick started for him, but Brodie appeared out of the haze, sword raised, and quickly dispatched the man with a slice to his leg.

Dashing toward Reena, Frederick slammed the butt of his pistol on the bolts, tore them from the chains, then lifted the top from her head and hands. She struggled to raise her head, and he circled around to lift her up. Strips of bloody flesh crisscrossed her back.

Another alarm sounded—accompanied by the thunder of horse hooves.

"Reena." He knelt and took her head in his hands.

Moaning, she pried her eyes open. "Freddy? What are you doing here?"

"My turn to rescue you, Kitten."

Wilson, Brodie, and Jo appeared beside him. Jo shrieked at the sight of Reena's back.

"Hurry." Frederick hoisted Reena up. Then slipping his arm beneath hers, he dragged her over the cobblestones.

"Nay!" She breathed out. "Wait!"

Ignoring her, Frederick continued.

She dug her heel into the dirt. "My friend. Henry. We can't leave him." She gestured with her head toward the other pillory.

Brodie glanced back. "We havena time, Captain. Come!"

"Nay!" She shouted with what Frederick assumed was the last of her strength. And if he knew one thing, 'twas not to argue with the woman when she got something stuck in her mind.

Jo cursed. "He's gettin' what he deserves."

"We bring him with us." Reena's voice lacked her usual strength, but her authority rang through. "That's an order!"

The woman's kind heart never failed to amaze Frederick as he gestured for Brodie and Wilson to get the man. From the moans and groans, he assumed Henry was in worse shape than Reena. In fact, it took both Brodie and Wilson to carry him across the square, then through the dark alleyways of town, stopping occasionally to avoid French troops. Frederick did not feel safe until they finally plunged into the jungle and emerged on shore to the boat Abraham had left for them.

Once aboard the *Reckless*, Abraham informed Frederick that, indeed, Antoine had made an attempt to board with a dozen men, but he and the crew had repelled them off successfully.

"Excellent." Frederick turned to Brodie, climbing aboard after him with Henry in his arms. "Settle him and then grab your bag and meet me in Reena's cabin." A thin gray line appeared on the horizon, announcing the arrival of the sun. They needed to make their escape now lest Antoine make another attempt.

"How's de cap'n?" Abraham must have finally seen her wounds and approached.

"They whipped her," Frederick said then shouted across the deck, "Lay aloft and loose all sails!" The crew scattered to obey as Abraham nodded his understanding and ordered them further to task.

Sweeping Reena in his arms—being ever so careful not to touch her back—Frederick climbed down the companionway, more angry at himself than he'd been in a long while. This would not have happened if he had remained with her. Was he being selfish to want to warn his family and friends? To get as far away from her as he could?

Kicking open her cabin door, he gently laid her on her side on the bed. Then, lighting a lantern, he held it above her. Frederick was not one to cry, but his eyes burned when he saw the stripes of shredded flesh. Forcing back his sorrow, he allowed his anger to rise instead. Toward himself, but mostly toward Antoine. In the past, when Frederick's raging temper was in full eruption, everyone in the vicinity had scattered. That old temper now entertained thoughts of murdering the villainous Frenchman in a variety of agonizing tortures.

CHAPTER TWENTY-SEVEN

Reena was dreaming. No doubt 'twas morning and she was receiving the remaining thirty-eight of her lashes. Hence, she blocked the horrendous event from her mind and instead dreamt of Freddy. Dreamt that he'd come to rescue her. But of course that couldn't be. Freddy was long gone.

She felt someone place her on a soft bed. The scent of spice and oak and Freddy drifted past her nose, bringing her senses to life. With great difficulty, she pried one eye open, and the shape of a man formed in her vision—a man kneeling beside her, holding her hand. "Freddy?"

"Aye, Kitten. Hush now. You are safe."

Safe. A foreign concept in her reckless way of life. "Where am I?" Yet she already knew. The familiar scent of wood, salt, rum, and lavender emanating from her pillow, the unique creak of timbers and snap of sails above…and Abraham's deep tenor floating above her—all melodies in a soothing orchestra emanating from her favorite place in all the world—the *Reckless*. But she wanted to hear it from his lips. Otherwise, she would know she'd gone mad.

"Your brig, of course, Kitten." He kissed her hand. "Rest now."

She tried to move, but her back screamed in agony. "Where are we going?"

"Far away from Antoine," Freddy muttered as footsteps pounded into the room and Brodie's brogue filled her ears, his tone one of concern. Freddy's presence left, and a stool scraped over the floor as Brodie took his place.

Fred squawked. "The traitorous carp!"

Beyond Brodie, Reena thought she saw Jo enter, Michael on her heels. The lad made a dash for her, but Freddy leapt in his path. "She's hurt bad, boy. Let the doctor do his work."

Jo set a basin of water and rags on the floor beside Brodie.

"How's Henry?" Reena managed to mutter.

"Henry?" Brodie asked. "Ach now, the man we brought wit' ye? He'll live, Captain. I'll tend tae him next." He dipped a rag into water. "This may hurt a wee bit. D'ye wish fer somethin' tae bite on?"

"Nay."

Fred fluttered his feathers. "As tough as any man, says I!"

She'd laugh if she weren't in such pain.

That pain instantly grew to near unbearable…a searing agony that burned across her back and rampaged through her body. Defying every attempt to remain strong, she screamed. Tears flooded her eyes and spilled down her cheeks.

Freddy took both her hands in his and squeezed them tight. His strength not only brought her comfort, but it leeched into her very being, soothing each nerve, as if they were one. She'd gladly suffer such pain if it would keep him by her side.

"Sorry, Lass." Brodie continued his torturous ministrations, and the throbbing misery overcame her. She felt herself drifting away to another place where pain and heartache did not exist. How long she was there she didn't know, but the next thing she heard was Brodie instructing Jo and Michael to keep her quiet and still and give her something to drink.

"She's going to be all right?" Freddy asked.

"Aye. If infection doesna set in. Right now, she needs rest."

Reena felt Jo touch her shoulder. "Take care. I will return."

She sensed Michael by her side as well. Longing to reassure him she would recover, she opened her eyes. His blue ones, so large and full of life, smiled at her. Odd, but he had the most peaceful look on his face. "I prayed for you, Captain. God protected you. He did." Then he rose and backed away. "I'll bring your chocolate in a bit."

She really must speak to Freddy about preaching to Michael.

Brodie packed up and ushered everyone out, leaving only Freddy. A chill raked across her skin, and she trembled.

Freddy must've noticed, for he grabbed a blanket and laid it over her. But she didn't want a blanket. She wanted to be in his arms, for only there did she truly feel safe.

His footsteps thudded across the deck. A chink and slush rang in her ears, and he returned with a glass of rum. "For the pain." Setting it down, he helped her lean on her elbow then handed it to her. The room spun, but she managed a couple sips. "I will leave you to your rest." Rising, he set the glass on the desk.

"Nay. Please don't leave me, Freddy. Come lay with me. I'm cold and frightened." She would never admit such a thing to anyone but him, but 'twas the truth. She'd almost lost everything—her brig, her life, and most of all, Freddy. She shifted on the bed, ignoring the pain.

Hesitation appeared on his face, but finally he lifted the blanket and slid beside her, laying his head just inches from hers on the pillow. His cross landed on the sheet between them, an ever-present reminder of what kept him from her. Regardless, she took his hands in hers and closed her eyes again.

"The pain will subside soon, Kitten."

"Some pirate captain I am, eh? Trembling like a babe."

He brushed fingers through her hair, easing it from her face… so gentle, it reminded her of their intimate moments together. And her heart nearly burst with love for this man.

"It pains me Antoine did this to you, Reena. I warned you about him."

She merely nodded. "You came for me."

"As fast as I could." He closed his eyes, and Reena took the opportunity to gaze at him. The dark stubble circling his mouth and angling up his jaw, his strong nose and cheeks, and the strands of dark hair dangling over his forehead. 'Twas just like old times, lying here beside him. Her heart soared so high she could barely feel the pain in her back anymore. Barely.

"I knew you still loved me," she said.

One corner of his lips rose. "You did, did you?"

At least he had not denied it. "Aye. 'Tis why you can't leave me, though you keep trying."

Fred squawked. "That be the truth o' it."

"Hmm," he mumbled.

A tremble waved through her again, and Freddy opened his eyes, rubbed her arms, then moved the blanket up to her shoulders. "Shush, now. All is well." Drawing a deep breath, he closed his eyes again.

"Freddy, I saw something in the plaza."

"Tell me tomorrow. You need your rest."

"'Twas a light, a man made of light, armed and standing next to me."

She felt Freddy flinch, yet he said nothing for several minutes. "What do you think it was?"

"I have no idea, but it seemed…I thought you might know since you oft see things others don't."

"In truth, I saw it as well," Freddy said, "while I waited to attack the soldiers."

"You did?" She attempted to rise, but Freddy nudged her back down.

"'Twas an angel, Reena. I've seen many over the years."

She wanted to laugh but it would hurt too much. "Why would an angel protect the likes of me?" A memory forced itself upon her thoughts—a blade of light that saved her from death during the mutiny. Could God have protected her then as well?

"Because God told him to protect you."

"You've lost all sense, Freddy." Yet, she could not deny the flicker of joy bubbling within her at the thought—the thought of being loved and cared for by the Creator of all. Especially when she was defying Him at every turn. Hadn't Michael told her he'd prayed for God to protect her?

"Is it so hard to believe that God loves you?" Freddy asked, his eyes still closed.

It was. Especially after the path she had taken.

Minutes passed as she relaxed beside Freddy, listening to the sound of the wind against the stern windows, the waves against the hull, the grind of wood, and Abraham's occasional shout above. The first ripple of dawn fluttered through the window and landed on the floor beside the bed. Dawn. She was so tired. So very tired.

But she didn't want to fall asleep. She wanted to relish every moment so close to Freddy—the heat of his body, his masculine scent, the sound of his voice. The way he laid there to protect and comfort her.

"Sedley is a traitor," she said.

"Indeed," Freddy mumbled. "He is a liar, Reena. I've seen it in the spirit realm."

Freddy claimed he saw visions and had dreams, but honestly, she never quite believed him. Until now.

"I want him locked up."

"Shh. Later. Rest now." Freddy's eyes remained closed.

"I must find the Fount before Antoine."

"It doesn't matter now, Kitten. You no longer have the maps."

Reena smiled. "That is not quite true. You see, the maps I gave Antoine were fake."

Come all who are thirsty,
Come to the waters,
The walls may be crumbling
But the children are singing
The key is tied and bound

CHAPTER TWENTY-EIGHT

*F*rederick knew the exact moment Reena fell asleep. He sensed her body relax, heard her breathing deepen, and her light snoring begin. He smiled, then quickly erased it from his lips. It wasn't the first time she'd fallen asleep in bed beside him. But it would be the last. Even now, her unique feminine scent was driving him mad, along with the feel of her soft skin. *And* her need for him, her dependence on him for protection and comfort. She had temporarily removed the cloak of stubborn pride and harshness she kept tightly around her. She had allowed him to see into her heart—where she was merely a little kitten in a world of lions. A frightened kitten who sought solace in youth, beauty, fame, and wealth—all things that didn't matter in the end. In truth, what she really needed, what she really sought, was acceptance, unconditional love, purpose, value, and destiny—all things God freely offered anyone who came to Him.

Thunderation! He had hoped with the loss of the maps, she'd be forced to end her foolish quest. But the woman was far smarter than he'd given her credit. He should have known she didn't trust anyone—not even him in the end.

She'd set a trap for Sedley, knowing he would betray her.

By now, Antoine had discovered his maps were false—at least the two she'd given him. Frederick smiled. He would have loved to have been there when the arrogant blowfish realized he'd been tricked by a mere woman.

Moving as gently and quietly as possible, Frederick backed away from her and eased off the bed. A slight moan escaped her lips, but she settled back into a deep sleep. Unable to stop himself, Frederick took a moment to gaze at her, the way her curves flowed over the bed like waves at sea, her pink lips slightly parted, her silky hair tumbling over her shoulder, and her ebony lashes splayed over her cheeks. She had been his first love. And in truth, his *only* love. He quickly repented of his desire to get back in bed with her. He also repented of his murderous fury toward Antoine. Finally, before he committed any other sins, he whirled about and left the cabin.

On deck, Abraham seemed to have things well in hand. A bright sun sat upon the eastern horizon, sending golden ribbons over the turquoise sea. A strong wind filled the sails, the crew went about their duties, and the *Reckless* sped close-hauled on a western tack. To Jamaica, Abraham had told him with a beaming grin. To which Frederick nodded his appreciation.

"And what of Sedley?"

Abraham's silver tooth gleamed in the sun. "Locked him in de hold. He ain't goin' nowheres till de Cap'n decides wha' t' do wit' him."

"Good man." Frederick nodded.

"Yuh should get some rest," Abraham said.

He should. Yet, instead of going below to his cabin, Frederick made his way to the stern to pray. His thoughts and emotions were far too agitated to fall asleep—much like the milky foam bubbling off the stern and trailing a creamy wake behind them.

Every time he tried to escape Reena, it seemed God put him right back on this brig. *Reckless.* He huffed. Reckless, indeed, for everything Reena did was reckless, and with each passing day he spent here, she drew him deeper into her recklessness. He'd only gone through half his prayers when Brodie eased up beside him, flask in hand, and handed it to him. Frederick shook his head, amazed the man could drink as much as he did.

Slipping his flask inside his coat, Brodie gripped the taffrail and squinted at the rising sun. "How fares our captain?"

"Sleeping. For now. Thank you for tending her."

"'Tis my job." Brodie smiled. "An' she's my friend. Been a good captain tae me."

Footsteps drew both their gazes to Jo and one of the gun crew approaching a swivel gun on the larboard quarter. Upon seeing them, she smiled and headed their way, and Frederick couldn't help but notice the sudden lift of Brodie's shoulders.

She leaned on the railing beside him, nodded at Frederick, but then turned to Brodie. "Thank ye fer saving my life yesterday."

"Ach now, that? 'Twas nothin'."

Frederick wondered what "that" was, but they didn't seem to notice his presence anymore.

"It were far more than that." Jo brushed a wayward curl from her face.

The brig slammed over a wave, and Brodie gripped her elbow, though the lady clearly didn't need the help.

"I didn't see that man wit' the pistol," she said, "until ye struck him o'er the 'ead."

Brodie only smiled at her.

"What's this?" Frederick leaned on the railing, enjoying their exchange.

She finally glanced his way. "We was gettin' ready t' toss the rest o' the grenades when a soldier found us an' were about t' shoot me." Her gaze shifted back to Brodie. "But Brodie charged 'im, knocked 'im out cold!"

Frederick slapped him on the back. "Well done."

But he was looking at Jo. "And I would dae it again. One thousand times."

Pink crept onto the lady's cheeks before she excused herself and went to assist her man.

"I believe you're quite smitten with our master gunner." Frederick smiled at the surgeon.

"Aye, she's a bonny lass. But she says I drink tae much."

Frederick rubbed the back of his neck. "She does have a point, you know."

Brodie patted his waistcoat where he'd hid his flask and laughed. "Weel, I suppose she does."

A wind, ripe with brine and salt, blasted over them and Frederick took a deep breath. "How did you end up in the West Indies? 'Tis a long way from Scotland."

"Aye." He squinted into the sun. "Had a row wit' my da an' went off tae war. Jacobite rebellion. Battle of Cromdale,

1690. It didna go weel. The British captured me…sent me to Barbados as an indentured servant."

Frederick assumed as much from what he'd heard, but it still surprised him.

"My master was good tae me, but then he turned me in tae the governor fer bein' sympathetic tae the French."

Sails thundered above as the brig veered slightly to larboard. "Sympathetic?"

"I treated a group of French sailors who shipwrecked on the island, an' I didna tell the authorities. But that wasna the real reason." Brodie scratched the stubble on his chin. "His wife didna hide her interest in me, if ye know what I mean." He grinned.

Frederick raised a brow. "I knew there had to be a woman involved."

"I ne'er touched her."

Frederick studied him for a moment. The man was many things, but he was no liar. "I believe you." The wind shifted and sails thundered above. "How did you escape?"

Brodie shrugged. "Wasna tae hard. The men were drunk who were transportin' me."

"And then Reena found you."

"Aye, right there by the docks." The brig heaved and Brodie gripped the taffrail.

"What about your parents? Do they know where you are?"

"Don't know. My da is a highland laird, so he might know."

"A lord?"

"Aye, you wouldna thought I come from wealth an' title, eh?" He grinned.

Nay, Frederick wouldn't have, but people never ceased to amaze him. Leaning on the railing, he watched the gurgling wake spread out toward the golden horizon. "I used to be just like you. Ladies' man, heavy drinker, seeking adventure."

"That's what Captain Reena said. But somethin' changed ye."

"'Twas God. He gave me a new purpose in life—a much better purpose—and He wiped the dirt from my soul."

Casting a glance over his shoulder at Jo, Brodie plucked the flask from his pocket and took another sip. "I'm not good enough fer sich a lady as Jo."

"You should tell her how you feel."

"Mibbe one day." He slipped the flask back in his pocket.

Michael dashed up to him, his eyes bright, his light hair askew. "Can you read the Bible to me again, Captain Carlton?"

Though Frederick's own eyes felt like anchors, he couldn't help but smile. A grand idea. He must grab any chance he had to share the good news, and he loved having an enthusiastic student.

Retrieving his Bible, he sat on a barrel on the main deck and read from the book of John, one of his favorites. Michael listened with rapt attention, asking appropriate questions loud enough for everyone close by to hear—as if he also was interested in saving these sailors. Curious.

Afterward, the lad ran off to his duties while Frederick leapt up the quarterdeck to assist Abraham. The quartermaster quickly relinquished command and stepped to the side, though Frederick had not requested it. Yet, standing there with the wind blasting over him, the brig heaving beneath him, and the smell of oak, tar and the sea in his nose, it felt good to be at the helm once again. The crew respected him, listened to him when he shouted orders, just like old times when he was the captain of this very brig. And though he had not slept last night, he felt renewed and exhilarated by the sparkling sea and majestic sails.

Michael leapt on deck again, a basin of water in his hands, and proceeded to move among the men, offering a ladle to each sailor he passed. Some took it freely. Most did not. Odd, since there was a barrel of rum-tainted water on the main deck for all to partake of at will.

Frederick leaned toward Abraham. "Why is Michael doing that?"

"Doin' wha', Cap'n?"

"Giving all the men a drink from that basin."

Abraham's gaze landed on the boy. "I don't see no basin o' water, Cap'n. Mebbe yuh better get some sleep." He chuckled.

Frederick rubbed his eyes and looked again. Michael stood talking with Jo, nothing in his hands. Indeed. He must be seeing things. Or was he?

Reena was in the one place on earth she longed to be—in Freddy's arms. She felt his warm embrace, his gentle caress, his lips on her forehead. He uttered words of love, called her "Kitten," and made her feel more safe than she had in a long, long while. If this was a dream, she wished she would never wake.

Yet… something outside her bliss—something important—beckoned her.

Sunlight angled over her eyelids as her bed swayed back and forth. The creak and groan of wood and swoosh of sea penetrated the gentle huff of Freddy's breath. His loving words faded. Nay! She must dive back into her slumber where Freddy awaited, where he held her…where he loved her again.

But a nagging thought slapped away the dense fog in her mind—the map! She had to remember it, write it down. With much difficulty she pried open her eyes. Her cabin blurred before her. Freddy was gone. With even more difficulty, she pushed herself to sit. A thousand brands seared across her back as if she were being marked as property by *many* masters. Tears pooled in her eyes, and she bit her lip. Carefully she swung her legs over the side. She was Reena Charlisse Hyde, Captain of the *Reckless*. And she could handle pain as well as any pirate captain.

Grimacing, she pushed from the bed and stood. The deck tilted. She stumbled but caught herself. Air from the hatch above swirled over her, pricking her stripes, causing new pain to rise. She swallowed down a shriek and made her way to the desk, grabbed a quill pen, dipped it in ink, and quickly sketched what she remembered—most of the shapes and the rhyme. The only thing she didn't recall were the shapes within the arc in the top left corner.

Fred chirped his greeting from his perch, and she tickled him with the feathers of her quill pen. He bobbed his head up and down and squawked even louder.

The door creaked open. Her heart sped up, hoping it might be Freddy. But it was Jo, smiling at her as she approached.

"I'm 'appy to see ye awake, Cap'n." She cocked a brow. "I figured ye wouldn't stay abed fer long, so I came to 'elp ye get dressed."

Kind lady. Setting down the pen, Reena smiled at her friend, only then noticing that the shirt she wore was not only ripped down the back but torn in several places in the front. Who of her crew had seen her state of undress? More importantly, why was she horrified at the thought? She'd never been one for modesty.

Jo grabbed Reena's wrist, held it for a moment, then released it. "No fever. Good. I'll call fer Brodie to look at yer wounds afore ye get dressed."

"No need. Help me on with a clean shirt."

Jo gave her a look of reprimand but did what she said.

It hurt. More than Reena revealed, but she finally had on a new shirt, clean breeches, and she even managed to ease into a waistcoat.

Michael entered with a mug of hot chocolate and a smile on his face.

"Ah, you are a Godsend, Michael. You always know what I need."

Michael said nothing, merely gave her his usual caring smile as he approached.

"What time is it?" Reena glanced toward the stern windows, blinking at the sunlight reflecting off the sea.

Jo gathered Reena's discarded clothes. "Ye slept the day away, Cap'n. It be near evenin'."

"Who's captaining the ship?"

"Captain Carlton." Michael handed her the steaming cup. "And he's doing a fine job."

Indeed. Due to the rush of the sea against the hull, he must have the *Reckless* at full sail. The deck tilted, and planting her boots apart, she made her way to the windows and scanned the horizon, sipping her hot chocolate. "We're heading west."

"Aye," Jo said. "Abraham set a course fer Jamaica."

"Jamaica?" Pain etched across her back, and she leaned a hand on the stern window seat. That would never do.

Jo appeared beside her and grabbed her cup before it spilled. "Ye need to rest, Cap'n."

Michael nodded. "Captain Carlton has it well in hand."

"That's what I'm afraid of." Turning, Reena hobbled to her desk, blinked back the pain, and studied her charts. "Turn the brig around at once."

"For what purpose?" Freddy's deep voice preceded him ducking and entering the cabin. Abraham followed, rubbing sleepy eyes.

Reena did her best to stand straight and lift her shoulders. "To retrieve the last and final map."

"Are you feverish, woman? You don't have the last one." Freddy came to feel her forehead.

She backed away, not wanting to quarrel with him, not wanting to dissolve the tender moments they shared last night. His eyes sharpened like emeralds, and she longed to please him, to give him whatever he wanted... if only he would cherish her forever.

"I got a good look at it before Antoine snatched it away. I remember the shapes and the rhyme."

She felt his displeasure heat the air between them before he released a heavy sigh. He gave her a look of chagrin and grabbed that infernal cross around his neck. "Blast your good memory, Reena! We are well on our way to Jamaica. I *will* get off near Kingston and then you can sail on whatever ludicrous adventure you please. You owe me at least that for saving your life."

Michael gazed excitedly up at Freddy. "Adventures are sometimes a good thing, Captain Carlton, aren't they? Even Jesus went on great adventures and many others in the Bible."

Fred flapped his wings. "Bring me that horizon!"

"See, the boy and Fred agree." Reena smiled.

Freddy gave her a pointed look.

Abraham shook his head. "Dere be a way what seemeth right t' a man, but de end dereof be death."

Freddy nodded toward the quartermaster.

Jo gave a ladylike snort.

Fred darted back and forth on his perch. "Death t' all mutineers!"

Picking up the other maps, Reena spread them on her desk, then added the third one she sketched from memory. "See." She pointed to it. "If you put maps two and three together, the entire string of islands becomes clearer. This has to be Barbados. I remember the red X on the spot where Bridgetown sits."

"*If* you remembered correctly." Freddy glanced at the map, while Abraham and Jo stepped closer. "'Twas dark, and you've been a bit dazed."

Ignoring him, she flattened her lips. "My memory is perfect. Just this section"—she pointed to the top left corner—"I can't seem to recall."

"Hmm." Abraham crossed arms over his chest. "Mebbe it be Barbados, mebbe not. But it be a big island. How d'ye know what yer lookin' fer?"

"Exactly," Freddy added.

Michael found Reena's cup of hot chocolate and handed it to her. She sipped it, relishing the rich flavor that always seemed to sooth her nerves.

"Ye should be in bed," Brodie said as he entered the cabin and cast a smile at Jo, who was on her way out.

"I'm all right. Quit your fussing." Though in truth, Reena was in quite a bit of pain at the moment. But the Fountain of Youth was so close, she could hardly give up now. "I remember the rhyme." She glanced over them all. "Come all who are thirsty, come to the waters, the walls may be crumbling, but the children are singing, the key is tied and bound."

Freddy snorted. "You remember all that from just a glance?"

Reena lifted her nose. "I do. And I also know enough of the Bible to know part of it comes from there."

Abraham nodded. "From de prophet Isaiah."

Brodie angled around Reena's desk to stand behind her. "I should check on yer bandages."

She waved him off with her hand.

"Thirsty for rum…thirsty for rum." Fred squawked.

Reena tossed him a slice of mango as the *Reckless* lurched over a wave.

"Ergo," she continued. "I'm thinking we are looking for a church."

"No doot a church wit' wee ones." Brodie moved to her sideboard and poured himself some rum.

"An old church," Michael piped in.

"Can't be too hard to find an old church with lots of children." Reena smiled at the lad and finished her chocolate before setting down the mug.

Abraham cocked his head. "Dis Antoine, won't he be headin' t' de same place?"

"Nay." Reena gave a victorious grin. "He doesn't have the other two maps. See,"—she pointed to where maps two and three intersected—"He may figure out 'tis a church he seeks, but he won't know the island."

Fred flapped his wings. "'Tis a fool's errand!"

"I quite agree," Freddy added.

"We are much closer to Barbados than Jamaica." Reena dared to glance at Freddy, afraid of the fury she'd find on his face. But other than his tight jaw and the fact that he stared out the stern windows, she couldn't discern his thoughts.

"Abraham, bring us about on a south-southeast course," she ordered.

Abraham gave Freddy a look of sympathy before he said, "Aye, Cap'n," and headed out the door.

"Weel, that be my signal tae leave." Brodie slammed his drink to the back of his throat and made haste to the door, no doubt hoping to miss the ensuing argument.

Reena didn't want to look at Freddy, for she knew she'd find no trace of the affection, the care, the tenderness she'd seen last night. But she didn't have to look at him to hear the fury in his tone.

"You *will* drop me off on Jamaica posthaste, Reena. This has gone far enough. I am not going to watch you get yourself killed for a foolish notion of eternal youth when you have eternity already in your grasp."

Reena had forgotten Michael was still there, but he stood looking at Freddy with such an admiring grin, it appeared he agreed with the man.

"Michael, please inform Cook that I'm famished, and I'll have my meal in my cabin posthaste."

Fred flapped his wings. "We'll feast on our enemy's bones tonight!"

"Aye, Captain." The lad dashed off.

"You may join me if you wish, Freddy. In fact, I'd like that very much."

Commands echoed above them, along with the pounding of feet. Sails snapped, tackle rattled, and the *Reckless* veered heavily to starboard.

Reena clung to her desk while Freddy leaned a hand against the bulkhead. The *Reckless* was making its turn, sealing her fate.

He finally looked at her, his eyes flaming, his lips tight. He shifted his boots over the canting deck. "I have no intention of joining you, Reena. Unless you plan on taking me to Jamaica."

"I *am* planning on it. Just not quite yet." She tried to inject strength in her tone, but it came out flat.

"You think you're different from Antoine du Casse, but you're just like him."

The insult sliced through her heart, but she gave no outward indication.

"Mark my words, Reena Hyde." He took a step toward her, shadowing her with his height and width, making her feel like a little girl again. "I could very well rally the crew and steal your brig. You've seen me do it to other captains before."

Reena swallowed. Indeed, she had.

"But I won't do that to you. God will not allow me." He raked back his hair and sighed. "I will, however, leave you at Barbados. And if you should find yourself caught and about to be hanged this time, you will find no champion in me." Then, turning, he marched from the room.

And she knew she'd lost him. Most likely forever.

CHAPTER TWENTY-NINE

*P*erhaps he was far too exhausted. Or perhaps he was far too angry, but either way Frederick found it difficult to sleep. His mind tossed and turned like a ship on a stormy sea, bereft of sails, and hurled hither and thither with no particular course or direction. Right before he had finally drifted into slumber, he'd asked the Lord what he was doing here, and why he could not get off this brig! No answer had come. Instead, he had fallen into a fitful sleep from which he awoke nearly every hour. Abraham snored on the bunk beside him—peaceful, God-fearing Abraham. So unlike Frederick— who much like his father—was engulfed in a constant battle between light and dark, good and evil. Had his father ever really changed? Or did he continue to wage battles in his old age?

The ship tilted this way and that. Frederick dug his fingers into the hard wood of the deck. He'd slept on the floor for over a year now, punishing himself for his past, hoping the discomfort would somehow pay a small penance for his crimes. Instead, he found himself right back on the brig with Reena, doing things he ought not to be doing as a preacher—as the man of God he longed to be.

Wind whistled against the porthole like a funeral dirge— his funeral—and he drifted back to sleep yet again with a prayer for Reena on his lips.

Fires lit the landscape all around him. Giant holes opened in the earth like hungry mouths, spewing lava into the darkness. Flaming cannon balls pummeled the barren landscape in fiery explosions. Freddy stumbled forward, his bare feet hurrying over the simmering coals of scorched earth. Thirsty. He was so thirsty! His throat was a rope, thick and scratchy. A blast of torrid wind scalded him, nearly pushing him over. But the worst thing of all were the screams—the agonizing cries, the sobs of despair, the howls of horror. They came from all around. Yet he could see no one.

He knew this place well. He'd visited once before.

Hell.

Terror like he'd never known threatened to crush him. Had he died? Was this to be his eternal destiny? Inching his way forward, he groped in darkness so thick it weighed heavy on his very soul. Another flame spurted from the ground, flashing light on the dreadful scene. And all the while Frederick made a desperate appeal to God—prayed that this was merely another vision. But why would God give him another dream of this horrid place? The last time he had dreamed of hell, the first thing he'd done upon waking was to say goodbye to Reena, get off the *Reckless,* make his way to his parents, and repent of everything he'd ever done wrong. Then, he'd rededicated his life to his Savior—the One who'd died in his place so Frederick would never have to endure such eternal torture.

The dream had shaken him to his core. And was doing so again. People appeared, wandering listlessly about. If you could call them people. Scars, open sores, huge lumps, and cysts covered skin that clung to skeletons that were twisted and malformed—as if all their sins had grown on them like malignant cancers, twisting and bending them out of shape. Some screamed and hissed at him. Others laughed and writhed on the ground as if they'd lost their minds. Still others wandered, sobbing, calling for loved ones, calling for anyone who would listen. But none of them could get close enough to speak a word to anyone else. Friends were within reach, but yet forever too far away. The comfort and love of friends and family only came from God.

And there was nothing of God in this place.

He tried to wake himself up, pinched himself until the pain was unbearable, hit himself in the head. But still he remained. Perhaps he was really here. A massive ball of fire shot through the air and landed a foot from him. The ground shook and flames flew at him. Dropping to the ground, he rolled to extinguish the sparks. His skin sizzled. Pain, so much pain!

Leaping up, he darted away, only to nearly fall into a hole that suddenly opened in the earth. He backed away. More flames shot forth. Hunger clawed his stomach, yet he knew that it would never be satisfied, for food came from God.

And there was none of God in this place.

Nor would he find light or flowers or grass or sunshine or water or the gorgeous Caribbean sea he loved so much. Neither would he find smiles, love, warm embraces, kind words, gentleness, goodness, patience, for all these things came from God. And every one of these tormented people had chosen not to accept God's free gift of salvation. Hence, they got what they chose—eternal separation from God and all His goodness.

Halting, Frederick glanced across the burning horizon, remembering so clearly the horror he'd felt the last time he'd been here. Still, when he'd awakened and ran back into God's arms, 'twas not out of fear. Nay, experiencing hell clearly revealed how wonderful God truly was, and Frederick couldn't get away from his wicked life fast enough.

A familiar scream scraped across his ears and tore at his soul. Hurrying in that direction, he came to an abrupt stop before a lake that extended as far as the eye could see. Not a lake of water, but one of liquid fire. Arms and legs flailed in the dancing flames as people struggled to get to shore. The scream blasted over him again, drawing his gaze. *Reena*! She slapped at the blaze surrounding her. Her head disappeared beneath the surface. Frederick charged forward to save her, but the fire engulfed him. Pain ravaged his body. Her head appeared again. Her hair was ablaze, her skin on fire and melting right in front of him.

"Reena!"

Frederick jerked to a sitting position. His breath came hard and fast. Sweat trickled down his forehead and neck.

"Are you alright, Captain Carlton?"

He rubbed his eyes and found Michael staring at him curiously. A wave of shame flooded him as he stood to his feet and ran a sleeve over his face. "Aye, lad. A bad dream 'tis all."

"You called the captain's name so loud, I thought perhaps she was in here with you. Or perhaps you were angry with her like you were last night."

Frederick grimaced. He had hoped he'd hidden his anger from the boy. Some witness for God he was.

"I brought water." Moving to the only table in the room, Michael poured water from his pitcher, then dipped a cloth in it and handed it to Frederick. "I don't blame you, Captain. She vowed to take you to Jamaica. But I know her. She'll end up taking you there as she promised."

"I hope you're right, Michael." Frederick ran the cloth over his neck, then moved to the basin.

"Are you sure you're not ill? You look pale."

Frederick splashed water on his face. "Aye." Embarrassed at his outburst, terrified by his dream, but not ill.

"Can I fetch you some tea, Captain, something to break your fast?"

Why was the boy being so kind when all Frederick wanted was for him to leave? He glanced out the porthole where the sun seemed awfully bright for dawn. "What time is it?"

"Almost noon, Captain. We should be at Barbados in an hour or two."

Frederick growled. He hadn't meant to sleep so long.

"Are you going to go ashore with the captain?" Michael asked excitedly.

In truth, following Reena on her quest was the last thing Frederick intended to do. He'd rather risk getting caught by the Royal Navy as he procured passage on another ship than risk his eternal soul with the likes of Reena Hyde.

Mayhap that was the message of the dream. Repent, return to God, and get as far away from Reena as he could.

"You should go with her." Michael said so matter-of-factly that Frederick turned to stare at him.

"And why is that?"

"Though she won't admit it, she needs you."

The boy said the words with such authority and yet such peace, it gave Frederick pause. Who was this young lad who seemed to possess an eternity of wisdom? Even now, his expression bore true humility. And something else—a confidence that came from truth.

Spinning back around, Frederick grabbed a towel and dried his face. He had no idea what he was going to do. He needed to pray and find out exactly what the nightmare meant. Mayhap it was merely to inform him that it was too late for Reena, and he should give up on her.

Nay. One thing he knew about God, as long as someone had breath, 'twas never too late.

Michael left, and Frederick lowered to sit on the cot and dropped his head in his hands. "Lord, what do You want me to do? Whatever it is, I will do it."

Several minutes passed as the sea gushed against the hull and sails thundered overhead. Frederick sought the answer deep within his spirit where God's Spirit lived. "I don't want her to go to hell, Lord."

Then help her.

It was more of a sensation than words, but it came through loud and clear.

Perhaps he was hearing things, making things up in his mind. "Lord, are you sure? You want me to stay with her and help her?"

The brig rose and plunged over a wave, its timbers creaking in protest.

Yes.

The voice was still and small.

Frederick released a deep sigh. "Father, I will obey. But just so you know, I am the last person who should be leading this woman to the light."

CHAPTER THIRTY

*T*hree things weighed heavy on Reena's mind as she stepped from the wobbly dock onto the sandy streets of Bridgetown. One, she felt ridiculous in the petticoats, mantua, and stomacher she'd forced herself to don, while at the same time, she felt completely naked without her weapons. Two was what Freddy had said about her being like Antoine. At the time, she had wanted to defend herself…to come up with a list of things which proved they were nothing alike, but she'd been hard-pressed to find any major difference in the areas that counted. Aye, she wanted to be a pirate, to live an adventurous life, but she was not someone who killed, lied, and cheated her way to get what she wanted. Was she? At least not to her friends. But hadn't she done that very thing to Freddy? The third thing that bothered her was Freddy walking beside her. Not that she was upset about the new development, but it completely baffled her. He had marched out of her cabin in such a defiant rage, vehemently declaring he would never join her on her madcap adventures. Yet, here he was, fully armed, and marching beside her on their way to find the church wherein lay the final clue to the location of the Fountain.

Abraham marched on her other side. She'd kept the shore party small so as not to attract attention, but also because Brodie might be recognized on the island where he'd been an indentured servant.

"Thought you didn't want anything to do with my foolish quest," she finally said to Freddy as they wove amongst wagons, carriages, and people mobbing the street. Afternoon sun simmered in hot waves off cobblestones and tin roofs.

"I don't." Taking her elbow, he led her around a pile of steaming horse droppings. "But you have a penchant for stepping in things you ought not, eh? Besides, I will have to answer to your parents, and I do not relish Captain Merrick's displeasure."

Reena glanced back at the manure and smiled.

Abraham chuckled.

Reena continued, "Alas, the truth comes out. Your care stems merely from an obligation to my parents."

He didn't answer. Instead, he proceeded, gaze shifting over the street as if looking for danger. He'd tied his hair behind him and donned a clean shirt, breeches, and a large floppy hat, no doubt hoping to appear less like a pirate and more like a preacher. But the cutlass strapped to his side and the pistol in his brace spoke otherwise.

A breeze tugged at the bun Jo had hastily pinned atop Reena's head and wafted the scents of tar, brine, wood smoke, and roasted pig around her. She shifted her back against renewed pain. Though Brodie had done his best to bandage her wounds, they still hurt every time she moved.

"Enough talk. Let us focus on finding this church," Freddy finally said.

His harsh tone bit another chunk out of her heart. She lifted her chin. "Henceforth, I relieve you of any obligation you may feel toward me, Freddy. I have no need of your protection or help." Reena yanked her elbow away, hastened her pace, and stepped onto a wooden walkway that extended along a string of stores, nearly bumping into a woman coming out of the weavers.

"Pardon," she shot back over her shoulder as she passed the apothecary, from which a plethora of bitter odors emanated.

Two Royal Naval officers strode down the street, just yards from them.

"Apparently you do," Freddy dipped his head beneath the shadows of his large hat.

"You shouldn't have come," she shot back. Not only was the city flooded with navy sailors but there was a Royal Navy Frigate and a three-decker 100-gun ship anchored in Carlisle Bay.

"And who's fault is it that I am here?" He snipped in return.

"He's got a point," Abraham said.

Reena passed the pottery house and stepped out onto the street again, anger flaring. Halting, she stabbed Freddy with her finger. "I rescued you from unending dullness and misery, and this is the thanks I get." Grabbing her skirts, she proceeded down the street. "Besides, I didn't ask you to come ashore. Hence, please do me the favor of not getting yourself caught."

She thought he'd be mad at her outburst. Instead he flashed her a witty grin. "Your concern cuts me to the quick, Kitten."

Black smoke from the coal forge puffed into the street, and Reena skirted it, coughing. Bare-chested slaves carried crates and barrels down to the docks, a sheen of sweat covering their ebony skin. She glanced at Abraham and found his sorrowful gaze locked upon them. If she could, she'd rescue all of them and give them positions on her brig. She may be a pirate, but being a slave owner was a far more cruel and sinful profession.

An ocean breeze spun around them, giving them a brief reprieve from the harsh sun, but also bringing the stench of spirits and sweat to Reena's nose. Up ahead, a band of men approached—sailors from the looks of them—their skin leathered, hair tied back, colorfully-attired, their swords and knives gleaming in the sun. They leered at Reena as if anticipating their next meal.

Freddy grabbed her arm and slipped it through his, glaring at the band. "You should have brought more men with you," he said.

"We are going to a church. I doubt there's going to be any trouble."

Freddy laughed, and Abraham joined him. "Dere's always trouble where yuh be, Cap'n."

"Indeed." Freddy's laughter faded, and he grabbed her elbow and tugged her to a stop. "How do we know where this church is?"

She gave him a sweet smile. "I merely had to get us to a better part of town." She glanced after the ruffians and frowned. Their presence certainly did much to disparage her statement. Drawing a deep breath, she glanced over the street. "Follow my lead." Clutching her skirts, she crossed the cobblestones, avoiding a passing carriage, and halted before a lady and gentleman—a very posh-looking couple who by all appearances were the epitome of politeness and decency.

The lady carried a parasol fringed in lace and wore a lovely walking dress of blue taffeta. White ruffles protruded from the gentleman's dark coat, while a waterfall of Mechlin lace bubbled at his neck.

Reena smiled at the woman. "Begging your pardon, if you please. We are new in town and seek a church. And you seem like God-fearing people."

This brought a huge smile to the man's face. "Why, yes, there are three fine churches in town. I assume you and your"—the man eyed Freddy with suspicion, then barely afforded a glance toward Abraham, who stood behind them.

"My husband," Reena slipped her hand in Freddy's.

"Ah, yes," the man said, and tapped his cane on the wood. "You are close to St. Michael's. 'Tis just over—"

"Nay." Reena waved her fan about her neck. "We seek a particular church. 'Tis rather old and has a large number of children associated with it."

The woman's delicate brow furled as she looked up at her husband who also was frowning. Finally his eyes widened. "You must refer to the old church on Roebuck at the edge of town. But I fear 'tis no longer a church, but rather an orphanage run by an elderly couple. What were their names, dear?" he asked his wife.

"The Radcliffs." The lady wiggled her nose. "A rather odd couple, if you ask me. Religiously extreme, but kind enough, I suppose."

"Thank you," Reena said. "I believe they are the very people we seek." She dipped her head and Freddy also thanked them before they started on their way again.

The scent of the sea mixed with loamy earth drifted beneath her nose as they turned on Roebuck and started up a small hill. Shops and warehouses dwindled away, leaving thick palms, sandbox trees, ferns, and vines encroaching upon the street on either side. Cobblestones gave way to sand. The song of a myriad birds sang from the green web, along with the sound of water trickling and the buzz of insects.

Just when Reena thought the posh couple had led them astray, a strange but wonderful sound joined the cacophony—children's laughter.

The joyous music infused strength into Reena's weary legs, and she hastened forward, rounded a corner, and caught a glimpse of a large stone building with a steepled roof and a bell tower. A large rusted bell that looked as though it hadn't been rung in years hung within. To the right of the crumbling structure, a garden covered the ground, bearing all manner of vegetables, while mango trees and plantains grew along the front of the property. Beyond the garden in an open space, an older lady was pulling a bucket from a well. Upon hearing them approach, she looked up and smiled, then grabbed the bucket and headed their way, baffling Reena.

For all the woman knew, they were here to murder them and take everything they had. Especially the way Freddy was armed.

"How can I help you fine people today?" the woman asked.

"We heard about your orphanage," Reena said. "And all the good you are doing and wished to pay a visit." 'Twas a ridiculous reason, but it was all she could come up with at the moment.

The woman smiled, creating creases beside her eyes and mouth. Short in stature, and round in figure, she wore a simple green cotton gown that was ripped across one sleeve. Stark blue eyes—that appeared younger than she obviously was—stared at Reena in confusion for a moment. "You are certainly welcome, though there's not much to see here 'cept an old couple an' lots of young'uns." She shifted her gaze to Freddy and then to Abraham, then down to the cutlass at Freddy's side.

Casting a frown at Reena, he stepped forward. "In truth, Madam, we need to look inside the church. There may be something hidden within that belongs to us."

Blast his honesty! Reena elbowed him in the ribs before she remembered his injury. Thankfully his groan was barely perceptible as he gently laid a hand over his chest.

Clearing her throat, she smiled at the woman. "Aye, we seek a map. It might be tied and bound somewhere inside your church. 'Twas left to me by one of my ancestors."

Abraham humphed.

Reena braced herself for the woman ordering them off her property. If she thought the map had value, she would never agree to allow them inside. Then, they'd have to wait until nightfall to sneak within.

Instead, the woman held out her hand. "My name's Mabel Radcliff. My husband and I bought this old church"—she glanced back at it fondly—"twenty years past. The pastor had left it vacant and it were being used by orphans and widows."

"Are you preachers then?" Freddy's tone bore excitement.

"Us?" She chuckled. "Nay. We's jist servants of God."

"I'm Reena Hyde, and this is Frederick Carlton and Abraham."

"Please t' meet you all."

Just then, a small boy no older than five darted up to the lady, grabbed her hand, and started to pull her away. "Ms. Radcliff, Ms. Radcliff, come see…come see what we've done."

The child barely glanced at them in his excitement. "You'll have to excuse me," she said. "Please come and meet my husband and the children." She laughed as the child continued to pull her along.

Following the woman, Reena leaned toward Freddy. "You shouldn't have told her we were looking for something."

"Honesty is always best, Reena. Besides, what did you expect them to do when we start rummaging around their church? They seem like decent people."

"Most people are not decent," Reena retorted. "I learned that the hard way."

They rounded a corner to the back of the church that opened up to a huge meadow framed by thick jungle on all sides. A bubbling creek cut across the grassy field dotted with wildflowers. *And* children. At least thirty of them—some barely walking, to others at least ten years of age—laughing and playing in wild abandon. Some kicked a ball to each other, a group of girls sat in the grass smelling flowers, while an older man taught a young lad how to chop wood.

Upon seeing his wife, the man stopped, wiped sweat from his brow, lowered his ax, and approached, reaching out for her. He took her hands in his, kissed her cheek, and uttered some ridiculous compliment about how her beauty outdid every flower in the field. Reena could only stare at the exchange in wonder.

Mrs. Radcliff blushed, then turned to introduce them. "Evan, this is Miss Hyde, Mr. Carlton, and Mr. Abraham."

It did not escape Reena's notice that the woman introduced Abraham with the same respect as any white man. Most people would have merely ignored his presence. And Reena found she already liked this lady and her husband who looked at his wife as if she were made of precious jewels.

Freddy shook the man's hand. "We didn't mean to take you from your duties." He nodded toward the church behind them. "I realize this is an imposition and quite unseemly, but if you would grant us permission to search your church, we won't be long, and we promise not to disturb anything or take anything that is not ours."

Reena wanted to laugh. No one in their right mind would allow strangers to search their home.

Mabel turned to her husband. "They believe an old family relic is hidden in our church. Isn't that fascinating?"

The man studied them each in turn, and Reena got the sensation he was looking far deeper than their mere appearance. "Where did you say it's hidden?"

"We do not know," Reena offered. "All we were told was that it's tied and bound."

Suspicion briefly made an appearance in the old man's eyes, but then he glanced over his shoulder at the children and shrugged. "Search all you wish. 'Tis an old building." He chuckled. "'Sides, we ain't got nothin' o' value."

Hiding her shock, Reena smiled. "That is most kind of you."

Thunder exploded out of nowhere and shook the ground. Lightning forked white-hot across the dark sky. Startled, Reena glanced up to see ominous, black clouds that weren't there a minute ago. Rain fell hard and heavy as if a dam had broken in the heavenlies. Screeching, Mrs. Radcliff grabbed her skirts and ran to the field shouting, "Children! Come in, hurry!" Mr. Radcliff joined her and together they herded the little ones back to the church like mother hens protecting their only chicks.

Reena scanned the field, still stunned by the sudden storm. She caught a glimpse of a small child, no older than two, crying at the edge of the field, heading toward the jungle. Thunder shook sky and land, and the poor babe cried even louder. Without thinking, Reena charged across the sodden meadow, her shoes sinking into the mud. Rain pelted her face and neck, her damp skirts tangled in her legs, but she slogged forward, nearly at the child now. "Come, little one! You are safe!" she shouted, reaching for the babe. Her foot struck something hard. Pain set her ankle on fire. She tumbled forward and landed in the mud with a splat.

Freddy's face filled her vision. Rain flattened his hair against his cheeks and dripped from his eyelashes. "Are you all right? Here." He circled her and thrust his arms beneath hers.

Lightning lit up the sky.

He tried to lift her, but the throbbing in her ankle shot up her leg and into her back, igniting further agony from her wounds. Ashamed of her incompetence, Reena withheld the cry of pain and instead pointed to the child, who was still crying and edging closer to the jungle.

"Wait here." Freddy dashed for the babe and swooped her up in his arms.

Mr. Radcliff came running and took the child from Freddy. "Better get her inside!" he yelled over the storm.

And before she knew it, Reena found herself in Freddy's arms as he sloshed across the field and into the church.

"I swears on me mother's grave, it be 'im." Sedley fumbled with his hat and glanced over his shoulder out the door. "'Is name be Frederick Carlton. Used t' be a pirate and then joined the Royal Navy. 'E were on HMS *Viper* when it were docked at Antigua." Being a pirate himself, Sedley didn't feel safe at the Royal Naval base at Bridgetown.

The man behind the desk had barely afforded Sedley a glance when he'd entered and the lieutenant announced him as having some vital information on a recent deserter.

Setting down his quill pen, the man stood, adjusted his blue coat, and finally gazed at Sedley with dark, brooding eyes. "And how would you come by this information?"

"'E boarded my mistresses' ship, *Reckless*."

He guffawed, nearly spitting in the process. "Isn't the *Reckless* a pirate ship?"

A tremble ran through Sedley, tying his tongue in a knot. Perhaps he shouldn't have come, but Antoine's promise of fortune…well, Sedley had ne'er had more than two shillings to his name.

"Which makes *you* a pirate." The officer gestured to the guard standing at the door.

"Nay, Sir…I mean, Captain. I escaped. She kept me captive. I were a mere sailor on a merchant ship when she captured our ship and took me 'ostage. I swears it." Sweat broke out on the back of his neck.

"A *woman* pirate captain?" The captain rubbed his chin. "So the rumors *are* true."

"Aye, and a fierce one she be at that."

"If she is so fierce, how did you escape?"

"Made a friend on board an' while she went ashore, 'e freed me."

The captain expelled a deep sigh and turned to face his window. "And where is this deserter now?"

Sedley smiled and licked his lips. "I can lead ye right to 'im."

CHAPTER THIRTY-ONE

A musty, sweet smell that reminded Reena of frankincense filled her nose as Freddy carried her inside the church—a holy, aged smell of old books, beeswax, and the sweet innocence of children. By the time Freddy set her down on a bench, Mrs. Radcliff had resurrected a fire in the hearth. The flames leapt and danced, crackling and sending out a warmth that drew the children around. Mr. Radcliff set the toddler down with them, and together, he and his wife began taking off the children's wet attire and wrapping them in warm blankets.

The quaint sanctuary exuded a sense of peace that immediately settled Reena. Divots speckled the wooden floor where pews must have once stood. Small tables, chairs, and bedraggled couches took their place, while a dais, harboring an old altar and benches rose at one end. Above it, three stained glass windows depicting the birth, crucifixion, and resurrection of Christ let in a fair amount of light. Hence, no lanterns were needed during the day. Along the sides of the room, blankets, pillows, and straw mattresses lay stacked and ready to be pulled out for the children to sleep upon at night. To the left of the hearth, a door led to another room, and to the right, a wide arched doorway opened to an alcove wherein Reena could see shelves of books and an old desk.

Freddy knelt beside her, his hair dripping onto his sodden shirt and waistcoat. "Let me see your ankle."

"I'm quite all right." She pushed him away. "In truth, I feel like a fool. I can balance on a heaving ship, but I trip and fall running across a field." She sighed.

He gave her one of his beguiling grins, his eyes shifting between hers and making her insides warm. "Regardless of your pride, I should—" Lifting her skirts slightly, he attempted to remove her boot. Pain speared up her leg. Before she could help it, a screech flew from her mouth.

Freddy stopped. "Check it."

Gritting her teeth, she nodded, knowing he was right. Yet that knowledge did naught to quell the ensuing pain as he slid off her boot and set it aside.

He gently laid her stockinged foot in his lap and examined it. Even in the dim light, she could tell it was swollen. Thunder bellowed, shaking the old church and sprinkling dust upon them from the rafters above. Rain tapped on the roof like a thousand marching soldiers.

Freddy turned her foot to the side.

"Ouch!"

"Don't be such a swab." He smiled up at her, then grew serious. "How is your back?"

"Better than my ankle at the moment."

Mrs. Radcliff rushed over and knelt beside them. "Are you all ri', Miss? I'm so sorry you slipped. Let me tend t' you." She all but pushed Freddy away. "A gentleman should not be lookin' at a lady's ankle. Would you assist Mr. Radcliff, Mr. Carlton?"

Freddy seemed taken aback at first, but then nodded and headed toward the children.

Mrs. Radcliff pressed gently on Reena's tender flesh, and then turned her foot slightly left to right, all the while watching Reena bite her tongue to keep from crying out.

"You sprained it, my dear. But 'tis not a break. You must stay off your feet for a few days, an' it will mend itself." She struggled to rise. "I'll find bandages to wrap it and keep it in place."

"I can't stay off it," Reena appealed to no one in particular. "I must find what we're looking for and leave immediately."

Sympathy poured from the woman's soft brown eyes. "Ah, goose livers! Nothin' is ever that important, Miss. An' the good Lord controls our time. 'Sides." She glanced toward the windows where rain pelted the panes. "Even should you find what you seek, 'twill be night soon. You and your gentlemen friends are welcome t' stay. In fact, we insist." She glanced toward Mr. Radcliff, who was heading her way. "Isn't that right, Mr. Radcliff?"

"Aye. Please stay—Miss Hyde, were it?—until you are able to walk. In the meantime, Mrs. Radcliff will cook us a feast." Rubbing his hands together, he smiled lovingly at his wife, then winked at Reena. "You haven't had a good meal until you've tasted my wife's cookin'. I and the children will help your friends find this relic you seek."

Mr. Radcliff kissed his wife on the cheek, and they both skittered away, leaving Reena stunned in their wake. Aside from her own family, she'd never met anyone so kind, so generous and caring to complete strangers.

Within minutes, Mrs. Radcliff returned with a long string of bandages that she quickly wrapped around Reena's ankle, making it as stiff as possible. "Now, then." She studied Reena with concern. "You poor dear, you're soaked to the bone. Let me fetch you some dry clothing. 'Twill no doubt be too large for you." She glanced down at her rounded figure then over at Reena and chuckled.

"Nay." Reena held up a hand. "No need. Thank you. I'll sit by the fire and dry quickly." Besides, she didn't wish the woman to see the lashes on her back.

The woman *tsked* and gave her a motherly look that no doubt sent the children running to do her bidding. But then she sighed and called Abraham over to help.

All but lifting her from the ground, he ushered Reena to a stuffed chair on the right side of the hearth, though not without enduring a barrage of her complaints. She hated being weak. Hated she couldn't walk without help. But there was naught to be done for it at the moment.

Besides, she was glad for the warmth of the fire that penetrated her wet gown and evicted the chill in her bones.

Freddy glanced her way and smiled, but continued to move from child to child, exchanging sodden attire for dry, and wrapping blankets around others. She had never seen him with children before. For such a rough pirate, he certainly had a tender touch with these wee ones—offering them a smile, tussling their hair, and even causing a few to giggle. She shook off the vision and leaned toward Abraham, stooping by the fire to add another log.

"We must find the map and be gone as soon as possible," she whispered.

Abraham stared at the flames. "I like it here, Cap'n. Dere's a sense o' God's presence in dis church, an' de Radcliff's be wonderful people. Why not stay de night?"

"Because Antoine may very well be on his way here right now."

He looked at her. "He don't have de map."

"Nay, not the real ones. But he's cunning and always seems ahead of me somehow." Reena sighed as another blast of thunder rumbled across the roof.

The littlest of the children squealed, their wide eyes gazing above. Kneeling, Freddy took several in his arms and drew them close. A little girl, no more than three, grabbed Reena's leg. Terror streaked across her eyes as she stared up at her. A bouquet of black curls surrounded an angelic face with skin the color of Reena's hot chocolate.

Unsure what to do, Reena patted the girl's back. "'Twill be okay. Naught to fear."

The child leapt into her arms, taking her by surprise. Reena had never been good with children, but as the trembling girl clung to her, she couldn't help but wrap her arms around her and squeeze tight. The poor thing shivered, her tiny frock wet and cold. Had they not changed her yet? "You are safe, little one."

"My name is Evie," the girl said without looking up.

"Very well, Evie. I'm Reena." Wind banged against the windows and whistled around the old stone walls as the rain continued to pound entrance into the warm church. The girl whimpered, and Reena looked over at Abraham and found him smiling at her. She wanted to ask how one calmed down a frightened child, but why would he know such a thing? A song, perhaps? Her mother used to sing to Reena when she was frightened. An old tune came to mind, and she hummed, drawing the gaze of several children.

After a few minutes, Evie melted in her arms.

"Come here, Evie." Mr. Radcliff appeared before them. "We must change you into somethin' dry before dinner." The man had quite the trouble prying the poor girl from Reena, but finally she relinquished her hold and smiled at Reena as the man ushered her away.

Gazing after the girl, Reena wondered if she would ever have children of her own. Which drew her focus to Freddy, holding a young lad in his lap. A longing filled her, a longing for a different life than the one she had planned. But 'twas a fantasy, a dream. For the life of a wife and mother was naught but hard work and sacrifice and one that aged a woman before her time.

"Help me up, Abraham, I wish to search." She lifted her hand and the quartermaster stood and assisted her. Leaning on his meaty arm, Reena kept weight off her bad ankle, though just the movement caused it to throb.

"May I look around a bit, Mr. Radcliff?"

He looked up from Evie. "Of course, Miss, but you shouldn't be on that foot." He raised a gray eyebrow.

"Abraham will assist me."

She thought she heard Freddy grunt.

Ignoring him and the pain in her ankle, she hobbled around the sanctuary. If she'd remembered the rhyme correctly, the map was tied and bound and had something to do with water. She looked for a basin, perhaps one used to baptize new converts, but found nothing of the sort. In truth, aside from the steeple and bell tower outside, the inside of the building looked naught like a church. Even the dais where the altar stood was filled with musical instruments meant for little hands.

With Abraham gripping her elbow, she felt her way around the walls, seeking any loose stones, though she doubted she would find the map hidden in the same way as the first one. Yet, this was a church, right? Shouldn't there be holy items lying about? Incense holders, cups for communion, tiny bells, vestments? In truth, she had no idea. All the church services she'd attended had been aboard the *Redemption* and were more like celebrations than solemn occasions.

She huffed out a sigh as Abraham, no doubt sensing her pain, wove around children and a dashing Mr. Radcliff, to a distant chair.

"What is upstairs?" she asked him as he passed.

Halting, he faced her and glanced up. "Storage—old books, farm tools, chairs, pots and pans. You're welcome to go up and see."

Reena accidentally put weight on her ankle, bit her lip, and fell into the chair in a huff of exasperation. "Would you mind if Abraham went up to look around?" She knew she was asking a great deal of these kind people, but how else to find the map?

Mr. Radcliff shrugged. "'Course not. There isn't anythin' o' value."

"You are most kind." Reena smiled up at the man, then turned to Abraham. "Look for something holy that has to do with water. Mayhap a baptismal."

One of the older children called for Mr. Radcliff.

"Nothin' like that up there," he said over his shoulder as he headed toward the child.

Abraham nodded and started off, disapproval in his eyes.

Thunder growled as if God were also displeased with her. Lightening flashed through the room. Her eyes wandered to Freddy comforting a small boy. In truth, she felt a pinch of jealousy at how much attention he was paying these children. She was the one with the twisted ankle! But that was selfish, wasn't it? And she could not deny that he was good with them. She smiled even now as two little ones crawled into his lap, and he embraced them as if they were his own.

The man was a dichotomy. Pirate, preacher, and now parent. Was there nothing he could not do and do well? So unlike her.

A delicious smell wafted into the room—all buttery and spicey and meaty.

Stomach rumbling, Reena set her foot up on another chair and tried to steady her anxious nerves. Was it the storm or being in this holy place that rattled her so? Nay, 'twas most likely being so close to the last piece of the puzzle that would make her dreams come true.

At least one of them. She glanced at her *other* dream, the man cuddling a group of children, and suddenly felt as if they were a world apart. The thought of losing him made her stomach fold in on itself. She could not.

She would not.

She leaned back in the chair and drew a deep breath, doing her best to keep her heavy eyelids from closing. They must have done so for a moment, for she jumped slightly at a touch to her leg. Blinking, she stared down at Evie. The girl said nothing, just lifted her arms toward Reena, and she felt a piece of her hardened pirate heart crack in two.

Smiling, she gathered the precious girl up in her arms and pressed her against her bosom, patting her hair. "Shh, 'tis just rain. 'Twill be over soon." A whimper escaped the girl's lips as she nestled against Reena. Embracing her even tighter, Reena glanced up and found Freddy smiling at her. Not a sarcastic or an *I-told-you-so* smile, but one that bore the admiration she had longed to see in those eyes for quite some time.

A group of children crowded around his feet. One little hand tugged on his breeches, drawing his gaze down. "Will you tell us a story, Mr. Carlton?"

And so he did. Gathering more of the wee ones around him, Freddy regaled them with a fascinating tale of pirates, mermaids, and sirens. Of course being a preacher, he had to interject God into everything. Hence, there was a fair share of miracles—raising the dead, calming the sea—along with angels and battles and a message of trusting in the Son of God for entrance into a heavenly kingdom.

The children loved it, staring at him with wide eyes. Mr. Radcliff smiled his approval as he went about lighting lanterns and candles against the encroaching night.

Descending the stairs, Abraham approached her, shaking his head, a look of remorse on his face, though she knew he cared not for the map. But he cared for her and that meant a great deal.

Soon Mr. Radcliff called the children to their seats around a large table, and he helped his wife deliver bowls of savory smelling stew to each one. Freddy brought a bowl to Reena, and she thought he might sit with her for the meal, but he sped off to assist the Radcliffs.

Forcing down her disappointment, she raised a spoonful of the meaty broth to her mouth when Mr. Radcliff cleared his throat. She glanced up, embarrassed, as he bowed his head and uttered the most heartfelt prayer she'd heard in a long while. He gave thanks for everything—the rain, the food, their humble home, their meager clothing—even though they barely had any possessions at all. How could this man be grateful to a God who provided them with so little?

Still, Mr. Radcliff had been right about one thing. The stew was the most delicious Reena had ever tasted, and she was sorry she was unable to help the woman clean up. But Mrs. Radcliff insisted she sit and heal her foot, waving a hand through the air, uttering that she'd done this task a thousand times before.

The storm finally passed, leaving naught but the sound of raindrops dripping from trees. As if to accompany the peaceful sound, Mr. Radcliff grabbed a fiddle, and together with his wife, led the children in song—old hymns that sounded familiar to Reena's ears. Freddy and Abraham joined in, and she found herself singing along as well. The joyous sound of little voices praising God filled the sanctuary, and Reena could not deny the cloak of peace and joy that settled over her. The candles even seemed to shine brighter, their glittering light dancing up to the rafters.

She shook away the sensations. She had a task to accomplish—an important task. As soon as her ankle stopped throbbing, she intended to search the entire church again.

In the meantime, Reena could hardly tear her gaze from Mr. and Mrs. Radcliff. They had to be well over sixty years, evidenced by the wrinkled skin that hung beneath their chin and jaw, their drooping eyelids, and gray, thinning hair. Mrs. Radcliff's youthful figure had plumped in some places and shriveled in others, while Mr. Radcliff bent over slightly and hobbled when he walked. Yet, they sat together on the couch, arm in arm. Mr. Radcliff whispered something in her ear, and she playfully slapped him and gazed up at him as if they were newlyweds. Then he did the strangest thing. He leaned over and kissed her full on the mouth. In fact they must've forgotten they had guests, for afterward, Mrs. Radcliff's eyes met hers across the room and a blush rose on her cheeks.

Reena had never seen the likes of such a thing—in a couple this old. Though, now that she thought about it, her own parents approached sixty. Memories surged of how affectionate they had always been with one another, and she wondered if they still were. Surely, you could still love someone in their old age, but feeling attraction and being affectionate was quite another thing. In truth, Reena enjoyed the looks she got from men, at least the respectable ones—the glances of admiration, appreciation, and even desire. All that would cease if she shriveled up in old age.

Finally, the singing stopped and the Radcliffs pulled out the bedding for the children.

Mrs. Radcliff approached, her face aflush and a smile on her lips. "How is your ankle, my dear? Do you need anythin'?"

Reena gestured for Abraham to help her stand. "Nay. Thank you. However, I was wondering…" She hesitated to impose on this woman's kindness further, almost hated herself for it. "Is there anything here—a statue, ornament, utensil— anything that was here when you first took over the church?"

Seemingly not put off at all, Mrs. Radcliff tapped her finger on her chin. "Not that I recall." She glanced over the room. "'Cept for the floors, walls, an' that altar over there. O' course we cook with the priest's utensils. Makes our food holy." She winked.

Abraham laughed.

Reena frowned. "Mayhap something small? An item you would never throw out. Something sacred?"

Mr. Radcliff looked up from where he was helping the children lay out the mattresses. "What 'bout that old Bible?"

Mrs. Radcliff nodded. "Aye. We found an old Bible. But I don't see how that could be what you're lookin' for. Lots of pages missin', some torn, others look as though they'd been scorched by fire. Can't hardly read it, neither, but we kept it, bein' a Bible an' all."

Reena's heart leapt within her. "Have you ever looked inside?"

"Jist peeked at it once. Didn't want any more pages to fall out."

"May I see it, please? You have my word I'll be careful."

Freddy approached and scoured her with a glare. "Nay. 'Tis too fragile. We wouldn't want to impose."

The old man gazed at his wife. "No imposition. I'll go fetch it." And off he hobbled up the cracked stone stairs.

Groaning. Freddy crossed arms over his chest, but she ignored him. 'Twas too important to worry about his displeasure.

The man returned, cradling a book in both hands as if it would crumble to dust at the slightest breath. A rope, tightly wrapped around it and knotted in front, held everything in place,

"Here 'tis, Miss. I do caution you t' be gentle."

"I will. Thank you, Mr. Radcliff." Tied and bound. 'Twas one of the clues!

No doubt as curious as she was, Abraham grabbed the lantern and sat beside her.

Oddly, the old Bible warmed in her hand—as if it were alive somehow. The leather cover was frayed and scratched so badly even the words Holy Bible could barely be made out. In all honesty, she feared to open it, feared that it would be the last sin on her list of sins that would seal her doom forever.

Freddy lowered to sit on her other side. "That has to be what you're looking for, Reena. Go ahead and open it."

She looked at him curiously. "Why would you say such a thing?"

He shrugged. "Should have figured it out. Something old and holy and filled with living water. That's the Word of God."

Reena remembered that Scripture well. She'd always wondered how words on the page could quench anyone's thirst. Taking a deep breath, she loosened the knot and opened the holy book. Pages crinkled and complained as if warning her not to continue. Gently, she flipped through them, carefully scanning each page. Mr. Radcliff was right. Whole chapters had been torn out, and some pages were burned on the edges.

Freddy leaned forward on his knees and stared at the floor as if not wanting to witness her blasphemy.

Finally, after what seemed like forever, she turned the page to the gospel of Matthew.

A piece of aged paper fluttered to the floor.

CHAPTER THIRTY-TWO

Frederick had just spent one of the most enjoyable afternoons and evenings in his remembrance. If ever there was a couple who exemplified God's grace, love, and generosity, it was Mr. and Mrs. Radcliff. They had not only shared their meager meal, opened their home to complete strangers, but they had allowed those strangers to rifle through their belongings. In addition, in their dotage, they cared for and loved orphaned children tirelessly day after day, sacrificing all their money, time, strength, and even sleep to ensure these wee ones grew up loved and knowing God.

In truth, after hanging out with pirates, they had restored Frederick's faith in mankind, for he'd truly begun to doubt whether there were any decent people left in the Caribbean.

God was in this place. Frederick could feel Him—the joy, peace, and love that only came when in the presence of the Almighty. Not to mention the angels. He'd seen at least three since he'd entered the church…hovering over the children, ministering to each one, blessing them, holding them in their arms when the Radcliffs were otherwise occupied. At first, Frederick thought they were merely helpers the Radcliffs had hired, but when he asked Mr. Radcliff how he could afford such assistance, the man had stared at Frederick oddly and insisted it was just him and his wife. After that, the angels drifted in and out of Frederick's vision, and each time, he thanked God for allowing him to see such things. These privileged peeks into the spirit realm bolstered his faith, kept him strong, kept him wanting to do the will of God more than anything else.

But exactly *what* His will was, Frederick wasn't sure.

He glanced over at Reena as she sat at a table, the new map spread out before her and Abraham at her side. She had asked Frederick to help her inspect it, but in truth, he had no interest. He'd much rather tuck the children into bed, help them say their prayers, and give them a kiss.

He smiled down at young Edwin as he moved the blanket up to his chin—a four-year-old boy with a freckled nose, blue eyes, and red hair. He'd been abandoned at only a month old on the front steps of the church. With one foot twisted and lame, Frederick assumed his parents decided it would be easier to give him up than try to raise him themselves.

He stroked the boy's cheek and kissed his forehead. The lad closed his eyes, and soon his breathing deepened. Placing his hands on the boy's foot, Frederick prayed for healing, hoping God would hear him and answer.

Hope isn't faith.

The words welled up inside him. Indeed. Frederick must have faith that God heard and answered. It said in God's Word that Jesus bore our infirmities on the cross. Hence, the price had already been paid for God's children to be well.

"Very well, Father. I *believe* You have healed this lad, and I thank You in advance."

Rising, Frederick scanned the room and found all the boys in bed and most already asleep.

Mrs. Radcliff descended the stairs where she'd tucked in the girls and approached him. Firelight glistened in her kind brown eyes and set her skin aglow. She blew out a sigh and pressed a hand on her back. "Thank you for your help, Mr. Carlton."

"'Twas my pleasure."

The lady smiled, and Frederick couldn't help but think how lovely she was, even in her advanced age.

"Then, I bid you good night, Sir. I hear my bed calling t' me." She chuckled then gestured toward her husband. "Mr. Radcliff will show you where you are to sleep. An' I've already instructed Miss Hyde t' join me upstairs wit' the girls when she's finished wit' her…well, wit' whatever has caught her attention."

Frederick glanced at Reena, but she was still absorbed in her map. "You and your husband have been more than generous. May the Lord bless you for it."

"Ah, 'tis nothin'. An' the Lord already blesses us, Mr. Carlton." She started off. "More than we deserve."

Frederick moved to the hearth, grabbed a log, and tossed it into the flames. Then pulling up a wooden chair, he sat down. Though his eyes weighed heavy and his body ached, his arms suddenly felt empty and cold without the warm embraces of the children. It surprised him how much he enjoyed caring for them and making them feel safe. He wondered if God felt that way about him…about *all* of His children. But of course He did. God was a Father who, out of His love, made the ultimate sacrifice so that those who received Him could live with Him forever.

Even when they continued to make mistakes. Or perhaps, *because* they did.

He smiled and stared into the flames. His biggest mistake, of course, was sitting at a table on the other side of the room making one of *her* biggest mistakes. Trouble was, Frederick was well aware of his failings, whereas Reena seemed oblivious to hers.

Caught up in his thoughts, Frederick didn't hear Mr. Radcliff approach until he sat down beside him with a groan.

"'Tis always good when the children retire so I can rest my weary bones." He smiled.

"You and your wife do wonderful work here, Mr. Radcliff. God must be very pleased."

The old man leaned back in the chair. "To honor Him is our utmost goal. 'Sides, Mrs. Radcliff and I love these children as if they were our own." He drew a deep breath. "They sure took to you right away. You're a natural father."

Though the comment sent a wave of delight through Frederick, he snorted. Him a father? A man worth looking up to? Respecting? Hardly.

"Perhaps you and your betrothed will have wee ones of your own someday."

Frederick chuckled. "Nay. We aren't betrothed. I'm merely assisting her in locating something she values."

"Could have fooled me. I saw she wears a ring. And the way you look at each other… well, reminds me of how Mrs. Radcliff and I looked at each other before we were married."

Frederick raised a brow. "You mean the way you *still* look at each other. I've never seen two people more in love."

"Going on thirty years now." Mr. Radcliff gazed into the fire as if remembering each one of those precious years. He chuckled. "I must apologize for our impropriety. We aren't used t' company." He glanced toward the stairs where his wife had disappeared. "She is the love of my life. An' more beautiful than the day I met her—inside *and* out."

Frederick leaned forward on his knees, sudden sorrow clipping at the joy of the day. He could only dream of having such enduring love. "You're a rarity, Mr. Radcliff. And an inspiration."

"Hmm." Mr. Radcliff stretched out his legs. "'Tis my guess that if you marry that lady..." He gestured toward Reena with his head. "That thirty years from now, you'll be as happy as Mrs. Radcliff and I."

An army of strange feelings battled within Freddy at the thought of marrying Reena—excitement, happiness, love, but also heartache, pain, and frustration.

Grabbing the poker, he stood and absently jabbed the wood on the fire. "In truth, I am trying to distance myself from her. She brings out the worst in me. Always has. And I want to follow God, stay on the straight path, preach the Gospel to those in need. Miss Hyde follows a different path." Even as he spoke the words, Frederick had no idea why he was sharing such intimacies with a stranger. But the man listened intently, his brow furrowed as if he truly cared.

Struggling to rise, Mr. Radcliff grabbed a pipe from the mantle, then stooped and lit it from a burning stick in the fire. He slid back on his seat and puffed. "You have great influence over her, and light always overcomes darkness."

The spicy, sweet scent of tobacco drifted past Frederick's nose. He snorted. "My light only dims in her presence." Shaking his head, he sat back down. "In truth, the blood that runs through my veins is anything but noble. My birth was not…honorable."

Instead of the expected disgust or shock, Mr. Radcliff laughed. "Whose birth *is* honorable? The Scripture says we are all born into sin, does it not?"

"Born into, mayhap, but not *from*," Frederick shot back. Obviously the man didn't understand. "Most babies are born out of love, within a committed marriage, and are wanted."

"Most?" Mr. Radcliff puffed on his pipe then pointed it around them. "There are thirty children here who say otherwise. I myself was an orphan."

Frederick studied the man.

"An' not left on church steps or given t' some parson as if my mother cared. Nay, she dumped me in a puddle of sewage in a back alley of town. I was but six months old."

Sewage? Anger caused Frederick's blood to pound. "How did you survive?"

"A trollop took pity on me. Cleaned me up, fed me, an' then brought me t' the nearest orphanage where I were raised."

Frederick may have been born out of violence, but at least his mother had wanted him. But to be tossed aside to die alone, what mother did that?

"How did you overcome it?" Frederick dared ask. "The shame, the feeling of not being loved or wanted."

Mr. Radcliff stared at the flames. "My mother were a trollop with a cold heart. But that has nothin' t' do with me. Has nothing t' do with who I am. God had plans for me that went far beyond the circumstances of my birth."

"But what if your birth was born out of violence? What if you have wickedness running through your heart?"

He chuckled. "Son, we all have wickedness running through our hearts. Don't matter who your parents were. Only Jesus lived a perfect life. An' that's why He offered Hisself up t' pay the penalty for our sins." He drew a puff from his pipe, then pointed it at him. "You are valuable to God. You are no accident. From before you were born, He knew you. Whether she wanted you or whether your father is the worst murderer ever to live, has nothin' t' do wit' you."

Frederick hung his head. "But I feel my father in my blood… in my bones. I can't seem to rid myself of my desire to do evil."

"Are you a believer? Have you trusted in Jesus to cover your sins?"

"Aye, of course." Frederick glanced at the man.

"Then you are a new man! That's what the Word says, don't it?" Mr. Radcliff smiled, excitement twinkling in his eyes. "The old is passed away. You are no longer of your earthly father, but of your heavenly one."

The man's words twisted through Frederick like threads of light weaving around the darkness, spinning a brilliant web that caught and devoured all his doubts and fears. Something else sprouted in their place—hope. Hope that, no matter who his father was or where he'd come from, he could be a better man, a *new* man. He wasn't his father. He didn't have to succumb to temptation, he didn't have to fail. Through the power of God, he could overcome evil and nothing would be impossible.

CHAPTER THIRTY-THREE

Something warm and soft rubbed against Reena. Wait. She always slept alone! Ever since Freddy had left her. It had taken months to get used to sleeping without his arms around her. But now? Was she dreaming? The person moved again and uttered a little moan. And Reena jerked her eyes open, reaching for the knife that was no longer at her side. Instead, a tangled mass of black curls tickled her chin, and she looked down to see Evie fast asleep in her arms. Reena's heart melted as, against her will, tears flooded her eyes. What would it be like to have a child such as this? To have someone to love and care for, someone who would snuggle up with her at night? Someone to mold and shape—*Nay*! She was in no position to mold and shape any young mind or heart. Nor did she wish her body to swell as big as a whale and become scarred and flabby.

Still…the sweet smell of innocence wafted up to her as a breeze blew through the window, fluttering gauze curtains that were stained and torn.

Outside, the golden hues of dawn crept over the brightening sky. The spicy scent of rain, damp earth, and flowers flooded the room, and Reena drew a deep breath, suddenly wishing she could stay in this church—this place of beauty and holiness—where she felt safe, where she didn't have to worry about ancient maps and Fountains of Youth and pirates trying to kill her. Where she didn't have to chase merchant ships loaded with goods or captain a crew that might stab her in the back while she slept. At least for a little while. With Freddy by her side, and this precious child in her arms, she could be happy. Couldn't she? If she and Freddy married, would they be happy like the Radcliffs? Would he love her even when she grew old and ugly?

Probably not. Most men were not like Mr. Radcliff. Most men looked at women with their fleshly eyes.

Soon, most of the young girls were awake, stretching and yawning, and Reena rose to help Mrs. Radcliff get them washed, dressed, and their hair brushed. Her back still pained her a great deal, and though she could put some weight on her ankle now, it hurt as well, so she settled for merely brushing the girls' hair, which she could do sitting down. What charming, sweet girls. So full of life and joy. Though Reena was anxious to be on her way, she had to admit she enjoyed every moment with them—the way they smiled at her, their silly songs, bubbling giggles, and how much they appreciated every touch, every hug, every gesture of affection.

When they were ready, Mrs. Radcliff lined up the girls and together they descended the stairs. Reena took up the rear, gripping the railing as she staggered down each step, thankful when Abraham met her halfway and helped her to a chair. She scanned the room and found Freddy, his eyes still crinkled with sleep and his hair askew, but handsome as always when he smiled her way. He and Mr. Radcliff assembled the children around the table, said grace, and then helped Mrs. Radcliff pass out pieces of stale bread with fresh bananas and mangoes. And water—my goodness, water that tasted fresher than Reena could remember—a rarity on board a ship.

After the meal, the children helped clean up, put away their mattresses, and then sat about the room singing, reading books, or playing with the few toys available. Reena sent Abraham out to make sure all was well in town and that the *Reckless* was still anchored in the bay. Not that she expected otherwise, but in this business, one never knew.

Freddy, looking less sleepy and with his hair raked back, finally joined her. "Sleep well?" He flipped a piece of mango in his mouth.

"I did, actually. Had a guest crawl into bed with me." She glanced at Evie, and he followed her gaze and smiled.

"They are wonderful children, aren't they?" His eyes searched hers the way he was prone to do, as if he plumbed the depths of her soul. But 'twas the way he looked at her—with intensity, not desire. But with something far deeper as if …

She shook her head and broke his gaze. She was dreaming again.

Clearing his throat, he gestured toward her foot. "How is your ankle?"

"Better. I can walk on it a bit." She held out her hand.

Taking it, he helped her to her feet. "Then I suppose you are in a hurry to leave."

She wanted to say no, she wasn't, that she felt something here in this place, something true and beautiful. But instead, she nodded.

Mrs. Radcliff approached. "I guess you'll be leavin' us now that you found your relic…paper?"

"Aye. We must." Reena wondered why she suddenly felt sad. "However, we are so grateful for your hospitality."

"And for allowing us to search through your things," Freddy added.

"Hospitality?" Mrs. Radcliff chortled. "We love the company, and the kids adore you both." She reached out and squeezed Reena's hand. "Please know you're welcome back anytime."

Reena warmed at the woman's sincere tone.

"Miss Reena, Miss Reena!" A little body crashed into Reena's legs, nearly toppling her.

"Evie, be careful," Mrs. Radcliff scolded. "Miss Hyde is injured."

"'Tis quite all right." Reena reached down and drew the little girl up in her arms, holding back a wince.

"Are you leaving?" Evie's bottom lip protruded even as her eyes grew moist.

Reena felt like sinking into the floor. "I fear I must, sweet one."

Evie leaned her head against Reena's shoulder. "Will you come back?"

Reena looked at Freddy, who arched a condemning brow at her. As if she didn't feel bad enough already.

She kissed the little girl on the forehead and hugged her. "I will try." That's all she could promise for now.

Mr. Radcliff, a little boy in his arms, rushed to them, his eyes bursting with wonder. "Mr. Carlton, have you seen Edwin this morning?"

Freddy turned and smiled at the boy, as Mr. Radcliff placed the lad down and gave him a slight nudge from behind. The boy took several steps, teetering and tottering as he went. But walking! Something he'd not *ever* done. Stopping, he beamed up at Freddy as if he'd accomplished a great feat.

Freddy gasped and knelt, gripping the boy and laughing. "God healed you!" He glanced up at Mr. Radcliff. "I prayed for him last night."

Mr. Radcliff clapped his hands and then raised them to the sky. "God be praised! We've been praying for him since we found him. But it took a complete stranger to heal him."

"Not me. Just a prayer of faith." Freddy embraced the lad. Giggling, he threw his arms around Freddy's neck.

Reena wasn't sure what to make of it all, but Freddy was no liar. And neither could she believe that of Mr. Radcliff.

"The Lord is so good." Mrs. Radcliff wiped a tear from her eye, then clapped her hands and shouted across the sanctuary. "Children, line up to go outside. Let us enjoy this fine mornin' before our lessons today." Reena put Evie down, and she and Edwin joined the children screaming in glee and forming a line at the door as if a grand miracle had not just occurred in their midst.

Mr. Radcliff opened the door, releasing a cascade of little ones. Then turning to his wife, he extended his elbow. "Shall we?"

Looping her arm through his, she smiled as he led her outside.

Freddy gripped Reena's arm, taking much of her weight, and helped her out the door.

Halting at the edge of the meadow, the Radcliffs turned to face them.

"We wish you Godspeed." Mr. Radcliff extended his hand.

Freddy shook it. "And to you as well."

Reena offered her hand as well, but Mrs. Radcliff drew her into a warm embrace that stung her back. But Reena didn't mind. "I pray you find what you seek."

"Thank you." Reena swallowed down a burst of emotion.

Then smiling one last time at them, the Radcliffs turned and walked, hand in hand, into the meadow to join the children.

Reena stared after them for a moment, wanting to remember this lovely couple.

A warm breeze fluttered loose strands of her hair into her face. She reached up to brush them aside when the world melted around her. Nay, not melted, exactly. It seemed as if an entirely different world was dropped atop this one, overlapping, yet not erasing. Flowers of every color filled the field that only a moment before was mostly grass. A silver creek laughed and tossed diamond drops in the air. The surrounding trees grew taller, stronger, and glimmered in the most varied and brilliant shades of green she'd ever seen. Plump, ripe fruit hung from each branch. The same precious children darted about, laughing and playing, but in place of rags, they wore clothing that shimmered like royal robes as they danced and frolicked through the flowers.

But Reena's gaze was locked upon Mr. and Mrs. Radcliff. Long, blond curls tumbled down the old woman's back, shimmering in the golden sunlight. Gone were the wrinkles, sags, the portly figure, and in their place was smooth skin and curves that would make any woman jealous. Sporting a head of dark hair and a muscled figure, Mr. Radcliff walked straight and tall beside his wife, with nary a stoop or hobble. He kissed her cheek, and she giggled as they grabbed each other's arms and danced.

Gasping, Reena stumbled backward. *What is going on?* She rubbed her eyes, hoping she'd not finally succumbed to madness.

"You all right?" Freddy caught her fall and held tight.

"Aye." She dared to peer around him. The vision was gone, and Mr. and Mrs. Radcliff were old once again.

No doubt she had not gotten as much sleep as she'd thought.

With a heavy sigh, Reena nodded at Freddy, and they skirted around the church and headed out into the street.

She heard the thumping of Abraham's boots before she saw him rush toward them, hand on the hilt of his sword. "Cap'n, Cap'n." His breath heaved as eyes, bursting with fear, shifted to Freddy.

"What is it, Abraham?" Reena's nerves tightened.

"British troops. Ten of dem. Comin' up de road now."

CHAPTER THIRTY-FOUR

"Thunderation!" Frederick raked a hand through his hair as two things occurred to him. One, he must not allow these troops to harass the Radcliffs, And two, Reena was in no condition to run.

She reached for the cutlass that normally hung at her hip, then let out a sigh of exasperation when she realized it was not there. "Hurry!" She jerked on Frederick's arm and gestured toward the jungle, a harried look on her face when he would not move.

Frederick glanced at Abraham. "They are after me, not you. Abraham, take her back to the *Reckless*. I'll draw them away."

Abraham gave a nod.

Reena tightened her grip on Frederick's arm. "You will do no such thing. We will fight them together."

"You can hardly walk, Reena. And even if you could, we can't overcome ten soldiers. Go back with Abraham. That's an order. I'll meet you on the *Reckless*." Frederick pried her fingers from his arm and handed her to Abraham, but she gripped his arm again.

"I take no orders from you," she spat out.

"You *will* today." Frederick used his harshest tone and gestured toward Abraham, who without hesitation, grabbed her by the waist and drew her beside him.

Terror streaked across her golden eyes. "You will come back to the brig. Promise me you won't leave me."

Until that moment, Frederick had not truly grasped the depth of Reena's need for him, the sense of utter loss that consumed her at the thought he would abandon her again.

Leaning toward her, he placed a kiss on her cheek. "You have my word." Though he had no idea how he would keep that promise. "Now go!" He nodded toward Abraham, and the large quartermaster dragged her toward the jungle lining the road.

She stared at him over her shoulder until the leaves swallowed her whole, the hurt in her eyes nearly undoing him.

But the sound of thumping boots brought him back to his predicament. Grabbing a fallen branch, he quickly wiped away Reena and Abraham's footprints, then pressed his boots deep into the mud as he made his way to the opposite side of the street. There, he dove into the brush and walked parallel to the road, making his way back to town. Hopefully, that would divert their attention from both Reena and the Radcliffs—while also allowing him to assess their strength before they realized where he'd gone.

Within minutes, their red coats appeared through the dense foliage, and he halted, stooped behind the trunk of a kapok tree and peered at the passing band—at least twenty soldiers now. Not good odds, even for his skill with the sword. After they passed, he leapt to his feet, pushed through the leaves, and sped out onto the street.

"Looking for me?" Grinning, he gripped the hilt of his sword.

The soldiers spun around, startled.

"That be 'im!" Sedley pointed.

"What you waiting for?" The man in charge shouted. "Arrest him at once!"

Whirling about, Frederick took off down the muddy street. The pounding of boots followed him. Soon, trees gave way to homes and warehouses and mud to sand and finally to cobblestones as he turned down Broad Street. Shops and taverns were just opening their doors. Servants and slaves rushed about, doing the bidding of their masters in the early morning, while only a few citizens were walking about.

Shouts for him to halt resounded behind him, along with the slap of boots on cobblestones. The rising sun shone in his eyes, blinding him temporarily as he hurried his pace. To where? He had no idea. But as far away from the Radcliffs and Reena as he could.

Their commander ordered them to split up. Ahead of him, more troops marched in formation, unaware as yet of the ensuing chase. He dove into an alley. The stench of rotted fish and sewage curled his nose as he emerged onto Victoria street. If only he could circle back around the troops and forge into the jungle again. There he could hide until they gave up the search and he could return to the *Reckless*. He just didn't know how far these troops would follow him. Or for how long.

An alarm bell rang from the fort, alerting more men to join the hunt. *Thunderation!* He hadn't seen that cullion, Sedley, until he pointed toward Frederick. How had he escaped the *Reckless*? He hadn't time to ponder the question as he turned right and darted down another alley—and was met with a brick wall.

He whirled about to head back the other way when three British marines dashed into the path in front of him and drew their swords.

He was cornered. And, by the gloating grins on their faces, they knew it too.

"So here's the wretched little deserter trapped like a spider in a web."

Frederick drew himself up, took a deep breath, and plucked his blade from its sheath. The eerie chime sliced through the morning mist. He'd rather die by the sword than be lashed, court marshaled, and possibly hung.

The men inched toward him. His thoughts sped to Reena. Would she even know what happened to him? Or would she think he had abandoned her yet again? *Father, take care of her.*

He met the first man's blade with a resounding clank, then swooped to avoid another sword and kicked the marine who approached from his left. The third man recovered and leapt behind Frederick. Keeping an eye on the other two, Frederick swept his blade blindly behind him. A yelp of pain told him he'd met his mark. The other two rushed at him, swords raised. Swerving his blade out before him, he cleaved it left then right, striking both their swords before he spun and dipped out of their way. Breath heaving, muscles aching, he had no idea how long he could keep these three at bay. From the corner of his eye, he saw two more men approach. Make that five to one—five well-trained men. No time to ponder his impending demise. As far as he knew, he was on good standing with the Almighty, and if this was his time to go home, then so be it.

The three advanced on him again. He crossed swords with the first, slashed the second man's blade aside, then thrust the tip of his sword into the third marine's leg. A line of red marched across his white breeches. Gasping, he hobbled backward. Frederick lifted his blade to meet the next attack when the two newcomers shouted and rushed toward the fray. The marines spun to face them. Frederick braced to take on five men, but the newcomers attacked the marines instead. Blades chimed. Grunts and groans filled the air.

He stole a quick glance at them. Couldn't be. Confusion clawed at his reason as he rejoined the fight, slashing this way and that, parrying with first one, then another of the marines. Two of the marines ran off, leaving their friend surrounded. Tossing down his sword, he fell to his knees before Frederick, quivering in fear.

"Go!" Frederick shouted at him, and leaping to his feet, the man disappeared around the corner.

Breath heaving, Frederick dared to turn and face his rescuers.

Captain Edmund Merrick smiled and cocked a brow at Frederick. And right beside him stood Frederick's father, Captain Kent Carlton.

⚓

"Father?" Frederick said the word but still could not believe he was staring at the man who had sired him, the vicious pirate who had ravished his mother, and yet the man who had loved him, raised him, taught him how to fish and hunt, shoot and swordfight.

The man who had taught him about God.

Kent Carlton, infamous pirate and missionary approached his son, his eyes filled with affection and a smile curving his lips. Grabbing Frederick by the shoulders, he drew him into a firm embrace that lasted a long while and grew tighter with every minute—as if he was trying to recover the distance lost between them and the years they'd spent apart. Then, nudging Frederick back, he stared at him with moist eyes.

Though approaching fifty years, his father had not aged a bit. Perhaps there were a few more streaks of gray at his temples and a few more lines on his cheeks, but he was as lean and muscled as always, and obviously still one of the best swordsmen in the West Indies.

"'Tis so good to see you, Son. We've been searching for you and Reena."

Captain Merrick approached, sheathed his sword, and smiled at Frederick. "You've gotten better at swordplay, I see."

Frederick huffed. "Spending time with your daughter has given me many chances to practice."

Merrick laughed, but Frederick detected a bit of sorrow in his mirth.

Sighing, Frederick glanced down the alley. "Thank you for your help. I fear I was in a bit of trouble."

"Aye, we heard you deserted." Kent rubbed the stubble on his stiff jaw and eyed Frederick with disapproval. "Why? I taught you better than that."

Ah, there it was—that all-too-familiar tone of disappointment and reprimand. The tone that told Frederick he would never live up to his father's expectations. Anger surged to join his shame. He leveled a defensive look at Kent. "Why can I never please you?"

"What?" Kent's brow furrowed. "Is that what you…?" Shock and sorrow filled his eyes as he let out a long sigh and rubbed his jaw. "I pushed you. I *did* push you. Forgive me." He gripped Frederick behind the neck and shook him, then drew him into another embrace. "I didn't want you to end up like me. I didn't want you to become a pirate."

Frederick swallowed the burning in his throat as his father released him and looked down. "The desertion was not my doing, Father. Reena *rescued* me."

"Rescued?" Merrick closed his eyes for a second then rubbed the back of his neck. "I can only imagine. How is she?"

"She is well. She is…the same."

The thump of marching troops joined the rattle of carriage wheels, snort of horses, and a bell clanging from the harbor.

Kent gestured for them to leave. "Come. The *Redemption* and *Restitution* are anchored nearby. 'Tis not safe here."

Though every fiber within Frederick longed to rejoin his family, how could he leave Reena? He'd promised her. "I cannot. Not right now." He heaved a sigh as shouts echoed down the alleyway. "Reena needs me. She's in trouble, and I can't abandon her."

"Then lead us to her." Merrick gripped the hilt of his sword, his intense eyes narrowing.

That would mean betraying her. And Frederick couldn't do that either. "She would never forgive me for that."

Frowning, Merrick arched a brow. "Charlisse may not forgive *me* for being this close to her and not bringing her home."

"She's not ready yet, Merrick." Frederick's dream of Reena in hell burned vividly in his thoughts. "She's in trouble, and I'm the only one who can help her."

"What kind of trouble?" Boots clapped over cobblestones, and Merrick glanced over his shoulder. "We are her family. We can *all* help her."

"Why is she sailing with Antoine du Casse?" Kent asked.

"Long story. Please. You must trust me." Frederick's gaze shifted between Merrick and his father. Both so different, yet so much alike—both pirates who used to be mortal enemies, who at one time had attempted to kill each other. Yet both redeemed by God.

"They are down here. This way!" Voices sounded—too close.

"Go! I'll boost you over." Kent dashed to the wall, threaded his fingers together, and lowered his hands.

Frederick shook his head. "You first."

"'Tis you they want." Kent's voice brooked no argument.

Slipping his boot into his father's hands, Frederick allowed him to hoist him on the top of the wall. Straddling it, he glanced down on the other side—another alleyway, empty at the moment. Above the roofs of shops and taverns, morning sun sparkled over Carlisle Bay and glistened over several bare masts rocking back and forth upon the water.

"Go!" Kent said.

"What of you?" he glanced down and was surprised by the combination of fear and affection he saw in his father's eyes.

"We can handle a few marines," Merrick said. "Go. Tell Reena we love her."

Frederick started to swing his other leg over the wall, but then glanced down at his father once again. "Wait! I have urgent news I must tell you."

"No time, Son. We'll stay here two days in case you can convince Reena otherwise. After that, meet us in Jamaica."

"Go save my daughter," Merrick locked gazes with Frederick. "Save her and bring her back to us."

A glimpse of red flashed in Frederick's vision, and he jumped onto the sandy dirt on the other side of the wall, hoping the troops had not seen him or they'd arrest his father and Merrick. He also prayed the men they'd just fought weren't among them.

Leaning back against the wall, he listened.

"You there! What are you doing here?"

"Us?" Frederick heard Merrick say in a slurred voice. "We're jisssst takin' a mornin' sssstroll."

"D'ye know wheres the Stinkheart pub be?" his father added in a drunken tone.

"Pishaw. Just besotted sailors." The first voice cursed. "Begone. Go sleep it off!"

Smiling, Frederick slipped down the alley.

Reena leaned on the railing of the *Reckless*, feeling more hopeless than she had in a long while. For one thing, it had been ten hours and still no sign of Freddy. She had sent sailors with the jolly boat back to shore to await him, but as each minute passed, she feared that he had, indeed, been captured. She was a great pirate and a good captain and her crew—what was left of them—were good fighters. Even so, she doubted they would be able to rescue Freddy from a British fort. She should have stayed, fought by his side, though most likely she would now be locked in irons as well. But to be chained alongside Freddy would be better than living without him.

The moon appeared over the horizon, creating a path of silvery turquoise on the water. Wavelets slapped the hull as palms ashore whispered in the breeze. Behind her, her crew shifted about the deck, some playing cards, another playing a fiddle.

The other thing that bothered her was that even with the three maps in her possession and her memory of the other one, she was unable to determine the exact location of the Fountain. She needed Antoine's map, for it contained the land masses in the center circle which would show them where it was. With only three parts to that circle, the Fount could be anywhere in the Caribbean.

Alas—she grabbed a strand of hair and spun it around her finger—not only did she not have Freddy with her, but now she would have to find Antoine, who was no doubt as furious with her for tricking him as she was for his betrayal.

Michael slid beside her. A salty breeze flipped through his hair while the moonlight glinted it in silver. He smiled up at her with that innocent smile of his that always seemed to set her at ease.

"Don't worry, Captain Reena. Captain Carlton is coming back."

He said it with such confidence that she almost believed he actually knew what the future held.

"I hope you're right, Michael, but 'tis been so long, and Freddy was outnumbered."

"But you forget, Captain. God is with him. I know you'll see him real soon."

Reena twirled the ring on her finger that Freddy had given her and was about to reprimand the lad for saying things he couldn't possibly know, when the slap of oars hitting the water reached her ears and a flickering light appeared in the distance. Heart pounding, she squinted through the darkness at the jolly boat arriving and held her breath as she counted how many people were aboard. Three. That meant Freddy was with them! Wait, there were four figures now.

She didn't know whether to be overjoyed or worried.

"De jolly boat approaches, Cap'n," Abraham said from the quarterdeck.

"In bows!" one of the sailors shouted from the boat, and turning, she gave orders for ropes to be tossed overboard.

"Boat your oars!" the order blared from below, and Reena peered over the railing, examining each face in the dim lantern light. Aye, 'twas Freddy! He stood and yanked another man up by the collar.

Sedley! Reena gasped as anger spun an eddy in her stomach. How did he…? Wasn't he in the hold? She exchanged a glance with Abraham, but he only shrugged.

Still, she could hardly believe it was Freddy until he swept his legs over the bulwarks and landed on the deck with a thump, all man and muscle, and none the worse for wear—save for the slice through his shirt on his right arm and a small gash on his face. He dragged Sedley over the side after him and tossed him to the deck before meeting her gaze. And for one brief precious moment, she saw a world of affection in his eyes. Throwing all propriety aside, she limped toward him and fell into his arms, ignoring the pain in her foot.

"I thought I had lost you."

Instead of pushing her away, he wrapped her in his embrace and kissed the top of her head just like he used to do. "Lost your confidence in my abilities?" he said as Abraham and Brodie approached.

Abraham gripped his hand. "Knew yuh'd elude dem redcoats,"

"Ach now," Brodie pointed at his wound. "I'll see tae that."

"'Tis nothing." Freddy waved him off.

Michael dashed toward him and hugged him, crowding Reena out. But she didn't mind. It reminded her of how much the children from the orphanage had adored him.

"Glad yer safe." Jo winked at him from the railing.

A strong wind swept the joy of the reunion away as Freddy glanced back at his prisoner.

"Where did you find him?" Reena asked.

"He's the Judas who betrayed me. 'Twas God's justice I ran into him."

Sedley gave a slanted smirk. "Just me luck."

Grabbing Sedley's blue neckerchief, Freddy hauled him to his feet. "I should string you up here and now."

Twilight, twilight fast comes the night
From the east you must take flight
In the reflection you must learn
Then the invisible will be seen

CHAPTER THIRTY-FIVE

With great difficulty Frederick did his best not to strangle Sedley right then and there. Terror shrieked from the maggot's face as he squirmed and winced, knowing he was doomed.

"How did you get out of the hold?" Reena fisted hands at her waist and scanned her crew.

"Answer the lady!" Frederick shook the man.

"Me door were unlocked. Don't knows 'ow. Ole Bellamy must've forgot t' lock it." Sedley's gaze shifted to the pirate who had brought him his food, but the man shook his head, his eyes widening.

"Don't think were me," he said.

"But yer always in yer cups, Bellamy," Fletcher said, and the crew laughed.

Reena cast a fierce gaze at Bellamy. "I'll deal with you later."

"Don't matter now." Frederick yanked Sedley to within an inch of his face. "You told the British where we were—where *I* was."

Sedley only shrugged. Drawing her knife, Reena hobbled toward him and held it to his throat. "You told that snake, Antoine, that I had my maps with me!" she seethed. "God knows what else you've done to stab me behind my back. I should gut you right here."

"Hang him from the yardarm!" one pirate shouted. The rest of her crew crowded around, spitting and cursing and thrusting fists in the air.

"Keelhaul 'im! Flog 'im, Tie 'im to the rack!" Others joined in.

Sedley gulped, his jittery eyes landing on Reena. "Mercy?" He pleaded in a squeaky voice. "He offered me more money than I ev'r seen in me life if I would keep an eye on ye an' tell him wha' yer doin'."

Reena pierced his neck with her blade. A trickle of blood stained his neckerchief. "You befriended my enemy! You spied on me!" She pressed the knife deeper.

Frederick stayed her hand and shook his head. Regardless of the man's betrayal, he'd not allow her—or anyone—to kill him. Though he had to admit, he was quite enjoying watching the man writhe like a ship in a storm.

Abraham crossed arms over his chest and eyed the proceedings while Brodie took out two of his knifes and sharpened their blades against each other. *Ching Ching Ching.* "Give him tae me fer an hour. I know ways tae make him suffer."

Frederick nodded with a grin. "Excellent idea."

"I quite agree," Reena said, sheathing her knife and waving a hand of dismissal at Sedley.

"But yer a godly man, a preacher." Sedley's breath came hard and fast. "Ye can't do that." He glanced at Abraham. "Nor ye. Ain't it against yer religion?"

"No rules against punishing the wicked." Frederick exchanged a glance with Abraham, who smiled, no doubt understanding what Frederick was doing.

Frederick handed the traitor off to Brodie, but Sedley withdrew with a shriek. "Wait! Wait! I knows where du Casse is."

Frederick gripped his neckerchief tighter. "I don't care if you know the whereabouts of the Queen of England."

Reena laid a hand on Frederick's arm, then glared at Sedley. "Then tell us. Where is the vile toad?"

"Will ye spare me life?" Sweat beaded on his forehead.

"If you speak the truth."

"I saw 'im in town."

Reena's brow furrowed even as fear scampered across her expression. "Bridgetown?"

"Aye. I swears it were him. An' the two brutes what stick t' 'im like barnacles." Sedley shrank back, no doubt expecting her to strike him.

Instead, she drew her sword and leveled it at his chest. "How would he know where the church was located? He doesn't have the real second map."

"I don't know, Cap'n. But it were him. I asked him fer me money, but he said not 'till he finds the last map, the loot-stealing cockroach."

Reena gritted her teeth and pressed her blade.

Frederick nudged the man out of her reach. "Never fear, Reena, he'll get what's coming to him." He shoved him toward Abraham. "Toss him back in the hold. Put a double lock on his cage. And nobody feeds him or visits him but you."

It took several hours for Frederick, along with Michael's help and some rum, to calm Reena down. She hated being betrayed nearly as much she hated being abandoned. He didn't blame her. 'Twas a hard thing to swallow—an enemy among one's friends.

Michael entered with another cup of tea into which Reena poured way too much rum. The lad smiled at them both, then gave Frederick a strange nod of encouragement before he left.

Frederick frowned. Encouragement for what?

Reena sipped her tea and stared out the stern windows at the darkness beyond.

"I know Sedley's duplicity has angered you, but what does it matter? We are all here, alive and safe."

"Aye, 'tis true. His vile plans did not succeed where you are concerned. Of which I am very pleased." She smiled at him, then hobbled to her desk and gazed down at the maps spread upon it. "But I fear I must find Antoine again."

"What?" Frederick leapt to his feet. "You have all the maps. What need have you of that mongrel?"

She glanced at him, her golden eyes glimmering in the lantern light. "The only thing on this new map is the image of a waterfall and another rhyme. I cannot remember part of the map in his possession. There's a section which fits in the center circle." She pointed to the empty place where it would fit. "When all the maps are together, it reveals the exact location of the island where the Fount is located." Sighing, she frowned and grabbed her tea again.

"After everything, you still intend to go after this ludicrous fountain?" Frederick squeezed the bridge of his nose, not believing the woman could be so stubborn.

"'Tis *because* of everything we've gone through that I cannot give up now. We are so close, Freddy, so close."

Frederick huffed. "Not *we*. You. This has all been your dream, your goal, Kitten. Not mine."

She set down her cup. "I merely need one more map."

Frederick stared at her. "And how do you propose to get it?"

"If Sedley is telling the truth and Antoine is in Bridgetown, I'll go ashore and find him."

"And he'll kill you for tricking him."

"Nay, he needs the map we found at the church. He'll be willing to barter for it."

"I thought you learned 'tis better not to make a deal with the devil."

"But if the devil holds the treasure, sometimes you must."

Fred spread out his feathers. "Thems that die be the lucky ones!"

"And what of the Radcliffs?" Frederick leaned his hands on her desk. "Did you consider what Antoine will do to them if he solves the riddle and finds them?" Something that had gnawed at him since Sedley's admission.

Limping around her desk, Reena leaned back on the top too close to Frederick for his comfort. "I did." She lowered her chin. "In truth, it has bothered me greatly. But Antoine is no monster. If he finds the church, the Radcliffs will tell him we already retrieved the map. He will have no reason to do them harm."

A breeze whistled through the stern windows, fluttering the lantern flame.

"That's where you will search for him, then. At the church?"

"Aye, tomorrow."

Pushing from the desk, he dropped into a chair and fingered the cross around his neck. *How do I reach her, Lord?* He gazed absently at the deck as it tittered over a wavelet. Memories surged of his encounter that day.

"I saw your father," he said.

A strange emotion appeared in her eyes. "Where? Why didn't you tell me?"

"I am." Frederick leaned forward on his knees. "He and my father helped me fight off a group of marines that had me cornered."

"*Your* father?" she breathed out in disbelief.

"Aye."

"How are they? Is my father well?"

Frederick leaned back and smiled. "Well enough to fight off trained soldiers."

She gave a sad grin.

"He said to tell you he and your mother miss you and love you."

At this, Reena stood, grabbed her tea, and limped to the windows again.

"He asked me to keep you safe and bring you home."

She brought the cup to her lips, saying nothing, but he thought he saw a quiver roll down her back. "Why did you not go with them? You've been trying to find them for weeks."

Frederick still could not believe he'd forgotten to tell them about Jean-Baptiste du Casse's planned attack on Jamaica. *Thunderation!* What a fool. He'd been so shocked to see his father, so overcome with emotion, it had completely evaded his thoughts.

"In truth, Reena, they asked me to go with them. When I wouldn't, they asked me to bring them to you."

She finally turned to face him, her eyes moist. "Why didn't you?"

"Because you've had enough betrayal for one day."

Reena set down her tea and hobbled toward him, more emotion than he'd seen in a long while clouding her expression. The deck shifted once again, and she stumbled to the side. Frederick leapt to his feet and caught her in his arms before she fell.

He stood here, holding her, feeling her warmth, breathing her sweet scent, and wanting nothing more than to keep her this close forever.

"Thank you for not leaving me," she finally whispered and looked up at him.

He brushed hair from her face, longing to dive into the golden pools of her eyes and get lost forever. "My sweet kitten." He ran a thumb down her jaw and onto her moist lips, soft as cushions.

She closed her eyes and breathed out a sigh of pleasure…a sigh of invitation.

And against his better judgment, Frederick accepted, lowering his lips onto hers…gently caressing at first, sampling her sweet taste. But hunger overtook him—hunger to know this woman in every way possible, to get as close to her as he could, to give her all the love he kept hidden for her in his heart.

She responded in kind, searching, exploring, drinking him in as if he were the finest of wines. She tasted of rum and cocoa and Reena, and he found his thirst for her unquenchable. He drew her tighter, felt her curves meld against him, felt her desperate need of him. Memories of their lovemaking filled his mind, and he longed to show her all his love again.

Instead, among the overwhelming passion, he found a speck of restraint, a spark of control, a smidgen of the wisdom that came from above…a wisdom that bespoke of commitment and real love—a love that took nothing that didn't belong to it and yet gave everything that was good.

He withdrew, but kept his lips close to hers. "I do love you, Reena. I always have."

"Then show me." She pressed her lips on his again, but he gripped her arms and nudged her back.

The pain in her eyes made him turn his face away. "I can't."

"'Tis your God again. Coming between us," she snapped as she made her way back to her desk.

"'Tis the life you have chosen. I cannot be a part of it."

"'Twas your life, too, before God intervened." She poured more rum into her tea, her tone bitter.

Frederick raked back his hair. "I thought when you saw how happy the Radcliffs were and how much more fulfilling a life of service is than a life of self-seeking pleasure, that you would give up your pirate ways. After you've seen how fickle people are, how depraved—people like Sedley and Antoine—how can you not see your need for God?" He dared approach her. "I make one final appeal to give up this foolish quest and return to the God, the eternal Father who loves you more than anything."

She stared at him for a moment as if she actually considered his proposal. But then a hard sheen covered her eyes, and she downed her tea in one gulp and set the cup on her desk with a clank.

"You're asking me to give up eternal youth and spend the rest of my life in poverty and servitude."

"Nay, I'm asking you to embrace eternal life and spend your time in this world being more blessed and more fulfilled than you can ever imagine."

She lowered her chin and swallowed. "I can't. I can't give up my quest now. Please don't ask me. Please,"—she looked up at him, her eyes misty and pleading—"let us find this Fountain together, taste its waters, and see what happens. Afterward, I promise to consider your proposal."

That's when Frederick knew he had lost her. Her heart was not ready. Mayhap it never would be. He stared at her in sorrow as she poured more rum, took a sip, and blinked back the dizziness it brought.

Shadows appeared, slinking around Reena, darker shadows than he remembered...*more* than he remembered...floating in between the weights of fear still perched on her shoulders and across her back. Yet now, added to their weight were heavy chains that bound those anchors to her chest. Her fears of growing old, of not being loved, of not fulfilling her dreams had only grown larger, heavier, dragging her down beneath their weight.

Had Frederick done any good here at all? He closed his eyes. "Then I am finished with this quest."

One of the hardest things he had ever had to do was leave Reena the first time. It had nearly sent him into a downward spiral of despair and depression. If not for God, he may have died there. But it was *because* of God that he knew he had to leave her again. He knew in his spirit that he had done all God had asked of him. He had loved Reena, protected her, resisted her temptations, joined in her quest, and—most of all—appealed for her to return to God.

The second hardest thing Frederick had to do was walk out of Reena's cabin at that very moment. Especially after seeing the agony in her eyes at his declaration. But what else could he do? She was encased in a prison of her own making—one from which only God could set her free.

He made his way up the quarterdeck ladder to the stern of the ship and sat down with his feet between the rails, watching the wind toss the trees on shore this way and that like his hopes for Reena's eternal soul.

Michael appeared beside him so suddenly, Frederick jumped.

"Beg your pardon, Captain Carlton. I thought you might like some tea." He sat down beside him and handed him a steaming cup.

Frederick took it. "You're a kind lad, Michael. You always seem to know what people need." He couldn't quite make out the boy's expression in the moonlight, but he felt him smiling.

"I won't stay long, Captain. I know you have to think and pray, but I thought you should know that Mack and Bellamy both committed their lives to God."

Frederick shook his head. Surely the trade winds had twisted the boy's words into nonsense.

"Aye, yesterday," Michael added. "And they are getting off the brig at the next port to start a new life." He rose to his feet. "It was your preaching and reading the Bible that convinced them."

Frederick searched his memory for those moments where he'd read the Bible out loud and the few sailors that had listened. Mack had been one of them, but he hadn't known about Bellamy. "I don't know what to say. Thank you for telling me."

"I knew it'd give you hope, Captain." Then as fast as he had come, Michael left.

Cupping the warm mug in his hands, Frederick bowed his head and thanked God for the two souls he'd helped to snatch from the fires of hell.

If only he could do the same for Reena. Sighing, he sipped the tea and set it aside, the guilt of his failures returning to haunt him.

You are no failure in My eyes.

"Is that you, Lord?" Frederick smiled and gazed at the pearl-tipped waves tumbling ashore.

Mr. Radcliffs' words filled his thoughts—words that Frederick was no accident, that not only had God created him unique, but that his life had been planned before he was born. That the circumstances of his birth did not define him, and as long as God lived within him, he was a new man.

Hadn't he just resisted yet another temptation with Reena? Hadn't he put her soul above his own physical needs? And what of those two sailors? Frederick was not like his father. He was a new man in Christ.

Forgive your father. The voice was so clear, so firm, that it spun a whirlwind of angst in Frederick's soul. He thought he had forgiven him long ago. But when he saw him today and felt all that anger return—even though the man had embraced him with such love—he knew that he hadn't. He hadn't forgiven his father for the violence he'd done to his mother, and he hadn't forgiven himself for being born out of that sinful act.

Wind tore over him, tossing his hair and bringing the scent of brine and earth to his nose. Frederick closed his eyes. A vision appeared—his father when he was younger. He sat on the shore, holding a babe in his arms, and Frederick knew it was him. His father lifted the child up toward heaven. "Father, I dedicate my son, Frederick, to You. May he always know You and Your love. May He always follow You and be filled to the fullness of all that is You. I break all the power of the enemy over him and claim Him for Your Kingdom." Then drawing little Frederick back into his arms, he nestled him close and kissed him on the forehead. "Help me to be the best father I can be. Help me to teach him all he needs to survive and especially about You. Help me to lead Him to You." Tears ran down his cheeks as he gazed at little Frederick in love. Then the vision disappeared. Frederick opened his eyes, his mind churning, his heart breaking. He swiped at the moisture on his face before someone saw.

He had no memory of that moment, of course. All he remembered of his father was his constant criticism. But perhaps that was because—as his father had told him today—he feared Frederick would turn out like him. God had truly changed his father's heart. He was a new creature, a new sort of being, a man filled with the Spirit of God, whose past was not only erased but forgotten. How could Frederick do any less?

You must also forgive yourself.

Frederick drew a deep breath and stared out over the ebony waters. "I forgive my father, and I forgive…I forgive…" Oddly, Frederick found the last part harder than the first. "I forgive *myself*."

A gust of wind spun around him, encasing him in warmth. He glanced up at a velvet sky, sprinkled with more stars than he remembered seeing, clusters of them scattered in a shimmering pattern of magnificence.

I love you, son.

Emotion clogged Frederick's throat. "I love you too, Father."

Smiling, he leapt to his feet, feeling freer than he had in a long, long time.

Now he knew what he had to do. And it wasn't going to be easy.

CHAPTER THIRTY-SIX

*R*eena woke, feeling as though she'd fought a battle all night. And lost. She could not shake the look in Freddy's eyes as he'd marched from her cabin—the one that said he'd finally had enough. She'd seen it once before, and what happened afterward had caused her more pain than she cared to admit. She'd wanted to run after him, to beg his forgiveness, to offer some compromise that would appease him. But she knew nothing short of giving up everything would bring him back to her.

Hence, she'd plied herself with rum and cried herself to sleep.

Now, as she stood staring at her image in the looking glass, with her head pounding and her heart breaking, she touched her lips, remembering the intimacy of Freddy's kiss. Tears filled her eyes at the thought it might have been his last one. She rubbed them away. Pirate captains did not cry.

She could do nothing about the shadows beneath her eyes, nor the reek of alcohol that seemed to permeate her skin. Not even the cup of hot chocolate Michael brought seemed to help settle her stomach. Or mayhap 'twas the lad's incriminating look—most unusual for him—that kept her agitated.

Regardless, after she made herself look as presentable as possible, she emerged onto the quarterdeck, squinting in the bright sun, and searched the deck for Freddy. She intended to apologize and somehow reach a compromise. Anything to keep him with her.

"Prepare the jolly boat, Abraham," she said to him in passing. "We will pay another visit to the Radcliffs this morning."

She found Freddy standing at the bow of the ship, fully armed and looking as if he had made up his mind about something. As she crept toward him, she noted there was something different about him—an odd peace and joy that hovered around him. Instead of his usual stern look, he was smiling as he stared off into the Caribbean… as if some weight had been lifted. And she suddenly feared that weight might be her.

She eased up beside him, shielding her eyes from the sun. "I must apologize for last night, Freddy. I know I upset you."

He shot a glance toward her then shook his head. "You were honest, Reena. You've always been honest with me. How can I fault you for that?"

She smiled, feeling hope rise. "You have my word that after I find the Fountain, we will sail to Jamaica and warn our families about the attack. Or did you already?" It suddenly occurred to her that he'd seen his father.

Freddy chuckled. "Can you believe I forgot?"

She laughed as a gust of wind swept over them. "Then we will warn them. And also"—she hesitated, unsure of what words to use to convince him—"I will consider committing myself to God again."

She thought he'd be thrilled. She thought he'd lift her off her feet, embrace her, shout for joy! Wasn't that what he wanted?

Instead, his lips drew into a somber line. "Reena, following God is not something you decide in your mind. 'Tis your heart He wants. Your heart must be willing—*completely* willing. And I fear yours is not."

Reena gripped the railing and glanced at the golden shores. She wanted to argue with him, but he was right.

He turned to face her and the look in his eyes nearly crumbled her on the spot. She'd seen that look before. Taking her hand in his, he fingered the ring he'd given her so long ago. "I'm getting off the *Reckless* and joining my father. The *Restitution* and the *Redemption* are anchored in Carlisle bay."

Reena did her best to hide the jarring split of her heart.

"Continue with your quest, Reena, but I want no part of it."

She grew desperate. "I'll come to Jamaica afterward. We can start over again there."

"Nay. You may certainly come there. In fact, I hope you do, but as far as anything else between us, that is not possible."

Tears filled her eyes and she turned her face away. "But your kiss last night. I thought…"

"Forgive me for that, Kitten."

"Nay!" She shoved down her fears. She had cried hysterically the first time he left, and—*bilge water*—she would not give him the satisfaction again. "You love me. You told me so last night."

"I do, but that doesn't mean I can be with you. I cannot be unequally yoked. Our lives are taking two very different paths."

Fear, sorrow, and agony spiraled through her, butchering her insides as sharply as any knife.

He tugged his hand from hers, but she held fast. She couldn't bear it. Not again. She would shrivel up and die. "Please, Freddy. Don't do this."

He finally retrieved his hand, and hers grew as cold as the bottom of the sea.

His jaw hardened to a grim line. "Goodbye, Kitten."

She planted her feet to keep from staggering. She wanted to tell him she'd give up her dream of eternal youth, she'd end her quest if only he'd stay. But she knew even *that* wouldn't be enough. He would never be her Freddy again. His God had seen to that.

"Sail ho!"

Gathering her wits and shoving down her emotions, Reena plucked her glass from her belt and held it to her eye. A three-masted frigate curved around the cape of the cove in which they hid, lowering its sails. She quickly shifted her focus to the hull where the word *Conquérant* appeared in bold letters.

"Antoine," Freddy announced before she had a chance.

Reena lowered her scope and excused herself. There was no time to mourn, no time to cry, no time to convince Freddy not to leave. She was a pirate captain, and an enemy ship headed toward them.

Or was it an enemy? By the time she uttered the command to hoist all sail and beat to quarters, Antoine had raised the white flag of truce and signaled that he wished a parlay.

Reena didn't trust him. She had never trusted him. But he had part of the map she needed, and she had a part he needed. Perhaps they could exchange the information in a civilized fashion—as civilized as pirates could be.

Hence, she belayed the order to set sail, commanded her crew to take up arms, and gave the signal for him to board. Soon the *Conquérant* dropped anchor and lowered a boat. All the while, her gaze kept shifting to Freddy, standing at the railing on the main deck. Did he really intend to leave her?

Reena scanned the deck. Jo surveyed her gun crew, ensuring they were ready to fire if necessary. Brodie took up a spot beside Freddy, alternating between taking sips from his flask and glancing at Jo, while Michael stood on his other side. The blasted man seemed to have stolen her friends as well as her heart.

"Looks like yuh will get yer map, Cap'n," Abraham said from beside her. "But, I would not trust dat man agin."

"I have no intention of trusting him. Using him for his map, perhaps." She winked at Abraham and gripped the hilt of her cutlass.

"Humph. An' Cap'n Carlton? Him leavin'?"

The words twisted a knife in her gut.

"Apparently." She swallowed down a burning lump. "He is free to go where he wants." Though the idea of locking him below had its appeal.

"Bes' ding e'er happened to ye, Cap'n."

Reena crossed arms over her chest. "Alas, he does not return the sentiment." Anger simmered, and she fanned the flames. Better to be angry than melt in a puddle of tears. "I'll hear no more about the illusive Captain Carlton, is that clear?"

One dark brow rose above Abraham's piercing eyes, but he remained silent.

That illusive captain leapt up the quarterdeck ladder and approached her. Her heart dared to skip a beat. Had he come to apologize, declare his love, inform her he was staying, especially now that Antoine was back?

"With your permission, Captain, since you have a boat ready, can your men row me ashore?"

Reena's heart shriveled. She inhaled a deep breath in the desperate hope of reviving it, but to no avail. Instead, she clung to her anger and faced him.

"If that is what you wish." She waved a hand of dismissal. "Begone with you. And Godspeed."

For the briefest of moments, pain appeared on Freddy's face, but then he stiffened his jaw, dipped his head toward her, and said. "Good day, Captain."

Then, spinning on his heels, he marched away, taking with him every ounce of her shattered heart.

With every slap of the oars in the turquoise waters, with every swish of the sea, Frederick's insides churned into a caustic brew. More than anything, he longed to order the sailors to turn about and return him to the *Reckless*—back to Reena's side. But he couldn't. He could do nothing more for her. She was in God's hands now.

And apparently Antoine's as well. Frederick dared a glance over his shoulder and saw Antoine's boat thud against the hull of the *Reckless*, watched as he and his men climbed the rope ladder and leapt aboard. Thankfully, Reena had assembled a greeting party of cutlass and pistols, but apparently from the sickly sweet French blathering on the wind, the weapons hadn't been necessary.

As long as Antoine needed something from Reena, he'd play nice. Frederick had thought to stick around and protect her from that blackguard, but Reena could take care of herself. For the most part.

Antoine's blue plume fluttered in the breeze as he bent over Reena's hand and placed a kiss upon it. Abraham waved at Frederick from the quarterdeck, while Brodie and Jo gazed after him from the railing. He'd had a chance to bid each of them farewell, but he didn't realize until now how much he'd miss them.

A bright light glimmered, drawing Frederick's gaze to the stern of the brig where he expected to see a knife or sword, something which caught the sun's reflection. Instead, Michael smiled and waved at him, and Frederick waved back.

The lad had come to him just before he'd climbed down into the boat.

"I'll watch over her, Captain Carlton. Never fear." He had said the words with such authority and assurance that it shocked Frederick. But then again, the boy was full of surprises. Frederick would miss him most of all.

Turning, he faced the shore. Sunlight shimmered over white sand that led to a web of green beyond. He'd have to hide until nightfall and then make his way to the docks and out to the *Restitution*. He smiled at the impending reunion with his family and hoped some of his siblings were on board. And his mother, of course. But she rarely left his father's side.

The order for oars to raise was given, and the boat struck land. Thanking the men, Frederick leapt out and waded onto the sand. At the edge of the jungle, he turned one last time to look at the *Reckless*. Even at this distance, he saw Reena glance his way, could feel the bond stretching between them, tugging at both their hearts, forever taunting them with a love that could never be. Then tearing his gaze away, he shoved aside a branch and plunged into the greenery.

CHAPTER THIRTY-SEVEN

Even before Frederick's feet hit the deck of the *Restitution*, his mother dashed toward him and hugged him so hard he nearly fell back over the railing into the sea. Two lanterns at main and foremast provided the only light, along with a half moon and a plethora of stars that seemed to shine even brighter in the wee hours before dawn.

"My boy, my boy. I've missed you so much!" She sobbed against his waistcoat and refused to let him go. Her familiar sweet scent drew out memories of how tenderly she had loved and cared for him all the years of his youth. Where his father had been harsh, his mother had been a soft net, a place to land after Kent had berated him for some infraction. Like a mother hen, she had covered Frederick with her feathers of comfort and love.

He nudged her back and ran his thumb over the tears streaming down her cheeks. The few creases that lined her face only enhanced her beauty—a beauty that spilled from green eyes still sharp and full of wisdom.

"I have missed you too, Mother."

His father strode up to him, placing one arm around Frederick and one around his mother, and drew them together in a family embrace. Overcome, Frederick could only stand there, surrounded by their love, and wonder why he'd stayed away so long—why he hadn't returned to them after he'd left Reena the first time.

A gentle breeze swirled about them, flapping loose sails, as the *Restitution* creaked over a wavelet. Hiding in town, Frederick had waited until the pubs and taverns grew quiet and most of their patrons had succumbed to an overindulgence in spirits. He had waited until nary a sound crept along the city streets, save the whisk of wind and slosh of water. Then, he'd made his way to the docks, where he'd bartered with a fisherman to row him out to the *Restitution*.

He hadn't expected anyone save the watchmen to be awake on board, but before he'd rowed to within ten yards of the brig, he'd spotted his parents on deck.

"What are you doing up at this hour?" he asked.

"Waiting for you, of course," his mother replied, her voice cracking with emotion.

"But how did you—"

Kent swiped the moisture from his face, then gripped Frederick's shoulder. "God told us you would come."

Frederick blew out a sigh of wonder. "I've finally made my peace with Him."

Kent shut his eyes for a moment and uttered a "Praise His name!" while his mother started crying again. "'Tis what we've been praying for."

"Forgive me for wandering so far away." Frederick gripped the cross around his neck and faced his father. "You were tough on me, Father. In truth, I resented you for it. I resented you for what you did to"—he shifted his gaze to his mother, then hung his head. "I was wrong."

"I don't fault you." Kent frowned and glanced over the bay. "I am not proud of my past. I hate that it caused you so much pain. That's"—he raked back his hair and growled— "exactly what I didn't want to happen."

Frederick clasped his father's arm. "I forgive you, Father. Say you'll forgive me as well."

Kent grabbed him by the nape of the neck and drew him close. "Of course."

Dabbing her eyes with a handkerchief, Frederick's mother laughed and cried at the same time. Wind gusted around them in a warm embrace as if Father God joined in their reunion.

Footsteps preceded a feminine shriek as a figure appeared from the hatch and rushed toward them.

"Freddy, Freddy! You're finally home." Phoebe crashed into him, her auburn curls bouncing and eyes shimmering in the moonlight.

"Greetings, Little Pea." Hoisting her off her feet, he twirled her around, her skirts fluttering in the breeze. "What are you doing awake?"

"I missed you so much! Put me down, you rascal!" She wiggled in his arms.

Frederick set her gently on the deck and stood back to look at his youngest sister.

"I'm not a little pea anymore." She pouted and slapped him playfully.

Frederick studied her. A good foot shorter than he was, she'd inherited her mother's auburn hair and jade green eyes. But she was her father's daughter through and through—tricking, teasing, and taunting Frederick since she'd taken her first step. Yet…her curves were more prominent, her skin glowing.

"Indeed, you have grown into a lovely woman. But"—he tapped her on the nose and winked—"You will always be my Little Pea."

Another shadow emerged from the companionway. "Freddy!" His brother Elon stepped into the lantern light, rubbing his eyes. "Mother said you would come."

Frederick opened his arms, but Elon hesitated.

"What?" Frederick teased. "Too grown up to hug your brother?"

"I'm a man now. Fifteen," Elon stated with pride.

Frederick smiled at his attempt to stand taller than he was, and though his voice had deepened, there was nary a whisker on his chin.

"Then perhaps a handshake?" Frederick extended his hand, but when Elon gripped it, Frederick drew him close and hugged him.

"Aww." Elon pushed from him, laughing. "Good to see you, brother."

The *Restitution* rolled over a swell, and Frederick glanced over the shadowy deck as memories crept out from hiding—most of them good. He'd grown up on this brig. Spent more of his childhood on the sea rather than land.

"Where's Levi and Lydia?" he asked.

His mother looped her arm through his. "Home. Attending their studies. But they will be thrilled to see you when we return."

"And Captain Merrick?" He fully expected to see the infamous captain lurking in the shadows, especially since they'd been expecting Frederick.

"On his way." Kent gestured over the railing. "We signaled them as soon as we spotted you."

Indeed, Frederick could make out the *Redemption* rocking in the bay off their starboard quarter and a boat headed their way.

Within minutes, Captain Edmund Merrick, his wife Charlisse, and their daughter Gabrielle climbed aboard.

Grabbing her skirts, Charlisse darted to him. "Where's Reena?" The desperate look in her eyes caused his heart to pinch.

Frederick shook his head. "On the *Reckless*. She wouldn't come with me."

The lady turned aside, and Merrick eased an arm around her, drawing her close. She gazed up at her husband. "We must go to her."

"Nay," Frederick said. "She sails with Antoine du Casse again."

Merrick snorted. "We have three ships. I think we can handle one Frenchman."

"Three?" Frederick asked, glancing over the dark bay.

"We are to meet the *Reckoning* here tomorrow," Kent said. "Alex, Juliana, Morgan, and Rowan were helping with our search for you."

"Juliana, Morgan, and Rowan? I see I have new family members to meet." Frederick smiled.

"And a new niece! Esther," Charlisse added, leaning back on her husband as he wrapped arms around her waist.

Frederick smiled. "What grand news!"

"But pray, tell us how Reena fares. Truly," Merrick asked. "Why does she continue to run?"

Wind whistled through lines and sheets above as Frederick released a heavy sigh. "I did all I could. She refuses to see the light." He shifted his stance. "The best thing—the only thing—we can do for her now is pray."

Charlisse opened her mouth, no doubt to protest, but Merrick placed a finger on her lips and nodded. "Then pray we will."

Sashaying up to Frederick, Gabrielle kissed him on the cheek, her blonde curls glimmering in the moonlight. "Good to see you've returned, Frederick."

"And you… look at how you've grown. I'm surprised some fortunate gentleman has not snatched you away."

If possible to see a blush in the moonlight, one rose on the fair lady's cheeks. His parents had always wanted Frederick to choose Gabrielle, the good daughter, the chaste daughter, the one who followed after God. But Reena had been the one who captured his heart—wild, adventurous Reena. His heart pained at the thought of her.

Shoving aside his sorrow, he glanced over them all. "I have important news. Jean Baptiste du Casse plans to attack Kingston."

Merrick's jaw stiffened as all eyes focused on Frederick. "When?"

"Soon. Within a week or two."

"How do you know this?" Kent asked.

"Antoine blathered about it one night when he was deep in his rum."

The deck tilted and Merrick shifted his stance. "And you believe him?"

"I don't believe much of what the man says, but aye, he'd have no reason to lie."

Merrick fisted hands at his twaist. "Then as soon as the *Reckoning* appears, we will make haste back home. We must warn the governor and fortify the city and fort."

Frederick nodded. "My thinking exactly."

CHAPTER THIRTY-EIGHT

*R*eena took another sip of rum and glanced over her guests who were laughing, cursing, and partaking of their meal around the table in her cabin. They blurred in her vision. Even their words were muffled, nonsensical and…if she were forced to admit, meaningless. Nothing made sense anymore. Not since Freddy had left her.

Antoine took her hand and lifted it to his lips for a kiss. Numbly, she allowed it, for she didn't have the strength to pull it back. His sickly-sweet lemon pomade threatened to force the food she'd eaten back up her throat.

"You seem…how do you say *désemparé*…distraught tonight, Mademoiselle Pirate?" He caressed her fingers. "How can that be when we know the location of the Fount at last?"

Amazing that the man could fawn over her like some sycophant after he'd left her to hang on Martinique. But he had waved away the "regrettable" incident as if it were simply part of the game. When she inquired how he'd discovered the final island was Barbados, he'd said 'twas a simple task from his one good map.

After she saw it, she could see why. Her hastily made copy from memory was missing several important details.

He leaned toward her, grinning like a hungry shark. "You aren't still angry that we quarreled, *ma chérie*."

Quarreled? She'd laugh if her head didn't feel like it was floating toward the deckhead. Instead, she tried to focus on his face that was blurring in and out of her vision—his snakelike eyes, the regal line of his pointy nose, and the fountain of lace bubbling at his neck. She fully expected a long, forked tongue to poke out of his mouth at any moment. A deal with the devil, indeed. Just as Freddy had said.

"To the devil with the blaggard!" Fred squawked from his perch as if he could read her mind.

She chuckled. "I fear I am merely tired, Antoine. 'Tis been a long day." She shifted her gaze to Brodie and Jo deep in conversation on the other side of the table, their chairs unusually close. Then over to Abraham, who sat stiffly on Reena's other side, arms crossed over his chest, a frown on his face, and an uneaten plate of food before him. Michael, however, had gulped down his usual two helpings as a young growing lad should. As if sensing her attention, he lifted his head and smiled, an unusual twinkle in his eyes as if he knew a grand secret.

Antoine was still slobbering on her hand. His two men stood behind him, ready to shoot anyone who crossed their master. Which was the only reason the foul miscreant remained alive at the moment. That, and the fact that Freddy would disapprove if she keelhauled him.

Reena had also invited Fletcher, her helmsmen, and Hastings, her carpenter, to join them, hoping to fill the void left by Sedley and Freddy and keep the festivities going. But she was not in a very festive mood. At least, everyone save Abraham appeared to be enjoying themselves. Fletcher and Hastings were well into their cups, laughing at every joke and gasping at each outlandish story Antoine told of his exploits. Brodie and Jo seemed oblivious to anyone but each other.

Yet despite the delicious meal, the overabundance of rum, and the cause for celebration, Reena felt like she was being dragged along the bottom of the sea. With an anchor chained to her heart.

True, they had put their pieces of the map together, creating the final diagram in the center. 'Twas obvious now—the location of the Fount. Oddly, it appeared to be on an island off the southeast coast of Spanish Florida. But Reena knew of no island that existed there. Nor did Antoine. In addition, the rhyme on the map she'd retrieved from the church was rather illusive—something to do with a certain time of day, a bright reflection, and an angle of entrance. She would think on it further when her head was clear.

Antoine had taken his piece of the map back, along with one of hers, as soon as they had charted their course. She couldn't blame him. Neither of them trusted the other. And with good reason. If something went wrong, if the island wasn't there, she'd need his maps to recalculate. She hated that she still needed him, hated that she couldn't leave him on an island somewhere to rot. But his well-gunned frigate followed close behind, ready to sink the *Reckless* to the depths if she made one false move.

Pushing aside her half-eaten meal, Reena retrieved her hand, grabbed a bottle, and poured more rum into her glass, ignoring the scowl that deepened on Abraham's face. She should be excited that her quest was almost over—that her dream of eternal youth was within reach.

Then why was she so miserable?

Antoine struggled to rise, then scooted back his chair, the scraping sound grating over Reena. "I will leave you to your rest, *ma chérie*. We should be at the Fount when the sun rises." Then with a snap of his fingers, he stumbled out the door. Oddly, Michael darted out before him without begging her leave, while Antoine's men followed in his wake.

Fred stretched out his wings. "Good riddance t' the bilge-sucker!"

Her sentiments exactly. At least she had one thing to be thankful for—the sniveling maggot was too inebriated to suggest anything untoward.

Fletcher and Hastings, their entertainment having abandoned them, also rose, thanked Reena and staggered away.

Abraham grunted and shoved to his feet. "Yuh should go after Cap'n Carlton. He's good fer yuh."

She wanted to tell him that Freddy no longer wanted her, but saying the words out loud would sever what remained of her heart. Instead, she stared numbly at the candles dancing in a breeze that squeezed through the stern window panes.

Abraham marched off, leaving her alone. Or so she thought until Brodie and Jo appeared before her, hand in hand, silly grins on their faces.

Reena gazed up at them curiously, thinking perhaps she was seeing things.

"Cap'n," Brodie began nervously, his eyes skittering about the cabin before he glanced down at Jo. The lady smiled up at him as if he were the only person in the room.

"We would like yer permission and yer blessin'."

Reena rubbed her temples where a headache formed. "My blessing?"

He smiled at Jo again. "I hae asked Jo tae be my wife. An' we would like yer blessin', ye bein' our cap'n and all. Also, we want ye tae come to our weddin'."

To say Reena was shocked would be an understatement. She knew the two had affection for one another, but marriage? Jo was at least ten years Brodie's senior with nary a coin to her name. Nor even a name to be spoken of and a rather sordid past to boot. Word was Brodie hailed from both title and land in Scotland where he could return one day and marry well.

Placing her hands on the table, Reena attempted to stand. Brodie reached to help her, but she pushed him away and rose, blinking back the dizziness threatening to swallow her whole.

Her gaze oscillated between the two of them. "I can't say that I saw this coming, though I should have. 'Tis been obvious—your affection for one another. Though you have no need of my blessing, you have it, along with my congratulations. And I would be overjoyed to attend your wedding."

Uttering an unusual squeal, Jo embraced her. "Thank ye, Cap'n. I ne'er thought to be this 'appy." She looked at Reena, tears in her eyes. "But it were all yer doin'—rescuin' me an' bringin' me on yer ship, givin' me a chance at life."

Brodie swallowed, a dozen emotions swimming in his eyes. "Thank ye, Cap'n. We hope tae stay on yer brig after we are married, if ye still want us."

"Of course." Reena gripped his hand. "You are both my friends."

The couple turned and left, gazing at each other with such love that Reena felt more alone than she had in a long while.

Alone forever.

She couldn't move. The cabin spun around her in a disturbing gyration of darkness and light. She focused on the candles again, flickering back and forth with the teetering of the brig.

Something moved toward the far end of the table. Plucking her pistol from her belt, Reena squinted in that direction, blinking to clear her vision.

"Only me, Captain." Michael stood and smiled her way.

"Forgive me, lad. I thought you'd left." She shoved the pistol back in her belt.

"Good news about Brodie and Jo, ain't it? They truly love each other." He glanced out the door where they'd just left.

"Indeed." Reena dropped back into her chair, suddenly wishing to be alone, embarrassed by her drunken state. "You should get some sleep, Michael. We have a long day tomorrow."

Instead of leaving, the young boy approached and gazed at her curiously. Yet there was no judgment in his eyes, only...*love*? Reaching in the pocket of his coat, he pulled out two pieces of parchment and laid them gently on the table.

"What is this?" She rubbed her eyes, trying to focus on the paper. Grabbing the pieces, she unfolded them.

The lines came into view, blurred, then came back into view. "'Tis Antoine's sections of the map." She gazed up at Michael and found a beaming grin on his face and a light in his eyes that seemed to reflect in a circle around him.

She shook her head. "Where...?" She glanced back at the maps. "How...?"

"'Twas easy, Captain. No one notices a boy. When Antoine stumbled down the companionway, the brig tipped, and I purposely bumped into him, reached in his pocket, and grabbed them. Thought they might give you an advantage over him. I don't like the way he looks at you." Michael's lips puckered as if he tasted something sour.

Rising, Reena stumbled, gripped the table, and then drew Michael close. She kissed the top of his head that smelled of sunshine and the sea. "I can't believe you did this. Thank you, Michael. I don't deserve your kindness."

"None of us deserve anything, Captain. It's only God who loves, forgives, and blesses us above what we can imagine." Then pushing back from her, he smiled yet again. "I best get to bed. God bless you, Captain." And off he darted out the door, closing it behind them.

"If God be fer us, who can be against us?" Fred bobbed his head up and down, and Reena gaped at him, wondering who had taught the bird Scripture.

Freddy, no doubt. If only to torture her in his absence. Huffing, Reena gently folded the maps and tucked them inside her waistcoat with the others. Then grabbing a bottle of rum, she turned and sat on the stern window ledge, staring over the endless charcoal sea. Moonlight laced the waves with pearls—far too beautiful for her dour mood.

She didn't have the heart to tell Michael that having possession of all the maps would do her no good if they found the Fount tomorrow. Still, his concern for her warmed her greatly. And she'd certainly enjoy watching Antoine's temper explode when he found them missing. Regardless, it wouldn't be long before, Fount or no, she'd rid herself of the bloated vermin and his inglorious frigate, *Conquérant*.

Lifting the bottle to her lips, she took another sip and scanned the horizon, her thoughts drifting to Freddy as they always did. Was he on board his father's ship by now? Reunited with his loved ones? Among his own kind again—the *godly* kind? Did he even think of her, long for her?

Tears burned behind her eyes, but she shoved them back. Even if she found the Fount, drank from its miraculous waters, and then returned to Jamaica, he had said they were finished. And she knew he meant it.

She rubbed the bottle and took another sip. Though why, she had no idea. The alcohol numbed her senses but only enhanced her pain. "How am I to live without you, Freddy?" At least the year she had searched for him, she'd had hope—hope that when she found him, he'd change his mind. But now, her hope was gone, sunk to the bottom of the sea, along with all her dreams.

Freddy had changed. She hadn't counted on that. He was not the Freddy she'd known. He was kinder, stronger, more honorable. He no longer lost his temper like he used to do. He was gentle and patient, and he never drank overmuch. Plus, he resisted her every temptation! Such control and self-sacrifice she'd not seen the likes of in any man. Was it truly God who had changed him? There was a new light in his eyes, an inner joy that had naught to do with circumstance—a purpose that went beyond the next adventure. Nor could she deny the desperation in his eyes for her to know this God of his. To follow Him as he did.

The events of the past month passed across her memory. The miracles on the island, how Freddy had said they would be rescued, and against all odds, they were; the bright sword she had seen protecting her during the mutiny; the incredible transformation of Castries, Saint Lucia, after her parents had ministered there for years. And how could she forget Crimson Jack's grave, his inglorious resting place—the disgraceful end of fame, fortune, and power? And what of the angel she'd seen while in the pillory on Martinique? How Freddy had healed that young lad's twisted foot? And of course, the Radcliffs, so happy and in love after all these years. She could not shake her vision of them, her peek into the spirit realm—to see them as they truly were, young and beautiful. She huffed. And then of course, Brodie and Jo, so in love—regardless of age, fame, name, and fortune.

Had Reena been wrong all along? The world shouted at her day and night that fortune, beauty, youth, and fame were what mattered—were all that could make one truly happy. Yet everything she'd seen in the past few weeks had proved all of that was a lie, a brilliant deception forced upon mankind in order to lead them down the wrong path.

A tear slid down her cheek, and she swiped it away as she gazed over the dark expanse above her. "Am I on the wrong path?" As expected, no answer came, save the purl of water against the hull and creak and grind of her timbers. Somewhere on deck, a fiddle played a sad tune. Yet how could saving herself and others from death be wrong?

She let out a long sigh. Mayhap everything Freddy had told her was true—that a life serving God and others was the only path to true fulfillment, joy, and peace. How could that be? It made no sense. Yet she could not deny all the things she'd seen in the past month.

"God, are you there? Do You actually care about me?" She waited to hear a trumpet blast or a deep voice that shook the bulkhead, but nothing came. What did she expect? She was far too evil, had done too many hideous things for God to take note of her. She took another sip of rum and felt something stir deep within her… as if someone had lit a candle and it sparked ever so slightly.

God?

Precious one. The words rose up within her—not audible, yet distinct and full of love.

More tears spilled down her cheeks. "If that is You, tell me what to do."

Yet even as she said it, she wondered if she could obey if He asked her to give up pirating, to give up the Fount. Freddy had told her she already had eternal life, and that where she spent that eternity depended on whom she served—God or Satan. There was no in between. Perhaps living forever in this evil world wasn't the best idea, after all. Not if there was a better world waiting for her and those she loved.

Rising, she stumbled over to her looking glass hanging on the wall, picked up a candle, and held it to her face. Indeed, she was still beautiful and young, but was this skin just a covering—a garment, a piece of clothing that would age and fade and someday be taken off? Was her real self beneath the surface? And if so, wasn't that the only part of her that mattered?

Seeing the Radcliffs as they really were in eternity had been a gift from God. No doubt to show her that no matter how old or ugly one became on the outside, if one's spirit was joined with God, they were beautiful and strong on the inside. Perhaps that was the beauty the Radcliffs saw when they gazed at each other—the inside, not the outside.

It was too much to consider. Rubbing her eyes, she wandered back to her seat, set down the candle, and blew it out. She wanted to pray but didn't know how. Would God even hear her in her inebriation?

"God, help."

Follow Me and live.

"I want to. I really do…" But how could she give up her dreams?

I have better dreams for you.

More tears streamed down her cheeks, dropping onto her breeches. She batted them away, hating her weakness, hoping nobody entered the cabin to witness it.

Follow Me, the voice said again. *And I will give you abundant life.*

Abundant life. She wanted that. She longed for that—something real, something eternal, the joy and purpose she'd seen in Freddy, that she saw in Abraham and Michael. What did all the youth and vitality in the world mean if she was alone and miserable forever?

"You win, God…*Father.*" Though she hesitated to call him that. "I submit myself to You. I receive Jesus, your Son, and the sacrifice He made to pay for my sin. I receive it and cling to it and trust and believe in You and You alone." She knew the words to say, had heard them from her parents. But this time she meant them from her heart.

The candle she had blown out sparked to life yet again. She stared at the flame spurting and flickering. How? *Impossible.* Yet suddenly she felt as if that lit candle had been placed in her soul, burning brighter and brighter, rushing life-giving light through her veins, through her pores, to every fiber of her being, scattering the darkness forever.

A weight lifted from her shoulders—a weight she hadn't realized was there, but in its absence she felt as though she could float up into the night sky.

"Thank you, thank you, thank you, Father!" She kept saying over and over and over again, alternating between bowing her head in reverence and staring at the stars in worship of their Creator. Love fell upon her like warm waves of the sea, so overwhelming she thought she would drown for the joy of it.

Is this what Freddy had been trying to tell her?

I love you, Daughter.

"I love You, too, Father." Minutes passed as she sat, basking in her Father's love. She tossed the bottle of rum away, no longer needing it. "But what am I to do, now? With Antoine?"

Suddenly a glorious, devious, wonderful idea occurred to her.

She smiled. This was going to be fun.

CHAPTER THIRTY-NINE

*D*awn's light found Reena standing at the bow of the ship, boots sturdy against the heaving deck, loose hair fluttering behind her with every blast of the trade winds. She drew a deep breath and gripped the hilt of her cutlass, relishing in the scent of the sea…and something else…a new scent—the sweet scent of freedom. She'd not slept all night, had spent every minute praising her newfound Father, bathing in His love and the light that now lit her soul…in His Spirit that filled her and gave her new life and purpose. She could hardly contain it. She also prayed for Freddy, for her family, and for the events of the day about to begin. Regardless of her new life, she still had to clean up her old mess, and that would be no easy task.

She adjusted the pouch over her shoulder and glanced up at the topmen furling canvas above. They'd sailed all night and finally reached the destination marked on the maps—the location of the island that contained the Fountain of Youth. Though she could see no such island, not even as the predawn light began to push aside the darkness, she knew it was there—hidden away from all but those who solved the final rhyme.

The sun blasted over the horizon, spearing shards of light over the sea, bold and unafraid of the darkness, pushing it back like the tip of a spear forced back an enemy. The pad of footsteps spun her around to see Michael climbing the foredeck ladder, a cup of steaming chocolate in his hand. Taking it from him, she smiled, noting the extra glimmer in his eyes, the knowing look he gave her.

"How do you know?" she asked.

Sunlight glinted off his teeth. "I'm so happy for you, Captain. There's a grand celebration going on in heaven in your honor!" He glanced up at the brightening sky as if he could actually see such a thing.

"There is, is there?" She shook her head at his boyish delusions. "And how would you know such a thing?"

"I prayed for you last night."

"Thank you." She sipped her chocolate and longed to speak with him about how he came to his own faith, but sailors popped up from the hatches, and Abraham hailed her from the quarterdeck. She must face the day.

"Let us talk later." She finished her drink and handed him the cup.

Michael smiled. "You have nothing to fear" was all he said before he scrambled away.

With all sails lowered, the *Reckless* eased to a slow drift as Reena made her way down the foredeck ladder to the main deck. She had almost reached the quarterdeck ladder when Antoine popped up from the hatch, his two brutes behind him. His face was redder than usual and a bit swollen, but 'twas his eyes that gripped her—narrow and seething like a volcano about to erupt.

Halting, she swallowed her fear and fisted hands at her waist. "Didn't sleep well?"

"*Où sont mes cartes?*" He raged toward her, but two of her crew leapt in his path. Abraham flew down the quarterdeck ladder and took a position by her side.

She cocked her head. "I fear my French is lacking, monsieur. Something about maps?"

"You know exactly what I said, Mademoiselle *Pirate*." He stepped back from the sailors and pointed a loaded finger at her. "You stole my maps!"

"Me?" She laid a hand on the pouch at her side and felt the bottle within, then shrugged. "What difference does it make? We are already at the location of the island, and surely you remember the rhyme?" She arched a sarcastic brow.

"*Bien sûr.*" He snarled. "Regardless, I trusted you, and you stole my maps yet again."

Wind swirled the odor of his lemon pomade beneath her nose, and she gave a tight smile. "I believe 'twas you who stole my maps to begin with."

"And *you* who stole the first one from my home!"

"Come now, Antoine," she returned nonchalantly. "You yourself admitted that we are both pirates."

He held out his beefy fingers. "Hand them over, and I will forgive you, *ma chouette*."

"I neither need nor desire your forgiveness, *mon rat*."

He fingered his chin. "*Mais* you do, mademoiselle. Or you and your brig will be blasted to bits." His glance took in the frigate drifting off their starboard quarter. "As you said, we are here. Let us put aside our differences, examine the maps, and determine the meaning of the rhyme, non?"

"You mean *I* will determine the meaning. You haven't the brains for it."

He grimaced. "And I will be by your side when you do. Then we will both find the Fount."

Reena breathed out a sigh. "I fear, monsieur, we will not find the Fount today." Drawing the pouch forward, she opened it and pulled out the maps, fanning them out before him to give him a good view.

"*Sacré bleu!*" Antoine reached to pluck them from her hands, but she whisked them away and stepped back. Pulling an empty bottle of rum from her pouch, she stuffed them inside and shoved the cork on top.

"*Que fais-tu?*" Antoine fingered the butt of his pistol while his men took a stance by his side, hands on the pommels of their swords.

"What am I doing?" she repeated his question. "Why, 'tis all our precious maps, stuffed in this bottle for safekeeping." A ray of sunlight struck the bottle, revealing the maps for what they were—old parchment covered with naught but scribblings.

Abraham gave her a sideways glance of confusion.

"*Bon*," Antoine said. "Give it to me." Once again, he held out his hand. With the other, he drew his pistol and leveled it at her chest. The chime of Abraham's sword, along with several others pierced the otherwise peaceful dawn.

"I fear I cannot do that, Antoine. You may shoot me if you wish, but my men will also shoot you and your men."

The deck canted over a wave as wind flapped loose canvas above.

Confusion twisted Antoine's expression. "If you do not wish to find the Fount, then why not give me the maps and allow me to do so."

"Because if I have realized one thing this past month, 'tis that no one as evil as you should live forever in this place."

Abraham chuckled.

Sweat beaded on Antoine's forehead as he glanced around, no doubt realizing that he was sorely outnumbered. "I will signal my ship to fire upon you."

Reena shrugged. "'Tis your choice." Then gazing up to heaven, she smiled at the puffy clouds floating across a bowl of cerulean blue and did her best to peer beyond to her Father in heaven.

Though she could not see Him, she could sense Him smiling back at her.

Then lowering her gaze, and without a moment's hesitation, she hurled the bottle into the sea.

The crack of a pistol echoed across the deck. Reena did not move. No doubt her time on earth had come to an end. Everything became muddled and slow. She braced for the bullet to rip through her heart. A bright light blinded her. She blinked and spotted the light flashing across the deck. And then it was gone. She glanced to her left. Only Michael stood by her side. Smoke curled from Antoine's pistol. Where was the pain? She patted her chest, waiting to feel the blood drain from her heart. She felt her head, arms, and looked down at her breeches. No blood appeared.

Antoine tossed his pistol to the deck and rushed to the railing. "Are you mad?"

"Nay, I believe I've finally come to my senses," she replied curtly.

Abraham smiled.

Whirling about, Antoine glared at her, fire and fury spitting from his face. "Those are not the real maps!"

Reena shrugged. "And yet you saw them with your own eyes."

He studied her for a moment as if assessing her sanity. "Why would you give up now? When we are so close?"

"I find I have no need to live forever in this place." She smiled.

He stared back at the bottle, bobbing in the waves. "But the rhyme. I don't remember it all."

"And I have forgotten it as well." Reena gave a sarcastic sigh.

Growling, Antoine snapped his fingers at his men, then leapt onto the bulwarks and jumped into the water. A mighty splash sounded, and Reena, along with Abraham and Michael darted to the railing to watch.

His two buffoons rushed to follow their master, hesitating only to cast her a smoldering glance before they jumped in after him.

Antoine swam toward the bottle, which had drifted a good distance away, kicking and splashing up a hailstorm of foam. His men didn't fare as well as they floundered in the water, merely trying to stay afloat.

Reena laughed harder than she had in a long while. Abraham and Michael joined her as her crew cheered and assembled at the railing to watch.

"I do believe Sedley should join them, don't you think?" She winked at Abraham, and smiling, he turned to issue the order.

Within minutes, the traitorous scamp appeared on deck, blinking from the bright sun and trembling in fear.

The sailor dragged him to the railing to stand before Reena.

"Since you prefer Antoine's command over mine, Sedley, you may join him."

Sedley's eyes darted to the three men thrashing in the water below and gulped. "Please, Cap'n. I swears I'll change."

"I pray you do, Sedley. But for now, off with you." She gestured toward Abraham, and he picked Sedley up by the belt and tossed him into the sea. Arms flailing, the man struck hard, disappeared beneath the water, but finally surfaced.

"Cap'n!" one of her crew gestured toward Antoine's frigate.

Gun ports flew open, and the charred muzzles of ten guns bid them welcome.

"Time to go! Lay aloft, topmen!" Reena spun on her heels, took the quarterdeck ladder in two leaps, and moved to her command position. In truth, she doubted the frigate would dare to fire her guns and risk hitting their captain swimming so close.

"Do yuh think he'll get it?" Abraham called up from the main deck as the crew scrambled aloft to unfurl sail.

"Nay." Shielding her eyes from the sun, she glanced toward the bottle, sparkling in the rising sun. "'Tis too far by now. And it will eventually sink to the bottom of the sea where it belongs."

Nodding, Abraham turned to issue further orders. "Man de royal halliards an' sheets. Haul taut!"

Michael tugged on her sleeve, drawing her gaze. "I must leave you now."

Reena stared at him. "What? Why would you say that?"

The thunderous flap of canvas filled her ears.

"My work is done." He smiled and reached for her. She took his hand in hers, small and blistered from hard work. But then, the boy grew, taller and taller, filling out in bone and muscle. His hand stretched within hers until it consumed her feminine fingers. She blinked. Was the rum still affecting her vision? But still, he grew, stopping when he towered at least two feet above her. She could hardly breathe. *What?* A light, brighter than any she'd seen, drew a circle around him, so bright she could no longer make out his face. The last thing she saw was a gleaming sword sheathed at his side…

Then he disappeared.

Reena glanced over the main deck, the foredeck, and then behind her where Fletcher stood at the tiller. But he was looking down, paying no attention.

Fighting back tears, she stared into the sky. *You sent him to protect me. All this time…Even when I was at my worst, You loved me.*

"Heave! Heave!" her linesmen shouted, drawing Reena's attention back to the deck. She hadn't time to ponder what had just happened. Swiping the moisture from her eyes, she studied the frigate, her guns still aimed at the *Reckless*. Soon sails caught the wind in a roaring snap, and the brig jerked forward and sped on her way.

Boom! Boom! Boom! Cannons exploded, and she turned to see their shots splash into the sea off the *Reckless'* stern.

Extending her hand in a flourish, she offered the frigate a sardonic bow as more sails glutted with wind and the *Reckless* swept out of their range.

"Where to, Cap'n?" Fletcher said from the tiller.

Gathering herself, she put hands on her waist and faced forward. "Jamaica. We have an island to protect."

CHAPTER FORTY

June 28th, 1694, Kingston, Jamaica

Frederick stood upon the stone battlements of Fort Charles, gazing out over the narrow inlet that led from the sea to Kingston Harbor. Governor Beeston had assigned him and his father the task of refortifying the fort under the command of Colonel Beckford. During the past week they'd rebuilt one of the damaged bastions, laid a line of nineteen culverins pointed to the east and five to the west, and ensured the gun crews were proficient in loading, firing, and aiming.

Captain Merrick and his son Alex fitted out a vessel as a fireship and helped to navigate all the merchant ships in the area into a defensive line before the harbor. Captain Dutton, who was Alex's brother-in-law, had positioned his ship, the *Reckoning* before the fort—all guns run out and ready to do battle. Inside the harbor, Lady Charlisse and Lady Isabel commanded the *Redemption* and the *Restitution* in case the French were able to slip by Fort Charles.

Kingston was ready for Admiral Jean Baptiste du Casse. And the scoundrel knew it, for though seventeen of his ships came within sight of Port Royal on Monday last, they soon sailed away, only to anchor at Cow Bay, and then later at Carlisle Bay. Fortunately, having been warned by the governor, the citizens of St. David and St. Thomas had all but left and were huddled amongst friends and family in Kingston.

Frederick ground his teeth. Regardless, the French had landed hundreds of troops to the west of Kingston and plundered, burnt, and destroyed everything in their path— killed cattle, drove flocks of sheep into houses and set them on fire, burnt fields of sugar cane, pulled up herbs and even cut down fruit trees. But the worst was the news that some of the straggling citizens had been tortured, murdered, and the women ravished.

Even from Fort Charles, he could hear the cannon fire and gunshot echoing through the jungle, and it irked him to no end that he could not join the battle. But he had his assignment, and he knew he'd be needed here if the French dared to attack the fort.

His father came to stand beside him, his coal-black hair striped in gray blowing behind him in the fierce wind. Frederick searched for the familiar bitterness and resentment he always felt in the man's presence, but it had dissipated, along with Frederick's fear he was just like him. In truth, he *was* just like him, for, despite an evil beginning, his father was a new man, good and honorable, following the true path of a God who loved him, who loved them all. And Frederick was on that path now, as well.

Kent drew a deep breath. "Hard to stand by and not assist."

Frederick nodded. "Beeston has called troops to St. Dorothy. Do you think they'll attempt to land there?"

"Who knows with this madman du Casse?"

"You think *he's* unhinged, you should meet his nephew." Frederick chuckled.

Kent smiled.

Frederick glanced over the waves of maroon, gold, and orange floating above the horizon, amazed how such beauty could exist when such evil was being perpetrated. "The sun sets. 'Tis a good sign we have not heard of any further fighting."

"Indeed." Kent's gaze sped to the *Reckoning*, guarding the entrance to the harbor. "Mayhap we scared them off." He gripped his son by the shoulder. "Without your warning, Kingston would have been caught off guard, and our families, our friends, and possibly our homes would have been destroyed."

"I suppose you should thank Reena, for I wouldn't have known about the attack had she not kidnapped me." The sound of her name brought yet another pang to his heart, and he wondered if she had found her precious Fountain of Youth. He pictured her and Antoine dipping cups into its waters, laughing and drinking their fill.

As if his father knew his thoughts, he said, "We have been praying for her. God will not let go of her. Have faith, Son."

Clang! Clang! Clang! The fort's bell rang. A trumpet sounded and Frederick and Kent swung about to see Colonel Beckford climbing the ladder to the battlements.

"They are sailing away!" He beamed as he approached. "Admiral du Casse has given up!"

Marines and sailors alike cheered, laughed, and tossed "Huzzahs" into the air.

Frederick could hardly believe it. "How can you be sure?"

Beckford removed his hat and swiped his sleeve over his forehead. "We thought they were coming ashore at Port Morant, but instead they gathered wood and water, put ashore several prisoners, and then sailed away!"

"Prisoners?" Kent smiled and glanced over the sea. "Then, aye, they are indeed leaving."

"We couldn't have done it without you, Mr. Carlton." Beckford extended his hand. "You took a huge risk coming here."

Frederick shook his hand. "I am glad to help."

"A ship approaches!" one of the marines shouted from his post, and all eyes turned toward the sea. Two white sails appeared on the turquoise waters, growing larger and larger against the setting sun.

Beckford marched down the line. "Norwell, Rogers, ready cannons one and two and await my order."

"Wait." Frederick plucked a telescope from his father's belt and held it to his eye. White foam shot up from the bow of the brig as she hastened toward them. He shifted the glass to her deck, where blurry figures appeared, and then up to her ensign. "She's flying the Union Jack!" he shouted.

"It could be a trick," Kent said. "Mayhap a fireship."

Frederick focused the scope yet again, longing to see what his heart already told him was true. He could hear the cannonballs as they were placed inside the muzzles, hear their eerie grate as they slid down the bores.

"Stand down!" he shouted. "I know this brig. 'Tis the *Reckless*."

Reena knew she was taking a huge risk sailing straight toward Port Royal and Kingston Harbor. Especially when they were no doubt on alert for Admiral du Casse's fleet to return. Especially when she was a known pirate in these waters. But she knew of no other way to announce herself and to see Freddy and her family as soon as possible. She had much to explain. She had much for which to apologize. And she could not wait another minute to do so.

She had not made it in time to help with the battle, for she had seen du Casse's fleet sailing away. She couldn't help but smile at the sight. Freddy had made it in time, and their city, their home, and their island had been saved. Gripping the quarterdeck railing, she gazed aloft at the sky fading to gray as the sun touched the horizon and thanked her newfound Father for his rich mercy and grace.

"Deys pointin' deir cannons at us, Cap'n," Abraham said from her side.

"Indeed. Can you blame them?"

He grinned. "I like dis new Cap'n. God sure do answer prayer in de most astoundin' ways."

"That He does, Abraham. That He does."

Though her crew still obeyed her, they seemed a bit jittery sailing straight into a British port. Naval authorities most often looked the other way at pirates who preyed on their enemies, but they were known to capture those without letters of marque. Hence, there was still a chance she and her crew would be arrested on the spot. She had promised them that if fired upon, they'd sail down the coast, where they could leave her ashore.

Brodie, however, found the entire adventure fascinating as he and Jo leaned on the quarterdeck railing and gazed toward

Fort Charles. Jo was not of the same mind. She'd all but begged Reena to allow her to ready the guns. But Reena had ordered her to stand down. Now, as the woman smiled up at her fiancé, 'twould seem she'd forgotten all her fears. Reena's heart swelled at the sight of them, noting that Brodie no longer carried around his flask. Indeed, God *did* work in the most astounding ways.

The *Reckless* listed to starboard, rising and plunging through the seas, creaking and groaning as she went. Reena flung her loose hair behind her and balanced on the jolting deck as wind blasted her with the sweet smell of jungle, tropical flowers…and home. They were now within firing range, and she could clearly see the dark muzzles of three cannons pointed her way. To her right just below the fort, a brig lay becalmed abreast of the island. Raising the scope, she spotted the words *Reckoning* on its hull. The famous pirate ship, *Reckoning*? But how could that be?

"Shorten sail!" she shouted as they entered the inlet, and Abraham complimented her order with a string of further commands.

Reena kept her eye on the *Reckoning*. No guns had been run out, and her crew sat idly by on the main deck. All save a man and woman who waved at her as she passed. *Waved*? A sign of friendship or a trap?

"Lord, help me," she whispered.

Drawing a deep breath to steady her nerves, she glanced up as they passed beneath the fort. Several men peered down at her from the battlements above. Her heart both leapt and froze at the same time. Freddy? Could that be Freddy? Yet how could she mistake his dark hair blowing in the wind, the cut of his jaw, and that intense stare of his. Before she could grab her scope, he was gone…as if she'd only conjured him up to ease her pain.

It only enhanced it. Her heart sank back to her chest as she faced forward again.

With main sails lowered, the *Reckless* eased over the water under topsails alone and entered Kingston Harbor without incident. Reena would never get used to the new Port Royal, a third of which had been cast into the sea during the earthquake two years past. Though they were attempting to rebuild it, she doubted the city would ever be the same. Across the glittering turquoise bay, the city of Kingston had grown since she'd last been here—encroaching upon the green hills like a mighty crab emerging from the sea.

Her father's ship, the *Redemption,* along with the *Restitution* were anchored toward the middle of the harbor, no doubt to protect the city. Nerves pinched at the thought of facing her family after all these years, of the shame and disappointment she'd see on their faces. But she must endure the consequences of her actions.

"Is dat Cap'n Carlton?" Abraham's voice snapped her gaze back to Port Royal where a dark-haired man ran along the shore, waving at her. Freddy? Aye, it *was* Freddy! Excitement buzzed through her.

"Sheet home! Lower topsails!" she bellowed. "Let go the anchor." She eased the *Reckless* to within twenty yards of the shores of Port Royal.

Brodie turned to face her. "Ach now, seems Cap'n Carlton is nae angry wit' ye anymore." He lifted his brows.

Jo smiled. "Go to 'im, Reen—I mean Cap'n. Looks like 'e 'as somethin' to say."

Reena glanced up at Abraham, who gave a nod of approval. "I'll stay wit' de ship, Cap'n." Then cupping his hands, he gave the order for a boat to be lowered.

Doing her best not to hope for anything from Freddy save what she deserved—a severe chastening, Reena climbed into the jolly boat and gave the order for her men to start rowing. A myriad of confounding emotions battled within her, love being the foremost—hope, fear, sorrow, and shame among the others.

Freddy halted on shore and waited her arrival, but she couldn't make out his expression. She shifted in her seat, hugged herself, then wrung her hands together, hardly able to wait another minute. What was taking so long? The edge of the sun slipped behind the horizon, drawing more light with it. She squinted, desperate to see whether love or anger lined his face. Wait…could it be? She could take it no longer. Standing, she caught her balance for a moment, then jumped over the side of the boat and plunged into the water.

CHAPTER FORTY-ONE

*F*or the life of him, Frederick couldn't understand why Reena was here. Had she found the Fountain of Youth already? Come to gloat about her newfound eternal life? Or mayhap she'd come to beg him to join her yet again. None of those made any sense, for she certainly would not sail straight into Kingston Harbor, risking her crew and brig in a battle with the French. Nor would she return to a place where her parents lived, especially a British Naval post where she was wanted for piracy. Yet, as he continued to stare at her from the top of Fort Charles, a wonderful, glorious thought occurred, rising up through his spirit and causing his legs to dart down the ladder, through the fort, past the barricades, and down to the shore, where she would see him as she sailed past.

She did. The anchor was tossed with a mighty splash, and the *Reckless* slid to a halt just twenty yards offshore—some distance from her father's brig, which he expected. What he didn't expect was the pounding of his heart as she climbed into a boat and headed toward him. Confusion and oddly, hope, battled within him. Hope for what? That she had come to her senses, that she had returned to God? Absolutely! Yet there was something more he didn't wish to admit, for he'd told her in no uncertain terms that they could never be.

And still she came. With every slap of the oars into the water, every heave of the boat through the waves, her expression became more and more clear. Not one of angst, worry, or anger, as was her normal state, but one of… dare he say, joy and peace? With a hint of nervousness… vulnerability. Nay, not Reena. He rubbed his eyes to clear the vision when a splash brought his gaze back up to see Reena swimming toward him. Was she mad? But he already knew the answer to that. Aye, she was incredibly, magnificently, and deliciously mad! Before he came to his senses, he ripped off his boots and dove into the warm waters to meet her.

They splashed toward one another for what seemed an eternity before he took her in his arms and drew her close. They sank beneath the waves, but resurfaced a moment later, both gasping and treading water. Her golden eyes searched his, reaching out to him like a light in the darkness, before tears filled them.

Clapping sounded from the *Reckless* where Abraham, Brodie, Jo, and the rest of the crew cheered from the railing. Laughing, Reena faced Frederick again.

"Freddy…Forgive me. Please forgive me. I love you!"

And at that moment, he knew. He knew that she had given her life to the Lord, that she had finally seen the light. "Come." Turning, he swam to shore. She followed and as soon as his feet struck sand, he stood and pulled her up beside him.

She took a step back, unsure, as waves swirled about their feet. Water dripped from her hair hanging to her waist, from her waistcoat, her cheeks and chin. It beaded in her lashes, sparkling in the setting sun. If mermaids existed, she was by far the most beautiful of them all.

"Seems we are destined to reunite in the sea, Kitten." He eased a wet strand of hair from her cheek. "Reminds me of the night you kidnapped me from HMS *Viper*."

She arched a sodden brow. "You mean rescued."

He held out a hand for her, and as she took it, her smile melted every part of him, every resistance he'd built up against this precious woman. "I love you, Reena Charlisse Hyde. I always have and I always will."

A tear spilled down her cheek as she fell into his arms and kissed him…long and deep and more full of love then he ever remembered. Finally, he forced himself to withdraw. Yet she remained, lips parted, eyes closed, breath puffing between them as if she were in a dream she didn't wish to end.

"What of your Fountain?" he asked.

Slowly, she opened her eyes, drew a deep breath, and gazed over the harbor. "What need have I of a Fountain when I already have eternal life with my Father in heaven?" She lowered her chin. "I hope you can forgive me, Freddy. I was wrong. I was so wrong about everything."

Frederick could hardly contain himself. He'd been right. Praise God! "Of course, I forgive you." He kissed her forehead and drew her against him.

"So, am I to understand from that kiss that you are not done with me yet?" she teased with a grin.

But before he could answer, a throat clearing drew both their gazes to Frederick's father standing on shore, arms crossed over his chest, but with a smile on his face. Taking Reena's hand in his, Frederick sloshed through the surf and onto dry sand.

"Greetings, Reena," Kent said, studying her. "I see you've found your way home."

"Aye, Sir. Better late than never." She glanced toward the fort. "Though I had hoped to join the fight."

"We took care of that Frenchman. Thanks to Frederick here."

A squeal echoed over the water and Frederick spotted Charlisse heading toward them in a boat from the *Redemption*, looking as though she might jump into the water just as her daughter had done.

Reena stiffened beside him, and he knew 'twould be difficult for her to face the people she had so wronged over the years.

The boat struck sand, and before the sailors could settle it, Charlisse leapt out and stormed toward her daughter.

The look of love on her mother's face after all Reena had done, after all her rebellion, after the years she'd kept her distance, nearly made her crumble to the sand. Despite Reena's sodden, dripping attire, Charlisse hugged her so tight, she thought she'd squeeze all the sea from her clothes.

"My baby girl. My baby girl!" Her mother nudged her backward and examined her as if she could fix any wounds, any flaws with merely the love in her eyes.

She smelled like beauty and sunshine, her unique scent invoking memories of the way she had loved and cared for Reena when she was little. And Reena could contain her tears no longer. They came streaming down her cheeks and fell to join the sea in her shirt. "Forgive me, Mama."

"I know. I know, dearest. I forgive you." She shook her head, her graying blond curls blowing in the wind. "I'm just so happy to see you." She wiped Reena's tears with her thumb.

"What's this? The prodigal has returned?"

Reena knew that voice—deep, resounding, and authoritative. Able to command a fleet of men and scatter a dozen pirates with nary a spark of resistance. Gathering her courage, she turned to face her father, Captain Edmund Merrick.

His jaw tight, his eyes impenetrable, he walked toward her. Lowering her gaze, she braced herself for the berating of a lifetime. Which was what she deserved. And more.

Instead, strong arms gripped her shoulders and drew her close. The unique scent of her father—musk and the sea—rekindled feelings of protection and safety.

"Precious, precious daughter. We have been praying for you." He forced her back, his expression now one of love and acceptance.

"Oh, Papa." She blinked back tears. "I've been such a fool."

Charlisse eased an arm around Reena's waist. "But you are home now. And looking more like a pirate, I might say, than our daughter." One brow rose.

Freddy laughed and Reena couldn't help but smile. "I take after you, Mother."

Grinning, Merrick winked at his wife. "She has a point, love."

"I have so much to tell you all." Reena said as a bell rang from the fort. "But wait." Her eyes shifted to Freddy, sudden fear pinching her. "You are wanted for desertion."

He snorted. "No thanks to you."

"Why haven't they arrested you? You must leave immediately." She tugged on his arm, but Freddy was looking at Captain Merrick.

"I may be a pirate-preacher," Merrick began with a smile. "But I am still an Earl of the Realm, and one who has the ear of the Admiralty. As providence determined, a judge from the Court happened to be in Kingston, and once I explained to him the circumstances surrounding Frederick's *kidnapping*"—he turned a sardonic eye toward Reena—"he absolved him of all charges. In fact, he has been released from further naval service as well. On one condition, however."

"And what might that be?" Reena asked, suddenly concerned he may be shipped far away from her in service of the crown.

"That they could count on him *and* the rest of the family"—Merrick glanced at Kent and Charlisse—"to be privateers during wartime, should the need arise."

Reena's heart felt like it would explode for the happiness that filled it.

Charlisse looped her arm through Reena's. "Now, daughter, you must come home at once. We will plan a huge feast in your honor. Gabrielle and Alex are here, and you've yet to meet Juliana, Rowan, and Morgan, and of course, little Esther!" She glanced toward the *Restitution*. "And Isabel and Freddy's brothers and sisters as well. Oh, 'tis too good to be true. My family is all together at last!"

Reena kissed her mother's cheek. "I cannot wait." Yet... she paused and looked up at Freddy. How she longed to hear his answer to her question, to know whether there was a chance for them to be together. True, he had kissed her. Quite passionately in fact. But he'd also done so when he'd been determined to leave her.

Charlisse glanced at Frederick and back at Reena, then nudged her husband away. "We'll meet you at the house."

Merrick's brow furrowed. "But why not take them with us now? We have fresh attire at home."

"Come now, husband." Charlisse winked at Reena over her shoulder as she all but dragged Merrick and Kent away.

Drawing a deep breath, Reena faced Freddy. Water still dripped from his hair onto an open collared shirt, whose tie strings flapped in the breeze. Sodden breeches clung to his muscular legs as he shifted his bare feet in the sand.

"You never answered my question," she said.

"What question was that?"

"Whether you are done with me or not." She couldn't look at him, didn't want to see the answer on his face before he spoke. "And truly I don't blame you after all I've put you through. Also, you must know I didn't turn back to God because—"

Freddy's lips covered hers. Not just covered but consumed like a man long deprived of his most valuable treasure.

Minutes passed. Minutes in which the warmth inside her grew to a ball of flaming heat that spread through every ounce of her, making her yearn all the more to be a part of him. Finally, he withdrew. His breath filled the air between them as he lifted her chin with his finger until their eyes were but inches apart—those stark green eyes of his examining every speck of her face. A strand of dark hair dangled over his stubbled jaw. Reena couldn't breathe.

"Kitten, how can I be done with someone whom I'm asking to be my wife?"

"Wife...wife..." She stuttered, her thoughts spinning. She started to wobble, but Freddy steadied her with a touch. "Are you asking...?" Dare she hope? Dare she dream?

He lowered to one knee, took her hand, and placed a kiss upon it. "I am."

"Yes! Yes! Forever yes!" She pulled him up and leapt into his arms, and together they whirled around, laughing.

Was it possible to die from happiness? If so, she was in grave danger. But this was the kind of danger she could get used to. And what an adventure it would be—living with this man, loving this man, and serving a God who made all their dreams come true.

If you enjoyed this book, you might enjoy the other books in the series, **The Redemption**, **The Reliance**, **The Restitution**, **The Ransom**, **The Reckoning**, **The Reckless**.

Author's Historical Note

On June 17th, 1694, Admiral Jean-Baptiste du Casse in command of a French fleet of ships sailed up to the Jamaican coast with the intent to attack Port Royal and Kingston and win them for France. However, after seeing Port Royal so well fortified, the French anchored in Cow Bay, seven leagues to the east of the city. Fortunately, Governor Beeston had been duly warned of the impending attack and had ordered the people living at St. David and St. Thomas to come to Kingston for safety. Still, the French landed and proceeded to plunder the cities, along with the crops, and tortured the citizens who had remained behind.

Having done all the damage they could, they then set sail to Carlisle Bay, where they anchored in the afternoon of the 18th. The next day, the French threw up balls of wild fire from every ship as signals for landing, and by daylight had landed what was estimated to be up to 1,500 men. They fell upon the breastwork under the command of Colonel Sutton of the Clarendon Regiment, but it had been ill-made and bore very little provisions. Hence the French easily ran off the British, who lost several of their officers. Reinforcements came and fought bravely, but they were unable to force back the French, who marched forward, doing their usual plundering and setting fire to the town of Carlisle.

According to Governor Beeston, "At their first coming they boasted that they would destroy all the country before them to St. Catherine's, plunder and burn that also, and then cut off the water from Port Royal, starve it out and so secure the whole country; but at the same time they took care to let our people know that all who would enlist to the King of France and to King James should have their goods preserved to them, which few believed."

Yet the French had not expected the resistance they encountered, nor the reinforcements at Port Royal, nor that most of the people had moved to the safety of Kingston. Therefore, despite the fact that they destroyed much of the towns, harassed the remaining citizens, and engaged in multiple battles, they were unable to get near Port Royal or Kingston to achieve their goal, Hence, Admiral du Casse, after having refitting his ships with provisions ashore and releasing prisoners, sailed away on Saturday the 28th.

Governor Beeston wrote, "I cannot yet procure a certain account of the losses on either side, but we reckon ours at sixty killed and wounded since the first landing of the French. From what we can gather from released prisoners the French have about 350 killed and wounded men, besides many dead of sickness in the ships, so that it is supposed that they will find 700 men wanting. I have since ascertained that Hubbard's house was first garrisoned and held by order of Major Lloyd. We have lost about 100 killed and wounded of all sorts, Christians, Jews and negroes, 50 sugar works destroyed and many other plantations in St. David's, St. Thomas's and St. Mary's, over 200 houses burnt besides in Vere and St. George's, and about 1,300 negroes carried off, besides other spoil." [*Signed*. Wm. Beeston. *Copy*. 9 *pp. America and West Indies*. 540. *Nos*. 41, 41 I.]

About the Author

AWARD WINNING AND BEST-SELLING AUTHOR, MARYLU TYNDALL dreamt of pirates and sea-faring adventures during her childhood days on Florida's Coast. With more than fifteen books published, she makes no excuses for the deep spiritual themes embedded within her romantic adventures. Her hope is that readers will not only be entertained but will be brought closer to the Creator who loves them beyond measure. In a culture that accepts the occult, wizards, zombies, and vampires without batting an eye, MaryLu hopes to show the awesome present and powerful acts of God in a dying world. A Christy award nominee, MaryLu makes her home with her husband, six children, four grandchildren, and several stray cats on the California coast.

If you enjoyed this book, one of the nicest ways to say "thank you" to an author and help them be able to continue writing is to leave a favorable review on Amazon! Barnes and Noble, Bookbub, Goodreads (And elsewhere, too!) I would appreciate it if you would take a moment to do so. Thanks so much!

Comments? Questions? I love hearing from my readers, so feel free to contact me via my website:
https://www.marylutyndall.com/
Or email me at: marylu_tyndall@yahoo.com

Follow me on:
BLOG https://crossandcutlass.blogspot.com/
PINTEREST: http://www.pinterest.com/mltyndall/
BOOKBUB:https://www.bookbub.com/authors/marylu-tyndall
AMAZON: https://www.amazon.com/MaryLu-Tyndall/e/B002BOG7JG
Instagram: https://www.instagram.com/marylu_tyndall/

To hear news about special prices and new releases sign up for my newsletter on my website Or follow me on Bookbub!
https://crossandcutlass.blogspot.com/p/newsletter-signup.html
https://www.bookbub.com/authors/marylu-tyndall

To hear news about special prices and new releases that only my subscribers receive, sign up for my newsletter on my website or blog

Check out my **Reckless Pinterest Board** as you read!